Kaji Sukoshi & The Shining One

CONNIE BAILEY

Dreamspinner Press

Published by
Dreamspinner Press
4760 Preston Road
Suite 244-149
Frisco, TX 75034
http://www.dreamspinnerpress.com/

Kaji Sukoshi and The Shining One

Cover Art by Anne Cain   annecain.art@gmail.com
Cover Design by Mara McKennen

ISBN: 978-1-61581-013-0

Printed in the United States of America
First Edition
June, 2009

eBook edition available
eBook ISBN: 978-1-61581-014-7

To my sisters.

Author's Note:

I've done my best to add a bit of Eastern flavor to my story; kindly forgive any gaffes.

Chapter One

*H*e never told me in so many words, but I know what attracted the Shining One's attention to my lads. Hayate was more than a group of musicians; they were friends. They enjoyed playing together and it showed. Furthermore, they had the knack of including the audience in their camaraderie. I'd seen it every time they played live and the performance I'm talking about was no exception. They had filled warehouse-sized Big Time Otaku and turned the popular bar into their private clubhouse for the night. The lads were all over Otaku's three-tier stage, running, leaping, and teasing the fans without missing a note.

Shirtless, with the gleam of silver piercing his nipples, Michi kept the beat behind his big black drum kit. Bassist Tsubasa, with streaks of electric blue in his dark mane, mirrored the moves of the lead guitarist, leaning back to back. Fingers blurring on the strings of his red Gibson, Sora turned and pressed his crotch to Tsubasa's hip, grinding as a stream of impossibly fast arpeggios stabbed the air. The crowd roared, applauding the antics as the bass player grinned over his shoulder and received a sweaty kiss from Sora. Kaji, the lead singer, ambushed Sora from the top of a speaker, jumping onto his back, clinging tightly with his knees as he launched into the chorus. The guitarist knelt and Kaji vaulted over him, turning to pull Sora's head to his crotch. Kaji rolled his hips, tossing his dark, waist-length hair, his voice a purring siren call to forbidden pleasures. Unwilling to be left out, Tsubasa moved behind

I

him, chewing on Kaji's neck as he dry-humped him. Engaged fore and aft, undaunted, Kaji delivered the last lyrics with all the power and glory of a climax after a long dry spell.

It always came to this, as the heady rush of doing what they did best overtook them and they had to release the joy that bubbled up through the rock like a crystal spring. Anyone who's been in the zone understands the transcendent feeling of flying high on the wings of your talent, of being in love with everyone and everything for as long as the flight lasts. The lads were irrepressible on stage, charged with energy and bleeding it off to the fans, making a celebration of each show. And every time they played, the crowd grew larger. Looking around at this one, I wondered if the club would still be standing at the end of the night. I wasn't sure it would survive the mass orgy that was threatening to break out.

As I smiled to myself in the darkness, proud and, yes, possessive, I noticed someone else who wasn't carried away by the giddy hurricane of sight and sound. With his long coat, hat, and sunglasses, he looked like a spy, and almost as soon as I saw him, he faded into the mob as if feeling the pressure of my gaze. Maybe if I'd been suspicious, or at least curious, I'd have saved myself and those I loved a lot of trouble. In the bright tumult of my memories of the night, he was a matte-black shadow, but I didn't give him another thought until Sato came calling.

Ichiro Sato, or Sato Ichiro in the eastern style, was the manager of Japan's most adored male pop idol and he was calling on me, the manager of a band still shopping for a label. How could I turn him down? I couldn't, of course. I wanted my boys to be the biggest act in Japan, just for a start, and I was willing to do anything to reach that goal. I would not be hampered by the fact that I was an Englishman in the Orient; I believed in music and I believed in the group of talented young men that I'd been shepherding for the past couple of years. That explains the eagerness with which I invited Mr. Sato into my excuse for an office. He took the briefest look at the converted petrol station/garage and made no comments on the spare, battered furnishings, but he did pull his magnificent mohair trench coat closer around his body and he sat very gingerly, on what I considered my best chair. He wore sunglasses so dark that I could barely see the gleam of his eyes and he never took them off during the entire interview. Other than that eccentricity, he behaved in the normal fashion of an ambitious Asian man moving into his thirties like me.

"I am here to speak on behalf of Kazuki to the benefit of both our charges." Sato got right to business, which is how we do it in the world of rock 'n' roll, even in Japan.

"I would be most interested to hear what you have to say," I replied, wishing I had more to offer him than the flat soda or bottled water that he'd graciously declined. "Kazuki is much admired."

Sato inclined his head in acknowledgment of the compliment, his blue-black hair almost iridescent under the fluorescent light. "Yes, much admired," he said with a trace of smugness. He could well afford his complacency; he represented a phenomenon, a comet that had blazed in the sky of the music world for almost ten years and showed no sign of dimming. I had never seen anyone quite like Sato's ageless client before, with the possible exception of one androgynous English rock star, but even that icon of my adolescence could not compare to this shimmering, half-mythical creature.

As everyone knew, he was born Naoki Murakami, but they called him Kazuki, the Shining One. It only took a glance at one of his many publicity photos to see why. His hair, currently a rich cinnabar, was thick and glossy. His features were perfectly shaped, his body covered with supple glowing skin, and he moved with all the grace of the average jaguar. If you saw nothing of him but that porcelain face, you could easily mistake him for a beautiful woman. His body, however, was indisputably male despite the smoothness of his skin. He was tall and broad-shouldered, with an aura of innate power that made his languid poses even more striking. He was quite deliberately seductive and the blatant nature of his smoldering mien gave it an element of farce, a joke you were in on, playing the game with him. He often averted his gaze to let the onlooker appreciate unobserved the classic oval shape of his face, the high cheekbones and full lips of a geisha, but when he stared directly into your eyes, you got the full effect of his startling gaze, pale green and cloudy as jade from the sea. He sang like a fallen angel and danced like a dervish on fire. He was worshiped by millions; what did he want with us?

"Hayate has come to Kazuki's attention," Sato said. "Very promising, he says. He likes the name and says it is appropriate."

"Thank you. We thought Hurricane suited the band, but it's very kind of him to say so."

"Kind?" A smile was caught in one corner of Sato's mouth. "Kazuki-san is truthful."

"Ah… well, then, please thank him for his honest esteem of my clients."

Sato nodded again. "Kazuki has been a star since he was sixteen, but he wishes for more fame. He wishes for his fame to stretch across oceans."

"I don't see why not. He's got it all; he's the total package."

Sato half-rose in an abbreviated bow. "*Arigato*," he thanked me.

"I'm just being honest." I smiled. "What can Hayate do for Kazuki?"

Sato smiled back, knowing that I knew that Kazuki could do a lot more for Hayate than vice versa. "We are both privileged to work with very special people. They have the necessary talent for success. It remains for us to bring their gifts to the public."

"That was very nicely put. I'd like to hear your ideas on the subject of publicity."

Finally unbending a bit, Sato unbuttoned his floor-sweeping purple coat to reveal a suit so white I was tempted to reach for my sunglasses as well. Expensive, but flashy, stocky Sato's clothes made him look like a boxer who'd done well as he leaned forward as though to share a confidence. "Kazuki's image, you understand, is deliberately ambiguous."

I waited for a moment, certain he was not finished, but he was obviously waiting for me to reply. "Ambiguous," I repeated. "Are we talking about his political views?"

"We are talking about his sexual orientation."

"Right. Well, I had formed the opinion that Mr. Kazuki was bisexual, or more likely, omnisexual. Of course, I know people who believe emphatically that he's a woman in disguise. They claim to have evidence that the nude photos of him are faked."

"Yes, Kazuki finds such tales very amusing. He does not care if people believe he is gay or a woman or a robot. He only cares that they find him… interesting."

"And you've thought of a way to make him more interesting?"

"*Hai*," he confirmed. "Research indicates that Kazuki's most loyal fans are women and that the most loyal of the women prefer to believe he is a bisexual. I want to give him a boyfriend."

"I see," I said, though I wasn't sure that I did.

"We have seen Hayate and Kazuki agrees with me that your vocalist would be a good boyfriend for him. He is shorter than Kazuki and he is also very beautiful as well as a known homosexual. They will look very fine together in photos."

I agreed with his assessment of our lead singer. As it happened, Kaji was very attractive, and he was very openly gay, but I was a bit taken aback by the baldness of Sato's approach. "Do you think I can just tell Kaji to be with Kazuki?"

"Doesn't he want to be famous?"

I saw his point. "Of course, I'll have to discuss this with the lads."

"We did not expect an immediate answer," he said, though I think he did. "Here is my private number. Please call me as soon as you have decided." He stood and I realized that the meeting was over.

"I'll do that," I said, as I walked him to the door. "Thank you for your time."

He bowed briefly and went to his chauffeur-driven Mercedes. Before the car pulled away, he rolled down the window. "One more thing, Mr. Blume: your singer will need to change his hair color. Blond would be best."

At a loss for an answer to that, I lifted a hand in goodbye. When the big car turned the corner, I went to find the lads. I couldn't decide if Kaji was going to go ballistic or laugh his arse off, but I couldn't wait to find out. As it happened, he did neither, though his bandmates did both. With uncharacteristic gravity, Hayate's resident spitfire agreed that the publicity would be extremely good for the group and if pretending to be the famous Kazuki's lover in a few public appearances would help, he'd make the sacrifice. After this improbably altruistic statement, the rest of the lads were struck dumb for approximately half a second before they pelted Kaji with verbal abuse and whatever else was handy. The latter eventually included their bodies, which they piled on their vocalist in a laughing, tickling, writhing heap. I watched with an indulgent smile until Sora hooked my ankle and pulled me into the group snuggle. There are worse ways to celebrate good news.

I went to bed happy that night, optimistic for Hayate's future. In the morning, I phoned Mr. Sato and he gave me the details of the scheme. In three days, Kazuki would fly in to Tokyo after a brief vacation on the island of Phuket. His return would be the perfect opportunity to stir the public's curiosity.

*N*arita Airport is always crowded, but that day one of the concourses was packed to the point that security had to force paths through the throng for departing passengers. At the front were the reporters and camera operators dispatched to film a beloved celebrity returning home. Kazuki was back from a much-needed break after suffering exhaustion brought on by his devotion to his fans; at least that's what it said in the press release.

I stood in the front row with Mr. Sato and representatives from Zennousha Music, just to the left of the lovely girl holding the gigantic bouquet. Even though I was in on the planning of the charade about to be enacted, or maybe because of it, I shared the mounting excitement of the crowd as they counted down the minutes until they would see their idol in the flesh. The tension grew as the private jet touched down and the fans realized the Shining One was only a few dozen yards away. The intermittent screaming became a sustained keening of desire. Keyed to a fever pitch, every sense heightened, the throng turned as one when a door opened to the left of the cordoned area.

I was waiting for it and so I was the first to spot the slight figure approaching the ranks of the press like a tomcat kitten on the prowl. Five and a half feet of pure dynamite, he wore an arterial red sweatshirt two sizes too big, bulky sleeves dangling almost to his fingertips. As he strode forward, the ripped neck hole slipped off one shoulder, baring tattoos inspired by Egyptian hieroglyphs. His spiky, recently bleached and chopped mop-top shadowed kohl-rimmed eyes as dark and gleaming as the leather jeans that clung to his legs. I was probably beaming like a proud parent, but I was the one who had discovered him and named him *Kaji Sukoshi*, Little Fire, and he was everything I loved about rock 'n' roll in concentrated form. I think I might be excused a wee amount of paternal pride even if I hadn't quite reached puberty the year he was born.

The members of the press took immediate note of Kaji's entrance. Who was this striking stranger who arrived by a secret way just in time to greet Kazuki? The curiosity of the crowd was an almost palpable thing as the photographers recorded the interloper's smallest movement like naturalists studying a gazelle at a water hole. He looked once at the fans, just a quick glance that appeared to surprise him. His demeanor went from unabashed cockiness to shy uncertainty and the cameras ate it up. As the reporters began to shout questions, the door they'd been watching so avidly for hours finally opened behind them. In a split second, the air was thick with the sound of Kazuki's name and the cameras turned to follow him.

I had seen hundreds of pictures and probably a dozen videos of the Shining One and I knew he was beautiful with an otherworldly beauty that didn't seem quite real. However, it was a very different thing to be standing in the field of his charisma. As he passed by me, my mouth went dry as though a lion had brushed against me in the dark. Frozen, I watched him pass by the press, the corporate greeters, and the fans. The huge room fell silent around me as Kazuki hurried to where Kaji waited. Kaji stood his ground, ready to recite a little speech of welcome, after which he and Kazuki would disappear slowly enough to allow plenty of photos. His lips parted as he took a deep breath and then Kazuki was on him like a tsunami, sweeping him up in a fierce embrace. The hush was preternatural as Kaji was pulled up onto his toes by the force of Kazuki's greeting. *"Gomen nasai,"* Kazuki whispered an apology, just before he claimed Kaji's mouth in a hungry kiss that unleashed a tumult of screams, sighs, and shouts of disbelief.

The snog was not in the script we'd discussed with Mr. Sato and I saw Kaji's eyes go wide with shock when Kazuki's tongue slid between his lips. Kazuki held Kaji tightly through the instinctive reaction to pull away, bending him backward until he was off-balance. Kaji put his arms around Kazuki's neck to keep from falling and after a moment, his eyelids drifted down as he surrendered to the kiss. To say that the crowd went wild would be an understatement of monumental proportions. As if just now noticing the deafening roar, Kazuki lifted his head and scanned the front rows of the masses. Holding up one hand, he shoved Kaji behind him with the other as he gave his fans a sheepish smile. He waved and blew kisses, but backed steadily toward the door Kaji had used. Their hasty exit was captured by dozens of cameras, probably hundreds if you count phones. The door closed on a glimpse of Kazuki pinning Kaji to the wall with amorous intent and pandemonium erupted again.

I turned to look at Mr. Sato as he glanced my way. Our eyes met in a moment of perfect rapport. We had just set off a nuclear bomb of publicity and it hadn't cost a thing. The crush of fans was so massive it was impossible for us to follow our clients, and it was nearly an hour before we caught up with them at the limo. I only needed one look at Kaji's face to know that in that time, his world had changed radically. I wanted to ask him what had happened while we were separated, but things were moving too quickly.

Sato had arranged for us to have dinner at one of Tokyo's most exclusive restaurants. It was atop one of the city's tallest buildings, a glass corona atop a tower of light, attracting celebrities and those that made a living off them. The meal was awkward to say the least. Kazuki and Kaji were under constant barrage by photographers and autograph seekers who stared curiously at Kaji when they could take their eyes off Kazuki. I reminded myself that this was exactly what we wanted, but I could see that Kaji was upset and trying hard to hide it. Having been in the path of Cyclone Kaji before, I didn't want his

7

anxiety to reach critical mass. So, when Sato suggested drinks at a trendy nightclub, I begged off.

"It's been a long day," I said. "I'd appreciate it if you'd have your driver take us home now."

Kaji, who'd not spoken more than five words during dinner, put his hand on my wrist in silent gratitude. His behavior was so out of character that it worried me. I glanced aside at him, but he was looking out of the limo window, his profile limned against the city lights. When I faced forward again, I caught Kazuki watching Kaji with an enigmatic expression on his drowsy feline features. Kazuki's eyes brushed mine and slid away, leaving me with the feeling that he hadn't actually seen me. I was starting to get a little creeped out by his mannequin-like calm. It made me feel as though he wasn't really there at all; that his spirit was on some astral journey, leaving this beautiful shell illuminated but uninhabited. I hoped that was the case since my other theory involved the misuse of some heavy-duty drugs. No way would I allow that shite around my lads.

Sato was disappointed that I cut the evening short. He wanted the fans to see pictures of Kazuki and Kaji dancing together. I reminded him that it was better to offer several small tastes rather than a banquet to whet the appetite and he had the driver take us home. I told Sato I would talk with him in the morning and got out of the car. Kaji climbed out after me and we started up the drive. Before we'd gone two steps, Kazuki got out and caught Kaji by the elbow. Bending slightly, Kazuki said something of which I heard only the word *takara*—treasure. Kaji didn't look at the other man as his lips moved in reply. Kazuki kissed the top of Kaji's head and slid back into the limo as the other three members of Hayate burst from the garage that served as our living quarters, practice space, and corporate office. After a few moments of teasing, Kaji's friends quieted when they realized he wasn't responding. I asked them to give us some time alone, and they left to hit a few clubs. As we entered the big open space of the garage, Kaji whipped the red shirt over his head and flung it at a threadbare sofa.

"I am so… screwed," he wailed.

"Take it easy. I'll make some tea, and you tell me what's going on."

"It is a disaster," Kaji said, pulling his hair into tufts as he trailed me into the kitchen area.

"We don't have to keep playing this game if we don't want to. If it bothers you to lie to the public, I can understand that."

"What are you talking about? I don't want to quit." Kaji paused, biting his lower lip in thought. "I should quit. This will not turn out well."

"Tell me what you want and I'll tell Mr. Sato."

"Kazuki."

"Right. I'll tell him too."

"No!" Kaji shook his head. "You asked me what I want and I said Kazuki."

I put the kettle on the stove and turned to look at him. I still wasn't used to the platinum-blond hair, but it was striking with his Asian features and dark eyes. "Why don't you tell me exactly what you mean by that so I won't misunderstand?" For the first time since I'd met him two years ago, a skinny, nervy seventeen-year-old punk with a voice too big for his body, he was hesitant to speak. "Come on, Susumu." I called him by his real name to emphasize my seriousness. "Tell me what's happening with you."

"I am… in love with Kazuki."

"Bollocks! You just met him a few hours ago."

"I know, but…." Kaji finally met my eyes. "Will you promise me you will not tell the other lads?" he asked in the slightly stilted English the band members always used with me. I spoke their Nihongo, but had to translate in my head first, which slowed me down considerably. The other members of Hayate collected English slang like truffle hounds, but Kaji tended to front less. It was an endearing trait of his to tailor his speech to the listener out of respect. He called me Benny-chan as though I were a beloved child and didn't care who thought he was being sappy. He was intelligent, sweet natured, and fiercely talented; how could I not love him?

"Your secrets are safe with me," I said.

"When I was thirteen, Kazuki became a big star and I had to accept the truth that I liked boys. I bought all his music and put his picture on my bedroom wall. Many times—"

"Bloody hell, Kaji! Did you used to wank to pictures of Kazuki?"

Kaji nodded.

"Well, never mind, mate. I used to flog my bishop to photos of a blond film star I won't name. It's no big deal, so don't let it throw you."

"I am thrown." Kaji picked up the discarded sweatshirt and buried his face in it. "It still smells of him."

9

"You've definitely got a big crush, but why is that a bad thing?"

He stared at me as though I'd gone mad. "Because he will never love me back. My heart will be broken and the best I can hope is that I will write a good song from it."

"Kaji," I said softly, putting a hand on his shoulder. "Why wouldn't he love you back?"

"He is Kazuki," Kaji said, as though that explained everything.

"From the way he kissed you, I'd say there's some interest there."

"That was for publicity. He was being very kind, but I could see that it was part of his job."

"Maybe it's just leftover infatuation," I tried putting another spin on it. "When you become a big star, you'll laugh about the time you thought you were in love with the Shining One."

Kaji rested his forehead against my shoulder. "When he kissed me, I forgot that we were being watched by hundreds of people. I forgot where I was. I almost forgot *who* I was."

"That good, huh?"

"I want him so much, Benny-chan."

"Well, there's not a lot we can do about that. We want what we want, however...." I cupped Kaji's chin in my hand and looked into his eyes. "We can decide for ourselves if what we want is good for us."

"Hai," Kaji assented. "I understand."

"No matter what you decide, you're still my *ichiban.*"

"You are my number one also." Kaji smiled up at me, tilting his head to rest his cheek against my palm.

After two years, I was still getting used to the lads' openly affectionate behavior. They had none of the personal space issues of the typical British or American male and were even more demonstrative than the Europeans were. Sora told me it was a samurai thing, but didn't elaborate. Whatever the source of their untrammeled displays of affection, I wholeheartedly approved. I'm not attracted to pretty boys, as it happens, but Hayate taught me that it's possible to be physically close with someone without needing to have it off with them. Furthermore, I will say that a good hug cannot be rated highly enough for the simple warmth and comfort it brings to body and soul. Call me a soft bugger, but it's the truth.

"Come here, you cheeky monkey." I pulled Kaji into an embrace. "You're bloody gorgeous and sexy as hell. I love you. The lads love you. Why wouldn't this Kazuki bloke love you too?"

"I just have a bad feeling."

"Well, shake it off. You're Kaji Sukoshi, the little fire. Let's see you shine."

"For you, Benny-chan, I will burn brightly."

I let him go with a kiss on the forehead and he went to his bed in the loft. I stayed up for a while with my thoughts. Mr. Sato's plan had not gone exactly as we'd mapped it out, and I thought he should have warned us that his client was prone to improvise. Now it was a tangled web with my young friend dangling from one of the threads. I took the emotional health of my lads as seriously as the condition of their musical equipment and Mr. Sato had just made my job harder. I couldn't help feeling some resentment toward him and if this silly publicity stunt resulted in a broken heart for Kaji, I'd never forgive him, or myself.

Chapter Two

I was so preoccupied that I never turned on the television before I went to bed to see if we made the late news. In the morning, I was immediately made aware of the fact that the media had adopted Kaji without stint or reserve. Every iota of information on Hayate had been ferreted out, winkled forth, and served up for the edification of Kazuki's fans and anyone else with eyes and ears. We were besieged and found it impossible to leave the garage until Mr. Sato sent a platoon of bodyguards in a fleet of luxury SUVs with the Zennousha logo on little flags. This, of course, set off anther tsunami of speculation. Answering the storm of questions with a single statement, the forbidding figure of the chief bodyguard tersely informed the press that Kazuki-san was lonely for his friend. The paparazzi found this extremely provocative in light of the way the Shining One had greeted his friend at the airport.

As per Mr. Sato's instructions, which were very detailed, Kaji wore a sleeveless red shirt that bared the bracelets of tattoos around his wrists and upper arms. He combined the eye-catching garment with tight white jeans, bright yellow boots, and a black and silver scarf around his neck. According to the agreed upon agenda, he would meet Kazuki at the zoo and have lunch with him. The wall of bodyguards around them was an addition necessitated by the incredible response to our hoax. We'd expected attention, but this was far beyond anything we'd foreseen. In fact, the lads and I were able to follow most of Kaji's progress that day as one of the entertainment channels kept up a nearly constant live feed. Sora, Michi, and Tsubasa opened beers and had great fun watching the show, but I found myself scrutinizing Kaji's face for signs of stress.

I had to give Kazuki his due as an actor. If I didn't know better, I'd swear he was a man head over heels in love. It wasn't so much the adoring looks, the tender caresses or sweet attentiveness, but the way his body instinctively oriented itself relative to Kaji's position like an attendant moon... or a stalking predator. The other band members noted Kaji's atypical demeanor, commenting hilariously on their fireball friend's shyly downcast eyes, demure posture, and closed mouth. They roared with laughter when Kazuki tried earnestly to coax a smile from Kaji. Kazuki ducked his head to look into Kaji's eyes. Kazuki did a funny little dance. Kazuki juggled two apples and a pear from their picnic lunch. Under the hooting laughter of the lads, I fancied I could hear the swelling screams of a legion of Kazuki fans.

My phone roared like a lion and Michi dissolved in giggles. Apparently, he'd resumed his ringtone prank campaign. I shot him a warning look as I answered. Mr. Sato greeted me and expressed his happiness with Kaji's presentation. He'd arranged for the band and all their equipment to be moved to a location away from the media storm so they could get on with the creative process. If I agreed, the wheels would start turning immediately. Of course, I agreed, and one hour and forty minutes later, we were watching Kaji on an enormous flat screen in a plush house with a private recording studio.

Over the next few days, public interest in the adorable couple swelled unabated. This was Japan, birthplace of the cult of cute, of the concept of *kawaii*, and there was nothing else around as perfectly cute as the Kazuki/Kaji matchup. Nor did the Shining One's publicity machine miss an opportunity. When Hayate was invited to play one of their songs on an afternoon talk show, Kazuki paid a surprise visit. After joining in on the final chorus, he exuberantly lifted Kaji in his arms and rained kisses all over his face. Fans that turned up to see Kazuki introduce the latest model of a popular sports car were treated to the sight of him driving away in one with his arm around Kaji. During an exclusive magazine interview, Kazuki was asked what was most important in life and he pulled out a picture of Kaji to kiss reverently. *Friends*, he said. *Especially one true friend.* Despite constant questioning by the media, neither Kazuki nor Kaji would confirm or deny anything, letting their actions speak for them.

Offers for Hayate poured in from all sides. I needed to be at the top of my form to catch the current while the stream flowed strongly, but I was often distracted by nagging doubts. Kaji never complained, or indicated in any way that he was unhappy—quite the opposite—but still I couldn't dismiss the notion that something was wrong. Haunted by the thought that without a contract it could all go away in a blink, I threw myself deeper into negotiations.

When we finally decided, as a group, to accept a contract with Zennousha, the company threw a party to celebrate. The event was hosted by Kazuki at a corporate-owned Western-style mansion and the press was invited to attend. The extensive grounds were covered with exquisite gardens where the guests were entertained, but only Zennousha personnel and people on the security list were admitted into the house. Sora, Michi, and Tsubasa stuck around for the introductions to the executives and their families, but quickly scattered to bask in the congratulations of the media folk outside. The Zennousha bigwigs and staffers soon graciously withdrew leaving Kaji and me with Kazuki and Sato.

"Please come." Sato bowed. "I have arranged a quiet dinner for us. No more photos tonight."

Kazuki was already walking away down the broad hall, his floor-length white silk coat billowing out like wings, a creature of the heights unwillingly confined to the earth, haughty and sullen. I was still having trouble thinking of him as a flesh-and-blood person, though Kaji assured me he was satiny-fleshed and hot-blooded. Looking over at Kaji, I caught him gazing at Kazuki's retreating figure with an expression that could only be described as yearning. I felt guilty for not being around in case he needed to talk, but I also felt that my duty lay in getting the best deal possible for my lads. I told myself that if Kaji were troubled, he would come to me. The thought did little to soothe my pangs of conscience and I made up my mind to have a chat with him as soon as we were alone.

Dinner was excellent as were the vintages that accompanied it. I drank a glass with each course, and why not? This was a celebration. I wasn't legless, but I'd had a bit by the time the four of us retired to a balcony where we could watch the party without being part of it. Sato poured brandy for everyone, offered cigars, and we sat back in our comfortable chairs.

"To our great success," Sato toasted, and we all drank.

I noticed that Kazuki barely wet his lips before setting his glass down. I also noticed the way Kaji's eyes lingered on Kazuki's sensuous mouth, and that Kazuki was ignoring Kaji. But of course, there were no cameras around, so why should he perform? My mood turned bitter, reminding me why I seldom drank alcohol these days. Though neither Kazuki nor Sato had ever lied about their intentions, I was angry with both of them, but especially with Kazuki. After all, he was the one who appeared to be breaking my Kaji's heart.

Sato raised his glass again. "To Kaji Sukoshi, who has played his part faithfully."

Kazuki swept his drink from the table where it shattered on the marble tile. Sato gave his client a sharp look, but Kazuki didn't see it. His face was a mask of ivory, jeweled eyes gazing sightlessly into the middle distance. *Wanker* , I thought. *Drama queen.* I was definitely drunk and any respect I had for this poser was evaporating.

"To Kaji," I said, as I rose unsteadily. "A *genuine* talent."

Sato drank with me, but Kaji pretended to check his pockets for the cigarettes he'd given up last year. Kazuki stood in a sinuous play of muscles and stalked away without a word. A moment later, Kaji hurried after him. I started to follow, tripped over a *chaise longue*, and fortunately landed on it.

"Let him go," Sato advised me as he tamped soft cigar ash into a crystal ashtray. "He won't find any trouble with Kazuki."

"He'd better not," I said darkly.

"Rest, Blume-san," Sato said. "I will get you some water."

"I'm not…." My words trailed off. Why deny I was pissed as a fart when it was so obvious? I could probably use some water. "Thanks."

Sato bowed slightly and walked away. I must have been more tired than I thought because five minutes later, I was sound asleep. When I woke, I'd been moved to a sofa indoors and covered with a blanket. On the table in front of me was a sweating bottle of water. I took several long gulps before I stood up and went in search of my lads. The party was still going strong and when I looked at my phone, I saw that it was barely midnight. Figuring the band was still celebrating, I tried to decide what I should do now. I was only kidding myself; I knew I was going to look for Kaji. I found him less than ten minutes later, but of course, he wasn't alone.

At the end of a broad slate-tiled hall, glass doors opened on a huge atrium filled with green plants, large, artfully arranged rocks and the plangent music of a fountain. Moonlight poured through the glass ceiling, limning in argent radiance the two men locked in an embrace. Though I was certain that I was awake, the scene had the flickering underwater quality of a dream. As I stood there staring, Kazuki's eyes opened and met mine over Kaji's shoulder. I was rooted to the spot with shame at being caught spying, but he didn't give me away by word or gesture. Wrapping his arms around Kaji, Kazuki lifted him to the top of a smooth waist-high boulder. Moving to stand between Kaji's thighs, the Shining One leaned into him. Kaji lay back, pulling the other man to cover him like a blanket. Taking Kazuki's mouth in a passionate kiss, my lad bent his knees, planted the soles of his boots against the rock, and thrust his pelvis forward. Kazuki's grip tightened on Kaji's hips, leather creaking as his fingers sank into muscle. However, despite this evidence of ardor, he remained largely passive after setting Kaji on the table rock. Kaji was happy to take the lead, letting Kazuki know by every means he possessed just how much he wanted him.

I couldn't watch anymore, not because it was wrong to spy, though it was, but because it hurt me. Kaji was too fine to throw away on a two-dimensional icon who would never feel what he felt. I couldn't bear to watch the shiny pastel vampire absorb my lad's adoration like a great river accepting a drop of rain. I turned and crept away as quietly as I could manage. Yet, I couldn't help taking one backward glance and the moonlit tableau stole my breath.

Kaji had slid to the ground with his back against the granite, face upturned, worshipful as his hands slid up Kazuki's thighs. Kazuki stood motionless, gazing straight ahead, as though trying to ignore what was happening. They were both so beautiful, but the scene brought no joy to my heart. Kaji was being used and not just for publicity. Anger bloomed in me and I nearly turned back to give Kazuki a piece of my mind. Only the fear that Kaji would never speak to me again kept me from making a fool of myself. Feeling terribly weary of a sudden, I left them alone and trudged off to the room set aside for me in the mansion. Things would look better in the morning when I was rested and divested of the effects of alcohol.

I was a bit too optimistic. The newspapers that arrived with my breakfast in bed were entertainment journals, no surprise, but the front-page photos on each nearly stopped my heart. In black and white and full color, each featured a large picture of Kaji on his knees, face planted in Kazuki's crotch. Kazuki stood stiffly as though posing for a catalog, serene face tilted to the best angle to catch the moonlight. After the initial shock wore off, I leapt from bed and pulled on enough clothing to be decent before slamming out of the door in search of Sato. A staffer informed me that Sato-san had gone early to the city.

Foiled, I steamed off to find someone to vent my outrage on. I was quite un-British in the way I went about it, tearing around, walking into rooms uninvited, and being generally impolite to all and sundry. My rage didn't deflate until I peered into a bedroom and saw Kaji sleeping peacefully, sprawled on his stomach and strangling his pillow as usual. He was as perfect as anything nature had ever cast in flesh and I wasn't going to let him be blighted. I would rather let Hayate sink without a whimper than buy fame at this price. The cost was far too dear.

A shadow moved across Kaji's sleeping form and I heard the sound of a sliding door opening and closing. Before I could think better of it, I slipped into the bedroom, walking swiftly to the glass doors that made up the far wall. Beyond was an enclosed garden and I saw a flash of Kazuki's fox-brush hair against the green. Without stopping, I entered the courtyard and followed the other man, bare feet cringing from the gravel of the path. Stands of bamboo and the winding trail conspired to give me only glimmering glimpses of my quarry. I didn't realize he was stark naked until he emerged from the foliage into a clearing with a pool. Before I could speak, he dove into the water, entering it cleanly in a shallow dive, gleaming like a school of koi as he glided the length without surfacing. He rose from the far end as graceful and unlikely as a merman sighting. I didn't think I'd made a sound, but he glanced over his shoulder, his eyes those of a hunted animal. Water droplets beaded his smooth skin, making it appear that he was weeping from every pore as he turned and disappeared, swallowed whole by the miniature jungle. I could have gone around the pool and perhaps caught up with him, but I no longer wanted to. What would be the good of it? What was done was done and if I had any character, I'd stop brooding about the unfairness of it all and deal with the consequences.

Kazuki did not reappear before it was time for Hayate to go home. Kaji was fidgety as we waited in the foyer for the car to be brought around. In contrast to his bandmates, who were in high spirits despite their hangovers, Kaji was subdued and brushed off all attempts to drag him into their play. I breathed a sigh of relief when the limo appeared and hustled my charges into the big car. The look on Kaji's face when we drove away without a farewell hurt me more than an ice pick to the heart. I knew without doubt that Kazuki had had my lad, taking Kaji the same way he'd eat an ice cream cone. It was time to end the farce. No more publicity stunts.

I asked the driver to take us home to our garage and I was walking into the office when my phone rang. Mr. Sato wondered if Hayate had enjoyed their stay at the corporate estate. After a few pleasantries, he thanked me for all my help and asked me to extend his gratitude to Kaji. It was a few seconds before the sense of what he was saying penetrated. Though I agreed that it was high time the charade was over, I was infuriated by his words.

"So I take it that you and Kazuki have no more need of Kaji."

"*Hai.* That is correct."

"Just like that."

"I do not understand."

"No, I don't suppose you do and neither does that bloodless android you operate. I'm not a bit happy about those pictures in the papers this morning. You told us there would be no more photographs last night."

"I am sorry you are upset, Blume-san, but your client signed a release for all photographs with Kazuki. Nothing unethical has transpired."

"That's shite!" I was provoked into saying. "You know it was an underhanded trick. You had your show pony seduce my—"

"I think this conversation will not be productive," Sato interrupted smoothly. "Please bring Hayate back to the studio tomorrow morning so they may begin recording. *Konichiwa.*"

Sato hung up and I stared at my phone for a long time before I put it away. I was starting to feel as if we'd all been had, but I knew I couldn't let it show in front of the lads. I gathered them and told them we were going to start recording tomorrow and did my best to share their excitement. Kaji joined in, but I could see that he was keeping up a brave face for his friends, much as I was. When the band decided to go out and buy some party supplies, Kaji opted to stay with me.

"Tell me, Benny-chan," he said, when the others were gone. "What is making you frown so?"

I would rather have cut off a finger than say what I had to say, but better that he heard it from me than someone who didn't care about him. "Mr. Sato called." Before I could go on, Kaji interrupted.

"Did Kazuki send for me?"

It was going to be even harder than I'd imagined. "No, Kaji. Sato called to tell me that Kazuki doesn't need a boyfriend anymore. You did your job so well that he reckons you can retire."

Kaji blinked and gave a little shake of his head. "In public, yes?"

I knew exactly what he meant. "I think he was speaking in general. I'm sorry, *ichiban.*" Not knowing what else to say, I held out my arms in a wordless offer of comfort. Kaji didn't rush to be held and the cold lump of lead in my stomach got heavier.

"Perhaps you mistook Sato-san's meaning. I know my friendship with Kazuki began as pretending, but when we are alone, I believe he is sincere. He would not… fire me."

"Maybe you're right. I hope so, if that's what you want, but I'm not sure the Shining One is capable of feeling love or anything other than disdain."

"You do not know him."

"Having sex is not the same as getting to know someone."

"Why do you assume I am having sex with Kazuki?"

"Let's not play this game. You made it perfectly clear that you'd roll over if he whistled and—" I stopped in mid-sentence, horrified by the words that poured out of me. "I didn't mean that, Su-chan. That was my anger talking."

"Why are you angry with me?" he asked.

"I'm not angry with you. I'm angry with Sato… and Kazuki."

Kaji's delicate features set in rigid lines of careful control. I was reminded that the blood of samurai flowed in his veins, but his voice was soft when he spoke. "I wish you would not be angry with Kazuki."

"You know how I feel about you. How can I help but be upset with the way he's treated you?"

"You do not understand. You have not heard what he whispers in my ear when we are alone: *anata*, *takara*, *ame*. You have not seen how loving he is, how fierce and tender and greedy for me." Kaji gave me a bittersweet smile. "I am a man in love with a dragon."

"It hurts me to see you in pain."

He came to me then and put his arms around me, laying his cheek on my chest. I was surprised again by the strength in his slight frame as he held me tightly. "You have been as a beloved uncle to me and a big brother as well. You have watched over me and worked for my happiness, giving me discipline when I needed it and praise when deserved. I honor you, Blume-san." He paused. "However, I am a man and you must allow me my own mistakes."

"You're not a delinquent kid anymore, that's for certain." I sighed as I returned his hug. "Can you forgive me?"

"There is no need to ask." Kaji stepped back and caught sight of his reflection in the mirror behind me. "*Baka*," he hissed.

"You're not a fool," I said quickly.

"Are you sure, Benny-chan? Look at my hair."

I chuckled as he wished, though I too missed his glossy waist-length hair. "Don't worry about it. It'll grow back, and, meanwhile, it's impossible for you to look bad."

"*Hai*," he agreed playfully, still trying to cheer me up. "I am going to the loft. There is a melody in my head that I want to figure out on guitar."

Kaji's bandmates left him alone as long as they could stand it and then the siren call of the plucked notes drew them up the ladder. In an all-night session, they tossed ideas back and forth until they had something they all agreed on. By morning, the lads had bashed out a version of a new song with the working title "Bed of Thorns." It was their first ballad and I thought it was the best thing they'd written to date. I liked it so much that I insisted they use their studio time to perfect it, instead of recording an existing song. Mr. Sato was not happy… until he heard the first raw mix.

"Excellent," he said on the phone. "Please continue. I will arrange to make a video."

Stunned, I told the lads the news. Not only was the new song accepted, it was going to get the royal treatment. The band was ecstatic, though Kaji was distracted. He expected Kazuki to call or show up at any moment and when that didn't happen, he drew in on himself. The rest of the guys noticed, but had the grace for once to leave him alone.

Two more days went by, in which time Hayate polished and recorded their first song. Mr. Sato stopped by with congratulations, bottles of champagne, and the information that he had contracted Miss Shiori, a popular maker of music videos. Filming would begin as soon as a concept was hammered out. As usual, the lads maintained a respectful silence around Mr. Sato, but as the executive was leaving, Kaji called after him. With a look of mild surprise, Sato stopped and waited.

"Will Kazuki-san be there?" Kaji asked.

"There is no reason for his presence," Sato replied. With a curt little nod, he went on his way.

Kaji's face didn't change, but I knew how deeply he'd been cut. Casting a significant glance at Sora, I put an arm around Kaji's shoulders and led him out to our old van. He leaned against the side farthest from the building and stared at the dumpster a few yards away. His eyes grew shiny with tears, but he blinked them away.

"I want to tell you a story," I began. "Would that be all right?"

Kaji nodded as he patted his pockets for nonexistent cigarettes.

"I was your age once. Hard to believe, I know, but I was a young man on fire to rule the world of rock 'n' roll. As it happened, I didn't have the necessary musical gifts, but I loved the life. London was…. Oh, man, how can I tell you about London in those days? It was wild and wide open. Anything went. Musically and sexually."

"It sounds like Tokyo."

"Yes. Yes, it does. I suppose that's why I like it here so much. I came to London from a much smaller town and I was bowled over. I walked around with my tongue dragging the ground just soaking it all up. I tried it all: all the drugs, all the rock, all the sex."

Kaji smiled a bit to imagine this old man of thirty-three out on the town.

"I met my first real lover when I was twenty. He was the lead singer for a band with a big local following. His family had moved to England from Norway and he was tall and golden as a Viking prince. I would have followed him to the end of the earth carrying his luggage. I threw myself at him and he was happy to catch me." I met Kaji's eyes. "Once upon a time, I was considered a pretty boy, not as pretty as you, of course, but I had my admirers."

"I can see that, Benny-chan."

"As I mentioned, I couldn't do enough for him. I catered to his every whim, in and out of bed. I thought it would make him love me, but it just made him take me for granted."

"Is this a sad story?"

I nodded. "He cheated on me because I didn't excite him anymore. I was a known quantity, and besides, he knew I'd always be there, ready and willing to please him. He didn't respect me. I'm not excusing him; he betrayed my trust. However, I did make it easy for him."

Kaji nodded his understanding.

"I regret the way I behaved," I said. "I was so willful and set on having what I wanted. I never bothered to think it through. I just did whatever I was moved to do on a moment-by-moment basis."

"Rock 'n' roll." Kaji pumped a fist in the air, surprising a laugh out of me.

"Yeah. Rock 'n' roll. True enough." I lifted the ornate cross he wore around his neck. "Thanks for reminding me that it's a crazy life. Why else would a Buddhist be wearing this?"

Kaji wrapped his fingers around mine on the silver-and-black-enamel pendant. "Because it's cool, man."

"How about us?"

Kaji took my hand between both of his and kissed my palm. Closing my fingers, he smiled up at me. "We're cool," he said. "Thank you for the story. I still feel like a fool, but at least I am not the only one."

"*Ichiban*," I said as I stroked his hair, "you're surrounded."

"When did you start to feel better about your Viking?"

"Not for a very long time, and to be perfectly honest, I've never completely gotten over him. I left without a word while he was on tour. I know from mutual friends that he tried to find me, but it suited me to imagine him suffering and I never once contacted him. If he didn't realize my worth, then he wasn't worthy of me... and the same goes for you and Kazuki. If he can just drop you like this, then he doesn't really care about you. Cut your losses, little fire, and get on with your life."

"I will think carefully about what you've said." Kaji chewed his lower lip. "How do you make it stop hurting?"

I pulled him to me with a hand on the back of his neck and hugged him close. "It's one of those things that have to go away on their own. After a while, you'll notice that the pain is duller and then one day, you'll realize you didn't think about him even once the day before, and so on. It will always be part of you, but it won't consume you. All right?"

Kaji nodded, squeezed me hard, and let me go. "The lads will be wondering," he said. "We shouldn't make them worry."

"Right." I fell into step with him. "By the way, that's a hell of a song you wrote, *ichiban*."

Kaji slipped an arm around my waist and all was right with the world for a little while.

Chapter Three

A week slid into the past and Miss Shiori's assistant called to set up a meeting with the band. We climbed into our new van with the sharp-looking Hayate logo on the doors and drove to the address I'd been given. Twenty-Third Century Video was housed in a former industrial district in a gutted row of yellow brick warehouses. The walls at the end of each huge structure had been removed and they were connected by a new roof into a continuous space as long as three footy fields.

The main set for "Bed of Thorns" was curtained off with layered hangings of diaphanous white silk and gauzy muslin. Against this numinous backdrop, a large Baroque bed carved of dark wood sat atop a marble dais like an altar awaiting a sacrifice. Miss Shiori's assistant director, Rik, described the planned effects for us: the showers of rose petals, the bloodstains that would appear on the snowy linen, the way the images would glow in grainy black and white accented by selected splashes of rich, vivid crimson. The lads loved the concept immediately.

Miss Shiori joined us. She was a surprisingly tall woman with close-cropped black hair and mother-of-pearl-framed glasses. She spoke with each of the band members, exclaiming at their attractiveness, clicking off pictures with her phone, and putting us all at ease with her straightforward manner. Tea was brought, along with cola drinks, and we discussed the project in a

23

little more depth. Shiori was open to suggestions, but it was plain that she had her own vision and it would take a lot to sway her. I liked her right away.

"I have a young woman in mind to play the part of your lover," she told Kaji. "However, if there is no chemistry between you, we will find someone else. Perhaps there is someone you would like to suggest?"

Kaji glanced at me before he shook his head.

"We will see how it goes then, okay?" Shiori stood and handed her smartphone to her assistant. "Download these pictures to my laptop," she said briskly before turning back to us. "I have a very good feeling about this production and I am very excited to work with you."

I thanked her and an assistant showed us out. Once we were on the sidewalk, the lads burst into excited chatter. What would they wear? How would they fix their hair? Which looked better, the barbed wire halo or the studded leather corset? This was one of the best parts of my chosen profession, being part of the fellowship, and I reveled in it as I drove.

Dropping them off at the garage to plan their wardrobes, I continued to the little market that stocked my favorite coffee. As I exited by the rear door, I saw a familiar blaze of red. There was no mistaking the imperial carriage of the figure that vanished through the reed fence across the alley. Calling myself nine kinds of fool, I tossed my bag in the van and followed Kazuki. "*O jama shimasu!*" *Sorry to disturb you*, I called out as I opened the gate and stepped through.

I was in a charming little garden of flowers and herbs bordered on three sides by the thick bundles of reeds and on the fourth by the rough stone wall of a tiny house. The muted music of bamboo wind chimes accompanied the sound of moving water that miraculously blocked the noise of the street. Kazuki was standing a few yards away, gazing up at the passing clouds through a pair of wraparound sunglasses. Even when I stopped in front of him, he didn't lower his head. Like the statues on Easter Island, he looked as though he might stand there for all time with the same fixed expression.

"I'd like to talk to you if you have a few minutes."

"Would even a million… be enough?" he murmured.

"Probably not, but would you do me the courtesy of listening?"

"Courtesy," he repeated, even more softly.

"Would it kill you to look at me?"

"I… do not know."

It occurred to me that he might not have the command of English I'd become used to with Kaji and the lads. "I'm afraid my Nihongo isn't up to this conversation," I said. "I'll have to speak in English."

At last, he pulled his gaze from the sky and looked at me. I couldn't see his eyes behind the smoky shades, but at least I felt like I had part of his attention. "I am listening," he said.

"Bloody hell, mate. You're not the divine emperor on the throne, you know."

"I know that." Kazuki tilted his head at a birdlike angle. "How is Kaji?"

"You've got hide; I'll give you that." I marveled at his nerve. "You led him on and threw him away like rubbish. How do you think he is?"

Kazuki's chin drooped toward his chest. A second later, something splashed his collar, making a spot of deeper gray. He didn't turn away, just stood there with tears running from under his sunglasses and down his cheeks, not making a sound. It was eerie, like seeing someone exhibiting signs of stigmata.

"What is this place?" I blurted out.

"It was my mother's house."

Maybe the trick was to ask him direct questions. "She's not around anymore?"

"She died... a long time ago. I was away. When I made enough money, I bought it back, hired caretakers, and made all as it was."

"It's very peaceful."

"*Hai.*" His concurrence was a sigh.

"So you're human after all."

Kazuki cocked his head at me again. "Now you will tell me how is Kaji?"

"You broke his heart and nearly broke his spirit. I can see that you've got some issues of your own that you're dealing with, but it's difficult for me to feel anything but anger toward you."

"Sure." Kazuki nodded.

"You're very odd, you know that?"

Kazuki nodded again.

"Right. I just wondered if you were aware of it. So, would you tell me something just for my peace of mind? How could you take a bright spark like

Kaji and try to snuff him? Why would someone do something like that? I'm really terribly interested for my own reasons."

"I wish Kaji was here."

"That's not really an answer."

"For me it is."

"Well," I spread my arms in exasperation, "you're too much for me, mate. I came here to tell you off, but I can see I'm wasting my breath and your time." I turned from him and walked to the gate.

"Blume-san! Tell Kaji—"

"No," I said, with my back to him. "No, I won't tell Kaji anything for you. He calls you dragon, so I'm sure you've got the balls to tell him yourself."

The Shining One didn't deign to reply. I unlatched the gate and crossed the alley to the van. The confrontation with Kazuki hadn't gone as I'd imagined. Instead of feeling as if justice had been served, I was hollow with something akin to despair.

When I got home, Sora told me that Miss Shiori had phoned. I returned the call immediately and then collected Kaji for a meeting with the actress Shiori had chosen. At a café halfway between the garage and the video company, I pulled into the tiny parking lot and we got a table. Shiori arrived scant minutes later with an elfin lass called Chikako. After introductions and drink orders, Shiori asked me to walk with her.

"It's only that I want to give Kaji and Chikako some time unobserved by their elders, okay?"

"Okay," I said, liking the way she took my arm as we traversed the sidewalk, a sweet old-fashioned gesture that made me feel quite easy with her. "Though I'm not sure I'm an elder."

Shiori giggled. "Compared to Kaji and Chikako?"

"You win." I stopped with her as she looked in a shop window. "The lads are really looking forward to doing the video."

"Me too! Such cute boys. *Chou kawaii!* They'll film well."

"I won't argue with you. I think they've got everything it takes to be stars."

"Well, we will do what we can to help that along, okay?" she said as we began walking again. "Do you think Kaji will like Chikako?" Before I could frame an answer, she continued. "Because if he doesn't like girls that way, we can find a boy. I don't mind. I have been waiting for the right excuse to make a *yaoi*-style video."

"You'd have a better chance of generating some heat with a guy. I hate to disappoint Chikako, but—"

"I understand. What kind of man does Kaji prefer?"

"Someone like Kazuki," I muttered.

Shiori giggled again. "Everyone wants Kazuki, but there is no one else like Kazuki."

"Thank God."

She gasped melodramatically, bouncing a little with her hands on my forearm. "You do not love Kazuki-sama? But… you *must* love him. *Everyone* loves him."

"I *liked* him until I got to know him better."

I wasn't falling in with her humor and her bright smile faded. "You think you know Kazuki? Let's walk a little more, okay?" She took a right-hand cross street and we entered one of Tokyo's many parks. "I grew up in the same poor neighborhood as Murakami Naoki. We weren't friends, but I knew about him, because he was so different. The way my mother told the story, when Naoki was born, his father took one look at the baby's green eyes and threw his wife into the street. He kept the older son and remarried. When Naoki was old enough, he insisted on using his mother's name. Otherwise, he would be Sato Naoki."

"Sato! Kazuki's manager is his brother?"

"Half-brother."

"Right. So what's the story there?"

"Naoki was thirteen before he realized how his mother earned money. She was very beautiful and she missed having company, so I suppose things happened rather naturally, but her son did not understand. Things were bad in their house and Naoki grew wild and disrespectful. Then about a year later, the firstborn came to visit. Ichiro was nineteen, living on his own, and curious to see his mother. Understand that Ichiro was providing security for a boy band that was popular just then. He saw how much money they made and when he met his little brother, he saw an opportunity."

"I'm sure he did."

"Yes, so, Ichiro tells Naoki he will pay for singing and dancing lessons if Naoki will agree to do as Ichiro says. Naoki said yes just to get away from home."

"And he became a big star."

Shiori nodded. "He never went back to his mother's house. She died while he was on tour in Thailand."

"Ouch! No wonder he looked so.... Hey, Shiori-san, do you know what kind of relationship Sato and Kazuki have now?"

"Not precisely, but I hear stories. One story is that Sato signed him to a twenty-year contract. Another story says Sato controls Kazuki's career completely. And some really crazy stories are about Sato keeping Kazuki chained up when he is not in public. Kazuki is everyone's angelic schoolboy and depraved sex demon all in one."

"How old is he anyway? Because I'm damned if I can tell by looking at him."

"He is twenty-five."

"So if legend is true, his contract won't be up for several more years."

"Perhaps it was a fifty-year contract," she said with a straight face.

I laughed and began guiding us back toward the café. "Would you mind walking ahead a bit? I need to make an urgent personal call." I had no idea if he'd talk to me, but my sense of fairness would nag me until I tried. Using the number Kaji had programmed into my phone several weeks ago, I waited to see if anyone would answer.

"Moshi moshi."

"Kazuki?"

"Blume-san?"

"Yeah, it's me. On the off chance that you actually do care about Kaji, write down this information." I finished what I had to say and hung up. I didn't need to hear his answer. I'd meddled enough.

*K*aji and I were ambushed the second we entered Twenty-Third Century Video the next morning. "Hello! This is Jun Lin. What do think of him for a lover?" Miss Shiori looked expectantly at Kaji.

Jun Lin was a young Chinese actor with wispy clay-red hair and eyes like an Aleut. His build hinted that he was a dancer as well as a thespian and it was apparent from his expression that he didn't understand the Nihongo that Shiori was speaking.

"He's fine," Kaji replied in English.

Shiori spoke to Jun in Cantonese and he smiled at Kaji like a man seeing his dream lover in the flesh. Kaji glanced at me and then back at the actor. Jun playfully extended a hand in an ultra-romantic pleading gesture and I nudged Kaji forward. "Go to work, *ichiban*," I grinned.

Shiori took several pictures of the two young men together to figure out the best angles to light them and then blocked out their scenes together. By the time we broke for lunch, she was ready to shoot some film of Kaji and Jun in costume. They bolted their food and sat for makeup, hair, and wardrobe artists. If Kaji had been my type, I would've shagged him silly on the spot when I saw the result.

His platinum mane had been dusted with the same pearlescent powder that made his face pale as the new moon. His dark eyes and brows were outlined Egyptian style to match his tattoos, but without the hard lines. The black color blurred at the edges as though brushed on with butterfly wings, fading subtly into the silvery pallor of his skin. A billowing white shirt with hundreds of tiny ribbon ties floated over a pair of white silk trousers. Dozens of silver bangles hung from his wrists and ankles, catching the light with a soft gleam. He was barefoot and from his shoulders sprang a pair of snowy-feathered wings supported by a harness under his shirt. Hesitantly, he took a couple of steps to feel the difference they made in his balance.

"You look utterly amazing," I told him.

"I look like host-boy angel."

"Like I said… amazing."

Kaji bowed and nearly tipped over. Jun Lin steadied him with a hand under his elbow, smiling largely when Kaji looked up at him. The puppy-dog look on Jun's face clashed with the fangs and the dark bat wings that were part of his costume. The poor guy couldn't have been more obvious; another unintentional conquest who had fallen for Kaji's innate charm. Even straight men who met him had to respond to him in some way, and I was poised to intervene when Shiori's assistant made an announcement.

"Everyone ready? Please come to the set."

I watched from the sidelines, fascinated by the process and doing my best to stay out of the way. After about fifteen minutes of filming Kaji with the wings, they were removed and his hair, makeup, and wardrobe were refreshed. Later, digital effects would make it appear as though the wings had been burned from his back in a burst of silvery flames, so he had to stand very still for several minutes while he was filmed from every conceivable angle. In the next bit, after some bittersweet kisses, Jun Lin pulled Kaji onto the bed. Rose petals began to rain down, changing from white to red as the action became rougher and Jun Lin simulated taking Kaji from behind. Kaji threw his head back as though baying at the moon, white teeth gleaming, as he pushed back against Jun's crotch. I was starting to feel rather warm, when the shoot was interrupted.

"Stop!" Kazuki called out as he strode in front of the cameras. "Stop it!"

Kaji's perplexed look changed to one of horror, and he shoved Jun violently away. "Kazu," he gasped.

"Excuse me!" Shiori said loudly. "This is my studio."

Kazuki spun toward her and bowed smartly. "Please forgive my intrusion, but I must speak with Sukoshi-san."

"So you want to speak to him, do you?" she said. "Is that all?"

"Do not tease me, or I will call you by the special name you earned that day at school when—"

"Okay!" Shiori stepped back and turned off the camera. "We are taking a break."

People moved away from the set, but short of going outside, there was no way to leave the room. Kazuki and Kaji had forgotten the rest of us existed, but it was impossible not to steal glances at them. Kazuki had dropped to one knee beside the altar/bed, the long skirts of his leather coat crumpling around his boots. Taking off his glove, he reached for Kaji's hand. Kaji stared him down, and Kazuki bowed his head. I turned quickly away from the pain on the Shining One's face.

"I wish I could be filming this," Shiori whispered.

I looked back at the set as Kaji moved to sit on the edge of the bed directly in front of Kazuki. He said something and Kazuki answered. Abruptly, Kaji pulled Kazuki's head to his chest with an expression of utter relief. Kazuki put his arms around Kaji's waist and the tension went out of his long frame. Tenderly, Kaji kissed the top of Kazuki's head and rested his cheek there. I saw Kazuki's lips form an apology several times in a row before Kaji put a hand over his mouth. Raising Kazuki's head, Kaji took his lips in a kiss that mingled passion and forgiveness. He pressed his forehead against the other man's for a few moments before he called to me.

"Come hear the news."

I didn't wait for him to ask twice. "Hello, Kazuki," I said as I stopped beside the bed.

Kazuki shot me a glance that managed to convey his gratitude for letting him know where Kaji would be today. "*Konichiwa*," he said simply, before returning his gaze to Kaji.

"Get up please," Kaji told him. "It makes me think you are about to propose marriage. What would the paparazzi make of that?"

"God forbid," I blurted out.

Kaji smiled up at me as he got to his feet. "Could you handle another artist's career, do you think?"

"That depends on who it is."

Kaji's eyes slid toward Kazuki.

"You're joking! What happened to Sato?"

"Ichiro forbids me to see Kaji anymore," Kazuki said. "I obey, as always, but… it made me… very sad to be without my *takara*. I have never disrespected my big brother. I owe him so much."

"Not that much," I said.

"Today I ask him again to let me see Kaji. He hit me and called me ungrateful. He reminded me that he saved me from a bad life. He called me whore like my mother."

"The filthy bugger," I swore. "I hope you sorted him out."

"I said nothing. I ran away like a coward."

Kaji put his arms around Kazuki's waist and looked up at him. "Sato feared he was losing control of you and that is why he made you stop seeing me. You have made his worst fear come true by leaving against his orders. You are not a coward, but if you need to prove you are brave, then do not go back."

"You don't know him," Kazuki said. "He will use his power to harm you. He could find reason not to honor your contract. He could spread rumors and give you a bad name so no one will want Hayate."

"Do you love me?" Kaji asked.

31

"I am… embarrassing." Kazuki flicked a glance at me. "I know I cannot live without you, *takara*. To me, that is love. *Aishiteru*."

"Then forget your fears. Tell me what you would do if you were free."

Kazuki smiled. "This bed is a convenience."

"Excuse me. Are we going to film any more today?" Shiori called out.

"If I were free, I would do this video with you," Kazuki said.

Kaji gasped in delight. "We have to do it! Miss Shiori, would you mind changing Jun Lin for Kazuki?"

"I would kill for it," she said, grinning cheerfully at the oblivious Chinese actor. "And I will see that Jun does not lose out on his fee."

Kaji laced his fingers behind Kazuki's neck and went limp, falling onto the bed and taking the other man with him. Kazuki landed atop Kaji in a surprised tangle of long limbs. When he recovered his aplomb, he stretched out like a panther on a branch, gazing into Kaji's fathomless eyes. Seeing that they were likely to remain that way for a while, I turned away.

"Benny-chan," Kaji said softly behind me. "*Arigato. Domo arigato*."

"For what?" I shrugged and kept walking.

Maybe I had made a mistake, but only time would tell, and meanwhile, Kaji was happy, even though, as Kazuki predicted, Sato made trouble. When Kazuki's half-brother couldn't manage to have Hayate's contract negated, and found he couldn't influence Miss Shiori, he sowed doubt in the minds of the executive directors of Hasu, parent company of Zennousha Music.

My moment of glory came when I convinced the board not to throw away the money they'd already spent on the video. They finally agreed to finish paying for it, gambling that it would eventually show a profit in terms of CD sales. It wasn't an easy pitch, but to clinch my closing remarks, Shiori had helped me put together a little video of public response to Kazuki and Kaji's pseudo-dates.

When the video for "Bed of Thorns" debuted three weeks later, pre-orders of Hayate's CD reached the half-million mark before it was even pressed. Sato lost a lot of standing with the company. Kazuki had made them a lot of money, but now they wondered how much more might have been made with a different manager. With the help of Hasu corporate lawyers, Kazuki was freed of his contract with Ichiro Sato, and I found myself with Japan's two hottest acts as clients.

Chapter Four

"Benny-chan?"

I clicked the pause button and looked inquiringly at Kaji. His gaze drifted to the freeze frame where Kazuki was ravishing Kaji's doppelganger in a blizzard of black and white feathers. His nose wrinkled as he made a face at the screen.

"You are watching that video again?"

"I love this video and until you make another one, it's all I've got."

"You can watch me in person." Kaji moon-walked fluidly over to the couch and collapsed next to me, feet up with his legs stretched out. I put an arm around him and he shifted until he was half-lying in my lap, warm, smooth, and silky. It was impossible not to cuddle him.

"May I continue watching?"

"*Hai.*" Kaji waved a hand in one of Kazuki's regal gestures. Despite professing boredom with the video, he turned his eyes to the screen when I pushed play.

"I could never get tired of this," I murmured.

"Pervert. You just like watching me and Kazuki getting busy."

"I cannot argue with you."

On the television, a bat-winged impossibly beautiful demon had his way with a waifish angel as a strong wind blew away the feathers and petals and blood seeped up through the white silk sheets. Kazuki and Kaji had bared a brave amount of flesh for the scene where a tornado of invisible claws tore at them, shredding their clothing.

"At least my butt looks good," Kaji drawled.

"Who are you showing your butt to?"

"Hello, Kazuki," I said as boot heels clicked to a stop behind the couch. "How are you today?"

Kaji stifled a chuckle. "It is my butt to show," he told Kazuki.

Quick as a cobra, Kazuki grabbed Kaji by the wrist and hauled him up. If I hadn't seen them play like this before, I would've been alarmed by the abrupt violence of the action. However, in the past ten days, I'd ceased being startled and come to trust Kazuki, at least on certain issues. He was trained in dance, fencing, and martial arts; I knew I could trust his control of his muscles and reflexes to keep Kaji from physical injury. It was Kaji's emotional health I worried about. While I didn't think Kazuki meant any harm, I wasn't about to try to predict his actions. Rejected by his father, practically raised on the streets, and then whisked away to rarefied isolation behind walls of money and fame, he'd never had any sort of normal life. I reminded myself of this whenever his high-handedness got under my skin. So what if he was arrogant? It was hardly his fault; though privately, I thought he was quite old enough to see that he should amend his behavior. Kaji adored his lover's haughtiness and wouldn't brook the vaguest criticism of the Shining One.

"This fine ass belongs to me," Kazuki said, running his free hand over Kaji's bubble butt.

Kaji squirmed like a puppy, and I got off the couch. I'd taken too many accidental hits to the crotch to stick around when the horseplay started. Kazuki's style was a lot less snuggly than the other lads, and I made sure to grab my bottle of imported Guinness as I moved out of range. Limber as a gymnast, Kaji pushed off with his feet and did a backflip using Kazuki's forearm for leverage. Kaji was quick, but Kazuki was too, and he had a longer reach. Lunging over the back of the couch, Kazuki caught Kaji in midair, before tumbling with him to the carpet. Kaji pinned Kazuki's wrists to the floor, clamping his knees to his lover's ribs as he crouched over him.

"Now who owns?" Kaji grinned. "No, don't give me those eyes. I will not have mercy on you."

Kazuki locked his legs around Kaji's waist and started to squeeze. Kaji blew him a kiss and slid easily out of the hold. Kazuki made a grab for him and got nothing but a handful of air. Kaji shook a finger at Kazuki as his lover rose from the ground. All the fight drained out of Kazuki like water from a cracked pitcher. Gently taking Kaji's hand in his, he wrapped his lips around Kaji's finger and sucked on it.

"*Kuso!*" Sora cursed mildly as he entered the garage. "Tell them, Benny-sama."

"Get a room," I told Kazuki and Kaji.

"But I thought you enjoyed watching." Kaji shivered as Kazuki licked his palm, tongue darting into the spaces between his fingers.

"On TV," I clarified. "I'm afraid a live sex act might make an Englishman implode."

Kaji chuckled, tilting his head back to give Kazuki more kissing room on his neck. Michi and Tsubasa came in behind Sora and began loudly discussing the Shining One's technique in the colorful, overheated manner of a pair of sportscasters. Kazuki shot them one evil look and went back to giving Kaji a hickey. The drummer and bass player broke up with laughter, leaning on each other as they passed into the kitchen area. Sora shook his head at their departing pleas that Kazuki not kill and devour them. I raised my eyebrows at the guitarist when he turned to me.

"How long are we going to live like this?" Sora asked.

"What? Aren't you enjoying yourself?" Kaji asked. "We are real rockers now. Living the life."

"We have always been rockers," Sora replied.

Kazuki's remark was unintelligible, his voice muffled against Kaji's throat.

"Did you have a point?" I asked Sora as I handed him a beer.

"I'm wondering if anybody else wants to move like Michi, Tsubasa, and me."

"Move where?" Kaji wanted to know.

"Anywhere we can't hear the two of you all night."

Kazuki turned his head to look at the guitarist. "Jealous, Sora?"

Sora scoffed and took a long drink of his beer. "I am very happy that Kaji-hime is having so much wonderful sex, but he is *loud*."

"I am... well-adjusted," Kaji told his bandmate. "And don't call me princess."

Sora stared at him bug-eyed before turning the same exaggerated expression on me. "What does he mean? Well-adjusted? I've seen his *katana*. It's normal size."

"You're thinking of *well hung*. He's just saying that he's comfortable with expressing his sexuality," I replied. "I think."

"You *are* jealous, Sora," Kaji said. "Kazuki is a super ultra fantastic lover. When you have one, you will understand, and I will tease you."

Sora scoffed again. "I have had lovers."

I couldn't resist. "Sure, mate, but were they super ultra fantastic?"

"Come on." Kaji took Kazuki's hand. "Let's find some place to finish this where we won't offend their ears."

"It's not me," I protested. "I like the way you scream. It reminds me of a roller coaster."

Kazuki blinked at me and then laughed the first real laugh I'd heard out of him. "Ro-lah-co-stah," he repeated, cracking up again. Kaji punched him lightly in the ribs, but that set him off again. Kazuki laughed until tears ran down his face.

"It is not that funny," Kaji insisted.

Kazuki nodded and then shook his head, giggling helplessly. "Whee," he managed to say between gasps for breath. Kaji grabbed him by the belt and dragged him toward the loft.

"Enjoy the ride," I called after them.

"Hey, wait," Sora said. "Instead of having more useless sex, why don't you try to write a song?"

"What a wonderful idea," I said. "Channel all that energy into something creative."

"We are very creative, Ben-kun," Kaji said over his shoulder. His gaze slid to Kazuki's hot-eyed stare. "But maybe Sora is right. Maybe I am not being fair."

Sora rolled his eyes. "Shout your lungs out. I was only teasing you."

But he wasn't. I could see it in the way he glared at Kazuki's back. I'd thought the firmly heterosexual Sora was over his man-crush on Kaji, but maybe I'd misread him. "This probably isn't the right time, but maybe we *should* talk about getting a bigger place with proper rooms with doors that shut."

"That doesn't sound like any fun at all." Kaji twisted around on the ladder to face me. "I like our family."

"We'll talk about it. So… are you lads going to jam? Or are you going to… jam," I finished lamely.

Kaji sighed and tugged at Kazuki's hair. Kazuki left off nuzzling Kaji's crotch and looked up. "Let's make music," Kaji said.

"*Aishiteru*," Kazuki murmured against Kaji's fingers.

"I love you too," Kaji said. "And I want you fiercely, but let's see what we can do with it. Help me to fly."

Kazuki wrapped his arms around Kaji's hips and pulled him away from the ladder. Kaji spread his arms as Kazuki pivoted slowly, raising his lover one-handed over his head in a standard dance lift, and incidentally, an impressive display of strength.

"Show-off," Sora muttered as Kazuki lowered a grinning Kaji to the ground.

"Yeah, but doesn't he look good doing it?"

Before Sora could reply, my phone rang like a firehouse alarm. I frowned at Michi as I turned away to answer it, which made him laugh harder. The lads went to the back of the garage and I took refuge from the amplified sounds in my office. "Hello?"

"This is Sato Ichiro."

"What do you want, Mr. Sato?"

"I wish to speak with Kazuki."

"Then call his phone."

"He has changed phones."

"I don't blame him really. Goodbye, Mr. Sato."

"Do not hang up. Do you think you have won a prize with him? Few people can deal with Kazuki. You are not firm enough."

"My firmness is between me and the mattress. I'm hanging up now."

"You will regret it."

"That was a threat, was it?" I said as I ended the call. I smiled to imagine his shock when he realized I'd hung up. It was an old and juvenile trick, asking a question and then ringing off, but it was a satisfying one.

I did some work on my new laptop until I was lured out of the office by the music. It was a melody I hadn't heard before, full of quick, bright chord changes like small birds taking flight. I was intrigued, but I gave the lads a bit more time to play while I heated up some pizza. By the time it was ready, they were ready for it, diving on the slices and bottles of beer. I hung around while they bashed out the bridge for the new song that Kaji called "Cinnamon Kiss." Kazuki wasn't shy with his opinions, which grated a bit, but his musical instincts were unerring. The song was undeniably better for his influence, even if the edge was a bit softer than Hayate's usual chrome razor style. A little after two in the morning, I went to bed, falling asleep to a raucous lullaby.

When I woke a few hours later, the big building was quiet. I left my closet bedroom behind the office and crept out to put the kettle on. I saw Kaji asleep on the couch and wondered why I didn't see Kazuki. Guessing that he was having a piss, I went out to get a breath of the morning air while the water heated. I peered around the edge of the side door before stepping out. The paparazzi gave us periodic breaks, but you never knew when you'd find someone waiting to take a picture of you in your knickers. The coast was clear and I took a deep breath of the crisp air as I looked up and down the disused alleyway. We kept a grill and a few lawn chairs out here, and the lads had added potted plants one by one until they covered the top of the concrete wall on the other side. I took another deep breath, let it out, and bent over to touch my toes. I caught a flash of white in my peripheral vision and turned to my left. When I realized what I was seeing, I straightened up and began to run.

"Kazuki!" I shouted, as the broken asphalt bit into my bare feet. All I could see was one leg, stretched out across the mouth of the alley, but I knew it was Kazuki. What I didn't understand was why he was on the ground. And why so still? When I slid to a stop next to him, those questions were answered. "Ah no, laddie," I breathed, my North Country accent coming out in my stress. "Ah, fook no. No, no, no." I dropped to my knees, but once I was down there, I didn't know what to do with my hands. Each time I reached out, I shrank back, afraid I would hurt him more with my clumsiness. Where was my cell phone? The thought finally penetrated the shock of seeing so much blood, of seeing that perfect face battered. Getting to my feet, I ran back inside.

"What's going on?" Kaji asked as his head rose above the back of the couch.

"Where's my bloody phone?" I shouted. "Do you have your phone?"

Kaji blinked drowsily at me. "There is a phone in your office."

I pelted into the office and dialed emergency services. As I was giving the operator the information she asked for, I glanced up and saw Kaji in the doorway. His big dark eyes were solemn and the oversized shirt of Kazuki's he was wearing made him look like a child woken from a nightmare. "That's right," I said into the phone. "We need immediate help. We have a badly injured man here." Kaji spun away and disappeared like a wraith in the sunlight. The aching in my chest nearly choked me as I stayed on the line long enough to be sure they were sending an ambulance right away.

"What's all the noise?" Sora called from the loft.

I started to answer, but was preempted by an eerie sound that shattered the morning quiet into shivering shards. The wailing resolved itself into Kazuki's name and Sora nearly broke a leg coming down the ladder. Michi and Tsubasa tumbled down after him and followed me outside. Everyone but me stopped short in shock. I knew what I was going to see and sank down at Kazuki's side opposite Kaji. Kaji had drawn the other man's head into his lap, stroking the blood-tacky hair and begging him to wake up. Tears pricked my eyelids and began flowing down my cheeks. I paid them no mind. Taking Kazuki's hand, I felt for his pulse and found it. He'd been badly beaten by the looks of it, but he was alive. I said as much to Kaji, though I knew it was little comfort just then. I moved closer and pulled his head down to my shoulder, disregarding the blood that stained both of us. Kaji stopped sobbing and made a visible effort to be strong.

We heard a faint siren that grew louder by the second until the emergency services crew stopped in front of the garage. Swiftly, efficiently, they examined Kazuki, loaded him on a stretcher and put him in the vehicle. They sped away, leaving us dazed, staring at the flashing lights as they receded. As the ambulance turned the corner, Kaji started to run after it. I caught him by the arm and swung him around. He pushed at my chest, leaving a bloody handprint, but I held on to him.

"It'll be quicker if we take the van," I said. "Sora, get the keys."

Kaji got hold of himself again and apologized for striking me. I hugged him, told him Kazuki was going to be fine, and got him into the van. Sora came back and we drove to the hospital. The nurses at the front desk thought

Kaji and I had been in an accident, and only then did I realize what we must look like. Kaji was wearing what he'd fallen asleep in: pencil-slim black jeans and a tuxedo shirt of Kazuki's that he favored, the ruffled front soaked with blood. I was resplendent in my navy track pants with the red stripes up the sides and a vintage Albert Hall T-shirt with numerous holes, also soaked in blood. It took several minutes to extract the information we wanted, but eventually we learned that Kazuki was in X-ray and we were welcome to go to the waiting room there.

"What was Kazuki doing out?" I asked Kaji as we settled in.

"Cigarettes for me." Kaji sighed. "I fell asleep waiting for him to come back. I should have gone with him."

"Don't do that," I said. "If you'd known Kazuki was going to be attacked and didn't do anything that would make you a bad person. But that isn't the case, is it? I don't think it's good that you're smoking again, but that doesn't make you bad."

Kaji drew his knees up under his chin and folded his arms, feet perched on the edge of the plastic chair. "Why would someone do this to him?"

"It could be a random gay-bashing."

"Do you really think so?"

"No, not really. Not in our neighborhood anyway."

"I think it must be a gang though. Kazuki would not be easy to beat in a fight unless there was more than one guy against him."

"I believe you. All he'd have to do is give me that snake-eyed look and I'd back off."

"My dragon," Kaji said. "He has to be all right. You have to know him as I do. I want you to be friends."

"We'll be friends if that's what you want."

"Oh bloody hell." Michi used one of my favorite curses. "Reporters."

"Bloody hell!" I echoed. "Come on, lads, down the back stairs."

"I don't want to leave Kazuki," Kaji said.

"Do you want to answer a lot of insensitive questions with cameras in your face right now?"

Kaji saw my point and we found an exit to the radiology wing. We only went as far as the van, which I moved to a parking space down a side street. When I returned, we went to the hospital cafeteria and bought cups of tea. The press didn't find us there, but they did get Kazuki's name from an intern. In another half-hour, the hospital was swarming with media. We decided it would be best to leave and slipped out the service door of the cafeteria. Using the dumpsters as cover, we nearly made it out of the parking lot before someone spotted us. The reporters were too far away to catch up, but the photographers with telephoto lenses got some sensational shots of Kaji's blood-spattered form. The photos on TV made him look like the victim of a rabid vampire attack. The hospital refused to give out any details and the press was forced to make up more wild stories to add to Kazuki's legendary exploits of excess. They speculated that he'd wrecked his motorcycle going two hundred miles an hour, that he'd been beaten by a famous actress's husband when he was caught in her bedroom, that he and Kaji had made a botched suicide pact.

Kaji couldn't sit still and he wouldn't allow me to turn off the television. I spent a lot of time on the phone trying to get information on Kazuki's condition. Finally, I reached a woman in administration who noticed that Murakami "Kazuki" Naoki's insurance form listed Akihashi Susumu aka Kaji Sukoshi as next of kin. When she heard my plight, she kindly coordinated with the police to give us an escort back to the hospital. I put down the phone and looked up to see Sora put his arms around Kaji from behind, stopping his friend's pacing. Michi and Tsubasa moved in from either side, cocooning their friend in a comforting embrace.

"It's okay," I said. "You can see him." Kaji held out a hand to me and I went to join the group hug.

When the unmarked police car arrived, Kaji had changed into a black shirt and trousers. He asked me to go with him, so I did. At the head of the hall where Kazuki's room was located, I spotted Sato and without a shred of evidence, I knew who was responsible for the beating. I pointed him out to the police officers that escorted us past the press. "That man is not to be allowed to see my client," I said as forcefully as I could. I restated this to the nurse at the station, ignoring Sato's attempts to speak to me. The officers kept him at bay, as Kaji and I walked into Kazuki's private room.

Two doctors looked up as we entered and then returned their attention to their patient. Most of the blood had been washed away and bruises stood out starkly against Kazuki's pale skin. His face was terribly swollen, his eyes mere slits, and his lips looked pulped. Kaji stood at a respectful distance for as long as he could stand it before moving to the end of Kazuki's bed. He put his hand on Kazuki's foot and some of the tension went out of him.

"You are the family?" the older doctor asked. "I am Dr. Matsumoto and this is Dr. Tanaka."

Kaji bowed. "Akihashi Susumu," he introduced himself.

"Akihashi-san, I am glad to tell you that Murakami-san is stable."

It would be the first time, I thought, but kept the opinion to myself as the doctor spoke again.

"His nose is broken, as well as his collarbone and several fingers. His jaw was dislocated, and he has fractures of some of the long bones, but no breaks, and these will heal quickly. As you can see, there are many bruises and abrasions but these will also heal quickly. There was no internal damage. Our only worry is the injury to his skull. Closed head wounds are unpredictable, but we think he will be fine when the swelling recedes. If it does not, we will have to operate."

"Brain surgery?" I blurted out.

Kaji glanced at me and then back at Dr. Matsumoto. "May I come closer?" Dr. Tanaka moved aside and Kaji came to stand by Kazuki's head. Hesitantly, he put a hand over Kazuki's chest, not quite daring to touch him. "*Ryu*," he whispered brokenly. *Dragon.* "Wake up."

"He is breathing on his own," Dr. Tanaka said. "That is a good sign."

Kaji's head was bowed over Kazuki and he gave no sign he'd heard. "Please." A tear fell on the sheets and then another. "I don't want to be without you."

I put a hand on Kaji's shoulder. "He's very healthy and very strong and he wants to be with you. He's going to wake up and he'll be fine again in no time."

"I must ask you to leave now," Dr. Matsumoto said. "Someone will call you if there is any change."

"I want to stay with him," Kaji said.

"That is not possible now. Someone will call when you can see him again."

"I will be right outside the door."

"Kaji, come on, man." I put an arm around his shoulders. "You need something to eat. I need something to eat. They'll call us as soon as anything happens."

Kaji let me lead him away, but his heart stayed in that hospital room. We ended up hanging out in the stairwell after I fetched coffee and cake from the cafeteria self-serve line. I wolfed down the sweet cake chased with bitter coffee. Kaji paced the small landing until he realized he was driving me crazy. Putting his back to the wall, he slid down to sit under the fire extinguisher. "I love him so much," he sighed.

"I can see that. Try not to worry so much. He's going to be fine." I said the words to comfort Kaji, but I honestly couldn't understand why Kazuki inspired such deep feelings in my lad.

Kaji must have sensed my doubts because he began to speak softly as if he were reciting lyrics. "When he looks at me, my heart beats so fast. When he touches me, I feel as though I'm going to explode like fireworks. He smells like spring rain, his kiss tastes of cinnamon, and he excites me more than anything besides rock 'n' roll, but there is more to it than heat. He fills me with glorious light, until I feel I could float up and soar on the wind. I could reach out and pluck stars to make a crown for his head."

"Yeah." My voice caught in my throat. "That's a fine feeling all right. I vaguely remember it."

"I hope you will feel it again."

"The same to you, *ichiban*." I licked the last stickiness of the icing from my fingers and took out my phone. Nine missed calls. I resolutely put my phone away without answering any of them. I had more immediate concerns. "Let's go see your dragon."

Four hours later, Kazuki went into surgery to relieve the pressure on his brain. As designated proxy for next of kin, Kaji gave permission for the procedure and spent the entire time in agony. I broke a personal tenet and went out to buy cigarettes for him, but after a few drags in the parking lot, he spit the butt out on the ground. Pulling his collar up, he gazed up the side of the hospital building as if planning to scale it. Without a word spoken, we started walking at the same time. I looked at my watch; Kaji had been outside a total of seventeen minutes. A couple of kids in the lift recognized the rock star, but they were too polite to do more than steal looks at him. I don't think Kaji even knew they were there. He stared at the panel of lights, willing them to change faster.

Our timing was good; Dr. Matsumoto came to speak with us as we reached the waiting room. He told us that the surgery went well and Kazuki was in recovery. It would still be some time before we could see him, and the doctor advised us to go home for a while. Kaji refused to leave without seeing Kazuki and not even the chief of neurology was proof against his potent personality. Swayed by the depth of emotion in Kaji's eyes, Matsumoto let him look through the observation window at the critical care nurses' station. Kaji flattened his hand on the glass and stood for long moments in silent prayer. With a last look at Kazuki's still form, Kaji thanked the doctor and led the way out to the van.

"They cut his hair," Kaji said, staring through the windscreen at the rising sun.

"Shaved it, more like." I backed the van onto the street and turned west. "Fancy a decent cup of coffee?"

"Yes." Kaji was quiet for several moments before he spoke again. "Kazuki is sure going to be pissed off about his hair."

I glanced over at Kaji. He grinned at me and I grinned back, both of us imagining Kazuki's reaction. Abruptly, we were both laughing hysterically and I had to pull over. The bout left us feeling drained but relaxed. We bought takeaway coffee and breakfast for the whole band and went home.

Chapter Five

he next day I sent Sora, Michi, and Tsubasa to an appearance on a kid's game show, while I went with Kaji to the hospital. The staff was extraordinarily kind and helpful now that word had gone around about Kazuki-sama's special friend. Kaji was ushered into a private room adjoining Kazuki's where he could wait in relative comfort until the doctors gave permission for a visit. Around two o'clock, masked and gowned, Kaji was allowed into Kazuki's room for a few minutes. With the option of hanging around all on my own or grabbing a snack, I went down to the cafeteria. As I exited the lift on my way back, I froze with a chocolate bar between my teeth. My words were therefore a trifle garbled when I called out.

Sato turned and saw me. "Blume-san," he said. "The man I wish to see."

"I've no wish to see you, mate." The caramel and peanuts were tasteless as I swallowed.

"Kazuki is still my brother."

"Half-brother."

"I have a right to see him."

"No, not really. I thought I had a copy of his instructions sent 'round to your office. In them, Kazuki specifically states that he doesn't want to see you."

"*Bakabakashii.*"

"No, I don't think it's ridiculous that he wouldn't want to see you. You've twisted him like a paper clip and getting out from under your thumb is the best thing that could happen to him."

"You speak in ignorance."

"I thought I'd be courteous and use your native tongue." I hadn't had a good bash at anyone in a long time, not since I'd left England, and this bastard was begging for it.

Sato wasn't fazed. "You do not know Kazuki. I raised him after our mother botched the job. I know his moods and his needs and how to handle all of them."

"He's twenty-five, a quarter of a century old. He doesn't need a nanny."

"That is true, but he does need constant supervision and strict discipline. You do not look like the one to give him that. It's certain that singer of yours is not the man for it."

"Are you about to insult Kaji?"

"I thought I already had, but I wish to add that I am sorry." Sato smiled at me. "I am sorry I did not plow his ass when I had the chance."

"That's it, mate." The rest of my candy hit the floor. "Get the hell out of here."

Sato's smile broadened. "You amuse me, Blume-san. I thought that cowboys were from America."

"In England, we have knights. If you don't remove yourself from my sight in three seconds, I'll have to thrash you, or at least try."

"No need for that. I will go." The hall was broad enough for him to pass without coming within arm's length of me and we kept our distance as he went to the lift. "I will get him back," Sato said. "He will have whatever surgery he needs to restore his beauty before I launch the next phase of his career. It is time for Kazuki to move on. I think he will be a very popular actor."

"When he recovers, he's going to do as he bloody well pleases. He's a grown man, Sato."

"He is my creation."

"Goodbye, Dr. Frankenstein," I said, as the lift doors started to close.

"I made him," were Sato's final words. "And he is mine."

I gave a low whistle as I turned away. "Somebody's got a God complex."

Kaji bounced out of his chair when I walked through the door and flung his arms around me. "Kazuki looked at me," he said.

I hugged him tight. "Lucky sod to have you as his first sight."

"He looked annoyed."

"Then he's well on his way back to normal. I'm happy for you, *ichiban*."

Kaji leaned heavily against me. "I am very tired."

"In the last fifty or so hours, you've had less than two of sleep. You need rest."

"I don't want to go. What if he wakes and I am not there?"

"Do you want to look like a slag when he opens his eyes again?"

Kaji reached blindly up and gave me a token slap. "Bad Benny-chan. I think I will rest on the couch for a while. You too." Taking my hand, he pulled me to the small sofa and let me get settled with my legs stretched out. I opened my arms and gathered him in, pulling his head to my chest and letting him sprawl across me. "I can hear your heart," he said and fell into sleep.

I let him drift without mentioning Sato's visit. There would be plenty of time for unpleasant news after Kaji had some rest. I finessed my phone from my pocket without disturbing him and called Sora. I told him the surgery went fine and he told me the band's appearance as judges of a dance contest had gone fine as well. Sora sounded upbeat, but things were different now and it was hard for him to hide that he didn't like all of the changes. The band was no longer the most important thing in Kaji's life and we all felt the repercussions. I told Sora he was doing a marvelous job as deputy manager and he made a rude noise at me. Kaji moved restlessly and I said goodbye to Sora. Lulled by the regular sound of Kaji's breathing, I joined him in sleep.

I woke to the sound of someone knocking on the door and my phone told me that it was ten minutes after nine in the morning. I roused Kaji from a sound sleep and shifted him aside. Leaving my shoes beside the couch, I went to answer the door.

"Is Mr. Akihashi Susumu here?"

"Why do you want to know?"

The man in the three-piece suit, shirt buttoned to the top, bowed crisply. "I am Shin Yoshiro, Kazuki-san's private attorney."

47

"Can you wait just a moment?" I looked over my shoulder. "Kaji! Kazuki's lawyer is here. Do you feel like talking to him?"

"What are you doing? Let him in."

The attorney entered and bowed deeply to Kaji. Startled, Kaji bowed in return. His clothing was rumpled, and his hair stood out in all directions like dandelion fluff, but Mr. Shin behaved as though the young man was as fresh and soberly attired as he was. "Please forgive my intrusion at this time, but there are matters that will not wait. May I be… frank?"

Kaji nodded as he sat down.

"Mr. Murakami met with me last week and had me change several legal documents to reflect his wish that you be designated his next of kin, as if, so he said, you were his husband. I did this and filed the papers. They cannot be disputed."

"What does this mean?"

"Until Mr. Murakami is able to make decisions, you are in control of his companies and his bank accounts. There are things that must be decided, if that is convenient."

Kaji met my eyes, his mouth hanging open in disbelief. "What should I do?"

"I believe I'd let Mr. Shin make the decisions for now."

"It is true that I often make decisions for Mr. Murakami when he is too busy. If that is what you wish, I will be happy to do so for you."

"I know nothing of running a company," Kaji said.

"That is not your calling, Mr. Akihashi. You have a great talent."

"You like our music?"

"I have not had the pleasure of hearing it. I referred to your ability to make Mr. Murakami happy. He spoke of you when he explained why he wished to give his power of attorney to you, and he seemed quite… happy."

"He said nothing to me of this."

"He feared you would think he was trying to buy you, but the reason he chose you is that he trusts you to protect his interests as you would your own. And I am not speaking of mere finance. When he signed the papers, he put his life in your hands."

"He couldn't have made a better choice," I said. "Kaji cares more for Kazuki than he does for himself."

The attorney nodded. "Like a husband." He rose without having opened his briefcase once. "I have intruded long enough. Here is my card. Call me at any hour at the second number." He bowed again to Kaji and then to me. "Thank you, Mr. Blume," he said, though he didn't say what for.

"Thank you," I replied, opening the door for him.

"We will speak again when circumstances are not so… grim," he said. "Meanwhile, I have taken it on myself to arrange things with the hospital and the police. Mr. Akihashi need not worry about details. Here is another number." He handed me a card from his breast pocket. "Whatever you need."

"Whatever?"

Mr. Shin nodded. "If you need a limo, or a passport, or a doctor, or anything. This service will find you whatever you need."

"Ninjas?" I joked.

"Let us hope you will not need ninjas." Mr. Shin smiled. "However, if you do, simply call the number." He bowed once more and walked away like a man with a purpose.

"Well, that was unexpected," I said, as I returned to the couch and plopped down.

Kaji was running his fingers through his hair in front of the mirror, trying to mold it into something that didn't make him look possessed. "I can't think about it," he said. "I would start crying and never stop."

"What did you think of Yoshiro Shin?"

"I think there are two Shins: one for the office and one for time off."

"Can we trust him, do you think?"

Kaji came out of the loo to frown at me.

I tried to explain. "What if he and Sato are…?"

"Kazuki trusts him."

"Kazuki's not exactly a sterling judge of character." I paused. "Sorry. I didn't mean to sound sharp."

"You are tired, Benny-chan."

"I only meant that Kazuki was probably brainwashed by his puppet-master brother and his view of reality might be a bit skewed in some areas."

"You think he's crazy?"

"Of course not." I was lying just a little. "I think he needs to hang around more with you and the lads so he can see how humans behave. He'll catch on."

Kaji punched me lightly over my heart. "He means no harm, you know."

"Right. It's not intentional. I've heard that one before. When your heart's in pieces, it doesn't much matter if it the breakage was unintentional. You're still shattered."

"Let go of that old pain, *ichiban*," he said, as he picked his jacket up off the floor. "You know, Shin Yoshiro was a little bit handsome, wasn't he?"

"Yes, he was, and I can see right through you. No matchmaking; I forbid it."

A knock at the connecting door sent Kaji running to answer it. With a little wave to me, he went to spend a few minutes with Kazuki. When he returned, his cheeks were wet, but he was smiling. "He spoke to me," he announced. "He told me to go and put on some makeup."

"If he's feeling well enough to be cheeky, we'll have him home in no time."

Kaji stretched his arms over his head and bent to touch his palms to the floor. He straightened up with a deep sigh. "I want a bath," he said.

"You *need* a bath," I corrected.

"At least I got a boyfriend."

"Ouch!" I clutched my chest as I opened the door and reeled out into the hall.

Kaji followed, aiming his fingers at me as I staggered to the elevators. A nurse on rounds gave us a disapproving glance that reminded us where we were. The giddiness evaporated, but miraculously, the gloom did not return. I felt tired and sore from sleeping on that miniature couch, but I no longer felt as though the sky was falling. Kazuki would recover, and we would get on with our lives.

W hen Kazuki came home, his hair was about a quarter-inch long all over his well-shaped skull, as sleek as wet seal fur. It grew out in his natural color, a rich black as iridescent as a raven's feathers, and he seemed content to leave it that way for now. I thought he'd never looked better, despite the hospital pallor. In fact, it suited him. All in black with big dark sunglasses hiding half his face, he was glamour itself as he left the hospital leaning on Kaji's arm under the scrutiny of the media.

We had moved from the garage to a place Kazuki owned on the outskirts of the city. It wasn't quite rural any longer, but it was quiet, separated from the neighbors by empty fields, and the former barn was now a recording studio. I could tell the lads missed the rhythms of Tokyo, but Kaji wasn't going to leave Kazuki's side, and this was where the Shining One had chosen to convalesce.

"You look well," I said, as I sat down next to Kazuki on the back terrace.

He turned his basilisk stare on me. "You think I look well?"

"Considering your injuries, I think you look very well. You're healing incredibly fast."

"Look at my nose!"

"Dr. Matsumoto said it would be fine. The scars will fade. You won't even need plastic surgery."

"I can't look at myself."

I glanced back at the house where Kaji was putting lunch together. "I'll tell you this for nothing, mate. Even as you are, most blokes would kill to be as handsome."

"No one calls me handsome. They always say beautiful or pretty."

"Does that bother you?"

"I am not a woman."

"No, but you *are* beautiful."

Kazuki made an impatient sound. "Speak of something else."

"You sound like you're fully recovered to me," I said as I stood. "I'm going to go help Kaji."

Kaji smiled at me as I entered the kitchen. Takeaway containers were piled on every surface and it looked as though he'd taken every dish from the cabinets. I began arranging things, as is my habit, while Kaji poured juice in glasses.

"Are you going with the lads tomorrow?"

Kaji set down the pitcher, picked it up again and put it in the refrigerator. "I would rather not leave Kazuki on his first day."

"You've missed a lot of appearances, *ichiban*."

51

"I know, but thank you for reminding me."

"Don't make me the enemy. I'm your manager. It's my job to tell you these things."

Kaji gazed through the open door at the terrace. "I do not want to be anywhere but where he is."

"You can't just stop your life. You have obligations. What about your career?"

"None of that seems important to me now."

So my fears were not baseless after all. "And the lads?"

"They will understand."

"You're probably right, but I wouldn't expect them to be joyful. Are you saying that you want to quit the band?"

"I cannot think of anything but Kazuki right now."

"You're making a mistake. Mr. Shin has already arranged for a nursing staff. Kazuki will be fine if you leave him for a few hours."

"I know, but I do not *want* to leave him."

"Yeah, I get that." I sighed. "Just please remember my advice. Don't make him your world."

"I am not making him anything. He *is* my world."

"Damn, it, Kaji! Stop being such a—" I stopped, immediately regretting the outburst. "I'm sorry. I'm just frustrated."

"We're all frustrated," Sora said from the doorway.

"Is everyone against me?" Kaji asked.

"No one is against you, Sukoshi Kaji-hime." Sora came into the room. "We miss you. Kazuki owns all of your time now and all of your love. We just want our Little Princess Fire back."

Kaji's brows drew together over his dark eyes, but he let Sora slide for calling him princess this time. "Am I being unfair?" he wondered aloud.

Sora crossed his arms. "Your old friends feel as though you have deserted them for this new friend."

"No, it is just that Kazuki needs me now. He depends on me."

"We need you too." Sora put his arm around Kaji's drooping shoulders. "You are the heart of Hayate."

Kaji took a deep breath. "It is time for lunch," he said, avoiding the issue, but I knew he'd think about what we'd said.

The next morning, when the lads assembled for the drive into the city, Kaji joined them. By the end of the ride, he was one of the boys again and the promotional appearance was a resounding success. Each member of Hayate posed for pictures and answered questions put by the host of the live cable show. When asked if he was enjoying himself, Kaji delighted fans when he answered quite honestly that he'd rather be with Kazuki. The overwhelmingly positive response from the studio audience surprised a smile out of Kaji and I could almost feel tender young hearts melting. It was a crass thought, but it occurred to me that Kaji's concern for Kazuki made him a terribly romantic figure to the fans. Every sigh, every faraway stare was a token of his sorrow at being parted from his beloved. I only wished he were pretending. He truly suffered when he had to be away from Kazuki for more than a few hours.

I lost patience with him again a few days later when he was unprepared for rehearsal. "How do you bloody expect us to fulfill our engagements?" I asked in exasperation.

Kaji glanced around and saw that Sora, Michi, and Tsubasa were as edgy as I was. "I thought the tour was in two weeks."

"If you were at practice, you would know what the schedule is," Sora said.

"I try."

"I know," I said. "But it's time to make a decision, Kaji. Either you're committed to Hayate or you're not. Kazuki is perfectly capable of surviving for a few days with the serving and nursing staff."

"He would miss me."

"That's part of life, sausage. The two of you can't be together every minute of every day."

"No, but they try," Michi put in.

"Seriously, Susu-kun," Sora said. "Every day you disappear for hours into Kazuki's rooms."

"You know, I don't think I've seen Kazuki today," I said. "Is he doing all right?"

Kaji, being Kaji, didn't remind me of my promise to be Kazuki's friend. He was grateful that I'd asked about his lover, and that stung more than any reproach could have. "He is not... happy," Kaji said slowly. "Though he is stronger every day. I tell him how well he looks. He does not believe me."

"Everyone needs time to get over something that traumatic," I said. "We haven't heard from the police either. I don't think they're going to catch the bastards that thrashed him."

"If they were in my hands—" Kaji stopped in mid-sentence and unclenched his fists. "Is there no chance the tour can be postponed?"

"Of course, but by then we'd have lost the heat from the video."

"We need to go now," Sora said. "There is a demand for us and we ought to be filling it."

"Nobody fills better than us," Michi said.

Tsubasa took Kaji by the shoulders and shook him. "Snap out of it! Since when are you so submissive anyway? Let Kazuki fetch his own lip gloss for a few days."

"Come play with us!" Michi kissed the back of Kaji's neck and continued around the side until he got to Tsubasa. Giving the drummer a snog as well, Michi bounced once as Sora joined them.

"Come on, baby," Sora purred, vamping cheesily, bumping and grinding around the three-way hug. "Been too long since we did this in front of a bunch of people."

Kaji giggled as Sora stuck his tongue in his ear. "If I don't say yes, you will probably kidnap me anyway."

"I hadn't thought of that," I said. "But thanks for the suggestion."

"Yeah!" Michi said. "We can just tie you up and throw you in the car."

"Pervert!" Kaji laughed as Tsubasa tickled him.

If I'd been part of the group grope, I wouldn't have seen Kazuki. However, I was standing between the kitchen and sitting room, and had a clear line of sight to the hall. I just got a glimpse of his back as he hurried away, but I knew that he had been standing behind us for a little while at least. Leaving the lads to jolly Kaji, I went to face the dragon in his lair. Kazuki-style, he refused to turn and look at me as I joined him on his private deck. I had to walk around and block his view to get his attention.

"Hello, Kazuki." I made a point of mapping his face before meeting his eyes. "You look good."

"Why do you... mock me?"

"A more interesting question might be: why do you think my compliment is mockery?"

"Because you hate me."

"I do not!"

The Shining One sneered at me. "Yes you do, all of you."

"I can't speak for everyone, but *I* don't hate you." I paused. "Sora might, but he claims to hate a lot of people."

"This is not a joke for me."

"You need to loosen up a little. There's more to life than hit songs and popularity. I rather thought that once you got away from Sato you'd change, but you're still a stick."

Kazuki cocked his head at me. "Stick?"

"Let's not get into that right now. If I can accept that you love Kaji, then maybe you can accept that I don't hate you."

He narrowed those winter-wolf eyes at me skeptically.

"Look, Kazuki, we have to find a way to work together or at least coexist for Kaji's sake."

"I am doing nothing."

"Right, and Kaji's doing nothing right along with you. You don't want him to fail, do you?" I waited several seconds for a reply that didn't come. "Is that what you want? Do you want him to stop singing and attend you twenty-four hours a day?" Kazuki smiled dreamily and I had the urge to smack him. "Are you on pain meds?" I gave him the benefit of the doubt.

"Hayate has a tour." He ignored my question.

"Yes, Hayate has a tour," I said slowly. "They're supposed to leave for the mainland next Monday."

"They seem very happy to go away and leave me behind."

"You're not exactly endearing yourself to anyone. You hide in here all the time."

"I don't want to be seen."

"This again? Come on, mate, you're more than a pretty face."

Kazuki blinked and performed his out-of-body trick. His eyes went soft focus and fixed on a point somewhere between us.

"I just don't get you," I said. I might have elaborated, but Kaji joined us.

He came to stand by Kazuki's side, slipping an arm around his waist. Kazuki pulled Kaji close, bending to kiss the top of his head. *"Takara,"* he murmured. *Treasure.*

"What is going on here?" Kaji asked, looking pleased to see us together.

"Just getting to know each other better," I said. "I should go back to work now."

"I hope you two aren't having secrets from me," Kaji said as I left.

"No danger of that," I called back.

I spent the afternoon calling promoters and double-checking that everything was lined up in each city Hayate would visit. It was a lightning two-week loop, ending with a special concert in Tokyo at one of the city's largest venues. We were on a bill with two other bands, but we didn't care. The arena held 20,000 seats and 17,000 tickets had already been sold. That was ten times the largest number of people the band had performed in front of. The lads alternated between anxious and ebullient. I kept plowing ahead as if everything would turn out the way it was supposed to, but if Kaji got cold feet at the last minute we'd be screwed, blued and tattooed.

I shouldn't have doubted my *ichiban*, but I could see that it was a struggle of monumental proportions for him. He was a poet deeply and romantically in love for the first time and his emotions swept through his slight frame like gale-force gusts. I wouldn't have changed him for the world, but I worried sometimes that he'd expire from excess of passion, just spontaneously combust in a glorious blaze. It never occurred to Kaji to take life at anything other than full throttle, something that James Dean would've understood. Shaking off the morbid thought that the good die young, I looked up and noticed it had grown dark while I gathered wool.

I was taking a bottle of water from the refrigerator door when I heard a loud crash from the east side of the house. "Kaji," I said under my breath like an abbreviated prayer for the safety of a loved one. As I walked down the hall toward Kazuki's suite, I heard tinkling noises and another crash. Picking up my pace, I reached the main door to Kazuki's rooms in four strides. "Is everything all right in there?" I called out as I put my hand on the doorknob.

"Everything is fine," Kaji answered.

"What was that noise?"

"Something broke."

"Is anyone hurt?" I waited. "Kaji? Is anyone hurt?" When I didn't get a reply, I opened the door and walked in. An antique silvered-glass mirror that had formed part of a vaguely Gothic mixed-media sculpture lay in ruins on the floor. Kazuki crouched amid the glittering fragments while Kaji stood over him, holding tight to Kazuki's wrists. The bony grip of dread squeezed my heart as I hurried over, but though there was blood, there wasn't an ocean of it. I don't know if Kazuki was attempting suicide, but my lad obviously wasn't taking chances. "What the hell happened?" I asked.

Kaji's eyes were locked on Kazuki's and it was a long moment before he spoke. "The mirror broke."

"By itself? Or was there poltergeist activity?"

Kazuki pulled away from Kaji's hold and rose to his feet. "I broke it."

"I had a feeling that might be the case," I said, without looking at him. I was intent on assessing Kaji's injuries. Taking his hands, I turned them over and inspected them. Down the outside of his left palm was a long gash, the source of the blood that dappled the wooden floor. "Well, this is lovely."

Kaji pulled his sleeve down to stanch the flow of red. "Are you all right?" he asked Kazuki.

Kazuki rolled his head on his neck with an audible popping noise. Without a word, he spun smoothly on his heel and walked away over the jagged debris. He flinched when Kaji called his name, but he kept going into his bedroom. Kaji started after him, but stopped when I asked him to.

"Come on, Kaji. Let me see to that cut." I went in search of the first aid kit and he followed me. The nursing staff kept extra stock in one of the linen closets and I found everything I needed there. I told Kaji to hop up on the kitchen counter and wash his hands in the sink. Once the blood was cleaned away, the wound wasn't nearly as bad as it looked. "You'll live," I told him. "But it's going to be sore."

He sat quietly, not wincing once as I cleaned more deeply with hydrogen peroxide and a pair of tweezers. A few tiny bright splinters went into the sink and I applied antibiotic salve. The cut wasn't deep enough for stitches but it was long enough to need a proper bandage. When I was finished, Kaji held up his hand and looked at the white gauze. "Makes me look dangerous," he said.

"Or careless." I busied myself putting away the supplies in the same way I'd found them.

"It was an accident."

"I didn't say it wasn't."

Kaji sucked in his lower lip, tucking his chin and looking up at me from under his long lashes. "You've always been truthful with me before," he said.

"We're leaving in the morning. I just didn't want to get into a big drama tonight."

"Kazuki is big drama for sure."

"Try not to look so pleased." I got a bottle of water and handed one to Kaji. "Is he seeing someone about those mood swings?"

"Those on the nursing staff are trained therapists."

"I suppose they know what they're doing then. What set Kazuki off?"

"I told him I was going on tour."

"He already knew."

"Yes, I have told him many times, but this time, he heard me when I asked him to come with me."

"Is it worth it?" I asked abruptly.

"Of course, Benny-chan. I love him and he loves me. Whatever problems he has, we'll work them out together. He won't always be like this." Kaji paused. "I cannot imagine greater happiness than being with the one I love, or a greater sorrow than being alone."

"You're wise beyond your years. Hey, where are you going?"

"We are waking early so I am going to bed now."

"It's barely eight o'clock."

"I am not going directly to sleep." Kaji winked.

"Are you insane?"

"Make-up sex, Benny-chan."

I made a show of putting my fingers in my ears. "I don't hear this."

Kaji laughed and started to walk away.

"I'm serious," I said. "I think you're insane if you go back in there tonight."

"My dragon won't hurt me... unless I ask him to."

"That's not funny at the moment. You already have one bandaged body part."

"I am not afraid of him."

"Maybe you should be," I muttered.

58

Kaji came back to take my hand and hold it between his. "I wish you knew my Kazuki," he said. "You would believe me when I say he couldn't hurt me." I gestured to his hand and Kaji smiled. "I did this to myself when I knocked a piece of glass aside. I am going to bed now. All right?"

"I have legitimate concerns here."

"Do what you think is right. I am going to be with Kazuki for as long as I can before I have to leave."

It was a long night for me.

Chapter Six

Nineteen shows in fifteen days, that's what we did. Five singles in China and two shows a night in Seoul, Bangkok, Manila, Taipei, Brunei, Osaka, and Nagano. We would arrive in town having traveled all night, grab a couple of hours' sleep in the hotel, do a sound check, get into stage clothes and makeup, give a kickass performance, tear down and start the process all over again. If the lads hadn't been nitro-powered Tasmanian devils with rubber bones and the uncanny ability to fall asleep anywhere, we wouldn't have made it. Other managers fed their charges on a diet of amphetamines, nicotine, and alcohol, but they should've known better. They were my age and had presumably been around the block a couple of times. I spurned short-term fixes and made sure there was always plenty of water and fruit around to supplement the regular meals. It wasn't easy, but it was worth it. Under their war paint, dye, and piercings, the lads' skin, hair, and eyes glowed with good health. Take it from me: there is no more effective beauty regimen than the right food and enough rest. Someday, I'll write a book.

Despite these measures, Hayate was on the ragged edge of exhaustion by the time we got to Nagano, last stop before returning home. Perversely, our run of luck deserted us. Not only were the hotel rooms not ready for us, the desk clerk had no record of our reservation. While I reasoned with him, I sent the band down to the venue. At least they wouldn't have to sit in a rented truck until things were worked out. With the help of the hotel manager, I secured two rooms in a place closer to the auditorium. Pleased with myself, I trotted down to the big old building to find my boys.

Michi and Tsubasa had captivated the cleaning staff of four women of varying ages. Surrounded by their mop-wielding admirers the bass player and drummer entertained them with outrageous stories of Hayate's fame and prowess. Sora was sitting at the edge of the stage with his guitar in his lap. It was still some time before we could expect technicians to arrive for a sound check, but he was strumming the unplugged instrument meditatively, as if trying to remember an elusive melody. I didn't see Kaji until I walked into the wing on the right of the stage. Our singer was fast asleep on a pile of folded velvet curtains, lying on his side with his knees drawn up, one hand under his cheek. Only the fact that he desperately needed rest kept me from tousling his hair. I just watched him breathe for a few moments and moved on, introducing myself to the manager of the theater. The promoter was scheduled to meet with me as well, but he didn't show up. Meanwhile, the techs had drifted in and begun a desultory check of their equipment. I shooed away Michi and Tsubasa's audience and sent the boys to join Sora before I went to wake Kaji. He was in the same position, deep in dreams, but someone had kindly thrown a coat over him. I recognized it right away.

The floor-length duster was an eye-catching garment of faux polar bear fur lined with pale blue silk. It was massive and it took skill to move around in it. Never intended as mere protection from the cold, it had been a prop in one of Kazuki's ethereal, fairy-tale videos and he sometimes wore it to premieres. Seeing it here was a shock. When I recovered, I looked quickly around as though I'd catch someone skulking. I didn't want to admit it, but the appearance of the coat shook me. It was just… weird.

"Kaji." I shook his shoulder. "Time to wake up."

He stirred and blinked at me, trying to remember where he was. "I had a strange dream," he yawned. "Why are you looking at me like that?"

I leaned over and rubbed the ball of my thumb over the smudged circle in the middle of his forehead. It was black and smeared like eyeliner and I thought one of the other lads must have put it there as a joke. Maybe Kaji had done it himself; he was forever doodling on his skin. I finished cleaning it off as Kaji ran a hand over the thick fake fur of the coat.

"This is Kazuki's," he said.

"Yeah, but I haven't seen him. The coat was here when I came to wake you."

"I have to find him."

"You have a sound check to do. I'll look for Kazuki, all right?"

Kaji stood as a flashing riff from Sora's amplified instrument made the air vibrate. "All right," he said, already turning toward the stage area. Once the music started, he was part of it and could no more resist the summons than an iron filing can refuse the magnet. "Please look for him for me?"

I took the coat he handed me and watched him dance off to join the other lads. The howl of a lovesick werewolf kicked off a song written three days ago in the bus. It was already tight and had the sound of platinum. With the assurance that Hayate would be occupied for the next hour, I unlimbered my phone and made a few calls. The staff at the country house had not seen Kazuki since yesterday evening, but didn't consider that unusual. The nurse I spoke to maintained her professional politeness, but it was plain that she had had enough of her famous patient. I insisted on remaining on the line while someone went to look for him. The nurse came back and reported that Kazuki-san's door was locked and that she was calling his doctor. I thanked her, hung up, and called the attorney, Mr. Shin.

"Ah, hello, most pleasant to speak with you again, Mr. Blume."

"I hope so. Sorry to be short, but do you know where Kazuki is?"

"I assume he is recuperating in the country."

"I don't want to be an alarmist, but could you have someone you trust check on him?"

"Of course! I have been too much... out of the loop, yes? Perhaps I should have a more... hands-on approach with my client?"

"Hands-on is a good policy in my book. I couldn't begin to guide Hayate if I didn't live among them."

"I will consider your words. Kazuki's world is a strange one to me. I am not sure I would do well there."

"You'll adapt; trust me."

"Perhaps you would guide me as well."

I was silent for a moment trying to decide if Yoshiro's words had a double meaning. "Are you coming on to me a little?"

"I would... come on to you more if I believed it were welcome."

"Why Mr. Shin, how very bold of you." He began to apologize and I cut him off. "That was a joke. It's been a while since I had any desire to play this game, but why don't we see how it goes?"

"Then, may I assume it will be possible to see you when you return to Tokyo?"

"I'm sure we can find some excuse to get together."

"I would like that very much." He paused. "I am sorry to raise this issue, but I assume you are what is called openly gay."

"I've never made an issue of it."

"Ah, good. Then there will be no need to fabricate reasons to be together."

"No, I suppose not." I said goodbye and moved on to my next call. Lunch was delivered and afterward, I sent the lads to the hotel for a lie-down. I was almost ready to join them, when the manager of the hall sent me a text. The promoter was in his office. I was tempted to blow off the meeting, but since the office was on my way out, I stopped in.

"Well, fuck me. Hello, Sunshine." A familiar voice drawled a profane greeting and I stared in disbelief at the man perched on the corner of the desk. "Don't you have a hug for an old friend?"

"Rune." His name fell off my numb lips. Hagen Rune, whose golden shadow had once loomed so large over every aspect of my life, was sitting less than two yards away from me. Suddenly, I was eighteen again, bright, beautiful, drunk on immortality with the common sense of a cat in season. I felt the heat that radiated from his honey-toned flesh and an answering fire blossomed outward from my loins. Yes, I used the word loins. It's a bit archaic, but believe me; it fits the primeval feeling of lust that swept through me. Carried through my bloodstream, the warm wave reached every part of me and all the memories I'd thought buried under the rubble rose up like souls on the day of the rapture. I remembered how it felt to rest in his arms, the sun on our bare skin, sated and slumberous, content. With an effort, I shook off the Rune Effect. I ignored the fact that at forty-two years of age, he had grown more rather than less handsome. I kept my eyes from dwelling on features so well cut they looked fresh from the sculptor's chisel. I disregarded the way the light made a crown of his fair hair. I absolutely refused to acknowledge that his eyes were still the exact blue of my heaven.

"Did someone tell you I died or something?" Rune hopped off the desk with the leonine ease that always sent sexual static racing along my nerves. "You look like you're seeing a ghost."

"Might as well be," I managed to say. "You've been dead to me for years."

"Still got that sharp tongue, I see."

The owner of the venue got in on the conversation. "I see you are acquainted and I have much work." He bowed briefly and left the room to us.

"Don't tell me you're the promoter."

"Why wouldn't I be?"

"Because you're hopeless when it comes to organization." I paused. "Of course, you are four hours late for this meeting. And what's the idea of using the name Hikage?"

"It's the name of my company. So what if I call myself that?"

"If I'd known I'd run into you—" He stopped in front of me, close enough to touch, and my words dried up in my mouth.

"I call myself Shadow, because that's what I am now."

I swallowed audibly. "You look solid enough to me."

"Always the flirt, Sunshine. I've missed you."

"How sad for you."

"You can't imagine how I felt when Mr. Li called to remind me of the meeting and mentioned your name. I drove so fast."

"Obviously, you have a different impression of the terms on which we parted." My speech became stilted as I tried to distance myself from Rune. "I'm not at all excited to see you."

"Liar." Rune purred the word in his raw silk voice. "I can see the pulse in your neck. I could always tell when you were nerved up."

"You were so often the cause."

"You look great. Why don't we have dinner before the show?"

"I don't have time."

"After the show?"

"I'm too busy."

"Breakfast tomorrow?"

"I'll be out of town."

"Are you enjoying this?"

"Immensely. Now, if you'll excuse me?"

"For running away now? Or a decade ago?"

"Running away!" I repeated in outrage. All the hot recriminations I'd stored up were scalding my tongue, but I choked them back. I was not going to have a soul-shredding session with him. I was going to look after my lads. "I've got work to do," I said and walked away on rubbery legs.

"I won't give up so easy," he called after me.

"I won't give in so easily," I replied, but I muttered it under my breath. No point in letting him know just how far under my skin he was.

I went to the hotel knowing I wouldn't be able to rest. The day had been fraught with ominous events, enough to rattle the legendary composure of the British. Kaji was awake and anxious for news of Kazuki, who was not answering his phone. I had nothing comforting to tell him. He brooded for a few minutes and then started on his makeup. I watched him finger-paint for a while before taking out my phone. I was shocked to see I'd missed a call from Yoshiro Shin, probably while under the influence of Rune. Mr. Shin assured me that he'd talked with Kazuki and that all was well. I left the mystery of the coat for another time, thanked him, and rang off. Kaji was relieved to hear that Kazuki was all right and I went to wake the rest of the band.

The show that night was Hayate's best performance to date. They'd grown tighter and more professional with each concert on the grueling schedule and they'd honed their stage show to a series of crowd-pleasing antics. Male and female fans alike appreciated the band's hard-driving brand of rock after dark, but the ladies screamed their loudest when the lads vented their overflowing emotions in displays of exuberant affection. Kaji used his bandmates as makeshift props and tumbling platforms for his more athletic moves, bouncing, strutting, sliding, hugging, throwing cartwheels and handsprings at the drop of a microphone, bestowing slaps and slapdash kisses. With the change of a song, he was a supersonic sprite, a delinquent demon, or an angel with a broken wing, and the crowd couldn't get enough of him. He owned them by intermission and the second half of the show was electric, the current between the band and the audience flowing strongly, each feeding the other, daring each other, soaring to greater and greater heights. During the last encore, Kaji did a limber backbend and Sora moved between his thighs. The guitarist lifted his instrument over his head, playing blindly as he thrust against Kaji's crotch. Kaji pumped his pelvis as he sang the final chorus, his voice an abandoned wail of fulfillment that climbed the scale until it ended abruptly as all the lights went out. The screams were deafening.

"I like your boys." Rune's breath tickled my ear in the dark.

"Would you mind not standing so close?"

"Yes I would. From here, I can smell your intoxicating scent."

"You are so full of shite. Don't talk to me if all you've got are lame pick-up lines."

"I really like your boys." He turned to a safe topic as the lights came back up on the stage.

"They're brilliant, aren't they?" I turned to watch Kaji ride by on Sora's shoulders.

"They're talented and they're appealing. I could go on, but what else could I add?" Rune paused. "Your lead singer is smoking hot. Pretty as a girl, but all boy."

"That's one way to put it. Stay away from him, by the way."

"Are you seriously warning me off him?"

"He's a kid, not in your league."

"I was joking, Sunshine."

"You have a bad track record with younger men."

"I didn't leave you. It was the other way 'round."

I turned my back on him. "I have somewhere to be," I said as I walked away. He followed me backstage. It was his event; he'd hired the security crew so there wasn't much I could do to stop him. However, at the door to the dressing room, I drew the line. I was being petty, but I didn't want him to meet my lads. I wanted him to stay in my past where he belonged.

"Have coffee with me," he bargained.

"Why would I do that?"

"Because you like coffee and I'll buy you the biggest pastry in the shop."

"Go away and take your big pastry with you."

"All right, but you've not seen the last of me. Now that I've found you, I'm not going to let you out of my sight until we're friends again."

I didn't dignify that with an answer. Slipping through the door, I shut it in his face.

*I*t was good to be back in Tokyo. We would only have a few hours' rest before we had to be at the arena, but we were happy that we'd be sleeping in our own beds. I was surprised to see Mr. Shin's

BMW in the drive when we pulled in, but it was a pleasant surprise. The attorney was talking with his client when we entered the house, but readily broke off the conversation to greet us. Kazuki nodded in our direction as he rose and walked away. Kaji swiftly followed.

"Hello, Mr. Shin," I said, as the other band members scattered to their rooms. "I didn't think I'd see you so soon." I could only imagine what I looked like after hours on the road.

"Forgive the intrusion." Yoshiro bowed. "I am taking your advice."

"I'm taking some scotch. Would you care for a snort?"

"Whatever you are having, Mr. Blume."

"You might as well start calling me…. What would you call me?"

"Ben-ja-min has a beautiful sound, but somewhat formal. May I call you Ben?"

"If you like." I poured two tumblers of single malt neat and handed him one. "In my wilder days, they called me Benj."

"Ben-juh?"

"It's a sort of pun on the English word binge. Look it up."

Yoshiro bowed again and sipped his drink. "Very fine," he said.

I sat down and he resumed his seat, perching on the edge. I was damned if I was going to let this be awkward. We weren't ignorant teenagers on a first date. Yet, my mind remained stubbornly blank as I sat in silence racking my brain for something to say. "How's Kazuki?"

"Kazuki is… difficult."

"I'd noticed actually."

"I heard from the police yesterday evening. They wanted to know when Mr. Kazuki could give his statement."

I stared at the lawyer. "He never talked to the police?"

"Apparently, he did not."

"And they didn't press him because he's a celebrity."

"*Hai.*" Yoshiro gazed into his glass. "He is very popular."

I nodded. "He has a huge and amazingly diverse fan base."

"Something for everyone."

"Nicely put. Don't you think, though, a person could reach the point where they've given so much of themselves away that they have nothing left? Sorry, I rather lost my grasp on that thought while I was talking. Do you know what I mean though?"

"Not precisely, but I very much enjoy listening to you speak."

My ears felt warm as I raised my glass for a drink. I hoped I wasn't blushing, but it had been a while since a man had said anything vaguely romantic to me. Rune's vulgar come-ons did not count. "You like a British accent?"

Yoshiro nodded. "Yours is not from London, is it?"

"No, I'm a country boy, a north-country boy."

Yoshiro nodded again. "You have lost most of your accent, but the… lilt?" He raised his eyebrows at me for confirmation. "The lilt is still there, the music that makes north English accents sound somewhat like Scottish brogues."

"You sound somewhat like Sherlock Holmes."

"*Arigato.*"

I smiled at his sincere thanks, but sobered again. "Seriously, Yoshiro—"

"Yoshi, please."

"Seriously, Yoshi. Do you think Kazuki is a danger to himself or maybe someone else?"

"Kazuki is a person of large emotions despite how he may seem on the surface. Hard to say what he will do. I have spoken to him about seeking counsel for the storm inside him."

I sat back and regarded him through narrowed eyes. Kaji had been right. There were two Mr. Shins; one was a model of the buttoned-down Asian white-collar worker, but the other seemed to have a mystical bent. "Do you think he'll listen to you and find someone to calm the storm?"

"For tonight, he has Akihashi-san."

"I'm going to be blunt. I'm afraid Kaji's going to get hurt, and I can't have that."

"I understand. He is the child of your heart."

"You're awfully perceptive."

"My parents wanted me to be a monk."

I laughed, nearly spraying my trousers with scotch. "Sorry. I'm very tired."

"Your laughter is most welcome. Please don't fear too much for your young friend. Kazuki is a raging sea, but Akihashi Susumu is the moon." He stood. "I should get back to the city."

"Thanks for drinking with me at the crack of dawn."

"A pleasure, Ben."

"What are you doing tonight?"

"I have no plans but working."

"Would you be my guest at Hayate's performance?"

"It would be my very great pleasure."

I told him where and when to meet me and took his hand as we said goodbye. His skin was soft and warm and for a moment, I imagined him touching me more intimately. I looked into his eyes and wondered if he felt the same curiosity. His smile persuaded me that he did. As the sound of his engine died away, I drifted through the rambling house to my room and surprised myself by falling asleep as soon as I lay down.

Chapter Seven

I t's a bloody good job you don't play piano, mate," I said, as I looked at Kaji's hand. The cut had healed well and on stage, he'd worn a glove over the bandages until he didn't need them.

"I play piano."

"I meant…. Oh, never mind."

"The hand has given me no trouble."

I swatted his bottom as he jumped down from the counter. "What about the dragon? Is he giving you any trouble?"

Kaji rolled his eyes at me. "Kazuki is going through a hard time. All he wishes is to be left alone until he is ready."

"Ready for what?"

Kaji shrugged. "Just ready."

"Is he going with us to the arena?"

"No. He will watch on television."

One less thing to worry about. "Did you ever ask him about the mystery coat?"

"I returned the coat to him and he tossed it into the closet without looking at it. When I asked, he changed the subject."

"Odd," I said. "Either he's sneaking out and following you, or…." I made weird noises, pulling my face into an expression of comic dread.

"Or what?" Sora said, as he came in to get a bottle of water.

"The coat is possessed," I said dramatically.

Kaji and Sora exchanged a glance and laughed at me. "Why don't you see the obvious?" Sora said. "Kazuki is a vampire with strange powers."

"Don't say such things." Kaji pulled Sora's hair. "Anyway, you have all seen him in daylight."

"True," Sora said. "But he is a very special sort of vampire, a demon vampire."

"It would please him to hear you say it."

"No doubt." Sora affectionately cuffed the back of Kaji's head on his way by. "No ordinary lovers for Kaji Sukoshi. He has to find the strangest one of all."

"Rock 'n' roll," Kaji replied.

"I hope you're walking around idly because you're packed and ready," I said to the departing guitarist.

"*Hai*," Sora said as he went to the front door.

"We're leaving in twenty minutes," I told Kaji. "When we're rich, maybe I'll buy a helicopter."

Kaji smiled at the notion of arriving for a show in a helicopter. "That would be max cool, Benny-chan."

I went to load my pockets with the small items that were the tools of my trade and returned to the front of the villa, ready to herd rock stars. In the large foyer, I found Kaji saying goodbye to Kazuki one more time. Kazuki sat on an upholstered bench, leaning against the wall behind him. Kaji faced him astride his thighs, hugging Kazuki's head to his chest as he palmed Kazuki's short hair. Kazuki tilted his head back, courting a kiss, and Kaji lowered his face to move his lips slowly against the other man's mouth. I saw how Kazuki drank in the affection and my ambivalent feelings about him shifted balance again. Was it possible that the Shining One was just an odd boy starved for love and too proud to ask for it? It seemed too pat, but I reminded myself that clichés become clichés for a reason and I renewed my resolve to give him the benefit of the doubt, if only for Kaji's sake.

Before I could make a noise to let them know they weren't alone, Kazuki slid his hands down the back of Kaji's purple cargo trousers and cupped his arse cheeks. Kaji raised his face to the ceiling, rising to a kneeling position, eyes closing in pleasure as Kazuki's fingers moved under the fabric. Kazuki pressed his face to Kaji's crotch, nuzzling aggressively, biting at the ridge of his lover's growing arousal. Kaji braced his hands on Kazuki's shoulders and pumped his pelvis languidly, rubbing his hard flesh against that lovely face. Feeling my deprived willy stir in interest, I left and used another door.

Sora was leaning against our shiny new van, tossing and catching a silver dagger he'd picked up in Bangkok. Michi and Tsubasa were laughing at a story the driver was telling, but they all looked at me as I walked around the corner of the sprawling house.

"Where's Kaji?" I asked innocently.

Sora cocked his head as if listening carefully. "Sounds like they're almost finished."

Michi smirked at Tsubasa, which inspired the bass player to grab his friend and pretend to hump him frantically. Tommy, the driver, cracked up and advised them to get in the van out of sight. Sora frowned at the front door, ignoring his bandmates' fooling about. I counted off two minutes and told Tommy to blow the horn. The door of the house opened and Kaji backed out, his hands busy at his waistband. As he fumbled with the metal buttons, Kazuki followed, welded to him at the lips. The lads reacted predictably: shouting mockery, encouragement, and reprimands. Kaji made a rude hand gesture over his shoulder, and I told him we were about to activate the kidnap option. Kazuki framed Kaji's face in his hands as his lover pulled away from him. The Shining One didn't plead and his expression was neutral, but the air between him and Kaji was almost luminous with the intensity of his emotion. For half a heartbeat, I was sure the two of them would disappear in a flash of blinding radiance, and then Kazuki dropped his hands, freeing Kaji. He turned without a backward look and went inside. Kaji stared at the closing door, chewing his lower lip until the horn sounded again. He ran to the van, and Michi yanked him inside. As Hayate teased their lead singer about his last-minute preparations for the show, we took the road to Tokyo.

*T*he arena was enormous and the event well funded by a big radio station and Zennousha Music. The featured bands received the red-carpet treatment and wallowed in it like true hedonists. The hospitality room was a fever-dream *bishōnen* harem of fourteen delicately handsome young men in leather and silk, laughing, bouncing and feeding one another from the sumptuous buffet. It was like seeing three tribes of the same nation meeting up at an oasis and declaring a feast day. They ran rampant and I was having the time of my life. I should have known it wouldn't last long.

"Surprise, Sunshine!" Rune stopped beside me and offered me one of the glasses in his hands.

I held up my drink so he could see that I already had one. I didn't need him for anything.

Rune tossed back one of his drinks, set the glass down, and started on the other. "I'll bet you didn't think you'd see me here."

"Hoped. I *hoped* I wouldn't see you here."

"So… you were thinking about me."

"Why are you doing this to me?"

"It's more something I'm doing *for* me than *to* you."

"Selfish as ever. Did it occur to you that I'm not interested?"

"Never."

"Bloody conceit!" I exclaimed. "Look, if you won't go, I will."

"It never occurred to me because we're *meant* to be together. When we were together before, I didn't know what I wanted, but now I do."

"Too late."

"Why? You're not in love with anyone."

"And how would you know that?"

"If you had someone in your life, you'd be able to give up the weird thing you have with your singer."

"I don't have a weird thing with Kaji, but I doubt you'd understand our relationship."

"I doubt you understand it." Rune finished his drink. "So what do you say, Sunshine? Will you at least give me a chance?"

Before I could say no, Mr. Shin in his black suit appeared from the throng like a priest blessing a flock of fallen angels. I waved him over and somewhat triumphantly, introduced him to Rune as my guest for the evening.

"An unrestrained and often excessive indulgence," Yoshiro said.

"I beg your pardon?"

"Spree," he replied. "A drunken revel."

"It is rather festive in here," Rune said, looking around the room.

Yoshiro smiled. "I looked up the meaning of binge."

I chuckled and relished Rune's frown when he saw there was a joke he wasn't in on. To my annoyance, he attached himself to us. Yoshiro was too polite to say anything and Rune ignored my hints. Even more irritating, Rune was on his best game, charming and affable, making you feel privileged to be in the company of such a delightful man. I glared at him whenever Yoshi was looking the other way.

"This is Sora, yes?" Yoshi pointed out our lead guitarist deep in conversation with a pink-maned androgyne in white lace.

I nodded and found the other band members for him. Michi was demonstrating his behind-the-back drumstick twirl and Tsubasa was stuffing his face with lobster puffs. I didn't see Kaji right away, because he was hidden behind the tallest man I'd yet seen in Japan. He wasn't at all familiar to me and my hackles rose as he lifted Kaji off his feet and threw him over his shoulder. Kaji was laughing , holding out his hands to Kaoru, lead guitarist of Burnt Incense, entreating his help. Kaoru backed away, holding a finger over his head to indicate the other man's gigantic stature. Onlookers chuckled as the stranger lifted Kaji as easily as a father lifts a child, demanding a kiss as toll for putting him down. Kaji got a hand on the top of the big guy's head, a foot on his chest, and flipped backward, landing on his feet. The big man laughed, feathery reddish hair trailing over his handsome features.

"How do you like my boy?" Rune asked. "Sung Ke Smith is the future of Asian rock 'n' roll."

"That's your opinion." I smiled at Kaji's good-natured rebuff of Sung's continued attempts to snog him. "If you want to see the real face of rock's future, there it is."

"I guess we'll see."

Yoshi would have to have been bereft of his senses not to feel the tension between Rune and I. "I'm a bit hungry," he said. "Would you like to get something from the buffet?"

"I'm going to talk to Kaji for a minute," I said. "I'll join you after, unless you want to go with me."

Yoshi opted to wait for me at the table and my expression warned Rune to behave. As I approached Kaji, Sung hooked his fingers in my lad's belt loops and lifted him until they were face to face. With a big smile, he leaned forward, but Kaji turned his head, still laughing. Damn, this big bloke was persistent.

"Kaji, I need to talk to you," I said over the ambient noise.

Sung looked at me like the herd stallion assessing a strange male. I ignored him and waited for Kaji to answer.

"Put me down," Kaji said. "This is my manager."

The big guy immediately set Kaji on his feet and bowed an apology at me. "See you later, honey cutie," he said, patting Kaji's head before moving away.

"Having fun?" I asked.

Kaji grinned. "Of course."

"Sung seems to like you."

"He'll get over it. It would be nice if Kazuki was here."

"Maybe it's better this way. If he were here, he'd own the room. Not on purpose maybe, but he'd still be the center of attention."

"True. He cannot help it."

"Tonight is Hayate's night. Enjoy it."

"It is also Burnt Incense night and Vudu Heat night."

"Do you have to be so literal?"

"I see Mr. Shin is here."

"As my guest. Is there anything you want to comment on?"

"No, Blume-sama. I am certain you have matters of business to discuss." He smiled impishly.

"Not really. I just like his company, but I still don't want to hear any shite about it from you and the lads, all right?"

"Michi might explode."

"I'll take the risk."

"I am not teasing you, I promise, but what about the other man?"

"What other man?"

"Don't pretend you don't know. That hot blond man who looks at you with such longing."

"That subject is not up for discussion."

"Is he the Viking?"

"Not another word, *ichiban*. It's time to do a last equipment check."

Kaji pursed his lips, but didn't ask any more questions as we gathered up Mr. Shin, Sora, Michi, and Tsubasa and went down to the auditorium. The other musicians trickled down to hang out backstage after assuring themselves that their instruments were waiting on one of the three rotating stages. My job was over until after the lads finished playing and I took the opportunity to soak up the buzz of being part of the show. I was the insider here and I enjoyed answering Yoshi's questions before Vudu Heat started their set and conversation became impossible.

Vudu's vibe was metallic and much darker than Hayate's quicksilver, vampire-cowboy style. Vudu's costumes were based on dominance gear and I suspected their lead singer was a genuine alien life form. Pale and painfully thin with yellow contacts and hair like a black and white chrysanthemum, Gekko was an arresting sight as he slalomed around the microphone stand and his bandmates like a stray cat made of smoke. I didn't care for his voice, which alternated between shrill sonar blips and grungy dirge growls, but the audience was buying his act and Sung Ke Smith was a genuine prodigy on guitar.

"Quite a spectacle," Yoshi commented when the last chord died away.

I smiled at him for reminding me that people will slow down to look at a car wreck. It was a petty thought, but I'm loyal to my lads. Politely, I congratulated the members of Vudu on a good set as they walked by on their way off-stage. Sung thanked me, smiling all the while at Kaji. Sora finally noticed the byplay and decided that it offended him. He leaned past Kaji, got in Sung's face, and in the briefest possible terms, inquired as to exactly what it was that Sung wanted. Sung recoiled like a puppy with a slapped nose, and Sora found himself the focus of everyone's attention. Kaji raised an eyebrow at his guitarist as the announcer introduced Hayate. Sora shrugged and put an arm around Kaji's shoulders. Together they bounded onto the stage with Michi and Tsubasa close behind.

Whether it was the feeling of being in the big time, the camaraderie of his peers, or the send-off that Kazuki had given him, Kaji was on fire for the entire forty minutes allotted to Hayate. The blaze spread among the band members and they lit up the stage, burning out of control for the last song, a blistering version of their club anthem "How Hot? Too Hot!" The crowd was still calling for Hayate when Burnt Incense took the stage. Sung Ke was waiting to pick Kaji up and swing him around until Sora got in his way. If there was to be any twirling of Kaji, it would be done by one of his bandmates, not some gorilla in black rubber. I looked up from hugging Michi and Tsubasa to see Sung and Sora chest-to-chest with Kaji calling both of them idiots.

"Some things do not change," Yoshi said. "Young men and their pride."

"I should go break that up."

"You will only add more wood to the fire. Not every problem is yours to solve, Ben. Let them decide how they wish to end this. Perhaps it will teach them a lesson about forethought."

"What are you doing?" Kaji asked Sora and Sung. "You don't dislike each other."

"He's too pushy," Sora said.

"You are a meddler," Sung shot back.

"You are no one," Sora topped him. "We are Clan Hayate. When some caveman tries to move on a brother, we don't stand by and watch without doing something."

"It's not like that, Sora," Kaji said. "Sung, if you want to be my friend, you will stop now."

Sung uncrossed his arms. "I meant no disrespect."

"Kaji is not a toy," Sora insisted.

"Are you sure?" Sung glanced at Kaji. "He could be a teddy bear."

Sora kept his war face on for another second before he grinned at Sung. "You're right. Ka-chan is very cute and nice to cuddle with."

Kaji looked from Sora to Sung and back to Sora. "Are you finished bonding now?"

Sora and Sung clapped one another on opposite shoulders and nodded curtly. "You should come by our place for a drink some time," Sora said. "We could jam or something."

"I am free now."

Kaji and Sora laughed at Sung's brashness. "Not tonight," Kaji said. "Another time."

"Any time, honey."

Sora shook his head with a look of exaggerated sadness. "Sung Ke, is it possible you don't know that Kaji has a boyfriend?"

"It doesn't surprise me since he's so cute and sexy, but if this boyfriend was smart, he wouldn't let Kaji-babo out on his own. He's taking a big risk."

"I don't think he's too worried," Michi laughed.

"When there's guys like me around?" Sung struck a bodybuilder pose.

"Oh, you poor fool." Michi giggled, hanging on Tsubasa. "Who wants to tell this *baka ka*?"

"Tell me what?" Sung asked. "Don't leave me hanging, man."

"You see," Yoshiro said to me. "They have resolved the matter honorably."

"If you say so." I smiled to let him know this was my attempt at humor. Glancing away, I caught Rune staring at me. Looking quickly aside, I saw Vudu's vocalist, Gekko, gazing at Kaji with an expression that would best be described as venomous. It didn't surprise me that the wafer-thin singer who called himself Moonlight was a bitch. As me mum used to say, hungry people are always cross.

"Kaji's out of your league, *chibi*," Tsubasa advised Sung.

Kaji came to stand next to me, wanting no part of the teasing. "I would like to go home," he said.

"You don't want to hear the rest of BI's set and go to the after party?"

"If you think I should, I will, but I would rather go home."

"That's fine. Let's check with the rest of the lads and we can go."

"You do not have to miss the fun."

"Don't worry about it. I'm knackered."

"Hey!" Kaji called to his bandmates. "Stop torturing Sung Ke for a minute. Do you want to stay here or go home?"

The rest of Hayate decided to stay in the city for what was shaping up to be the party of the year. Kaji and I were castigated as lightweights as we said good night.

"Wait, honey," Sung called after Kaji. "Tell me who your boyfriend is so I can take you away from him."

"Stop being so stupid all the time," Gekko told Sung. "Everybody knows Ka-chan is having a super *hentai* sex affair with Kazuki-sama."

"No way!" Sung exclaimed. "Hey, Kaji cutie! You need a real man for a boyfriend."

Sora snickered, but Kaji didn't acknowledge the comment as he moved away from the light and noise. Yoshi walked out to the van with us and said goodbye while Kaji and the driver waited in the vehicle.

"Sorry I'm running out on our date," I said. "I really am done in."

"I expected nothing, so your company was a great gift."

"I had a good time too."

"May I hope that we will see one another again like this?"

"If you're asking me out, I accept." The pleased look his face was humbling. We shouldn't have that much power over another person's emotions. It's a lot of responsibility to shoulder.

"I will call you."

"You know I never go anywhere without my trusty phone." I could see that he wasn't going to make a move, not in a million years, so I leaned toward him and brushed his lips with mine. It was nothing, a token good-night kiss, but it felt like a lot more. It felt like something had been put in motion that would keep running until it reached its conclusion. I suppose you could say the same of each action we take, but it felt right to kiss him, so I did. No need to make a big existential deal out of it.

I climbed into the van, ignoring Kaji's grin, and asked Tommy to take us home. When I looked back, Yoshi was standing in the same spot, fingers touching his lips as he watched us drive away. As I faced forward again, I caught Kaji's sparkling eyes.

"Not a word," I said.

Chapter Eight

*W*hen we reached the house, we were surprised to see sports cars and crotch-rocket motorcycles parked in the drive. We walked in and the jackhammer music of a German band currently in vogue assailed our ears. The noise was coming from the room with the biggest television and there we found a small but intense party going on. The room was thick with smoke of more than one kind and bottles and glasses stood on every horizontal surface. Thirty or so men and women were engaged in activities that ranged from merely shocking to prosecutable. I'm a rock 'n' roller, make no mistake, but even outlaws have standards. Before anyone at the party realized there were gatecrashers, my outrage carried me into the middle of the room. I slapped my hand down on a glass tray lined with white powder and looked into the face of the girl laying it out.

"The party's over!" I yelled over the train wreck of the music. "Get out and take this shite with you!"

The purple-haired purveyor of cocaine gave me a blank look until the vaguely familiar guy next to her whispered in her ear. She nodded, gathered her stuff, and left with a small train of bottom feeders in her wake. As I walked over to turn the sound down, other partygoers began drifting out and I saw Kaji moving determinedly against the current. Calculating his trajectory, I saw Kazuki enthroned on the leather couch with his fly open and an acolyte at his feet. When the kneeling figure slithered up to sit in his lap, I recognized fiery-haired Natsuko, the pixie lead singer of the pop band Strawburi. This wasn't going to be pretty, but I reckoned Kazuki deserved to be raked over the coals.

"I was listening to that," the Shining One said mildly when I turned the music off. Natsuko giggled a comment, lips moving against the side of Kazuki's neck as she zipped him up. Kaji stared at them in disbelief until Kazuki spoke again. "Why home so early? No after party?"

"What are you doing?" Kaji found his voice.

"Having a little party in honor of Hayate's success; what does it look like?"

"Why is Natsuko slobbering on you?"

"I like the way he tastes," she drawled. "You're right about the cinnamon."

Kaji met Kazuki's eyes and held them.

"We watched you on TV," Kazuki said. "Trend Thirteen had cameras everywhere." He leaned forward to pick up the remote, dislodging Natsuko from his lap. As she sulked prettily, Kazuki pressed play and on the giant screen, Sung Ke Smith manhandled Kaji. "Why didn't you bring your friend home? The four of us could have some real fun, if that's what you like."

"*Kuso* ! Are you that ready to distrust me?"

"Look at your face," Kazuki said, pointing to the screen. "Look!"

I saw what Kazuki saw, but he was misinterpreting Kaji's playful reaction to Sung's adoring assault. I opened my mouth to say so, but closed it again. Kaji could explain himself without help from me.

"We were just having fun," Kaji said. "There was nothing sexual happening."

"Talking about sex, are we all going to get busy at some point?" Natsuko broke in.

"You're sitting in my place," Kaji told her.

"Yes, and it's really nice."

"I know. Thanks for keeping it warm; now get out."

"Kazuki wants me to stay," Natsuko said, putting a hand on the Shining One's thigh.

Kazuki batted Natsuko's hand away. "This is not any longer... appropriate," he said.

Natsuko got to her feet as the last of the guests walked out the front door. "Tease," she said as she retrieved her scarf from the back of the couch. "You used to be fun, Zuki."

Kazuki didn't acknowledge the insult or the woman's angry exit. He wasn't aware of anything but Kaji now. "I am not a forgiving type," he said. "When I am struck, I strike back."

"That is your reason for putting that slut in my place?"

"I wanted to hurt you as much as you hurt me," Kazuki said flatly.

Perhaps one of the hardest things I've done in my life was to leave them alone, to accept that this was private, that I couldn't help, no matter how badly I wanted to. I had given Kaji the benefit of what little wisdom I had and now I had to trust him to handle his own love life. I walked out and slid the doors closed behind me. Kaji and Kazuki took breakfast in their room the next morning, but I didn't have long to brood over it.

The Hasu Corporation had decided to pick up Vudu Heat and assigned them as opening act for Hayate's upcoming tour of Japan. My mind was now consumed with the million and one details of readying the lads to go on the road again under the shadow of sharing the bill with Rune's band. The idea that he would be a daily presence was maddening. If I were ever going to lose my mind that would have been the time it went missing. However, I soldiered on, doing whatever needed doing, and not returning Rune's messages. After two days of nonstop organization, I felt confident that I'd prepared for any contingency. That's when Kaji told me Kazuki wanted to come with us.

"That's great," I said unconvincingly. "I'll just change all our travel arrangements."

Kaji laughed at me. "You are so easy to read, Benny-chan. Don't worry. Kazuki and Mr. Shin are making his arrangements."

"Good, because I just finished our itinerary."

"Mr. Shin asked me to greet you for him."

"He's a very polite man."

"*Hai.*" Kaji looked at me from the corners of his eyes. "I wonder what he looks like out of a suit."

"Do you really?"

"You must have noticed how handsome he is and his body looks fit. Perhaps we could go swimming together sometime."

"Don't match-make; it's a bad habit."

"Match-make?"

"You know what I mean."

"I just want you to have happiness."

"Speaking of that, are you still happy, *ichiban*?"

More gracious than I, he didn't pretend he didn't know what I was referring to. "Kazuki and I talked for a very long time last night. He understands now."

"Good. Jealousy is an ugly thing."

Kaji nodded. "Kazuki is very sorry about the way he behaved."

"Someone needs to tell him that life isn't like a soap opera."

"For him, life has been extreme always. I am trying to show him there is a place between the mountaintop and the valley."

"As if you've ever been there," I teased.

"It is true that I am an extreme rock-and-roll maniac," Kaji smiled. "But just now, Kazuki needs me to be the calm one."

"Kazuki is a lucky man."

"I am sure you will get lucky soon."

"Was that some sort of double entendre?"

Kaji gave me his perplexed look. "Just wishing you well."

"Right." I leaned back in my chair. "Are you all packed?"

"I never had time to unpack from the last trip. Besides, Kazuki wants me to go shopping with him, so I'll buy some new things, okay?"

"Absolutely. We have a wardrobe budget; go spend some of it."

"You know, maybe Hayate's manager should have a new image to go with our success." Kaji eyed my faded olive green corduroy trousers and baggy black jumper.

"I'm content as I am and I'm not the one the public wants to see."

Kaji came around the desk and invaded my space in a big way. Sitting sideways on my lap, he took over my PC and accessed his picture account. I actually flinched at the image he called up. There I was in all my sartorial glory in a scan of an ancient magazine layout of the decadent London club scene. The text under the photo described me as a willowy beanpole with the face of a Romance poet. I was wearing a rather elegant suit of matte black over a pink shirt with a wing collar. I remembered the scarf draped around my neck; Rune had bought it for me on a trip to Marrakech. It was so soft that Rune joked about it being spun from clouds as he drew it down my naked body. I stared into the heavy-lidded eyes of my younger self and tried to remember what I was thinking when the picture was taken. Most likely, I couldn't wait to get back to Rune or my next hit of Ecstasy.

"You're beautiful," Kaji said, resting his cheek against mine.

"I was very young in this photo."

Kaji put a finger to the screen to trace the curve of my hip. "And so sexy."

"If you say so."

"I say so."

"*Takara!*" Kazuki yelled from the front hall.

"You're being summoned," I said.

"Isn't he sweet the way he cannot wait?"

"Actually, we call that being spoiled, and it's not a good thing."

"My spoiled dragon." Kaji laughed as Kazuki called him again. "I am in here."

"No, no, no," I said, easing him off my lap. "There are breakables in here."

Kaji held on to me, grinning as Kazuki entered the room. Despite my protests, I was horribly abused as Kaji insisted on hiding behind me. Kazuki tried going around, over and through me, as I did my best to extricate myself. Kaji jumped up to wrap his arms around my neck and his legs around my waist. When his lips met Kazuki's over my shoulder, I yanked on a tuft of his hair hard enough to make him gasp.

"Enough," I said, when they broke the kiss. "Perverts."

Kaji rubbed his nose against my ear. "*Aishiteru.*" he laughed softly.

I expected Kazuki to have a tantrum, but he put his arms around me and rested his forehead against mine. "Friend of my beloved," he said a bit dramatically.

Nonplussed, I stood still as Kaji hugged me from behind. "We just want you to know you don't have to worry about us," he said. "You already have much to think about."

"*Hai,*" Kazuki said, his breath sweet as caramel.

"All right then. Thank you both. I'll just get back to work now."

Kaji and Kazuki left to go shopping, Kaji blowing me a kiss on the way out. I took a few moments to recover from the Shining One's unprecedented performance while I ignored the computer's notice that I had mail from Rune's Hikage Productions. Five minutes later, I received a call from Mr. Shin regarding his client's travel plans. I felt a lot better when Yoshi told me he'd be coming along. I enjoyed his company, and he'd be a buffer between Rune and me. If he could keep Kazuki in line, it would be a welcome bonus.

The equipment for the tour was traveling by truck, but the musicians would ride in private train coaches. We were scheduled to meet Vudu, who'd dropped the Heat from their name, at the station at nine. I'd asked Hayate to be at the van at eight and when I joined them, wearing a new suit, they whistled and carried on like loons. When we finally got on our way, Kazuki leaned across Kaji to tell me I looked sharp and I was absurdly pleased by the compliment.

The press had been notified, of course, and the two bands posed for photos at the station. Kazuki stood next to me in hat and sunglasses, watching the lads mug for the cameras. It was the first time I'd seen him in direct sunlight since he'd been discharged from the hospital. If I looked closely, I could discern faint scars, but I doubted anyone else would notice. I nudged him on the shoulder. "Go on, mate," I said, plucking the fedora from his head. "You know you want to."

Kazuki leveled his tranquil gaze on me. "Do you think I should?" He covered his face with black-gloved hands, inadvertently playing peek-a-boo with me.

"You're gorgeous and I'll bet your fans are hungry for a sight of you. Besides," I pointed, "are you really going to ignore that?"

We watched Sung throw Kaji over his shoulder and spank his bum. Before Sung's hand fell for the third time, the Shining One strode up like the wrath of heaven. Pulling Kaji away from Vudu's guitarist, Kazuki positioned himself between them and gave Sung a long cool stare before turning to the press. The photographers called Kazuki's name to get him to look at them as Kazuki moved behind Kaji, embracing him sweetly. Pressing his cheek to Kaji's, he smiled dreamily for the cameras. Kaji reached out and pulled Sora into the picture with one hand and Sung with the other. Despite my lad's efforts, the fickle press was only interested in the fact that the Shining One had surfaced. They shouted questions that went unanswered and clicked off hundreds of pictures until Kazuki ended the session in his inimitable manner.

Miming the need for a break, Kazuki swanned over to one of the benches under a bronze statue of a dog. Stretching out on his back, he let one booted foot dangle. With his forefinger, he beckoned to Kaji. When Kaji was close enough, Kazuki took his wrist and drew him down. With a look that clearly said *here we go again,* Kaji draped himself over Kazuki's supine form. Kazuki brushed a hanging lock of Kaji's hair behind his ear and cupped the back of Kaji's neck. With the slightest of pressure, whispering words only Kaji could hear, Kazuki coaxed him into a snog. Kaji kept his eyes open, and his doe-eyed gaze slid to the group of onlookers as his mouth moved on Kazuki's perfect lips. A few moments later, the kiss had morphed from an affectionate caress to full-blown necking with Kazuki's hands moving under Kaji's shirt. The number of people passing by grew and the photographers had to jockey for good angles as the oblivious couple collected a crowd. It was inevitable that Kazuki would be recognized and the sound of his name gathered more fans. If nothing happened to stem the tide, we'd be in danger of missing our train.

"Kaji," I called. "Time to rock."

Kaji climbed off Kazuki. Kazuki pulled him back. The fans loved it. After one more kiss, Kazuki rose with suave indifference to the fact that he was the cynosure of all eyes and sporting an erection that couldn't be missed. He smiled pretty for the cameras, one arm around Kaji's neck, holding him close to his side. His audience obligingly made way for the Shining One and his consort, opening a path to the station entrance. With a multitude of good wishes for their journey, Kazuki and Kaji strolled down the adoring gauntlet to the platform.

"Quite the little scene-stealer, isn't he?" Rune said at my shoulder.

"Stop sneaking up on me."

"It isn't intentional, Sunshine."

"No, of course not. How could it possibly be your fault? You don't accept blame. How silly of me to forget."

"How much coffee have you had today?"

"Why don't you worry about getting your band on the train?"

"My boys can take care of themselves."

"Excuse me." I walked briskly away, catching up with Sora and Sung, who had formed a mutual admiration society.

"Hey, Blume-san," Sora greeted me. "Some send-off, yes?"

Sung was goofing around, high-fiving people in the crowd and making grim heavy-metal faces. "I love it," he crowed. "I could do this every day."

The rest of our party followed Kazuki and Kaji's path to the private cars at the end of the train. The press and fans weren't allowed beyond a certain point, but they hung around until we were all on board. Only when the train began to pull away, and it was certain that Kazuki would not reappear, did they start to disperse.

"That should make a good story for the media," Mr. Shin said as I sat next to him.

"Good to see you again, Yoshi." I smiled warmly at him.

Rune sat down opposite us and nodded toward the front of the car. I glanced over my shoulder and saw Kazuki and Kaji disappearing into the next coach.

"Lovebirds." Rune winked. "So it's not just a show for the cameras?"

"Don't I wish," I sighed. "Sorry, Yoshi, but Kazuki's a real handful."

"This is not news to me."

Rune looked annoyed by our matching smiles. "I heard a rumor that you're managing Kazuki now," he said to me. "You didn't even mention it."

"It slipped my mind. In any case, Mr. Shin is handling Kazuki while he convalesces."

"He looked pretty damned healthy to me. What does he stuff his crotch with? The old banana in a sock?" When I didn't answer, Rune went on. "What exactly is he recovering from anyway?"

"That's his business."

"Wow, you're really holding on to this grudge."

Yoshiro gave me an inquiring look, offering to leave if I wanted privacy.

"On the contrary," I said. "I've moved on and I'd prefer not to talk about the past."

"Good luck with that," Rune said as he stood.

"Your past is with you always," Yoshi said when Rune was gone.

"Tell me about it." I sighed. "This should be the happiest time of my life."

"Then behave as though it is."

"That's the answer, is it?"

"It's my answer."

"I like you, Yoshi. Have I mentioned that?"

"You may remind me as often as you wish."

We had coffee in paper cups and chatted about anything that came into our heads, finding connection after connection in our interests. I was really looking forward to getting to know Yoshi better while he was traveling with us. As I was trying to talk him into changing his schedule to include the entire trip, Kaji and Kazuki returned. I eyed them both as they sat opposite Mr. Shin and me. They were the definition of well laid, with creamy smiles and languorous postures, unable to stop touching each other in small, tender caresses.

"The photographers should get a picture of you now," I joked.

Kazuki pulled out his Smartphone and held it at arm's length. Kaji leaned in close and Kazuki took their picture. "With a few clicks, I can post this at my official fan site," he said. Kaji's delighted laugh was all the encouragement the Shining One needed. Less than five minutes later, the afterglow photo, as I named it, was uploaded and subsequently downloaded half a million times. "I have more," Kazuki said. "Some we took a few minutes ago in the bathroom."

"You've shared enough for today," I told him. "That was a lovely bit of stuff you two gave the paps, by the way."

Kaji kissed Kazuki's hand where it rested on his shoulder. "I have no self-control once we get started. It's embarrassing sometimes when I remember we aren't alone."

"It doesn't bother you, does it?" I asked Kazuki, though I was already sure of the answer.

Kazuki shrugged and turned his attention to one necklace among the several Kaji was wearing.

"Seriously," I continued. "I've never seen anyone so good at pretending the rest of the world is a backdrop for his personal movie. Is that how you deal with your fame?"

Kazuki lifted the pendant from Kaji's chest and studied it intently.

"Are you thinking about your answer? Or just ignoring me."

"*Hai*," Kazuki answered absently. "*Takara*, where did you find this?"

Kaji unhooked the silver chain and held it up. "I've never seen this before."

"It was mine," Kazuki said, staring at the silver dragon's claw. "I lost it when I was sixteen and never saw it again."

"I did not know I had it on."

"How is that possible?" I asked.

Kaji looked at me. "I don't know, but I've never seen it before. I know I was not wearing it last night. This morning…," Kaji glanced at Kazuki, "I did not notice what I was wearing."

"That's just weird," I said.

"Excuse me, please," Yoshiro said as he took out his phone. Taking no chances, he made a call and arranged for a security detail to meet us at the next stop. Kazuki shifted to sit with his back to the window and put his long legs up on the bench seat. Kaji settled between Kazuki's thighs, nestling against his chest. Kazuki wrapped his arms around Kaji and closed his eyes.

"Shameless," I commented, as Yoshiro and I got up and walked to another seat.

"They are young and healthy," he said. "Why wouldn't they love one another whenever they have a chance?"

"No argument, but they're going to set some kind of record."

"You know, I have known Kazuki for some time, as his attorney of course."

"I heard a little of his history from Miss Shiori. I know about his dad abandoning him and how his brother exploited him."

"Sato-san is a shrewd businessman, but there was little affection between him and Kazuki."

"Little, as in *none*?"

"I believe that Sato cares for Kazuki the way a trainer cares for a very fast horse." Yoshi glanced at me, trying to gauge my mood. "However, I do not wish to bore you."

"I promise I'll let you know the second I feel a yawn coming on. Go on then; tell me about Kazuki."

"It is hard to imagine being him. Since he was fourteen, he has found his self-worth in the eyes of a faceless crowd. To so desire the love of people you will never know seems a sad thing to me. I have never understood the thirst for fame."

"I think some people want fame and some people *need* fame. It's a validation, if you like, proof of their worth and worthiness to be loved. I'm horrible at expressing myself."

"I think we are saying the same thing, Ben."

I felt a funny little pulse behind my pubic bone when he said my name. I hadn't felt that peculiar prelude in quite a while and I savored it for a bit. I knew then that I'd sleep with Yoshi given the chance, but I was able to enjoy the anticipation without needing to rush him to some dark corner. As the notion of snogging Yoshi went through my mind, it nearly gave the lie to my mature observation. If we had been alone, I'm not sure what would have happened.

"What are you thinking?" Yoshi asked.

"I'm predicting the future." I smiled at him. "Go on with what you were saying."

Yoshiro looked as though he'd like to know more about my abilities as a seer, but did as I asked. "Mr. Sato often spoke of the strict discipline needed to manage Kazuki, but never about his methods."

I leaned forward, my knees almost touching his. "I hesitate to say this aloud, but do you think it's possible that Sato abused Kazuki?"

"I believe that when young, Kazuki was very dependent on his brother and that Sato took advantage of the situation," Yoshiro said a bit primly.

"Look, I didn't mean to imply any sort of... sexual... abuse. I meant *emotionally*."

"It is a hard subject to speak of or conjecture about."

I nodded. "It's hard for me to even comprehend how a person can be deliberately cruel to another."

"Yet, you seem to care nothing for the pain you inflict on Rune-san."

I must have looked like a fish in the market as I gaped at him.

"Forgive me. That was too personal," he said.

"I'm just astounded that you see it that way. Hagen Rune hurt me so badly that it changed the course of my life. If I'm cold to him, it's because I wish he'd go away."

"Ben, you are a most attractive man in many ways, and it is my hope that I will be in your future, but you are still bound by your past."

"Everything would have been fine if Rune hadn't shown back up."

"Do you really believe that?"

"It's the truth."

"Is this one man really responsible for all your unhappiness?"

"I liked it better when we were talking about Kazuki."

Yoshiro inclined his head to me and sat back a little. "Kazuki takes with both hands, as my grandfather would have said, and the world is happy to offer up whatever he desires. He spent fourteen years in want, but has wanted for nothing since. I think he has tried to forget his childhood and to remake himself according to some design known only to him and Sato."

"He hasn't forgotten it entirely." I told Yoshiro of my meeting with Kazuki in the garden of his mother's old house.

"Most interesting." He paused for a long moment as if considering how much to tell me. "After Kazuki was attacked, I suggested he speak with a therapist and he refused. He wrote a statement at my urging, which I delivered to the police, but he will not speak of it. I wonder if Akihashi-san has said anything to you."

I shook my head. "If Kazuki told Kaji anything about the attack, Kaji hasn't shared it with me."

"I am worried."

I could see that it cost him to admit his concern. "So am I. Kazuki's pulled a couple of stunts that were way over the line, in my opinion. Maybe I'm being paranoid, but I get the idea that he might do something… irreversible in fit of rage."

"Or fear. He is so fond of Akihashi-san. His biggest fear now must be losing him."

"If you say so. Granted, he's very affectionate with Kaji, not to mention hot for his body, but I don't see the love."

"I think you underestimate the role of the moon."

"It's not a role to Kaji. It's real for him, but I don't think you can say the same for Kazuki."

"What is real, Ben?"

"Don't go all Zen on me."

Yoshiro smiled gently. "Are thoughts real? And what is love if not a collection of thoughts about someone special?"

"I don't have an answer for that. I'll have to think about it."

"I am only asking you to consider that Kazuki's feelings are as real to him as yours are to you."

"Ah, but will they last as long?"

"No one can know that."

"It's strange; we're so different, but we talk like we've known each other all our lives."

"And for all of our lives, if you believe in reincarnation as I do."

"Clever sausage," I said, touching his knee lightly. His eyes lit with pleasure at my prosaic compliment. I was definitely going to shag him before this tour ended.

Chapter Nine

The pictures of our departure stirred a new furor of interest among Kazuki's fans. Having suffered through a starvation diet of tiny news nuggets about Kazuki's "accident," they gorged on the feast of new facts laid on by the paparazzi. The Shining One was back and though there were no shows or new songs in the offing, he was posing for pictures and it was obvious that his astonishing beauty endured. It was also obvious that he was still infatuated with Kaji Sukoshi and his fans bought Hayate tickets in hopes of catching a glimpse of him at a concert. Every date on our tour was sold out by the time we reached our first destination.

The Yokohama press was waiting for us and I was glad Yoshiro had arranged for security. It took twice as long as I expected to go from the station to the hotel. There were dozens of messages waiting for us at the front desk, along with bouquets of flowers and a zoo of stuffed animals. A camera crew from the local entertainment channel was waiting by the lift and a young woman with very white teeth and very black hair thrust a microphone at us.

"Kazuki-sama, I am Akiko. Please tell your fans, are you here to perform?"

Kazuki shook his head. "I am here only to sex him up," he replied, patting Kaji's bum.

Akiko's jaw dropped as security hustled us into the elevators and my phone rang. As the doors closed, I saw the reporter with her phone to her ear. I'm not sure how she got my private number, but she also got me to agree to an exclusive interview with the boys as soon as we were settled. After getting the nod from the band, I invited her up.

The television crew consisted of the perky on-camera personality Akiko and a dreadlocked man with a large video camera on his shoulder. After introductions, Akiko interviewed each member of Hayate in turn, but I saw her eyes darting about for signs of Kazuki. With his usual knack for an entrance, the Shining One waited until Akiko began to speak with Kaji before he interrupted. The sound of a door slamming got everyone's attention and then Kazuki slouched into the suite's living room, shirtless and disheveled. The camera operator knew his job and turned the lens on the star's smooth, sculpted torso, panning up the cobbled abs and the hard curves of the pectoral planes to the famous face.

"Kaj-eeeee," Kazuki whined. "Why do you make me wait?"

Akiko closed her mouth, glanced at her partner to make sure he was filming, and held up her omni-directional microphone.

"We are doing an interview, remember?" Kaji said.

Kazuji leaned over the back of the couch. "But I need you *now*."

"Forgive me." Kaji shrugged at the reporter. "He does this."

"It is not a problem for me," she said.

Kazuki pinned her with his laser gaze for a split second before he jumped nimbly over the couch to sit next to Kaji. "I will help so this will go quickly and we can go—"

"Practice for the show?" Kaji supplied.

"Yes, practice," Kazuki purred.

Akiko was having a hard time keeping her eyes off Kazuki's smooth-skinned, rock-hard torso. "Your fans know that you follow a commendable program of exercise. You have inspired many of them to do the same."

Kazuki looked mildly amused. "I hope I can be a force for good in the lives of those who admire me," he said smoothly.

"I am very curious if you will ever perform again as Count Kuro?"

"That is a popular question." Kazuki gave her his self-effacing smile and she giggled. "It is possible that Kuro will rise from the grave, but I have no plans at this time."

Akiko sighed with disappointment; the vampire persona Kazuki had created for his Coffin Hammer tour was arguably his most popular, and five years on, still had legions of devoted fans. "May I ask about your friendship with Sukoshi-san?"

Kazuki turned to look into Kaji's eyes, seeking permission. "*Anata?*"

Akiko actually blushed when Kazuki used the pet name generally reserved for married couples. "If it would not be too personal," she added.

Kaji shrugged again, the epitome of insouciant retro cool in a black leather jacket and white T-shirt.

"Ka-chan is my most special friend," Kazuki said, pulling Kaji closer with an arm around his shoulders. "We write songs together. We make videos. What else do we do together?"

"Our makeup?" Kaji suggested.

Akiko giggled again. "Kazuki-sama, you like to kiss a lot with Kaji-sama, I think."

Kazuki turned to her, his eyes simmering like absinthe over a flame. "Yesss," he said, drawing out the affirmative syllable.

Akiko withstood his molten stare for about three seconds before she dropped her eyes. She seemed a bit flustered when she spoke again. "Do you think you will perform together?"

Kazuki and Kaji exchanged a glance. "Not until the interview is over," Kazuki said and looked vaguely puzzled when the rest of us laughed.

"What are your plans?" Akiko asked Kaji.

"No plans," he said. "I just want to rock."

Watching my Little Fire handle Kazuki and the interviewer with an effortlessness that was damned near undetectable, I knew his future in show business was unlimited. His ingenuous charm was so engaging because it wasn't forced. He wasn't projecting an image; he was living his music. Yoshiro must have felt the waves of pride emanating from me because he put his hand on my shoulder and gave it a little squeeze. That small gesture stood out in a day filled with many memorable moments. Yoshi understand how I felt, shared it, and acknowledged it. A small gesture, as I said, but filled with a wealth of complex emotions.

When the interviewer's time was up, I asked to speak with her. Aware that Yoshi could hear me, I advised Akiko to do another interview before she left the hotel. "Go to the suite at the end of the hall and talk to our opening act. You'll be glad you did."

"Are they good?"

"Would they be touring with Hayate if they weren't?"

Akiko thought that over and told her partner they were going to do one more interview. She thanked me, Kazuki, Kaji, and everyone else in the room. As the door closed behind her, Kazuki rose fluidly to his hands and knees and crouched over Kaji. Kaji fell back against the cushions, still grinning at Kazuki's answer to Akiko's last question. When she asked if he ever gave last-minute advice before Hayate went on stage, Kazuki had grabbed Kaji's crotch and solemnly explained, with a quick demonstration, how he never let his *takara* perform without a hard-on. His demeanor was so detached that his outrageous behavior took a moment to sink in. I wondered if the sequence would air uncut.

"What do you think, Yoshi?" I asked. "Enjoying the tour so far?"

"I am not bored."

"Lovely. I'll do my best to make sure you're not."

*A*fter the show that night, I cast aside my good intentions along with all my decorum and knocked on Yoshiro's door. He looked surprised, but terribly pleased to see me. Still wearing his shirt buttoned all the way to the top, he was having a breath of air on the balcony before retiring. I said I'd join him if he didn't mind. He didn't.

Still buzzed from the show, I leaned on the waist-high molded concrete railing and gazed out over Yokohama's downtown area. "I feel like I could jump off and soar over the city right now."

In a daring move, Yoshi came to stand behind me and put his hands over mine. "I cannot fly," he said. "So please stay here with me."

I turned in the circle of his arms and looked into his eyes. "Well, since you ask so nicely…."

The moment stretched out until it snapped and we leaned toward each other until our lips met. Chaste at first, the kiss went through stages of exploration until our tongues made acquaintance and hit it off. I hate to compare every man I bed to my first real lover; it's such a threadbare cliché. However, it cannot be denied that Hagen Rune was a sex god. I just happened to luck out on my first go, or not, depending on how you look at it. The Viking raider ruined me for the common run of selfish or inept bed partners, but Mr. Yoshiro Shin was showing early promise. His touch was respectful, light but sure, as we got to know each other's anatomy a little. We were tuned to the same pitch and moved to the same rhythm with no awkward fumbling or hurrying ahead. Though we'd done little but kiss, by the time his hand drifted anywhere near my crotch, my willy was as hard as it was ever going to get.

"Ben?" Yoshiro said, fingertips massaging my thigh through my trousers.

"Yes, it's all right to touch me there," I said.

"I was going to suggest that we stop for now."

"Were you really?" I pushed away from the rail. "And I thought it was going so well."

"This is not a rejection. It is the deferment of pleasure that intensifies the eventual act."

I took a deep shaky breath. "If that's what you want."

"I think perhaps it is wise to wait a little while. I would never want you to regret having slept with me too quickly."

"I don't think I'd regret it, but I respect your viewpoint."

"Do not be angry with me, Ben. I want this too, but I don't want to rush. I wish to savor each step in this courtship."

"That's a lovely thing to say." I sighed. "Why do I still feel rejected?"

"You're human." Yoshi embraced me, holding me close as the wind plucked at our hair and clothing. "We will continue this soon."

I walked the short distance from his room to mine, intending to have a wank, a shower, and a good night's sleep, in that order. I was not pleased to find Rune hanging about in the hallway. "Have you any idea of the time?" I asked sharply.

"Was that what you were doing? Getting the time from Shin?"

"It's really none of your business. Could you move away from the door?"

"Sure, Sunshine. I just wanted to thank you for sending that reporter our way."

"I'm sure she meant to interview Vudu all along."

"I'm still grateful."

"You needn't be. I'm going to bed now," I hinted broadly.

"Good night then."

Before I could move, he took hold of my jaw and kissed me, letting me feel his tongue at my lips, but going no farther. I pushed him away and swiped my key card in the lock, angry at my body's reaction to his. I was afraid if I didn't get inside and lock the door immediately, I would end up dragging him in with me. I was not going to let horniness lead me into a huge mistake, but bloody hell, he tasted good. Locking the door, I leaned my back against it and waited for Rune's footsteps to fade away. After a decade of brief amiable affairs and one-night stands, I had two men seriously interested in me, and each could make me quiver like a blancmange in an earthquake. *Great timing, Blume.*

*W*e played five cities in five days and took a day off in Kyoto. Naturally, everyone wanted to do something different: go to Mount Arashiyama and see the monkeys, visit the Golden Pavilion temple, the film studios, the Manga Museum, and on and on. When I told the lads to do as they pleased, they ended up sitting around the hotel, a testament to the exhausting schedule they'd kept for the past few months. They gathered in the living room of Kazuki's posh suite, lounging on the furniture and floor, channel surfing while testing the patience and ingenuity of room service. Only Kaji and Kazuki stuck to their original plan of going sailing on the big lake.

After I had breakfast with Yoshiro in the hotel restaurant, he and I set up our laptops on the balcony of his room and took care of our correspondence. A little before one, I walked over to Kazuki's rooms to look in on the boys, planning to return and seduce Yoshi into making out for a while before a late lunch. I found members of Hayate and Vudu sprawled in front of the enormous television screen, glued to the entertainment news channel.

"*Kisama!*" Sora swore as I entered.

"That was harsh, mate," I said.

"Not you, Blume-san." Sung Ke Smith, now Sora's sworn brother-in-rock, pointed to the telly.

I stepped carefully over Gekko, fearing for my ankles, and looked up at the screen. Strawburi's lead singer, Natsuko, was being interviewed by the music media's leading gossipmonger, a stocky drag queen called Mrs.

Shibuya. Natsuko's lips, painted the metallic red of a soda can, trembled as she replied to a question.

"Bloody hell!" I exclaimed. "Did she just say she was pregnant?" I knew what she'd said well enough; I just couldn't believe my ears. "And that Kazuki is the father?"

"This is too funny," Gekko said, rising from the floor. "I can't wait to see Kaji's face."

Sung said something in Korean to his lead singer. It didn't sound like a compliment.

"Man, can you imagine what it's going to be like the next time Kazuki goes outside?" Sora said.

Michi pretended to interview Tsubasa, who answered as the Shining One. They were trying to be as ridiculous as possible, but I had a feeling they weren't that far off the mark. Nothing was too ridiculous for the tabloids to print. Tsubasa was pretending he was a pregnant Kazuki— waddling elegantly across the lounge with a cushion under his shirt—when Kazuki and Kaji returned. It was plain from their smiles that the couple hadn't heard about Natsuko's announcement and silence fell in the room.

"Why is everyone so quiet suddenly?" Kaji asked.

Why did they all look at me? "Maybe we should do this privately," I suggested. "Can we go to your room?"

Kaji glanced at Sora and whatever he saw in his friend's face convinced him. "Sure; let's go." He closed the bedroom door behind us and sat on the foot of the rumpled bed. Kazuki went to the closet and pulled out articles of clothing, holding them up to the full-length mirror. I leaned against the dresser as I spoke on the phone to Yoshiro, figuring Kazuki's attorney should be here. None of us spoke until he arrived.

"A little while ago, Natsuko announced she's pregnant," I said bluntly. "And to put the cherry on the top, she claims Kazuki's the father."

"*Fukanou!*" Kazuki spun to stare at me.

"Impossible or not, that's what she said, and she said it on the telly."

Kaji turned to look at Kazuki. "Why would she say such a thing?"

"How would I know?"

"You were engaged to her once."

"So of course I can read her mind."

"Easy, lads," I said. "No one knows anything for certain." I glanced at Yoshiro, who was already dialing. "Let Mr. Shin see what he can find out."

"Natsuko is a stupid bitch," Kazuki said.

"What a way to speak of the possible mother of your child," Kaji said.

"How should I speak of her? She is telling a lie to hurt me."

"Are you really this conceited?" Kaji got to his feet. "Is everything a plot against you?"

Kazuki held out his hands, palms up. "This is a lie. I did not sleep with her for months, since before I met you."

"Why should I believe you?"

"Why is it so easy to doubt me?"

Kaji bit his lip. "You have lied to me many times. I said nothing because the lies had nothing to do with our love, but now they make it difficult for me to believe you." He took a couple of steps forward, but stopped well out of Kazuki's reach. "I want to believe you. I want to stand beside you when you call Natsuko a liar to her face." Kaji put a hand over his stomach. "I feel I am being disloyal and—" His words ended abruptly as he ran to the loo. The rest of us pretended we didn't hear him throwing up.

"I am not lying," Kazuki said to the air.

I didn't know whether to believe him. I watched the door until Kaji came back, pale but steady. Yoshiro finished his call and we turned our attention to him.

"Natsuko's legal staff has already contacted my office requesting a sample of Kazuki's DNA. Of course, I would have demanded a paternity test of the child in any case, but it is revealing that the young lady feels so confident."

"How long do we have to wait for proof?" I asked.

"We can get a court to order amniocentesis at the end of the second trimester. It is risky, but if we want to know as quickly as possible—"

"No," Kazuki said firmly. "Not until the baby is born." He paused. "If there is a baby."

"Tell me the truth," Kaji said. "When did you sleep with her last?"

"Do not make me say it, *takara*."

"No sweet talk. Just tell me the truth."

"The night Natsuko was at the house and I was so angry with you, I was a little crazy."

"That cannot be your excuse for everything."

"You don't understand. I have never loved a man before."

"How can you expect me to believe that?"

"I don't mean I haven't slept with men. Of course, I have. Many many. I wanted to be good at all kinds of sex so I practiced a lot. Ichiro's people made sure my bed was never empty."

"Murakami-san," Yoshiro began, but Kazuki cut him off with a look.

"I almost married twice, but when I kissed you that first time, I knew I had never really been in love before."

"You are so good at seduction," Kaji said as though reminding him of the fact.

Kazuki crossed the distance between them so quickly it was like trick photography. Taking Kaji by the shoulders, he locked eyes with him. "How can I make you believe me? I cannot feel this way for nine months."

Kaji shrugged out of Kazuki's grasp. "Tell me why being in love with me would drive you to sleep with that woman."

"I thought about it too much. You hurt me flirting with that muscle man guitar player; I thought you had sex with him. I could not stop thinking about you and him together and the images in my head were...." Kazuki paused. "Suddenly, it seemed crazy to me that I was having an affair with a guy and I had sex with the first woman I saw."

"That does sound crazy."

"I could only finish by pretending she was you. I swear it."

"All right," I butted in. "We're getting too much information now. Let's decide what we need to do." I turned to Yoshiro.

"I think it would be best if Kazuki-san and I return to Tokyo and confront Miss Fujiwara. If she is only doing this for publicity, perhaps we can persuade her to choose another story."

"I don't want to go to Tokyo," Kazuki said immediately.

"Nor do I, but perhaps we can stop this thing now and you will not have to wait nine months."

"Why must I go? You can take care of it."

"There are some things you have to take care of yourself," Kaji told him.

"Not if you can afford attorneys."

Kaji shook his head. "*Ryu,*" he said reproachfully. *Dragon.*

"Don't look at me that way." Abruptly, Kazuki clenched his fists and screamed in frustration, making everyone jump. "We were so happy this morning. Why is this happening?"

I exchanged a glance with Yoshiro. "Kaji," I said. "Let Mr. Shin talk with his client for a minute."

"No," Kazuki said, taking Kaji's hand. "I don't want you to go."

"It's only for a few minutes." Kaji kissed Kazuki's knuckles and stepped away from him.

I don't know what Yoshiro said to Kazuki, but the Shining One was subdued when we saw him a short time later. He and Kaji spent about an hour together in their room and then he emerged dressed for travel. I said goodbye to Yoshiro and he promised to keep me updated. The front desk called to say the limo had arrived, but Kazuki didn't want to let go of Kaji. I told him we'd be back in Tokyo in four days and pulled Kaji away. Yoshiro urged Kazuki to the door where the Shining One balked.

"*Takara,*" he said, stretching out his hand. I would have laughed at the melodramatic gesture, but it was plain that he was not faking his distress. Kaji left my side to go to him, enfolding him and holding him for several heartbeats before releasing him. "*Onegai, nanitozo onegai,*" Kazuki fastened his gaze on Kaji. "Please, don't send me away."

"I will be home soon," Kaji said. "I love you."

"Come," Yoshiro beckoned to Kazuki as the lift chimed. "Do not be the cause of worry for Akihashi-san."

Kazuki's anguish was gone as though a switch had been flipped. He composed his features back into a marmoreal mask, standing as upright as a daimyo giving an order to his best samurai. "Come back to me," he said to Kaji as he turned and followed his attorney.

"Are you all right, *ichiban?*" I asked, already knowing the answer.

Kaji threw his arms around me and the tears began to come. "How could he?"

"He sees these things differently; you know that." I stroked Kaji's hair. "Sex doesn't mean the same thing to him that it does to you and me."

"He knew it was wrong to sleep with someone when we were together."

"You're only right. But I think he's truly sorry. Not to mention truly confused."

"It hurts, Benny-chan."

"I know." I held him a little tighter.

"I am torn in half."

"I know." I could smell Kazuki's scent on my lad, an elusive sweetness that reminded me inexplicably of my family's once-a-year visit to Brighton Beach when I was a child. "Part of you wants to go with him and part of you knows you can't."

"*Hai.*" Kaji snuffled.

"Do not wipe your nose on my new suit." I startled a laugh out of him and kissed the top of his head. "Tell me about your day at the lake," I said in an attempt to divert him.

"Maybe not right now, okay?" Kaji looked past my shoulder. "Hello, Rune-san."

"I'm sorry," Rune said from the doorway. "The door was open."

"What is it?"

"My boys were wondering if Hayate wanted to have some dinner and go to a few clubs."

"I'll ask."

"Let us know soon," Rune said as he left. "Sora's down at our suite, by the way."

"What do you want to do, *ichiban*?"

Kaji looked up at me. "I want to dance with you."

"Now?"

"No, at a club. I will go out if you will."

"All right. I'll go for a little while."

"And you will let me choose your clothes."

Kaji seemed determined not to think about Kazuki and I did my best to help. I let him dress me in a white oxford shirt and a pair of Sora's faux snakeskin jeans. He hung a few of his trinkets around my neck and fastened a studded wristband on my arm. I drew the line at makeup, but let him add a little gel to my hair. "Sexy," he pronounced when he finished tugging at my stubbornly wavy locks. "Have a look." He opened the closet door and I looked at myself in the full-length mirror. I hadn't put on more than ten pounds since I was a teenager and I had to admit that the skinny trousers made my stork legs look good. The white shirt complemented my dark hair and olive skin. I felt a bit self-conscious, but my transformation cheered Kaji up. "Give it a rest," I yelped as he grabbed a handful of my arse and squeezed hard.

"You are in good shape, Benny-chan. Don't be shy to flaunt it."

"Some people are born to flaunt, but I'm not one of them."

"That is not true. I have seen footage of you dancing in a club in London."

"You're joking."

"Everything is uploaded these days. Did you call Rune-san yet?"

"Bloody hell!" I whipped out my phone and dialed. After a brief conversation, Kaji and I walked down the hall to Vudu's quarters. The look on Rune's face when he saw me was almost worth the ribbing I took from the lads. *Eat your heart out,* I thought.

We ate at a steakhouse that Yoshiro had recommended and strolled a few blocks to a street lined with nightclubs. Lurid signs lit by noble gases beckoned fun seekers to enter pleasure domes of light and music. At a trendy place called Modern 8, I made good on my promise to dance with Kaji. The lads teased us, of course, but eventually joined us on the floor and allowed that I was not a total turnoff as a dancer. I'd had enough alcohol to be loose, even smiling instead of snarling at Rune when his hip brushed mine by accident. The song ended and I tried to leave, but Kaji insisted on one more dance. To tell the truth, I was having a good time and past caring how silly I looked. When Sung tried to cut in, I raised my fists like a boxer and the three of us danced together for a while, pretending to fight. Other dancers joined in, throwing punches and kicks until the song ended. Laughing, I swung Kaji in a circle before I let him go. He promptly bent over and lost his dinner.

"Oh dear," I said, holding him up. "We'd better get you out of here."

He nodded, teeth tightly clenched in an effort to hold back another wave of vomiting. I got him to the men's room before he heaved again and stood outside the stall commiserating. When he didn't stop after several minutes, I took out the number Yoshiro had given me at our first meeting. A pleasant female voice answered and asked me to state my request. I told her where I was and what I needed. She told me to hang up and a doctor would be with me shortly. In less than ten minutes, a harried-looking young man was examining Kaji in the loo. After talking with us, the youthful doctor told us

Kaji had food poisoning. The physician gave him a shot of antibiotics and a bottle of pills. He left while I was thanking him.

"Are you feeling any better?" I asked my white-faced singer.

"A little," he lied.

"Let's go back to the hotel so you can lie down."

Kazuki called while Kaji was sleeping and I told him about the food poisoning. He was silent for a long time before he replied. After telling me to take care of Kaji, he rang off without saying goodbye.

Kaji slept through the night and woke up groggy. He wouldn't listen to any talk of canceling the show that night. The day went off as scheduled with Kaji calling Kazuki every time he had a few minutes' break. Kazuki wasn't answering and by show time, Cyclone Kaji was at Category 5. He took the stage and gave away every ounce of nervous energy in a bravado example of what a trouper really was. Drained, he collapsed while leaving the stage after the third encore. I mentally crossed the last date off the tour as my lad was taken to the casualty department. He was suffering from exhaustion, which surprised no one, and he was ordered home to rest and recuperate.

Chapter Ten

"When was the last time you saw him?" I asked, my anxiety mounting. Kaji was watching my face intently as I listened to the voice on the phone. "Yes, it would be all right if you came over. All right, I'll see you then." I hung up and Kaji spoke immediately.

"What did Shin-san say?"

I looked around the terrace of Kazuki's graceful country house. "It's not good, *ichiban*."

"Tell me."

"Yoshiro hasn't seen Kazuki since last night."

If Kaji hadn't been weak from his bout of intestinal trouble, I knew he would be pacing. Pale and lethargic, he closed his eyes for a long moment before he answered. "So no one knows where he is."

"It appears that way, but he'll turn up. You know how he is."

"That is why I am worried."

"Mr. Shin has reported him missing to the police and asked them to keep it quiet." I paused. "Bloody hell, how stupid am I?"

"*Nan?*"

"I think I know where Kazuki might be."

I called Yoshiro Shin from the van on the way to Kazuki's mother's house. We parked behind the market and walked across the street with no thought of waiting for Yoshiro or the police. I pushed open the gate and Kaji squeezed around me only to stop short. I put a comforting hand on his shoulder as we gazed at the destruction of the tranquil little garden. Pots were overturned, spilling dirt and plants over the slate stepping-stones, and the tiny fountain was choked with mud and grass. It looked as though someone had tried to obliterate peace itself.

Yoshiro arrived with a stocky man in a suit whose card identified him as Inspector Aizawa. The police officer wandered around the yard, making notes, as Yoshiro spoke with Kaji and me.

"This doesn't look good," I said, after he informed us that Kazuki's absence was being investigated by a special branch of the police force.

"No, it does not," Yoshiro agreed. "But we cannot know yet if Kazuki was here when the vandalism occurred."

"Vandalism?" Kaji spoke up. "No, it must have been the same people who attacked him before. Why did no one catch them?"

"Kazuki was not… cooperative," the attorney said. "He gave the police few details and would not sit for an interview with them."

"Foolish dragon," Kaji sighed. "He told me he had spoken with investigators many times."

"He is headstrong," Yoshiro replied. "And does not always know what is best for him." He met Kaji's eyes for a long moment before he turned to me. "I am sorry, Ben."

"You've nothing to be sorry for. You're doing everything you can to find him."

"I am the one who lost him."

"He's a grown man, Yoshi, not a kid in the park that ran off after his balloon."

"He is very upset over the pregnancy rumors. Miss Fujiwara states that Kazuki is the only man she has slept with."

"Has the pregnancy at least been confirmed?"

"I have a copy of a doctor's report," Yoshiro said neutrally.

"Which could easily be faked." I said it for him. "I want to get Kaji out of here. Do you have to stay with the inspector?"

"Not at all, but I do have business back at the office which will not wait. I am anxious to continue the conversation we began in Yokohama, so I hope I may call you later."

"I'd like that. Or come out to the house. Is it all right that we're staying there without Kazuki?"

"Of course. Akihashi-san is still Kazuki's heir."

"Do you think you'll ever call him Kaji?" I smiled.

"My regard for him is… complicated. I am not sure how best to address him and so I settle for simple respect."

"Why is it so complicated? Because he and Kazuki are lovers?"

"No." Yoshiro glanced to where Kaji sat on an overturned wooden bucket. "The love of one man for another is a beautiful and natural thing that has comforted warriors since time began."

"I thought maybe you thought that Kaji wasn't quite good enough for Kazuki."

"Good enough? There is no question of that. I know the tabloids like to say that their pairing is one of an aristocrat and a peasant, but that is pure romanticism. Kazuki and Kaji are modern men; class means nothing to them."

"It did bother me a bit when I read that shite. Some of those so-called journalists write as if Kazuki has a new pet called Kaji. Then there's the constant speculation over which one is the girl in the relationship. Isn't there anything else for the music press to talk about?" I rolled my eyes. "Someone told me two schoolgirls were expelled in the Shinjuku district yesterday for fighting over whether Kazuki is gay or not. It's out of hand."

"What do you wish to do?"

"What choice do I have? I'm going to do my job."

Yoshiro turned slightly, blocking me from view as he touched my hand. "There are always choices, Ben. You only see one path."

"I'm in a rut, am I?"

Yoshiro nodded.

"Perhaps you're right. I've been focused on moving forward for so long, I've forgotten what it's like to go sideways."

"Many interesting things lie beside the road."

"Are you telling me to stop and smell the roses?"

"That is a beautiful English saying, but not precisely what I meant. I will try to explain later. Now I must return to my office. You will be all right?"

"It's very kind of you to ask," I said, the warmth of my tone at odds with the formality of my words. "We'll be fine. Call me when you're free."

Yoshiro bowed over my hand before he let go of it. "That would be my fondest wish."

I watched him leave, an attorney with a fencer's body and the mind of a sage. Kaji smiled wistfully at me when I went to help him up.

"I hate being weak," he said wearily.

"The antibiotics are as bad as the food poisoning, but you'll be back to full amperage by tomorrow," I assured him. "I'm sorry we didn't find Kazuki."

"I do not understand how someone found him here. He told very few people about this place. Even Sato-san does not know Kazuki bought their mother's house."

"Maybe whoever it was followed him from somewhere else," I said as I got in the van.

"It was a beautiful garden," Kaji said, slumping in the passenger seat.

"Yeah, it was," I agreed, as I steered the vehicle onto the motorway. "Do you want to go anywhere while we're out?"

"No. I just want to go home and wait for Kazuki."

Kaji sat in the backyard for a while when we got back, smoking Sora's cigarettes and brooding. Sometime in late afternoon, he drifted into the house and I began to hear the plangent notes of a piano falling into the silence like drops of quicksilver into a well. He was working on a new song and as was their habit, the other lads joined him one by one, offering their contributions. Kaji called the composition "Hollow Day" and it was a haunting jagged lament like pieces of a broken mirror wrapped in silk. When Kaji started crying the third time through the chorus, Sora put down his guitar and cradled him to his chest. Michi and Tsubasa came to sit near, each with a hand on Kaji, wordlessly offering their support. It was even more touching to me, knowing Sora's dislike of Kazuki. I didn't think there was a finer bunch of young men in the world and I told them so.

Tommy ended the moment when he came in to tell me there was someone to see me. Informed that Mr. Rune was in the sitting room, I thanked Tommy and went to get the meeting over with.

"Sorry to drop in like this, Sunshine." Rune got to his feet when I walked in.

"Drop in? We're miles from the city."

"That's my boy; never give any slack."

"I'm tired, Rune. Can we make this quick?"

"I remember the last time you said that to me." His eyebrows wagged up and down.

"Unfortunately, so do I." I started to walk away, afraid he'd call me back and afraid he wouldn't. Why was I so weak where this man was concerned?

"Benjamin, wait. I had a purpose in coming here... apart from harassing you."

"All right then." I sat on one of the brightly upholstered ottomans and gestured to the couch opposite me. "What's your business?"

"I hear you've lost something priceless."

"If you have any information about Kazuki—"

"I have suspicions based on what I've seen."

"I see." I sighed. "And what will it cost me?"

"You know, Sunshine, you really are...," Rune began. He stared at me for a couple of seconds and then started over. "You should give people the benefit of the doubt once in a while."

"Perhaps I would, if they didn't keep disappointing me."

"Okay, we won't discuss your inability to forgive. I came here to tell you that if you want to find Kazuki, you should ask that attorney of his."

"I have. Mr. Shin has already called the police and a special unit is working on the disappearance. They're doing a good job of keeping the press out of it."

"Have you considered that he's shacked up somewhere and doesn't want to be found?"

"No."

"It happens."

"I'm well aware of that, but I don't think that's the case here."

"How well do you know Yoshiro Shin?"

"Why?"

"He strikes me as a facilitator. You know, the guy who can get you anything, anytime, anywhere. If Kazuki wanted to disappear for any reason, Shin would be the guy to set it up."

"That's absurd. Unlike some, Yoshiro cares about his clients."

"I really wish I hadn't been so stupid all those years ago," Rune said, changing gears. "If I'd known I was ruining any chance I'd have of ever being in your life, I would have done things differently."

"Thank you for that. I wish I'd been a little wiser as well, but there's nothing to be done about it now. And if you're trying to drive a wedge between Yoshi and me—"

"I'm not doing this out of jealousy," he interrupted. "I'll admit I'm jealous of Shin, but talking behind someone's back is not my way."

He was right. Of all his faults, backbiting wasn't one of them. "So far, your information is very vague. Just what are you saying about Yoshi?"

"I kept an eye on him, because, as I admitted, I'm jealous. He and Kazuki had a lot of secret meetings. I don't know what they were talking about, but it wasn't percentages."

"How do you know?"

"Have you forgotten how good I am at reading body language?"

"Rune," I said, making a warning of his name.

"When I saw them together, Shin was laying down the law and pretty boy was sulking, but he wasn't talking back. Maybe I don't know exactly what was said, but the lawyer was clearly giving orders. Kazuki didn't like it, but I could see that he was going to go along. Now, is it not possible that they cooked up this pregnancy thing with the girl for more publicity?"

I felt a chill and irrationally resented Rune for it. "They wouldn't be so callous."

"And why not?"

"Kazuki was as surprised as anyone."

"He's a very good actor, if you want my opinion."

The knot in the pit of my stomach extended cold tendrils. "I don't want to believe this."

"I understand. I just thought you should know there was a possibility that this is all a sham."

"Bloody hell, I never thought I'd be *hoping* the tart was knocked up." I paused. "I suppose I should thank you."

Rune shook his head, shaggy straw-pale hair catching the light. "Don't worry about it."

"Why did you do it? Why did you drive all the way out here to tell me? You don't owe me anything and I've been a proper bastard to you."

"It seemed like the right thing to do. That's been my policy for a while now. I did a wrong thing once and it ruined my life."

"Don't be maudlin. It doesn't suit you."

"That's better," Rune said. "Your gratitude confused me, but we're back on solid ground now."

"Everything's a joke with you, isn't it?"

"Sunshine, if I didn't laugh all the time, I'd be crying."

I made a rude noise that eloquently expressed my incredulity.

Rune shrugged. "At least you're speaking civilly with me now and I don't care how long it takes to win your forgiveness. I'm willing to put in the time and do the work."

"Why is it so important to you?"

"You're kidding, right?" Rune looked into my eyes. "I love you, Benjamin Lloyd Blume. I always have and I always will. Out of pride, I made a stupid, stupid mistake and I lost you. I swore I'd never let my ego rule me again and that if I ever found you again, I'd do my best to win you back."

"I did my best to make sure you couldn't find me, just in case you tried. I even changed my name. Then, about two years ago, I just got tired of it. I took my name back and got back into rock 'n' roll."

"You've done well."

"It's the lads; they're brilliant."

"So they are."

"Your lot aren't half bad. Mind you, that singer gives me the wobblies."

Rune chuckled and my groin vibrated in sympathy. "Gekko's very theatrical," he said.

"So that's what they're calling it now."

We were silent for a minute, and then Rune spoke softly. "It's still a blast, isn't it?"

I nodded. "Yeah, it still makes my heart beat faster when I hear the hum of an amp."

"It's in our blood, Sunshine."

"So why are you managing a band instead of fronting one?"

"Lost my nerve."

I made the rude noise again.

"All right, the real reason I stopped singing is because you weren't there to listen."

"Oh do put a sock in it. That's a bit much, even for you."

"I don't know how to get through to you." Rune looked down at the floor.

"Maybe you could just act like a normal person when you see me and I won't try and flay you with my tongue."

"I doubt it's possible, but I'll try. I suppose I'd better start back to Tokyo."

"Are you in the studio tomorrow?"

Rune nodded. "The guys are really excited."

"A pity you never got to make a record. You were so bloody good."

"Future generations have been deprived of my genius."

"A tragedy of epic proportions."

"Oh, the humanity."

And just like that, we were back in the old groove, riffing on each other in good-natured competition for the more clever remark. It happened without our noticing it as we were laughing and I remembered how easy we were together, meshing without effort. Tommy came back to see if we needed anything and the spell was broken, but too late. I had seen that Hagen Rune was not a heartless monster, just a man who'd made mistakes. Having seen this, I could no longer hold on to the grudge that had defined my life for so long.

"I'll probably run into you at the studio," I said, as I rose to my feet.

"Should I pretend I don't know you?"

I smiled. I couldn't help it. "You can say hello to me if you want. Look, about Kazuki, I don't think there's any deep, dark plot here; it's just a neurotic artiste indulging a taste for drama."

"What a whack job." Rune gave me his opinion of Kazuki as we reached the door.

"Kazuki's way past whack job. He's a full-blown loon." I paused. "Some of the time."

"And the rest of the time?"

"A bloody genius when he's working, a virtual savant. Singing is like breathing for him and lyrics are his native tongue. I've never seen a man with better moves, aside from you."

"I'm touched. So what's the most intriguing thing about him?"

"He smells sweet."

"He smells sweet?"

"Yeah. Not sickly sweet or old-lady sweet; it's not even a perfumey smell really. It's a bit like… if you could make candy floss of fresh-mown grass and sunbeams it would smell like Kazuki."

"That wasn't what I was expecting. I thought you'd tell me he slept hanging from the rafters or something."

"You should know better. I remember some of the stories that went around about you."

"I guess people like to exaggerate, make things a little grander."

Why is that? I wondered. *Isn't this world wonderful enough? Why do we yearn for something just beyond our reach at the edge of our vision?*

"Earth to Benjamin," Rune said.

"Sorry, I spaced for a second. See you tomorrow, all right?"

Rune was smiling as he got in his rental car and drove away. The space that used to be occupied by my hatred of him was empty, a blankness that yawned before me and froze me in place for several minutes. Everything was abruptly unfamiliar and I wasn't sure which way to go. The sound of an electric guitar being tuned penetrated my paralysis and reminded me of where and who I was. I was not a victim. I was not a martyr. I was just a man who had made mistakes.

Chapter Eleven

K aji was fully recovered and firing on all cylinders again the next morning, so we went in to Tokyo. The studio booked for us was deluxe to say the least. Behind the board was the talented technician who had mixed Kazuki's last platinum CD, *Talk Pretty to Me*. With a comfortable lounging area and well-stocked mini-bar at hand, there was no need to leave and Hayate made excellent progress, laying down a few tracks for "Hollow Day." Everyone was taking a short break, buzzing with the charge of doing good work, when my phone quacked like a very irritated duck. I bowed an apology for forgetting to turn it off as I gave Michi the finger for changing my ring tone again, and then I went out into the hall.

"Blume-san, so pleasant to speak with you again."

"Sato?"

"*Hai*. I am calling as a courtesy to tell you of a press conference I will hold in my office at two o'clock today. Kazuki and Natsuko will be present to make an announcement. I wished to give you the opportunity to attend."

"Where is Kazuki now?"

"He is approximately two meters away from me."

"Let me talk to him."

"That is not possible, but you may speak to him in my office before the press arrives."

"I'll be there in ten minutes." I dithered over it and finally decided that Kaji would kill me if I didn't take him along. It took slightly more than ten minutes to reach Sato's office in the building across the street, but not much more. A pretty secretary showed us into the private office right away. Ichiro Sato sat behind a glass and chrome desk in a black patent leather chair, but he rose politely to greet us. Kaji didn't even look at him. His eyes were on the couple sitting on the hot pink sofa.

"Blume-san, Akihashi-san, welcome." Sato bowed.

"I'm not in the mood for amenities," I said. "Call me a rude *gaijin*, but I'd like to get right down to it." I turned to look at Kazuki. "What's going on here?"

"Natsuko and Kazuki are overjoyed at the news that they will be parents," Sato said. "Of course, they plan to marry."

"Marry?" Kaji and I repeated simultaneously.

"Of course," Sato said. "The wedding of Japan's two most beloved pop stars will be the biggest event of the year."

"Just a bloody minute, mate," I said. "What do you have to do with anything?"

"Kazuki has decided to change management again." Sato turned to his half-brother.

"I have decided to change management again," Kazuki said without inflection.

"I won't claim my feelings are hurt, but would you mind telling me why?"

Kazuki looked at me, but didn't register my presence. "The experiment is over. I know now that Ichiro is the best manager for me. He knows me best."

"Where is Mr. Shin?" I asked. "Shouldn't he be at this meeting?"

"This meeting is not official," Sato said. "It is only a courtesy so that you may hear the news first."

Kaji had stood quietly at my side until now. "Kazuki, why are you doing this?" he asked calmly.

"It is the honorable thing."

"Then you are certain the child is yours?"

"I love Natsuko, and I will love her child as my own no matter the outcome."

"How can you say you love her?"

"I made a mistake with you," Kazuki said in the measured tones of someone speaking into a microphone. "It started as publicity, but it became confused. It is my nature to be affectionate and loving and you misunderstood my fondness. We were only ever friends, despite what you may have fantasized. I hope we will continue to be friends always and share our love of music."

Kaji stared at him when he finished, but Kazuki would not meet his eyes. "I do not think we were friends after all," was all he said. Tears welled up and ran down his cheeks, but he didn't carry on. If Sato had been hoping for a scene, Kaji disappointed him.

I didn't. "You're heartless bastards, the lot of you." I pointed at Kazuki. "But you take the cake, mate. To see you sitting there cool as gin and tonic as if you never burned like a fever for this lad…. I heard you tell him more than once that you loved him when there were no cameras around."

Natsuko finally spoke. "Surely no one really believes that Kazuki would sleep with a man? Even a man who looks like a *bishoju* princess."

I ignored her, addressing Kazuki again. "You'd better think very carefully about this, mate. You're making a life-altering decision here. Once Kaji walks away, I don't think he'll take you back. If you're doing this for publicity, or because you think you owe Sato something, you're going to regret it for the rest of your life. Be brave for Kaji if you can't do it for yourself."

"You have my respect, Blume-san," Kazuki said.

"That's it?"

Kazuki nodded, his eyes glittering like fool's gold.

"You're a bastard."

"*Hai*," he said softly. "My mother was… weak."

Kaji took my hand. "Blume-san, let's go."

"You don't have anything else to say?"

Kazuki tilted his head to the side. "What is there to say?"

"You could tell them all to go to hell."

"Our hell isn't like your English one," Sato said.

"Oh, so you've already been. That rather cheapens my little curse."

"There is nothing you can say or do to harm me."

"Right. You'd have to have feelings first."

"This has nothing to do with feelings. It is blood."

"*Onegai*," Kaji pleaded, tugging at my hand. "Please, let's go."

Kaji had always been a fighter. His diminutive stature dictated that he be either a mouse or a tiger, and he was ninety-eight percent tiger until he met Kazuki. Now he deferred to the other man in a way that set my teeth on edge. Not to get too whimsical, but it was as if the fire in Kaji's soul had been smothered.

"Are you certain?" I asked him. "If you want to, I'll stay here with you and make a shambles of this precious publicity stunt."

Kaji shook his head and we left before the press arrived. I called Yoshiro on the way to the van, got his voice mail, and left a message.

"I guess we'd better go pack," I said as I hung up.

Kaji nodded and his tears overflowed again.

I held out my arms and gathered him in. "Kazuki and his friends are complete wankers," I said into his hair. "They're not worth one of your tears." Kaji shook in my arms, his sobs muffled against my jacket as I held him. "I really am sorry."

"I want to go home," he said, when he could trust his voice. "Home to the garage."

"No problem." I gave him the van keys. "Why don't you get in and I'll go to the studio and see what the lads want to do?" I paused. "What should I tell them?"

"What difference does it make?"

"I'll be right back," I said, but I was being too optimistic. As I entered the building, I saw Rune. With his much-vaunted ability to read body language, he cleverly deduced that I was upset about something. I took about a minute to give him the bare facts, ending with, "You've got an *I told you so* coming to you, I reckon."

Rune shook his head. "I wish I'd been wrong about their underhandedness. How's your lad?"

"Wretched, but keeping up the brave face."

"He's aces," Rune said, bestowing one of his highest accolades. "He'll bounce back."

"Poor sod." I shook my head. "He's so in love."

"Kazuki is an incredibly convincing actor."

"He is, but he didn't have to try all that hard. Kaji was primed to fall in love with him."

"It's not your fault, Sunshine."

"I have to go," I said, moving past him. "We'll talk another time."

I left him and gathered up the lads. They weren't satisfied with my vague explanation that plans had changed, but I wasn't stupid enough to tell them what had happened while we were still within spitting distance of Kazuki. Not until it became obvious that we were heading into our old neighborhood did I tell them about the meeting. Predictably, all sorts of unflattering comparisons were made and the Shining One was the recipient of multiple death threats. When they settled down a little, I told them we were moving back into the garage for now. As Sora began to speak quietly with Kaji, I took out my phone and called Tommy at the country house. Tommy had already been informed of the change and told me kindly that our belongings were being packed. If I wished, he would arrange to have them delivered. I wished. He then told me that he'd enjoyed serving us while we were Kazuki-san's guests and I told him I'd miss him. He wished the band luck and we hung up.

Kaji went straight to the loft when I unlocked the garage. The rest of the lads gave him privacy for a couple of hours and then Sora went up. Using a combination of guilt and bullying, the guitarist got Kaji to come downstairs. He wasn't hungry, but he sat at the table with us. As we were finishing a subdued dinner, Yoshiro called me back.

"Forgive me for not calling sooner, but unexpected business came up. I regret to tell you that I am on my way to Sydney."

"Australia?"

"I am afraid I will not be able to come for dinner."

"Yoshi," I said, as I took the phone into my office. "Do you know about Kazuki's wedding plans?"

"Yes."

"How long have you known?"

"Ben, I am Kazuki's private attorney. Anything he might tell me in confidence is not mine to reveal."

My grip tightened on the phone. "I understand, but how long have you known what Sato and Kazuki were up to?"

"I cannot tell you that." His voice thickened with emotion.

"I see."

"Ben?"

"I'm still here."

"What Sato has done is... not honorable. Only to you will I say those words. I hope Akihashi-san is finding comfort with his worthy friends."

"He's strong," I said.

"Stronger than he knows. I am afraid I must go now."

"Goodbye, Yoshi."

"Ben, wait. May I call you another time?"

"Yes, I'd like that." I said goodbye again and hung up. So Sato and Kazuki had put Yoshiro out of the way while they pulled their dirty tricks. I was angry that Yoshi hadn't told me the minute he knew where Kazuki was, but I also understood the concept of attorney/client privilege. I didn't like it, but there was nothing to be done about it.

A little later, I saw photos and snippets of film from Kazuki and Natsuko's announcement of their engagement. They posed prettily together, but the pictures had no life. Though Kazuki's gaze was as direct and sultry as ever, it never kindled into the flash-fire of passion. There was not a drop of chemistry between the two people in the photos, and I wondered if anyone bought the lie they were selling.

Kaji drew into himself for a few days, smoking Sora's cigarettes until dawn, sleeping until two in the afternoon, existing on coffee and microwaved noodles. The rest of the lads continued working on "Hollow Day" until their singer rejoined them. The vocal track on the finished version was a raw-throated, elegiac plea for release from limbo that ended on a broken a capella note. Kaji pulled his sleeves over his hands and dried his eyes as the technician congratulated the lads on a job well done. As I joined them in the sound studio, Kaji was already over the congratulations phase and trying to talk to Sora about an idea for a new song. I knew the heartache was far from over, but my lad was beginning to heal in his own way.

By the time "Hollow Day" was released as a single, Hayate was already recording more music for a second CD. The first one, out for barely three months, had gone gold and was on its way to platinum. We didn't need Kazuki anymore, if we ever had, but I never let the thought seep into conversation. Kaji never spoke Kazuki's name, and by silent mutual agreement, no one else did either. We couldn't avoid seeing his image, not without retiring to a bomb shelter, but we never commented. Only once, after seeing Natsuko on a talk show geared to homemakers, did Michi remark that maybe Godzilla should take a paternity test.

For a couple of months, our days coasted past us like a shallow river, barely wetting our ankles as we strove mightily to reach the sky. More often than not, we succeeded and I was lit by the inner glow of due pride. Each member of Hayate was vastly gifted and the past two years of relentless practice and performing had honed them to a gleaming edge. They had always been good, but now they were exceptional; moreover, they were professionals. Despite the passions that flowed and surged in a room full of creative people, there were no tantrums, no door-slamming exits, no smashed instruments, no bouts of uncontrolled weeping, all of which behavior and worse had been exhibited in the past. If I had thought them committed to their craft before, they were fanatical now. Everything they did was in service to the new offering to their growing army of fans.

Mr. Sato called to invite Hayate to Kazuki's engagement party and I kept my cool. As if I received a dozen such invitations every day, I told him we were too busy, though saying we regretted not being able to attend was beyond my hypocrisy. When he called a week later to arrange a publicity shoot for Kazuki and Hayate at a music store opening, I gave him the same excuse in exactly the same words. He told me I was being foolish and not acting in the best interests of my clients. I told him he was the last person whose advice I'd take. He told me, in so many words, that I was in over my head. I told him to bugger off. I sincerely hope he understood the idiom. In any case, he didn't call again.

Kaji received a hand-addressed invitation to the wedding, scheduled a few weeks after the bride's due date. He dropped the creamy vellum envelope into the trash without opening it. I could swear I smelled Kazuki's honey and brine scent when I closed the bin bag. I knew that simply ignoring the fact that he existed would only hold for so long. Eventually, Kaji, and the rest of us affected by the breakup, would have to deal with it head on, but for now, all of our energy went into the project.

Kaji had written a song, virtually by himself, with minor additions to the bridge by Sora. He called it "Half-Moon Heart," and it was unlike anything I'd heard. Granted, it was not a new idea to mix a chamber group's violins and cellos with electric guitar and drums, but the arrangement alternated between pure symphonic, unadulterated rock and a chorus that was a seamless blend of both. A song about the moon that was both paean and lament from a man in love with a wolf, it set the tone for the entire album. The wolf is transformed into a man by the alchemy of love, but in the end, reverts to his natural form. The music conjured wild nights of running across snow with the pack, the electric shiver of fur against flesh, the siren call of the moon that drew answering howls from her worshipers. As soon as I heard it once from beginning to end, I told Hayate it was world class, a song for the ages, and then I took out my phone and called Miss Shiori.

*F*ive days later, after Shiori cleared a space on her calendar to accommodate Hayate, we met at Twenty-Third Century. The video artist was very excited about the concept of "Half-Moon Heart," confessing her weakness for werewolf stories. She'd already arranged for the rental of several snow machines for the blizzard sequence and hired a trained wolf and handler. We looked over her storyboards and found little fault. Kaji was a bit hesitant about the fur thong Shiori wanted him to wear in one scene, but she reminded him how quick the editing cuts would be in the lovemaking montage.

"A flash of bare booty is nice," she said, peering at Kaji over her mother-of-pearl frames.

"That's true," Sora said gravely. "We can all agree on this, yes?"

"*Hai*," Michi said. "Especially if it's Kaji's booty."

"*Hai*," Tsubasa agreed. "It's so round and firm."

"Eat your hearts out," Kaji quoted one of my favorite phrases.

"We do, Susu-chan," Michi said. "It is our sad fate to desire what we can never—"

"Shut up," Kaji suggested. "Miss Shiori's time is valuable."

"*Arigato*." Shiori nodded to Kaji. "You said you have someone in mind to play the wolf man?"

I spoke up. "A strapping lad called Sung Ke Smith. He's the guitarist for—"

"Vudu," Shiori finished for me. "Yes, I can imagine him turning into a wolf. A very large wolf. Rik!" Her assistant came to her side. "Call the wolf handler and find out how big a wolf we can get." Shiori smiled at us as Rik walked out of the room to make the call. "I am thrilled to have the excuse to work with a wolf," she said. "And with my favorite band again."

"We're thrilled, we didn't have to wait a year to work with you," I answered.

"Yeah, but why are we always cast as the bad guys?" Michi asked.

"Because you get to wear black and black is cool," Kaji told him.

Michi nodded. "Thanks. I forgot again," he said sheepishly.

Tsubasa cuffed him on the back of the head and got an elbow in the ribs in return. I gave them a sharp look that halted the incipient wrestling match. Miss Shiori had a lot of awfully nice things in her private office and several of them looked fragile. We agreed to meet the next day to shoot some footage of the band in costume and then our time was up. The lads wanted to go down the street for a bite and I waved them on as my phone started chirping at me. Despite my severe reprimands, Michi was still pulling his favorite trick of changing the ring tone of any unattended phone he came across. At least I recognized the number on the screen.

"Yoshi!" I said. "How wonderful to hear from you."

"I am sorry I have not called in so long."

"Mate, it's been thirty-six hours, not thirty-six years," I said lightly.

"I missed speaking with you at our regular time."

"Yes, I know."

Yoshi's soft laugh rubbed up against my ear. "No, Ben, I meant I *missed* speaking with you."

"I missed speaking with you as well. How long are they going to keep you there? It's nearly a month now."

"Until the job is finished. Not knowing the exact date is an exquisite torture."

"Indeed it is. We never finished that conversation we started in Yokohama."

"The anticipation has become quite hard to bear."

"Yes, and I'm getting tired of the temporary solution. I want to feel *your* hands on me instead of mine."

There was a brief silence from Yoshiro's end. "The picture in my mind right now is quite compelling. I will work harder so I may return to Japan as soon as possible."

"I'd like that."

"Ben, you know that if the anticipation becomes too great, you are free to seek relief with another. There is no arrangement between us."

"Seek relief with another?" I repeated in a posh accent. "You make it sound like a cure."

"The body needs what it needs. When you are hungry, you eat. When you are tired, you sleep. When you are cold—"

"I get the concept," I interrupted. "There just isn't anyone else I'm attracted to."

"Your words would be pearls if they were true."

"Are you calling me a liar?"

"Only because you are lying. You can lie with your tongue, Ben, but not with your face. I have seen the way you look at Rune-san. He is a good match for you."

"Oh, do you really think so?"

"I have offended you again."

"No, it's all right," I replied out of reflex. "You're right; Rune is catnip to me."

There was another silence from Yoshiro. "Perhaps we should speak of something else."

I saw Kaji come out of the noodle shop and cross the street. I waved and he shouted that he'd left his phone in Miss Shiori's office. "Sorry, Yoshi," I said. "Go on."

"Shall I call you later?"

"Mmm, right around bedtime would be nice."

"I will set the alarm on my watch. Do you think you could arrange to be in the bathtub?"

"I'll see what I can do. Goodbye for now." I rang off as Sora, Michi, and Tsubasa came out of the tiny shop. "Ready, lads? Have a seat in the van, and I'll fetch Kaji." I figured he was talking with Shiori, but I heard him before I got to the studio area.

"As I said, it is a generous offer, but I cannot accept."

"We could still work together." Kazuki's silk and sandpaper voice stopped me in my tracks.

"No, we could not," Kaji said firmly.

Kazuki leaned toward Kaji and spoke so softly, I could barely make out the words. "I wish I could speak with you in private."

"I have no wish to be alone with you. I don't know you."

124

"Don't say that."

"I don't know you," Kaji repeated. "You are not my dragon."

Loudly clearing my throat, I came around the corner. "Kaji, the lads are ready to go home. Hello, Kazuki. Making a video?"

Kazuki nodded. "Natsuko is making a video called "Married in Heaven," and I am in it."

"Good luck with that whole thing. Kaji, let's go."

"I miss you," Kazuki said as we turned away.

Kaji's stride broke, but he caught his balance and kept walking. As we rounded the corner, I heard Sato calling for Kazuki. "Miss Shiori is waiting for you. Why are you standing around like a halfwit?" And then we were through the lobby and walking out into the sunshine. Kaji took a deep breath of the brisk air and glanced at me. I gave him the thumbs-up sign and he smiled.

"What did he want?" I asked as we crossed to the van.

"He thinks we can have a professional relationship that will benefit both of us."

"Where have I heard that before? And how does his wife fit in?"

"I could barely look at him, Benny-chan. What has happened to him? Where is the man who took me like a dragon? How could he change so much?"

We were almost at the van and I spoke quickly, forcing myself to be fair. "Maybe he's still the same man. Maybe circumstances have forced him to behave in a despicable manner. Maybe someday, he'll see what he threw away. Then you'll have a big decision to make. But right now, if you want to hate him, go right ahead. You don't have to work with him ever again. Hayate will do just fine without his help."

Kaji nodded. "I will try to be more positive," he said, damn near breaking my heart. He opened the passenger door and tossed Sora out of the seat, precipitating a boisterous brawl. Kaji would be all right. He had his friends and something to focus on.

I wished I could hate Kazuki with the wholeheartedness of Sora, but I would never see things from only one perspective again. My revelation about Rune had opened my eyes to just how blind I'd been all my life. There is seldom one side to a story and most are as faceted as diamonds. Maybe everything that had happened since I met Sato had been a charade. Maybe

Kazuki had been privy to every twist and maybe not. Maybe Kazuki was being blackmailed by his brother. There was any number of variations. And since I didn't know the whole truth, I was unable to despise Kazuki as I wished for hurting my lad. Maybe he too was just a man who had made mistakes.

Chapter Twelve

"I love it," said Sung Ke Smith, looking at his altered visage in the mirror. "Wish you didn't have to clean it off."

The makeup artist agreed with him and then began removing the points from his ears. For one of the key shots of the new video, Sung's handsome features had been transformed into something halfway between man and wolf, savage and beautiful. In the process of returning to lupine form, he turns at the sound of his human lover calling to him and they gaze at each other across a gulf that cannot be bridged. That's what it said on the call sheet. Sung and Kaji had played it exactly the way Shiori envisioned it, Kaji standing nearly naked in the snowdrifts as flakes swirled around him in the moonlight, one hand stretched out in entreaty, Sung half-turned, his muscular torso and legs caught at their best vantage, a complicated expression on his in-between face, topaz eyes yearning and feral.

"Maybe I should keep the contacts," Sung said. ""What do you think, Blume-san?"

"I think you'd scare people."

"Excellent!"

"Yes, I guess it would be, given your stage show, but do you really want to compete with Gekko in the creepy department?"

"How would that be possible?" Sora asked as he changed out of his wolf hunter costume.

"Hey, be nice," Rune said from behind me.

"Bloody hell, I told you to stop sneaking up on me."

"Sorry." There was not a trace of contrition in Rune's voice.

"Hello, Rune-san," Kaji said, walking blithely past us in a flesh-colored thong.

"Hey," I said to Rune. "Eyes up here."

Rune dragged his gaze from Kaji's bare bum, divided by a string into two perfect hemispheres. "Sorry, but you have to admit, that's distracting."

"Yes, it is, but how could I pass up an opportunity to scold you?"

"To be honest, I think you're losing your edge."

"Do you really?"

"It wasn't a challenge. Want to go for coffee or something?"

I shook my head. "The lads are having a bit of a barbecue. Sung's coming along and you'd be welcome, as well."

"I'd really like that. What can I bring?"

"I think we have everything, unless you'd like to share the arcane elixir that keeps you from aging."

"That sounded like a compliment."

"Just an observation."

The lads finished changing into street clothes and we drove to the garage. Rune involved himself in the preparations, turning everything into a sideshow to the delight of the musicians. We had what Sora called a real American-style pig-out and lay about the place complaining about how full we were. Rune and I went into my office so he could show me Vudu's new Web site and we ended up hanging out there for a while.

"We should do another tour together," he said, taking the bottle of water I handed him.

"Mate, Vudu will be headliners next time 'round."

"It would be a great show and the guys all get along. They've done well in Japan, but we should let the rest of the world have a look at our boys."

"That's definitely in my plans, though it's not going to happen quite the way I thought it would. Hayate was scheduled to open for Kazuki on a world tour in spring. However, things went a bit awry."

"Speaking of Kazuki, have you noticed anything about his popularity lately?"

"I haven't paid him the slightest bit of attention."

Rune grinned. "I can't believe I get to tell you this. I thought you'd know already."

"Well, do go on."

"Well, it seems as though a significant number of Kazuki's fans are upset over the way he treated Kaji. A number of them have given up their membership in his club in protest and the online forums dedicated to him are raging with the controversy. Some think Kazuki did the honorable thing in standing by the mother of his child. Others think he's heartless for abandoning his best friend. Sales of Kazuki merchandise are actually going down. Sato's latest publicity scheme is backfiring on him."

"Serves them right."

"I knew it would put a smile on your face."

"I'd like to think there was some small penalty for shredding Kaji's heart."

"Hey, Sunshine? I just want you to know that I suffered without you. Each day, I felt your loss and I had to live with the fact that it was all my fault."

"No it wasn't." I leaned my elbows on the desk and met his eyes over my laced fingers. "I was partly to blame. I've seen myself as the innocent victim for so long that I forgot how it really was. Seeing Kaji with Kazuki brought it all back to me. I watched him make the same mistakes I made."

"Your biggest fault was loving me too much, but it doesn't excuse me cheating on you."

"No, it doesn't. And with that skanky Gawain Goldust. That really hurt."

"He looked like you."

"The hell he did."

"Everyone said so."

"Everyone being the tripped-out party monsters we hung around with?"

"I don't want to fight about what GiGi looked like, okay?"

"What *do* you want to fight about?" I tried to lighten things up again.

"Who's going to be on top?" he suggested.

I smacked him lightly on the cheek as I stood. "I'm going to the loo."

"Let me know if you need a hand with anything."

I groaned. "Do grow up."

Sora looked up from the television and waved as I passed through the living room area. Michi and Tsubasa remained engrossed in the footy game. The absence of Kaji and Sung should have been a clue, but I wasn't thinking beyond my need for the toilet and the growing warmth between Rune and I. Still, I should have noticed Sung's bulk before I ran into him. I just didn't expect him to be blocking the dark hallway that led to the toilet. And I really didn't expect him to be snogging like mad with Kaji.

"Sorry," I said. "I'm just going to the lav."

"No problem, Blume-san," Sung said, moving sideways.

When I came back out, Sung and Kaji had joined the others. Kaji sat between Sung and Sora, and the vagrant notion drifted through my head that Hayate would kick major arse with two smoking hot guitarists. It was only a fantasy though; I'd never poach from another band. Michi told me that if I was just going to stand there, I could at least get him a beer. I brought beer for everyone and called Rune to come sit with us. We pretended to watch the match while Rune attempted to embarrass me with tales of my youth. He largely succeeded.

"You had a three-way with Rune-san and Lorelei of the Sirens?" Sora gaped at me. "No way."

"You don't believe it because it was a threesome? Or because I slept with a girl?"

"All of it," Michi answered, putting his fingers in his ears. "I don't want to hear more."

"Seriously," Tsubasa said. "It's like hearing about my parents getting freaky."

"You're crazy," Sora told his bandmates. "This is prime blackmail material."

"Why would we blackmail Blume-san?" Michi asked.

"You never know when information will be useful," Sora replied.

"I am shocked, Benny-chan," Kaji said, fending Sung off with a palm to the sternum.

"I'm sure," I said. "I hope you're all having a nice laugh at my expense."

"I believe we are, thanks," Rune said.

My lads laughed like hyenas. I gave them a reproachful look that made them laugh harder.

"Come on," Sora said, when the hilarity died down. "Let's go up to the loft and jam."

"Don't stay up too late," I told them. "Miss Shiori will not be happy if you look tired tomorrow."

"We work in the best industry in the world," Rune said.

"No argument."

Rune turned to me and I could practically feel the brush of his eyes on my skin. "I want to kiss you so badly right now."

"You've never kissed badly in your life," I joked, annoyed by my accelerating heart rate.

"Don't you wonder, just a little, if the old magic is still there?"

"No."

"Really?"

"I don't have to wonder. I know."

"One kiss. What are you afraid of?"

"Are you actually daring me?"

"We're not kids, Benj. Do you want to stop playing games now?"

"What does that mean?"

"You know how I feel; I've laid it all on the line. I was hoping for maybe just one little clue from you."

"If you're asking me if I'll ever take you back—"

"No," Rune cut me off. "You wouldn't be taking me back. I'm not that guy anymore. If you take me, you'll be getting someone a lot smarter."

"You know I never like to say never, but I'm just getting used to being around you again. I think it's going well so far, but you can't expect me to jump into bed with you like I did the first time."

"As I recall, it was within an hour of meeting me."

"Yes, yes, you have an excellent memory, mummy's good boy," I said briskly.

"I'm not asking you to jump into bed, though I wouldn't refuse you. I'm just asking for a kiss."

The random noise of instruments being tuned turned into a choppy blues riff that chugged along for a few seconds before falling to rags. Sora did a count-in and Hayate began playing a witty acoustic version of their club stomper "How Hot? Too Hot!". The music got into me the way it always did and I rocked slightly in place. Gently, Rune slipped an arm around my waist and moved with me. It felt so good and so right that I simply closed my eyes and let him hold me as we swayed like reeds in a strong current. The smell and feel of him was like an insidious drug that beguiled me into a fever dream. My body remembered well the rapturous release he could draw from me, leaving me enervated and gasping for breath: full, sated, complete. I could achieve that sublime state once more; all I had to do was say yes.

A blast of strident marching band music blared out. "My phone," I said, my voice sounding distant in my ears. I realized that Rune's thigh was between my legs and that my indisputable hard-on was pressed against it.

"That's quite a ring tone, Sunshine."

"Michi's practical joke." I moved back as I dug in my pocket. My fingers were shaking so badly that I dropped the phone. Rune bent and retrieved it. "Thanks." I looked at the number on the screen. "I should take this."

"You can't be serious. We were making real progress."

"Pushing it will not win you points."

Rune held up his hands. "It's getting late," he said. "I'll just see what Sung wants to do and then I'll leave you in peace."

My phone went to voice mail and I spoke quickly. "It's all right, Rune. The dance was nice, but it wasn't foreplay." I was such a liar. "I'll see you tomorrow."

Looking a bit too pleased with himself, he went upstairs and I returned my call. "Hello, Yoshi," I said warmly. "I'm just going to draw a bath."

I would have to rate that bath as one of the best of my life. I emerged clean and rosy-cheeked, pleasantly tired and a little in awe of Yoshi's talent for eroticism. There were several mundane bathroom items that I will never look at in the same way again. I smiled as I ran my fingers through my damp hair on the way to my bed. When Kaji spoke from the darkness, I nearly dropped my towel. I turned and saw the glowing tip of a cigarette in the living room area.

"That's becoming a habit again," I said.

Kaji dropped the butt in a beer bottle and rose to chuck it in the bin. "You look happy," he said.

"It's theoretically possible to be happy for several moments at a time."

"So I am learning."

I said his name and then fell silent. I'm not sure what I thought I was going to say, but the words just weren't there. Maybe there aren't any words for what I wanted to say to him, or maybe it would take too many. Fortunately, he could read my silence.

"I am glad you are my friend, *ichiban*," he said.

"You're going to make me cry." My eyes were already filling with tears.

Kaji thumbed the moisture away. "I have spoiled your happiness."

"Not a chance. You're my number one; don't forget that. Nothing you could do would ever make me stop loving you."

"Now I will cry."

"It's forbidden," I said sternly.

Kaji smiled. "I think you would have more authority if your towel wasn't falling off."

I adjusted the terry cloth around my waist and dropped my cell again.

"Why did you have your phone in the bath?" Kaji asked.

"You know I take my baby everywhere," I said casually. "So, Sung is still pursuing you, is he?"

"I would say he has caught me."

"I see," I said automatically. "Well—"

"I know you don't care for Sung."

"It's not that; he seems like a good fellow. Just not precisely your type."

"I have a type?"

"I'm sorry. That was a condescending thing for me to say. I'm treating you like a child again."

"I don't mind so much." Kaji rose on his toes to kiss my cheek. "Don't worry about Sung, okay? He's a good guy. I told him I cannot care for anyone in that way right now, and he said he understands."

"Then why were you snogging each other's wits out?"

"Are you kidding, man?" He grinned as he walked away from me. "The same reason you took such a long bath."

I threw my balled-up towel and hit him squarely in the back of the head. He turned and I dashed into my office, locking the door behind me.

"Good night, Benny-chan," Kaji said sweetly through the door. "Someday, you meet my friend Payback."

"I hear she's a bitch," I couldn't resist saying.

"Sleep well."

I heard his footsteps fade away and went to my closet-sized bedroom. It was originally the storeroom for the garage office and once it was cleared out, there was enough room for a single bed and a nightstand. It served its purpose and I was never going to invite anyone to stay the night within shouting distance of the lads. They'd lose all respect for me if they ever heard me in the throes of ecstasy, as they say.

I was feeling quite wanton, having made out with one man and moved on to phone sex with another. My love life had two seasons: drought and flood. It would be lovely to have the same outlook that my lads did. Their craving for physical closeness was easily gratified; even the staunchly hetero Sora thought nothing of cuddling with his friends. They didn't let their affection for one another get tangled up with their sex drives. *I come from a different world* was my last thought as I fell into the well of sleep.

*W*e spent the next day at Twenty-Third Century and by two o'clock, Miss Shiori was satisfied with what she had to work with. The lads wouldn't be needed any longer, but for her, the work of cutting and editing the raw footage had just begun. In addition, several special effects had to be incorporated. Though I could see she was champing at the bit to get started, she took the time to show us the portfolio of stills her assistant had put together. "For you," she said. "Use them to start promoting the video." Then she was gone, her very expensive pumps tapping away on the onyx tiles.

The prints were of the highest quality, as I expected, but their power blew me away. Each photo Rik had chosen, and Shiori had approved, was charged with a lightning strike of emotion. The hatred in the faces of the hunters. The pure yearning love that shone in Kaji's face as he gazed on the sleeping wolf. The agony in the eyes of the creature of two worlds that now belonged fully in neither. And not least, the volcanic passion that exploded from the picture of

Sung and Kaji entwined on a pile of pelts as snowflakes melted on their bare skin.

"That's a nice picture," Rune said at my elbow.

I didn't even flinch this time. "Hello. What are you doing here?"

"Miss Shiori's assistant let me in." He paused. "I was looking for you."

"What's up?"

"I had an idea and wanted to see if you thought it was good."

"Why didn't you call?"

"I think your cell's turned off."

"Ridiculous." I fished the phone from my pocket. It was off. I instantly turned it on and rolled my eyes at the missed calls. "Well, this is just lovely." I must have turned it off after my long conversation with Yoshi last night, but it was strange that I hadn't turned it on this morning.

"Getting a bit forgetful, are we?"

"Stop reading my mind. It's not polite at all."

"Polite and rock 'n' roll have nothing to do with each other."

"Point taken. What's your idea?"

"I want to take some photos of Vudu and Hayate together."

"What about the ones from the train station?"

"Those are months old."

"I'm really rather busy, but—"

"You have the afternoon free; I checked."

"Perhaps the lads do, but I don't."

"Then do what you need to do and we'll take pictures."

I sighed. "Ask Hayate," I said. "If they want to hang out and have their pictures taken, which I'm sure they will, shameless camera whores that they are, then I won't stand in the way."

"That sounds like…," Rune looked inquiringly at me in an irritatingly adorable manner, "yes?"

"Take them, but return them in the same condition you found them."

"Have you considered having them shrink-wrapped?"

"Go," I shooed him. "I have calls to make."

"All right, Sunshine, but I'll see you later."

"I have no doubt," I said under my breath, but my sarcasm was vestigial at best. For better or worse, I had accepted him as part of my life. My annoyance stemmed from my reaction to his farewell. I was looking forward to seeing him again.

Rune showed up the next morning with a disc of photos for me to approve. The photographer, a young woman from New Zealand, had chosen a small amusement park as her backdrop. Her style was the opposite of static and the developing process she used produced colors so vivid they appeared to float off the surface of the print. There were no brooding, ominous images, just a bunch of attractive young men having a good time. Full of motion and gleaming highlights, the photos were the equivalent of a bullet train ride down Broadway.

"This is one of my favorites," Rune said as he clicked the next thumbnail.

The screen filled with a candy-colored scene of two young men on one carousel horse. Sung was in the gilded saddle. Kaji sat facing him, head tilted back, with his arms twined around the brass pole behind him. Sung's hand was splayed at the small of Kaji's back and he'd been caught in the act of drawing his tongue up Kaji's throat.

"Yeah, that's a good one," I said. The next picture was a close-up of Sung sucking Kaji's tongue into his mouth. "Are there more in this vein?"

"A few."

"Don't use them."

"They're not doing a sixty-nine or anything like that."

"If those pictures go public, the press will jump on them and stir up the whole Kazuki thing again. I won't put Kaji through that."

"Shouldn't that be Kaji's decision?"

I looked from the screen to Rune's face. "He's already decided, hasn't he?"

"He loves the idea. I don't know why we didn't think of it before."

"What's the point of trying to make Kazuki jealous?"

"Jealous? No. I think this is Kaji flipping Kazuki the bird, the old *who needs you?*."

"I don't much care for that either. I've learned my lesson about being deceitful."

Rune tapped the next picture of Kaji and Sung, captured in the moment before their lips met. Sung's eyes were fixed on Kaji's mouth, Kaji's gaze rested on Sung's lowered eyelids, and both of them were smiling slightly in anticipation. "Does that look faked?"

It didn't. It looked like two handsome lads in the first flush of sexual attraction. "If Kaji's okay with using them, I'll approve it, though I don't necessarily approve." I sighed. "He's just so smoking hot, isn't he?"

"Without even trying."

"Poor thing. He reminds me sometimes of the girl from that Dickens book where the young hero is so put upon."

"You've just described most of Dickens' books."

"It doesn't matter. When he's a boy, the hero meets this beautiful stuck-up girl and he falls for her, but he's not good enough. He meets her later, after she's married to some fabulously wealthy brute. Anyway, she tells the hero that all sorts of ugly bugs are attracted to candles and asks him if it's the candle's fault."

"Are you really comparing Sung to an insect?"

I laid on the sarcasm with a trowel. "Yes, Sung's a bug. That's my point exactly."

Rune chuckled. "How could I ever have doubted that you're the one for me?"

"Back to business, Romeo. Let's use all the photos we selected. What the hell."

"When are you planning on releasing the stills from the werewolf video?"

"It's already being done. I sent them off to Zennousha's press liaison while I was having coffee this morning. There's no reason you can't do the same with these."

"We should have something to promote though, don't you think?"

"Vudu has a CD coming out soon, and Sung is featured prominently in Hayate's upcoming video. It wouldn't hurt to give the fans an appetizer."

"You're a lot better at this than I am."

I turned and stared at him, a bit disconcerted that he was mere inches away. "You said that quite naturally," I marveled.

"It wasn't easy."

"That's because you belong on the stage, not in the wings."

"At my age?"

"Forty-two isn't exactly decrepit."

"Yeah? You think I still got what it takes?"

"You've always had more presence than ten men put together. Not only that, but you have a great voice and you used to write marvelous songs."

"Maybe I still do."

"Maybe you should do something with them."

"Maybe I will."

"I guess we'll see."

"You really enjoy teasing me."

"It's an acquired taste." He was right though. This time around, I felt like an equal in our evolving relationship. I was feeling my power and being a bit of a birk about it. "I'll help you, if you like," I said to make up for my teasing.

"It's just a vague notion."

"Well, when you're ready then. I'll click send if you're still happy with the selection."

Rune glanced quickly down the thumbnails. "Looks good to me."

I sent the file off and got a message back thanking me in less than two minutes. The e-mail also informed me that Hayate were nominees on the MTV Video Music Awards Japan as Best New Artist in a Video for "Bed of Thorns." I stared at the words for so long that Rune was compelled to read over my shoulder.

"Congratulations," he said.

"I'm stunned."

"Get over it. This is going to start happening on a regular basis."

"I've always believed that Hayate would make it to the top, but the reality of it is hard to take in. So many things happened in such a short time."

"It's not going to slow down for a long time." He smiled. "If you're lucky. Come on; it's what you've worked so hard for. Embrace it with open arms."

"Should I be taking advice from you?"

"Forty-two years of experience," he reminded me.

I smiled at him as I stood. "I'll start embracing it by telling the lads about the awards show."

He got up and followed me. "I just thought: Kazuki's in the video too, right?"

"So what? It's Hayate's song and Hayate's video. Kazuki was a guest star at best."

"Okay." Rune held up his hands. "I just wondered."

The boys were as stunned as I was when they heard the news, but they recovered quickly... actually, bounced back would be more apt. The furniture never had a chance.

"Let's go out and celebrate," Rune suggested when the pandemonium died down.

"Why pretend you're talking to anyone but Blume-san?" Sora said.

Rune grinned, unabashed. "Go out with me, Sunshine."

Now he'd done it. He'd called me by that awful nickname in front of my lads. "Must you continue to call me that? I'm not exactly a clueless airhead any longer." It was one of the few times I'd seen Rune shocked.

"I call you Sunshine because you're the light in my life," he said. "I treated you like a... clueless airhead, because I was blind and arrogant. But if you don't want me to call you that, I won't."

Kaji put a hand over his heart. "That was beautiful," he said. "How can you not go with him, Benny-chan?"

"I'm afraid to be alone with him."

They laughed as though I had made a joke. "We'll be your chaperones," Kaji said, taking Sung's hand.

"That's a truly absurd notion," I told him.

"Oh, just go get laid, will you?" Sora said with a dismissive gesture.

"A little respect for your elders, if you please."

"Here, Blume-san, let me help you with your beard so you don't trip over it," Michi said.

"*Hai*," Tsubasa chimed in. "Let me get your cane, grandfather."

"Yes, you're all quite amusing." I paused. "And genuine stars. Way to shine, lads. In six weeks' time, you'll be accepting your award for best new artist."

"Come on," Kaji said, taking my hand. "Let's go have some fun."

A couple of hours, one restaurant, and three clubs later, I stood in line with Kaji for the portable toilet at a warehouse rave. I was easily the oldest person within a hundred feet in any direction. The rap-metal fusion band was interesting, but I wished I'd had a pee before we got here. The thickhead who'd organized this gathering had ordered too few loos and the concrete floor would be awash in sickly sweet chemical/urine soup before the night was over. I wanted to be gone long before that occurred.

Kaji leaned closer to me. "Are you having a good time?" he asked.

"At this moment?" I smiled. "Actually, I am having a good time. Rune always was good company."

"He likes you."

"Yes, he's mentioned it." We finally inched our way to the front and I ducked inside one of the plastic booths. The smell was indescribable, but I'd expected that. I swear I'd rather smell honest piss any day than the perfume that's used to cover it up. I exited as quickly as possible and found Kaji waiting.

"What took you so long?"

"Your boyfriend was in there with me."

Kaji laughed and punched me lightly. "You want to go somewhere else?"

"Let's find Rune and Sung and see what they want to do. I can't believe he wanted me to see this band."

"They are... amusing," Kaji said. "But I think Rune-san wanted you to think he is cool."

"Of course, he's cool. Just look at him." I spotted Rune across the dance floor and motioned him toward the exit. He nodded and got Sung's attention. "Come on," I said to Kaji. "Let's find the stage door."

The amateur-looking security detail braced us when we walked backstage, but one of them recognized Kaji Sukoshi and grandly gave us leave to pass. We kept walking past the makeshift dressing rooms and out the loading-dock doors. We were at Rune's leased car well ahead of our friends and leaned on the fender to wait for them, staring up at the night sky.

"Weird how many radical changes we went through in less than half a year," I said.

Kaji nodded, his eyes on the stars. "Some crazy shit, man." He rarely cursed, but this was one of Sung's many cool-cat sayings.

"Are you doing okay, *ichiban*?"

"I am okay. I wish things were different, but I am okay."

"I regret ever talking to Sato. I'm sorry, Kaji. I've never asked your forgiveness for involving you in a silly publicity scheme."

"You could not have stopped me once I heard Kazuki's name. I wanted to meet him, to talk with him and do whatever else he wanted to do with me. That is the worst part. I have no one to blame but myself."

"Oh mate, do I know how you feel," I said sympathetically.

"But you have a chance to fix your mistake with Rune-san."

I thought for a long moment before I spoke again. "Would you take Kazuki back?"

"If he were free and could prove a good reason for his actions." Kaji met my eyes. "I would take him back. I love him, Benny-chan."

I couldn't think of anything to say other than, "I'm sorry."

He leaned against my side. "I miss him so much. Sometimes my whole body aches."

"It'll get easier; I promise you."

"Hey, are you hitting on my honey?" Sung called out as he spotted us.

"You didn't give me enough time," I answered.

"What's wrong, cutie?" Sung asked, when he was close enough to see our expressions. "That's not your happy face."

"We were just looking at the constellations and thinking about old friends," I said. "Let's get some ice cream before we go home."

"The one with two hundred flavors," Kaji quickly seconded me.

"Two hundred flavors?" Rune said as he got behind the wheel.

"A lot of them are combinations," I said, watching Kaji and Sung climb into the backseat. "Buckle up, boys," I told them.

"It's hard to make out with seat belts on."

"That is my fervent hope," I answered as I got in on the passenger side. I directed Rune to a park where the trees were festooned with tiny white lights. With Kaji's help, I located the shop and we chose our flavors. Sung and Kaji walked ahead of Rune and me as we strolled around, finishing our ice cream. I stopped to look at the light display in the fountain and Rune stopped as well.

"So, was the ice cream just a ploy to get me alone?" Rune said. "That's a joke, by the way."

"Kaji loves this place and I wanted to cheer him up."

"I think Sung's taking care of that."

"He's sweet, isn't he?"

"Yeah. The big badass act is just that. He's crazy about Kaji, obviously."

"It's hard not to love Kaji."

"Cute *and* sexy is hard to beat," Rune said. "There's just something about an overbite."

"When he smiles, I feel as though the world is a pretty sweet place after all."

"That's how I feel when I see you smile."

"We might as well do it." I finished my ice cream and dropped the napkin in one of the ubiquitous trash bins shaped like tranquilized dwarf orcas.

Rune gaped at me. "Here? Now?"

"I meant kiss, you hopeless mental case. Of course I'm not going to shag you here."

"Then there's the possibility you'll shag me somewhere?"

"The merest twinkling. Now, do you want a kiss or not?"

With this tacit permission, Rune swept me into his arms, his ice cream hitting the ground an inch from my foot. His lips covered mine and time slowed like shining ropes of candy on a taffy-pulling machine. I kept my eyes open, gazing into his, filled with a million reflections from the lights all around us. Our bodies aligned themselves, perfectly matched, like adjoining pieces of a jigsaw puzzle. The physical part of love had always come easy to us and that hadn't changed one iota. His hands spread across my back as mine cupped his arse. Straining toward each other, we pressed as close as possible. Tongues darted in warm, wet mouths, a vivid preview of further pleasures, as our cocks grew hard in readiness to back up the boasts.

"What am I doing?" I whispered, as he broke the kiss.

Rune nipped at my ear before he answered. "Sharing a romantic snog under the stars."

"What if you hurt me again?"

"What if *you* hurt *me*? *I'm* the one who should be worried. I want to be forgiven; you've got motive for revenge."

"You're a terribly silly man and that tickles."

"Yeah, I remember." He fluttered the tip of his tongue against my pulse again.

I shivered. "You're going to have to help me," I said. "I don't want to sleep with you right away, but I'm weak."

"You're kidding, right? You can't expect me to put on the brakes."

"I can and I do. If you want to earn my trust back—"

"Fine. I'll do it, but if you wanted vengeance, you got it. This is going to be torture."

"This is the way it should be. If I hadn't jumped you right after shaking hands, we might be celebrating an anniversary."

"I hope you know I'm serious about wanting you back. I'll do anything that doesn't compromise my self-respect."

I leaned back against the circle of his arms and looked into his eyes. "That was an awfully mature thing to say."

"I won't stand here and be insulted."

"Then let's go find the lads."

Rune groaned. "One kiss? That's it?"

"It was quite a kiss, in my opinion."

"Arousing is the word I'd use."

"I'm sure it is. You can hold my hand if you like." He dragged his feet like a little boy as I pulled him away from the fountain. I was vibrating at the same frequency he was, but I knew I was doing the right thing. It would be all too easy to enjoy a quick blowie in the bushes, but I didn't want that. If or when we slept together again, I wanted to take my time.

I expected to discover Kaji and Sung in flagrante, but I found them in a crowd of children. Kaji was performing tricks on a borrowed skateboard for an awed audience. Sung had a small child on each shoulder and more were swinging from his arms and clinging to his legs. Polite but wary parents watched from a short distance; they could see that these were just two larger kids joining in the fun. Rune and I waited until Sung caught sight of us and called to Kaji. Kaji did a kick-flip, caught the skateboard, and presented it to its young owner as though it were a family heirloom. The children applauded as Kaji and Sung walked away, calling out to them to come back soon. We piled back in the car and sang all the way home.

Chapter Thirteen

"Holy crap, dudes!" Michi said as he came into the half-finished recording studio at the back of the garage. "Have you heard Kazuki's new single?"

"Who cares?" I wanted to know.

"I think you will find it interesting," Michi said. "Its name is called 'You Are the Fire'."

"You're kidding." I put down my hammer and looked over at Kaji. Kaji met my eyes briefly and went back to helping Rune, who was quite clever with electronics and the like.

"Is it any good?" Sora asked.

"Yeah," Michi shrugged. "It's, you know, polished, but that's not the point. It's the words."

"What about them?"

"It's a full-on love song about Kaji."

"He wouldn't," I said sardonically. "Not because he has any tact, but because he's done with the whole gay experiment, remember?"

"Just listen," Michi said, plugging his MP3 player into the speakers.

"You downloaded it?" Sora was incredulous.

"It's really pretty good," Michi said apologetically. "I don't know if it's rock, but it's got…." He paused. "Anyway, you can dance to it."

The sound that swept from the speakers was airy yet lush, a rising, swirling rush of notes played on an entire symphony of instruments. Kazuki's voice soared on the back of the scintillating magic carpet of music, earnest and joyful. As I translated the words in my head, I heard what Michi heard.

> *You are the small fire that burns in my heart,*
> *Shelter from the cold winds that tore me apart.*
> *One word from your lips and the sun comes shining through.*
> *How did I live without you?*
>
> *Don't leave me in winter; bring me my spring.*
> *With you at my side, I can do anything.*
> *Ask me to fly and I'll chase away the clouds.*
> *Shouting I love you out loud.*
>
> *If I didn't have you, I would still be wandering lost.*
> *I'd still be paying without knowing the cost.*
> *If it weren't for you, I would sleep on bare floors.*
> *You're the one who can open all the doors.*
>
> *Don't leave me in winter; bring me my spring.*
> *With you at my side, I can do anything.*
> *Ask me to fly and I'll chase away the clouds.*
> *Shouting I love you out loud.*
>
> *You are the fire that never goes cold.*
> *You are the fire deep in my soul.*
> *You are the fire that descends from above.*
> *You are the fire of love.*

"Unbelievable," I said when the song ended.

"Still, it's pretty good," Sora said grudgingly. "It's not rock though."

"How could such an asshole write such a song?" Tsubasa asked. "It's not right."

"Kazuki is not an asshole," Kaji finally spoke.

"Yes, he is," Sora backed Tsubasa. "How bad does the *tanjo* have to hurt you before you hate him?"

"I am not like you, Sora. I cannot hate the way you do."

"Why are you so *kei wai*?" The guitarist got to his feet. "Take your head from the clouds and come live on Earth with the rest of us."

Kaji turned away from his oldest friend and went back to work.

"*Kuso!*" Sora swore as he grabbed his smokes and stomped out.

Michi stared after him. "Man, I'm glad I didn't show him this."

Our drummer held up the latest issue of an entertainment gossip rag called *Dish Paper* in English. On the cover was a picture of Natsuko and Kazuki in samurai and geisha drag. She was smiling, showing her teeth in a way a real geisha never would, self-satisfied and sure of herself. He looked like a very cleverly made wax figure. Inside was a brief pictorial about the expectant couple and an update on the wedding plans, outright puffery that Sato had probably paid for. The real goods were in the middle spread. Rune gave a low whistle as he gazed at the pictures over my shoulder. There were five: three from the photo session that Rune had arranged with Hayate and Vudu, one from the werewolf video, and one that didn't go with the others. Four were of Kaji and Sung; the one in the middle was Natsuko looking suspiciously prim.

"We didn't release that photo." I pointed to the one of Kaji and Sung entwined on a faux snow leopard skin. "That's captured from the video."

"Which is being released day after tomorrow, right?" Rune said.

"Yeah. I don't mind free publicity, but I don't like the idea that someone at Twenty-Third Century might be selling shots to this tabloid. And why is she here?"

"You really ought to learn to read," Tsubasa told me.

"I keep trying; it's not easy for someone who grew up with just twenty-six letters in his alphabet. Please just translate it for me."

"*Chikuso!*" Kaji cursed mildly as he grabbed the magazine from Michi. "I will read it for you." He scanned the vertical lines right to left for a moment. "So, it seems that I am a nasty *hentai* slut whose sushi bar is always open."

"It says that?" I was incredulous.

"No, Ben-kun," Michi shook his head. "Well, not exactly. Something like that though."

"Charming."

Michi moved closer to Kaji. "Here's the part where she says that Kazuki's friendship with such a low person was a sign of what a bad life he'd fallen into. She is saving him from that."

"That sounds familiar," I said. "That's the same line that Sato fed Kazuki."

"Poor dragon," Kaji said softly.

"He made his choice," I reminded Kaji.

"Sometimes we choose what looks like the only option," Rune said.

"Is it all right if I still feel sorry for him?" Kaji asked.

"You're a better person than I, *ichiban*."

"Not according to Natsuko," Tsubasa chimed in.

Kaji threw the magazine at the bass player. "I am going to make some lunch. Who wants my special noodles?"

"You'll be sorry you said that," I predicted. A few moments later, I grinned as Michi and Tsubasa chased Kaji into the kitchen trying to get hold of his "special noodle." I felt eyes on me and glanced at Rune. "What's that cheeky look for?"

"Just admiring you, Sun…. Sorry."

"What the hell," I said magnanimously. "You can call me Sunshine if you like."

"You know what I was thinking?"

"How you could bring up the subject of shagging?"

"Normally, yes, but just now I was thinking that Miss Natsuko must be royally hacked off about her fiancé's new song."

I sighed for effect. "Why can't we just have the music without all the muck?"

"Without the muck, there wouldn't be a reason for the music."

"Right, I forgot. Hey, we got the official notice from MTV about the Japan awards show. They gave us a block of seats. Kaji will probably ask Sung if he wants to go. Would you like to go along as well?"

"Are you asking me out?"

"Don't push it."

"I'd love to, but what if Shin comes back into town?"

"We're all adults, in theory anyway. I'm sure we'll handle it."

"I've avoided talking about it, but you really like him, don't you?"

"Yeah. He's smart, respectful, interesting, and good-looking."

"So he is."

"So are you. How's the CD going?"

"Good. I'd like to throw a little party when the recording wraps."

"Why don't you do it here?" I looked around the cavernous space. "We're having a killer sound system installed, you know."

"Yeah? These guys do good work?"

I nodded. "One of them is particularly good with his hands."

"Tell me more," Rune put his hands on my hips.

"He's a handsome devil as well," I said as he pulled me closer.

"Just handsome? Or devastatingly handsome?"

His lips were a breath away from mine. "Nuclear," I whispered.

"Gross, man," Michi said behind us. "Quit sucking face and come eat."

I smiled as Rune's mouth covered mine and we shared a lovely kiss with no strings. Kaji yelled from the kitchen and I pushed away from Rune. The lads smirked at us when we joined them at the indoor picnic table, but I didn't care. Since I'd let go of my ancient grudge, I felt tons lighter and able to deal with whatever cropped up. All I had to do was keep my wits, resist the urge to run screaming into the ether and face the problem squarely. It worked for me in my job as manager. Why shouldn't I apply it to my private life? I enjoyed having Rune around and if the kids wanted to tease me, I could take it.

"Maybe Natsuko can talk about Blume-san next," Tsubasa said with unlikely innocence, as he held out his bowl for more. Michi glanced at his partner in crime, eager to abet, but unsure where Tsubasa was headed. Sora shot the bass player a warning look that was blithely ignored. Kaji ladled out more spicy noodles for everyone except Tsubasa, who promptly stole Michi's bowl. Rune kept eating. "Well," Tsubasa continued. "If she's tired of letting people know what a super-skank Kaji is, she can talk about Blume-san's wicked ways."

"Two men at once!" Michi finally caught on. "Shameful!"

"Eat your heart out." I gave him my standard reply to such nonsense.

Kaji leaned across the table, the ladle poised in his right hand. "If you ever want to eat again," he threatened his bandmates.

"It's only a joke, man," Michi said.

"Have some respect for Blume-san," Kaji said. "You can't treat him as if he was one of us."

I put my hand on Kaji's forearm. "Little Fire, thanks for defending me, but we have a show tomorrow night, so please don't hurt them."

"Thank Blume-san for sparing you." Kaji pointed the big spoon at Michi and Tsubasa.

"*Arigato gozaimasu*, Blume-san," they said in unison.

"And honestly," I added, "I love being treated as one of you."

Kaji shook his head. "You are not just a musician. All we have to do is make music; you do all the rest. You work so hard and so well. We would be nowhere without you."

I looked up at him and it struck me that his bleach job had really grown out; his hair was almost half-and-half black and white and nearly down to his shoulders. He was starting to remind me of Cruella de Vil. "We need to get you to a salon," I said.

Kaji stared at me for a split second before he started laughing. "You see what I mean?" he asked as everyone around the table chuckled.

"I do appreciate the tribute, *ichiban*." I paused. "Do you like your hair that way? Because it actually looks rather spectacular. If you were to fluff it out a bit—"

"He'd look like a mini-Gekko," Michi crowed.

"Impossible," I said. "Kaji's not a mutant…. Sorry, Rune."

Rune swallowed a mouthful of noodles. "No offense taken. Gekko is Gekko. I don't get his trip and that suits me fine."

"I am going to dye it all black, I think," Kaji said. "Maybe."

"I think you should," Sora said. "It looks better black."

"I like red," Michi offered.

"You like whatever you can get," Sora answered.

"Easy, killer," I said.

Sora pushed away from the table. "I'm going outside for a smoke. Who wants to work on my song when I get back?"

"Everyone," I replied. "Rune and I can finish running wire."

Sora nodded and walked to the side door. He'd never believe it, but I loved his song. The music had been floating around for a while, composed piecemeal during stints in hotel rooms, and he'd finally put words to it. They were the first lyrics he'd written that weren't in collaboration with Kaji and if they lacked a certain poetry, they made up for it in sheer bravado. "Bust My Buttons" was Sora's tribute to the sexy swagger of rock 'n' roll. He claimed it was about a phenomenal boner he'd once had: classic Sora. As Rune said, anyone who could sit still while listening to it was not to be trusted. I was thrilled that the lads had a solid rocker to kick off their next CD, but Sora was having an attack of chronic doubt. Any praise was shrugged off as an attempt to make him feel better about the fact that he'd never be as good a composer as Kaji. My "apples versus oranges" talk did not impress him, and he went me one better. He admitted to the possibility that he was an apple, but if so, then Kaji was a fruit basket—no, the entire fruit market. My giggling didn't improve his mood, but then again, fruit doesn't have the same slang meaning in Japan as it does in England.

Rune and I finished the electrical work while listening to the lads having a bash at changing the tempo of "Buttons'" middle eight. We snacked on edamame washed down with crisp lager and I found myself missing Tommy, whose favorite snack it was. The jack-of-all-trades on the staff of Kazuki's country house had been in my life for such a short time, but he'd made everything so much easier that I'd started wondering if I didn't need an assistant. The thought had never occurred to me before and the novelty of it was beguiling. I didn't make up my mind right then, but the idea definitely took root.

"What are you thinking about?" Rune asked, coming back from throwing away our rubbish. "You have the oddest look on your face."

"I have an idea."

"Ah," he said, assuming a wise expression. "That explains your surprised look."

"Just for that, I'm not going to tell you what it is."

"Don't be childish."

I stuck my tongue out at him. It was all the provocation he needed. The world tilted and I ended up on my back across the mixing board. His mouth moved on mine with such sweet insistence that I opened to him, inviting his probing tongue deeper. As my tongue slid against his, he leaned in, pressing the hard muscle of his thigh against my crotch. The fierce ache in my groin drew a moan from me that he couldn't fail to interpret as favorable. His hands slid down to cup my bum cheeks as he covered every inch of exposed skin with meandering kisses. I wove my fingers into his silver-gilt hair and pulled him into another long kiss. My free hand was creeping under the back of his waistband when he stepped away from me.

"Is everything all right?" I asked a bit breathlessly.

"I'm just doing as you asked. I thought it was getting a little hot and heavy, so I called a halt."

"I asked you to do that?"

"In the park? After the ice cream?"

"Yes, I remember. I'm just surprised that *you* remembered."

"Well, the way I see it, it's your law and you can repeal it."

"No, you're right. We shouldn't just go for it on the first available horizontal surface."

"I said that?"

"No, but I'm sure that's what you meant. Call me an old queen, but I want it to be special."

"Old queen? That's not very PC of you." Rune touched my cheek and the playful tone was gone. "Bottom line: it'll be special for me if you're there. The place and the time don't matter as much to me."

"So you *do* think I'm an old queen."

Rune grinned at me. "Well, you're not old."

"Arse," I said as Rune squeezed mine. Naturally, my phone rang. Rune fished it out of my trouser pocket, taking his time about it. The call went to voice mail and I glanced at the number before finishing my thought. "It's not going to be like it was before, you know."

"I didn't think it would."

"I want to be clear about this: I won't be your love slave."

"Does this mean you want to be on top?"

"Sometimes, yes."

"I'll look forward to it."

"Oh, please! Not once in the sixteen months we were together did you ever bottom."

"You never implied that you wanted anything different."

"You never asked."

"Benj, come on. All you had to do was shift a few inches. I'd have gotten the hint."

I met his eyes and took a long slow breath as my fingers uncurled. "Are we really fighting just because we aren't screwing?"

"Well, all that tension has to go somewhere."

"And you have to go home. It's gotten late while we were busy." I straightened Rune's collar and ran a hand through his tumbled jackstraw hair. "Thank you for all the help."

"It felt good working with you. Maybe we can build a house together some day."

"The things you say," I marveled. "Go on then." I kissed his cheek and pushed him toward the door.

"The phone call you can't wait to return is from Shin, isn't it?"

"You were almost out the door." I sighed my disappointment at his jealous curiosity. "But you just had to ask. You know the answer, right?"

"It's none of my damned business?" he guessed.

"Bull's-eye. Good night, Rune." I held the phone to my ear as I turned away. Yoshiro answered in the middle of the second ring. "Where are you today?" I asked him as I walked down the hall to my office. "Rio? Really!" I shut my door and sat down in the chair behind my desk. "So how much longer do you think you'll be trotting the globe?"

"Zennousha is paving the way for Kazuki's world tour. That is why I called you earlier than usual. Sato-san wants me to visit several venues and acquaint the local promoters with Zennousha and Kazuki."

"You're greasing the wheels," I translated.

"Just so. Money is an excellent lubricant."

"Don't they have someone else that could do it?"

"It suits Sato-san to send a lawyer as his emissary."

"I'll say one thing for that man: he knows how to send a message."

"*Hai.*" Yoshiro's soft-voiced agreement stroked my ear.

"Yoshi," I said, determined to do the right thing before I lost my nerve. "I should tell you that I've been seeing Rune. And that I'm interested in him. I'm sure you'll think me a fool."

"Only for love, Ben. Perhaps you cannot see it, but when you are with Rune, the two of you have a shine about you. I think you still love each other."

"The bloody hell of it is that I still feel the same way about you."

"I do not envy you your divided heart."

"It sounds as though you've had experience with that."

"Who has not?"

"Your parents were right, you know. You should have been a monk."

"If only I were worthy. Are you in bed yet?"

"No. We worked late on the recording studio. I'm glad the lads voted to put our money into building it, rather than moving to a posher address."

"You've taught them well."

"Maybe I should've been a monk."

"If you were a monk, I would gladly be one too. Imagine us in a monastery in the mountains watching the valley turn pink with cherry blossoms."

"Are our heads shaved in this fantasy?"

Yoshiro chuckled. "Not you, Ben. I like your curly hair too much."

"I like yours as well, but I'll bet you'd look wicked with your head shaved."

"I shall remember that if I am ever called upon to look wicked."

I snorted. "I've never even seen you out of your suit. All right, I've seen you with your jacket off, but you've never so much as rolled up a sleeve or even unbuttoned your top button."

"When I return, you may unbutton it."

"I'd better go; I'm getting turned on."

"Perhaps I could talk you through it?"

"Not tonight, Yoshi, or whatever time of day it is where you are. I appreciate the thought, but is doesn't feel right."

"Then I will say *konbanwa*."

"Good night." I put my phone on the charger and went to the office door. I didn't hear music so the lads were taking a break or in bed. I went to mine. Rio de Janeiro. If I were more paranoid, I would have suspected Sato of deliberately keeping Yoshiro and me apart. However, I knew Sato had more important things than my love life to think about. And so did I. What on earth was I going to wear to an awards ceremony?

Chapter Fourteen

I wore the suit that Rune and Kaji picked for me. Black and slim-tailored, worn with a crisp white shirt and a red silk scarf tied in a bow, the suit made me look like a film star from the first days of the movies. Kaji was delighted that my hair had gone untended long enough to make a respectable ponytail, but pouted when I wouldn't let him spike it out. That look was killer on him with his thick straight hair in a spiny fan at the back of his head, but it simply wouldn't work on me. Kaji settled for fastening my hair back with a black leather strap studded with tiny chrome spikes. The look on Rune's face when he saw me turned the clock back a decade. I felt like a rebel, randy and ready to rock.

"You look good enough to stand next to me," Rune joked.

I let him get away with it. I didn't need verbal compliments; I'd already seen that look in his eyes. "Then I must look bloody fantastic," I answered as I gestured to him to spin around so I could see all of him. Only Rune would have chosen such a suit and only he could have pulled it off. "Are you going to fight a bull later?"

Rune tugged at the hem of his short dark jacket. The lapels, shoulders, and sleeves were thick with gold embroidery as was the collar of the red shirt he wore under it. The snug trousers were tucked into knee-high boots with stacked heels. "I was expecting a flamenco joke. I don't have an answer ready for a matador comment."

"How could you not see that you look like a matador?"

"Hey, Rune-san," Michi said as he entered the living room area of the garage. "Why are you dressed as a bullfighter?" I laughed so hard Michi took a step back and bumped into Sora.

"*Baka!*" Sora shoved Michi into Tsubasa. "You stepped on my boots." Sora's new silver-toed snakeskin cowboy boots were sacred.

"I still love you," Tsubasa reassured Michi as he caught him and steadied him on his feet.

"Is everyone ready?" I asked.

Rune took out his camera. "Let me get a shot of you."

"I think the press will take plenty of pictures," Tsubasa said.

"You should have a picture of your own to remember this night," Rune told him.

We arranged ourselves according to some arcane natural order: Kaji front and center, me on his right, Sora to the left with an arm around Kaji's neck, Michi and Tsubasa clowning behind us. Rune clicked off several shots and we went out to the waiting limousine. Sung was staying home with a cold, but the lads were so excited about the nomination that Kaji didn't have time to miss his lover. Among the things I was thankful for that night was the fact that the video for Kazuki's "You Are the Fire" hadn't been released in time for consideration. It was the first year in five that the Shining One wasn't up for an award, and I took a petty satisfaction in the thought.

"Champagne?" Rune asked as the limo pulled onto the main road.

"The lads don't drink a lot of wine," I said. "Why don't we toast with a shot? Who's with me?"

"Rock 'n' roll!" Kaji shouted, echoed by his bandmates.

I poured shots of bourbon into the crystal glasses provided by the car service and we tossed them back. Sora insisted on another toast, and then Rune made one. By the time we reached Tokyo Bay Arena, the jitters had been properly smoothed out. None of us was drunk, but we were definitely relaxed. "My God," I said, as I saw the line of limos and the crush of the press. "I can't believe we're about to walk the fabled red carpet."

"We would not do it without you," Kaji said. "And if we win, you are going to accept with us."

"*When* we win," Sora corrected him.

Kaji kissed the moody guitar player on the cheek as we rolled up to the entrance. The limo doors were opened and then we were out and walking. Sora, in Goth gunslinger drag, hung an arm around Kaji's neck as they sauntered past the crowds behind the ropes. Kaji's hair, a uniform shade of midnight now, looked tattered rather than cut into a layered mane that framed his face and neck. He wore a simple long-sleeved white T-shirt of knitted silk over black leather trousers and he outshone every rhinestone cowboy at this rodeo as he paused now and then to take someone's hand and thank them for being there. Michi and Tsubasa stopped several times to take cameras from fans. After snapping off shots of the cameras' owners, they struck poses and took pictures of one another. In bemused indulgence, I watched as Hayate hand-fed their fans and I never gave a thought to being nervous as I followed them into the building with Rune at my side.

Ushers helped us find our seats in the enormous arena and we watched people arrive until the show got under way. The male/female VJ host team was attractive and glib as you'd expect of on-air presenters, the ever-changing set was impressive, and the air of expectant excitement was intoxicating. As the evening progressed, it lived up to every dream I'd ever had about a night like this. Even if Hayate didn't win, I'd never forget this night. I leaned over and kissed Rune just to share how good I felt as the emcee announced the next category: Best New Artist in a Music Video. I glanced at the lads and met Kaji's eyes, all of us grinning at the outrageousness of it. We were here at the top and in a few minutes Hayate's name would be added to the list of stars.

"And presenting the award... Kazuki!"

The audience clapped wildly and my head snapped around as Kazuki descended from the rafters in a harness disguised as S & M gear. Dressed head to toe in supple bright red leather, half his face covered by mirrored sunglasses, he touched lightly down on one foot and smoothly hit the quick release. To music drowned out by the sound of applause, he did a three-minute dance routine that should have set off the fire alarms and then sashayed to the podium. Deftly opening the envelope without removing his red gloves, he read off the nominees as snippets from each video played on the giant screen behind him. I'd forgotten what a sexy mouth Kazuki had, but Kaji hadn't, by the look on his face. I reached over the armrest and took his hand. He took Sora's hand and in a moment, the entire band was holding hands, waiting for Kazuki to pronounce the winner.

"Hayate!" Kazuki announced, displaying a rare public grin. "For 'Bed of Thorns'!"

Behind Kazuki, another scene from the video was projected on the screen. This one featured a torrid kiss between the beautiful demon and the heartbroken angel. Kaji stared at it as though hypnotized.

"Get up!" I shook him. "Go get your award."

Kaji wouldn't let go of my hand. "You are coming too," he told me.

Rune stood to let us out and I was half-dragged down the aisle to the stage. With Sora on my right and Michi and Tsubasa behind me, there was nowhere to go but forward. I didn't trip on the steps, thus depriving Rune of hours of merriment, and then we were at the podium. A leggy young woman handed Kazuki something that looked vaguely like a gold brick and Kazuki presented it to Hayate. He leaned forward as he handed the trophy over and said something only Kaji heard. The audience quieted as the band, one by one, expressed their gratitude for the honor. I found Rune in the crowd and sent him a smile as we were conducted into the wings where Sato was waiting to take Kazuki by the arm and draw him away.

"Don't let this ruin the night for you, *ichiban*," I told Kaji.

Kaji was staring after Kazuki with such concentration that I was surprised he didn't will the Shining One back to his side. Only when the two men were out of his sight did he turn to me. "We have to help him," he said.

"Why would you believe him?" I asked, settling back in the limo.

"You will not help?" Kaji replied.

I glanced at Rune. Sora, Michi, and Tsubasa were partying with some of the other winners, but Rune had elected to stick by me when Kaji wanted to leave. No way was I going to let my *ichiban* go off alone.

"I don't think that's what Benj is saying," Rune said. "We just need to know a little more before we mount a rescue operation. Think how silly we'd look showing up with tanks and air support if Kazuki was just joking with you."

"Why would he joke about such a thing?"

I'd thought the Shining One was out of our lives, but he was still causing trouble. I couldn't think of a single individual who'd put me through so many twists and turns, including the magnificently mercurial Hagen Rune. "Who knows why he does anything?" I said, a bit exasperated.

"Because Sato tells him to." The tone of Kaji's voice told me I'd hurt him.

"I'm sorry; I know you don't want to believe anything bad about Kazuki, God knows why, but…." I glanced helplessly at Rune, unsure what to say.

"The thing is," Rune took the conversation, "that it would take a pretty far-fetched plot to explain everything Kazuki has done. Do you really think it's a case of mind control?"

"Please do not make fun of me."

"We're not," I said. "Think about it. Can you come up with a plausible reason for Kazuki's actions?"

"Sato," Kaji said, starting to pout a little.

"So half-brother Sato is an evil genius. Okay, I'll buy that, but Kazuki doesn't have to do as Sato says. He proved that once, remember?"

"Yes, I remember. We were happy for a while and then Sato forced him to come back."

"He wasn't even speaking to Sato at the time."

"Do you remember when Kazuki's coat showed up without Kazuki?"

I nodded. Of course I remembered; the incident had made me uneasy until I decided Kazuki had paid to have it delivered. It was exactly the sort of extravagant gesture the Shining One was prone to.

"Sato had one of his men take the coat and bring it to Nagano as a warning. The same with the necklace."

I recalled the necklace as well with its dragon-claw pendant. "Sato had someone put it around your neck while you were asleep? Why?"

"For the same reason he sent the coat: to scare Kazuki."

"I don't know. It's a little… indirect for Sato."

"Why won't you believe me?" Kaji asked. "Kazuki is trapped and has no one to help him."

"Mr. Shin cares about…," I began and then paused. Yoshiro Shin hadn't been anywhere near Kazuki in quite a while. Sato was making sure the private attorney stayed away from his client. "I think we need more facts."

"I still don't see how Sato could make Kazuki lie to your face," Rune told Kaji. "And I'm sorry to be so blunt, but how is Sung going to fit into this?"

Kaji dropped his eyes. "Sung knows how I feel about Kazuki," he mumbled.

I leaned across to take Kaji's hands. "I'll stand with you; you know that. I just don't want you to be suckered into another stupid publicity stunt."

"I will take the chance."

"And your friends will take it with you," Rune said. I couldn't tell if he meant it as reassurance or a warning.

I tried one more time to dissuade Kaji. "I just can't forget Kazuki saying he'd made a mistake with you and that you'd misinterpreted his kindness. What if that's true?"

"I know he is a good actor," Kaji replied. "But he was not *acting* gay. We made love many times, and it was not fake."

I glanced at Rune again before I spoke and realized I was treating him like a partner, looking to him for support and trying to gauge his reactions beforehand. "Some people can screw without feeling a thing," I said, knowing how cruel the words sounded.

Instead of looking stricken by the comment, Kaji's features set grimly. "Kazuki feels."

"All right," I sighed. "Forgive me for playing devil's advocate. It's the same old story; I just don't want to see you hurt."

"I do not want to be hurt."

"Are you sure?" Rune interjected. "Every time you break up, you write a hit song."

Kaji and I turned to stare at him; after a moment, we chuckled. "Thank you, Rune-san," Kaji said. "You are a true rocker."

"Yeah, sure, I'm Elvis," Rune scoffed, but he was pleased by the compliment. "Now how do we get to the bottom of this Kazuki cock-up?"

"I wish I had an idea. Kazu told me he agreed to be a presenter tonight so he could have a chance to speak to me without Sato being able to prevent it."

"This reminds me of that battered wife movie," Rune said. "You remember, Sunshine? That really beautiful brunette was in it, the one whose brother is an actor too. Her husband was a total bastard, wanted to control every minute of her life. Everything had to be just so or he'd flip out."

"I know the one. Don't recall the title though."

"Doesn't matter." Rune waved a hand dismissively. "My point is that the woman was terrified of doing anything other than what he told her to do. He had convinced her that she was a... what's that phrase? Oh yeah, he convinced her she was a useless airhead and he was only trying to help her improve herself. He had total control of her."

"And you see Kazuki in the role of the battered wife?"

"Why not? Isn't the theory far-fetched enough?"

I turned to Kaji. "How did Sato and Kazuki behave around each other when they were alone?"

"I was not there when they were alone and Sato never intruded on Kazuki and me. I thought it was polite of him. Now, I think he did not like seeing me with Kazuki."

"But it was his idea to put you two together."

"I am sure he regrets it."

My laugh was devoid of humor. "Good one, *ichiban*."

"We could have someone follow Kazuki," Rune said. "Maybe we'd find out something."

"Are you mad? It would take Zennousha's security people about three seconds to find and annihilate anyone who tried spying on their meal ticket."

"I should have thought that through before speaking," Rune admitted. "Anyone else have an idea?"

"Why don't we go in the front door?" I said.

"You have a plan," Rune stated, knowing well the look on my face.

I nodded. "Something so clever you could put a tail on it and call it a *kitsune*."

F eeling better after hearing my foxy plan, Kaji went directly to bed when we got home. I think he slept with the trophy. Rune watched me pour the last beer in the fridge into two glasses and I looked up to catch an odd expression on his face.

"Good Lord, what are you thinking about?" I asked as I handed him his beer.

"You." He raised his glass to me. "You're really quite spectacular."

I touched my glass to his. "That means an awful lot to me."

"Seriously, I was already impressed with you, but this… this idea of yours is brilliant. How can Sato say no?"

"He can't, not without the kind of publicity he doesn't want."

"Are you going to do it by phone or face to face?"

"Well, you know the cellular is my weapon of choice, but I have a better idea. I'm going to tell it to you, but I don't want you to go mental, all right?"

"Why would I?"

"I want to be a partner in Hikage Productions."

Rune shot out of his seat and sat back down. "I'm doing my best not to shout and leap about the room. Would you say it one more time so I can be sure I heard correctly?"

"I want to be a partner in Hikage Productions. I want to set up a label for the lads called Uzumaki. It means something like vortex according to Sora. I'm willing to buy in at whatever your assets amount to or we can talk about a sum."

"Whatever you like, but… why?"

"I just can't do it by myself anymore. For starters, I'd want you to handle Hayate's dealings with Sato."

"Excellent," he said immediately. "When?"

"Why wait? Tomorrow morning, you call his secretary and make an appointment as Hayate's new rep. I'll make sure you have a copy of the contract before you go in. Sato's been doing all the pushing up 'til now; let's see how he likes being leaned on."

"Oooh, you sound so gangster."

"Knock it off." I paused. "There is the formality of clearing these changes with the lads, but they have the bad taste to admire you, so I doubt they'll object."

"Since we're getting an early start, maybe I should stay the night."

"It's up to you. The couch is quite comfortable."

"Oh, come on. We can sleep together without sleeping together."

"But why torture ourselves? Go home and get a good night's sleep. I'm going to call Yoshiro and see if he'll talk about Kazuki."

"Are you sure that's a good idea? I know he's hot for you, but he *is* Kazuki's attorney. A man like Shin would see clearly where his duty lies."

"Yoshiro and I have an understanding," I said, making it obvious that I had nothing more to say on the subject.

"All right. See you in the morning."

Rune leaned toward me and I met him halfway. God that man could kiss. It took all my willpower to push him away. He stole one more, an almost subliminal pressure against my lips, there and gone, and he walked away humming a tune I didn't recognize.

"What is that?" I asked, intrigued.

"It's called 'When the Sun Didn't Shine'. I'll sing it for you some day." He closed the door and in a few seconds, I heard his car engine. I'd never heard of the song and after some thought, I realized it must be one of his own. With the melody stuck in my head, I went to call Yoshi. When I got his voice mail, I figured he was in a meeting, or maybe sleeping. I had no idea of the time where he was, or even *where* he was exactly. Sato might have sent him to the other side of the planet by now.

I fell asleep with Rune's wistful melody wandering around my head. I imagined it played on an acoustic guitar accompanying Rune's scratchy baritone. I didn't have any words to put to it, but the raw-honey sweetness of his voice was a potent lullaby. I dreamed of him and woke up in a wet spot.

Chapter Fifteen

I was thinking about the vivid dream when Sato called me, right on schedule. "Good morning, Sato-san," I said breezily, the tone I'd decided to adopt when I had to speak with him, as I inevitably would even with Rune blocking for me.

"You will have your way in this," he said without preamble.

"I beg your pardon?"

"Hayate will open for Kazuki on his world tour. That is what you wanted, yes?"

"I do remember discussing that possibility at one point in our relationship."

"Don't be coy. Your agent had a copy of the contract."

"Mr. Hagen Rune is my partner. You may deal with him as you would with me."

"You are making a mistake."

"Do you know something about Rune that I don't?"

"Very well, Blume-san. If you wish to pretend ignorance then that is your business. I don't know what you think you are accomplishing by holding Zennousha to this contract, but I can assure you that you will not change Kazuki's plans."

"You mean *your* plans, don't you? And what I'm accomplishing is exposure for my lads."

"Don't you think it will be painful for your juicy singer to work with Kazuki?"

"I'm sorry to derail the convo, but did you just refer to Kaji as *juicy*?"

"Is it incorrect?"

"Not strictly speaking. As opposed to dry, I suppose you could call him juicy, but it's an odd choice, nonetheless."

"Are you playing games with me? I mean juicy like a steak, yes?"

"Now you're making me uncomfortable. I think I'll hang up." I leaned back in my chair. I was enjoying this every bit as much as I'd thought I would. I'm a pleasant and easygoing bloke for the most part, but Sato brought out the worst in me. I'd need to be aware of that and not let it get the better of me. People tend to make mistakes when they react without thinking.

"Just a moment," Sato said quickly. "I want to know what Kazuki said to the boy last night."

"The *boy*? That's verging on disrespectful again, Sato-san."

"What do you wish me to call the little *hinin* whore?" When I didn't answer right away, he continued. "You are shocked, yes? Be prepared, *gaijin*. This is only a beginning. You may force me to work with you, but you will not enjoy it."

"That was a given," I found my voice.

"Now tell me what Kazuki said."

"Ask your show pony." I wanted to say, "Ask your own whore," but saw no reason to use vulgarity yet. Just the fact that I was balking him gave me the cool to stay polite.

Sato gave up on the question and delivered another veiled warning. "You should back out of this deal. It will not benefit your clients in the end."

"I think it will."

"Remember that I gave you a chance to walk away."

"Duly noted. Was there anything else?"

"*Hai*. When your Kaji is within my grasp next time, I will have him. Then I will know why Kazuki was willing to disobey me for the little *yarichin*. He must have an ass like—"

I hung up, cleansed my mind of the mental image Sato's hateful words conjured, and called Rune. He answered before the first ring finished pealing.

"I tried to call," he said. "Were you talking to Sato?"

"Of course. He squealed quite satisfyingly, the swine."

"I must protest that insult on behalf of all swine."

"Tell me about the meeting." I sat forward in my chair and listened to Rune's colorful account of Sato-san's reaction to the news that Hayate intended to enforce their contract. "That's lovely stuff, that is," I said when he'd finished. "Sato didn't mention it. Did he take Vudu?"

"Swallowed it whole. The lineup for the world tour will be Vudu, Hayate, and Kazuki."

"It actually worked."

"Why do you sound surprised? You said Sato couldn't refuse."

"Allow me my self-congratulatory moment."

"Bask away." Rune began humming. "Done yet?"

"Baby, I'm just gettin' started."

"Should I come over?"

The phone felt inexplicably warm against my ear. "For now, I think that concentrating on getting Vudu's CD out there should take priority. Wouldn't it be ultra if we had a duet by Kaji and Sung?"

"You're giving me gooseflesh."

"What about that tune you were whistling last night? I quite liked it. Think it would be suitable?"

Rune was quiet for a moment before he spoke. "I wrote that song for you."

"Oh... well, of course, I understand if you want to record it yourself."

Another, longer pause. "Let me think about it on the way over."

"You're coming here?"

"I want to play the song for you."

There was a time when the sun didn't shine.
When I lived in the darkness of my broken mind.
A man on a journey, I forgot to watch my step.

I wandered off the path and into regret.
Now I am falling. Can you hear me calling?
Do you still wish we'd never met?

I went for days with my head in a haze.
People were just characters in their own plays.
A man wearing blinders, I strayed from my way.
Now, I'm at your door and hoping I can stay.
I will keep waiting. Is your heart still breaking?
I've waited so long for this day.

Let me take your hand and feel that touch once more.
Let me take your heart and keep it safe this time.
Let me keep you near, whisper in your ear
Stay with me throughout the years and let the sun shine.

Will there come a time when you smile at me?
Unlocking the chains and setting me free.
A man filled with hope kneels at your feet.
Say you forgive me and make me complete.
I won't stop trying until you stop crying.
I'll show you the man I can be.

Let me take your hand and feel that touch once more.
Let me take your heart and keep it safe this time.
Let me keep you near, whisper in your ear
Stay with me throughout the years and let the sun shine.

"Well?" Rune raised his expressive eyebrows.

"I need to hear it again."

He looked more than a little bewildered by my calm reaction; after all, he'd poured out his heart to me, but all he said was, "That would be my very great pleasure." He settled the classical guitar more comfortably on his lap and his clever fingers picked out the notes of the opening bars. The early morning light collected in his gauzy blond hair like pearls of radiance. His skin was luminous as he raised his face and began to sing. I watched the ways his lips curved around the words, anticipating the way they'd feel moving against mine in a few minutes. My heart was beating so fast, beating against my ribs like a hummingbird in a cage. I needed those few minutes to collect myself, but as the last plaintive note died, I was still an emotional mess.

"Well?" Rune prompted.

I cleared my throat and began weeping like a beauty pageant winner. "Sorry," I managed to gasp.

Rune put down the guitar and drew me into his embrace. "So do you like your song or is it so horrible that it made you cry?"

"All that wasted time."

"You can't look at it that way, Sunny," Rune said in my ear. "What about your lads?"

I sniffled. "All right. It wasn't all wasted."

"And we're together now, a little older and a little wiser. Maybe it was always meant to be this way. I certainly appreciate you a lot more now."

"Hang on a moment. You have me in a weak state just now, but I'm not going to drop all my defenses just because you wrote me a song." I pulled away from him slightly. "I love you, but I still need a little time, especially with all that's going on."

"You just said you love me."

"Oh dear, are you going to make a big fuss about it?"

"You said you love me."

"And I'll say it again. I love you."

Rune's eyes sparkled with moisture as he pulled me into another hug. "Thank you," he said, and I got the feeling he wasn't speaking to me, but to Fate, the angels, or some other shadowy entity that bestowed good luck. "I won't make you sorry."

"Oh, I expect we'll make each other sorry on occasion. Butting blocks now and then will take off our sharp edges until we're like tumbled rocks in a river. We'll fit so smoothly—" My words ended as Rune's mouth covered mine. I've no doubt mentioned what a champion kisser he is, but that kiss turned my blood to napalm and melted my bones, not because of any technique, but because the sincerity of his passion was implicit in the caress. I felt loved without let or reservation, loved for who I was, not for what I could be, loved not blindly, but in the full light of all my flaws, loved.

When our lips parted, I leaned my forehead against his. "I'm still not a sure thing, you know," I said, rubbing my nose against his.

"As long as you know that I am."

"Great balls of fire!" Sung said as he stopped just inside the studio. "Should I come back later?"

"Are you hoping for work as a door?" Kaji said from behind Sung. "Keep moving. Ow! *Kuso!* Sora! Wait!" Sandwiched between the other two men, Kaji yelled at Sung to move. Sung turned to face Kaji and pressed against him, pulsing his hips, rocking Kaji into Sora. "That is not what I meant," Kaji said.

"I'm shielding you from the sight of our managers getting it on."

"No one's getting anything on, mate," I said, as I rose from my seat.

"Then you just enjoy the taste of Rune-san's tonsils?" Sung asked innocently.

Kaji dug his fingertips into the big guitarist's ribs. "*Baka yaro,*" Sung cursed, letting Kaji go.

"What is the big news today?" Kaji asked as he moved around Sung.

Sora slouched against the wall, tossing his weighted dagger; he'd gotten pretty good at juggling it and it had become his favorite prop. "Yes, tell us, Blume-san. Have we changed labels in the last five minutes? Our name perhaps?"

"How about changing your knickers?" I replied in kind. Sora was the only band member who hadn't reacted with wild enthusiasm when asked about the merger. He didn't disagree; he was just annoyed that he hadn't been consulted first. "And the news," I continued as Michi and Tsubasa came in, "is that Hayate and Vudu are opening for Kazuki on his world tour."

Gekko slunk in with the other three members of Vudu in time to hear. From the noise in the room, everyone seemed pleased with the idea.

"*Ichiban,*" Kaji said, coming over to hug me. "Have you been crying?" he asked in a whisper.

"Yeah, but in a good way."

Kaji glanced at Rune and back at me. "So did he ask you to marry him?"

I slapped him lightly on the cheek. "Lunatic."

169

"Count on it."

Sora came up behind Kaji, yanked his bandmate's head back and bit into the curve of his throat hard enough to leave an impression. "I will show you lunacy," he declared, brandishing the silver dagger.

"Save it for the show," I said. "You lads are going to have to up the ante. Make sure the Shining One has a hard act to follow."

Kaji rolled his eyes at me. "We are going to kick some major ass." His colleagues echoed this sentiment, each in his own way, and Kaji waited for the noise to die. "We will make Kazuki proud to have such an opening act."

I wanted to spank him and hug him at the same time. Instead, I put an arm casually around Rune. It was noticed, but no one remarked on it.

"Benj and me were talking over an idea when you lot came in," Rune said, instantly getting everyone's attention in that effortless way he has. "A duet by Sung and Kaji."

"Why not a duet with me and Kaji?" Gekko said. "I am the singer."

"Sung sings too," Rune said. "And I... *we* think that Sung and Kaji's voices would blend very nicely. We actually have a song for you to consider."

"If I am not needed," Gekko said, "I have things I could do."

"We all have a lot to do to get ready for this tour," Rune said. "Go ahead and get started. We really just need Sung and Kaji for now."

"Come on." Vudu's bassist Maru gestured to Kyo, the drummer. "Let's go tell everyone we know that we're doing a world tour."

Sora flopped into a chair with the demeanor of a man who plans to stay for a while. Michi and Tsubasa took seats on the floor and watched Rune expectantly. Sung and Kaji focused their attention on him as well.

"You'd better do something," I whispered loudly. "They look hungry."

Rune did what he'd always done best: captivated an audience. When he finished singing his song for the third time in an hour, there was silence in the room for several moments.

"Beautiful, Rune-san. It is not our style, but I would be proud to sing it," Kaji said.

"I would love to do this song with you, honey cutie," Sung chimed in. "It could be some fun to sing something folksy."

"It's not folksy," Rune said quickly. "It's just that I'm playing it on a—"

All of us turned at the loud sound of Sora striking his nails across the strings of his amplified guitar. "I can write a nova-hot arrangement of that tune," he said.

I raised an eyebrow at Rune.

"I guess it wouldn't hurt to try different versions," he said, bravely handing his baby to the wolves.

"Brilliant! Now, let's make copies of the lyrics and get to work. What's the good of having a home recording studio if all you use it for is karaoke?"

"That was low, Blume-san," Michi said. "I'm going to call for pizza. Who wants?"

Sung and Kaji ran through the lyrics together until they knew them and then started playing with harmonies. Sung was a competent vocalist with a bluesy growl to his lower notes; Kaji was a bell-pure virtuoso with a range that soared over four octaves. Together, they were an ear-catching combo. The contrast suited the subject of the song perfectly, in my opinion; Sung's solid melody line counterpointed by Kaji's floating harmony. Sora's stinging riffs should have sounded like machine-gun fire in a church, but somehow it worked. It not only worked, it was a stand-alone song that defied easy categorization.

"Well, what do you think?" I asked Rune. "Can we use your song?"

"It's yours, Sunshine."

"Don't be absurd. It belongs to Hikage Productions and royalties will be paid. Just because we're all in bed together doesn't mean we can skip the paperwork."

"I like the way you put that."

"I'm shocked. Hand me my phone, would you?" As I took it from Rune's hand, it began to yodel. "Michi!" Our drummer scuttled out of the room as I glared at him. "I wish he'd stop doing that," I grumped as I glanced at the number. I didn't recognize it, but I answered anyway, wondering how the caller got my private cell number. "Hello?"

"If you are smart, you will stay away from Kazuki."

"How does that follow?" I asked just for fun.

There was a brief silence from Sato's goon. "Stay away from Kazuki. If you do not—"

Abruptly, I recognized the thick voice. "Inspector Aizawa?" The caller disconnected, as clear a confirmation as I could wish. "That was odd," I said.

"Remember that detective that searched the garden behind Kazuki's mum's house? He just called and threatened me." I dug through my card wallet until I found the number the inspector had given me. I punched it in and waited. In a few seconds, a recording informed me that the number was unassigned. "Very odd." Being me, I called the main number for the Tokyo police and inquired after Aizawa. It took more than a few minutes, but I hung up having learned that no Inspector Aizawa had ever headed up a special squad to investigate Kazuki's disappearance. It was quite worrisome.

"Why would Sato hire a thug to impersonate a police officer?" Rune asked.

"So we'd think Kazuki's disappearance was being investigated?"

"That's the obvious answer, but I just can't make myself believe Sato would go to all that trouble. Kazuki wasn't kidnapped; he jumped ship and Sato could prove it easily. Why bother with all that set dressing and extras?"

"I don't know," I sighed. "I wish I did. I wish just one piece of this made sense to me. When Sato came to me the first time, I knew there was something off about his proposition, but I was so eager to see the lads get ahead that I ignored my instincts."

"I would've done the same. It was a golden opportunity."

"On some level, I knew it wasn't right."

Kaji moved from under Sung's arm to sit close to me. "We are not going to look for blame here," he said. "We all did what we wanted to do or what we thought we should do. Let's move forward."

I kissed the top of his head. "*Bonsai!*" I said.

"It's *banzai*, Blume-san," Sung corrected me, not being in on the private joke.

I tried to educate him. "Never say that word when Kaji's around."

"Why?" Sung asked just before the self-guided boy bomb hit him.

I watched Sung and Kaji wrestle for a few moments before turning to Rune. "Do you think we're being stupid in taking on Sato?"

"A bit late for that question, but what was your other choice? Let Sato continue in his campaign to bury Hayate? We'll just have to stay ballsy and keep our eyes open."

"This thing with the cop bothers me. It's the sort of thing big-shot criminals do in cheesy films."

"Maybe the phony cop was one of Sato's security people and all he wanted to do was keep you from going to the real police."

"Yeah, that makes sense. You know," I glanced at Kaji and Sung, now recumbent on the threadbare sofa, "as much as Sato pisses me off, it's Kazuki I'd like to throttle."

"His was the biggest betrayal," Rune sympathized, and then added, "or so it appears."

"You're defending him?"

"I'm keeping an open mind. That battered wife movie really affected me."

I ran a hand through his hair. "I really do love you, you know."

Rune took my hand and interlaced our fingers. "I don't know if I deserve this second chance, but I'm not going to arse it up. Maybe that's why I can give Kazuki the benefit of the doubt. If he loves Kaji, he's in hell right now."

That was a sobering thought. My feelings about Kazuki had been a seesaw from day one, but now they tilted to a precarious balance. "We can never know for sure, can we?" I said softly. "Even if we're present to witness an event, we'll never know what was going on in everyone's minds. It drives me mad that the truth can be so subjective."

"Yeah, that's a tough one, Sunny." Rune kissed the end of my nose.

"You might think I'm being paranoid, but it wasn't that long ago that Kazuki was beaten badly enough to need surgery."

"And still no word on who or why."

"Right. I'm beginning to wonder if the police even know he was attacked." I paused. "No, wait; Yoshi sent them a statement from Kazuki."

"Sato probably hushed it up. The papers were full of the story for a day and then it just went away. The wrong kind of publicity for Japan's sweetheart."

"I'm just getting the feeling that Sato was right when he told me I was in over my head."

"We're all in over our heads. The trick is to keep swimming."

I took a deep breath and, looking into his eyes, found my strength. "You're right; this is something I have to do. For Kaji."

Kaji looked up at the sound of his name, pulling his hair from Sung's fingers, half his head now covered in tiny braids. "What do we do next?" he asked.

"We have a tour to get ready for. That means new wardrobe, new hair, and new choreography. I'd also like to get that duet in the can and add it to the show."

"Come on." Kaji rose and held out a hand to Sung. "We have work to do."

"There's another worry," I said as the young men put on headphones.

"Sung?" Rune glanced at the lads. "Yeah, I know what you mean. He tells me that it doesn't bother him that Kaji isn't in love with him, that he's willing to wait until Kaji's over Kazuki, but that's shite. If Kaji gets what he wants, Sung is bound to be hurt."

"What does Kaji want?" I knew the answer, but I was interested in how Rune saw it.

"He wants Kazuki back, right?"

"I'm sure he'd like that, but I think he'd try to help Kazuki even if he knew he'd never see him again."

"Look, I didn't mean to say that Kaji is heartless or anything like that. He's been perfectly honest with Sung all the way."

"And I didn't mean to be so defensive. Why don't we get some work done?"

"Whatever you say, partner."

Chapter Sixteen

I had been to Nippon Budokan many times to hear other bands, looking forward to the day when Hayate would play at the big hall. It was there that Kazuki's *Pandemic Love* tour would start and it was there we went to rehearse. When we arrived, Kazuki was on stage practicing a dance routine with three women. Watching him spin and glide in clingy garments was mesmerizing. Whatever else he might be, Kazuki was a natural entertainer and it was almost impossible to look away from him. Like my Little Fire, the gods had imbued Kazuki with a measure of stardust. Call it charisma, call it charm, call it sex appeal, it's an ineffable, enchanting quality that has caused more strife than oil reserves. If only people didn't have to own what they find appealing, there would be a lot more peace in the world.

"Kazuki looks good," Kaji said, doing his best to sound casual.

"Good?" I took off my sunglasses and gave him my incredulous look. "I would say he's the definition of temptation."

"I'd do him," Sora said, leaning on Kaji. "From behind… if he promised not to turn around."

"Shut up," Kaji suggested, giving him an elbow in the ribs.

I looked around for Rune, who'd driven in ahead of us to meet up with Vudu. Seeing no sign of my partner, I called him and found he'd taken his lads around the corner for a bite.

"Rubbish. You're scheduled to use the space between twelve and two. It's one-forty."

"I can't dispute that, but neither can I tell Kazuki to get off the stage. It's his show."

"You let him get away with that?"

"Honestly, I didn't make an issue of it. We have three more days."

I bit my tongue before I could say something sharp. Rune was right. We still had plenty of time. I was just incensed by the lack of consideration. "True enough," I said. "Are you coming back here?"

"Yeah, the guys can always get in a couple of hours after Hayate's done. Want me to bring you anything?"

I felt warm all over just because he'd thought to ask. Hagen Rune being thoughtful: it boggled the mind. "I think we have everything we need right now."

"Call me if you think of anything," he said, but it sounded like *I love you*.

"I love you too," I said and rang off.

The music ended and Kazuki gestured to the dancers that he was through with them. Bending backward, he put his hands on the ground and did a slow walkover ending in a split. Leaning forward, he touched his forehead to his knee and stretched his arms out in front of him. Sora whistled softly, but whatever rude comment he was about to make concerning flexibility was preempted by the sound of a woman's voice. Natsuko hove into view from the wings and stood over Kazuki.

"Why did you let the dancers leave?" she asked.

"They are finished."

"I wanted to discuss some ideas for the routine before they left."

Kazuki rose to his feet without a reply and went to turn off the sound system. He picked up a hooded sweatshirt from a speaker and walked to the side of the stage.

"You are not listening to me," Natsuko said.

Kazuki kept going as though she hadn't spoken. As he reached the wings, he glanced out at the auditorium and saw us in the aisle. His eyes met Kaji's and he began to walk faster. A few seconds later, he reappeared from the stage door. I didn't say anything as Kaji bolted toward him. Kazuki quickened his step and they met several yards ahead of the rest of us.

"*Hisashiburi.* I am honored to be associated with such a talented group," Kazuki said as Natsuko dug her phone out of her handbag.

"Indeed, it has been some time since we last met," Kaji said in the same formal tone. "And it is we who are honored."

"I look forward to working with Hayate again."

"And Vudu," Kaji reminded him.

Something flickered in Kazuki's serene gaze like a cloud shadow passing over a still lake. "You are here to rehearse?"

"Yes, we are," I said, stopping beside Kaji. "You look very well, Kazuki-san."

"*Arigato,* Blume-san." He tilted his head to view me from a new angle. "You look different."

"Happens to the best of us. The lads should get to work, but you're welcome to hang out."

"My manager was not here to greet you, but I'm sure he will be here soon."

It seemed like a non sequitur, but I was sure it wasn't. "Are you threatening me, or are you afraid your manager will find out you were with Kaji?"

"I do not know who I can trust."

Over Kazuki's shoulder, I saw Natsuko put her phone away and walk toward the stage exit. "Look, if you're being blackmailed or something, just say it and we'll do whatever we can to help you."

The Shining One's jade eyes widened. "No," he hissed. "Do nothing."

"If you'd just tell us what's—"

"Kazuki!" Natsuko said peevishly as she came within earshot, one hand resting on her round belly. "Why didn't you wait for me?"

"I did not want you to come with me."

It struck me then that what I'd taken for Kazuki's breathtaking cruelty was nothing more than literalness. It also occurred to me that Natsuko should have known better than to ask the question. Nevertheless, the sight of a weeping pregnant woman can only inspire sympathy.

"*Nandesuka*!" Kaji gasped. "You are unbelievable! Have a care for her feelings."

"Why? She doesn't care for mine," Kazuki said. When he saw the look on Kaji's face, he reverted to his formal manner like a man changing a hat. "Please, all of you, accept my apology for my rudeness. Now I think we should be going."

Natsuko's tears turned off like a faucet as Kazuki took her hand and pulled her forward. "Forgive us," she murmured. "My fiancé is so impatient."

Kazuki looked back once as he held the door for Natsuko. His eyes met Kaji's, and I could almost smell the ozone charge of an imminent lightning strike. Then the Shining One was through the door and gone.

"You see," Kaji said to me. "He could not even speak in front of *his* fiancée. He is all alone."

"It certainly looked that way. No love lost between them, ay?"

"It is very sad."

Sora snorted. "It is pathetic," he said. "When will the Shining One grow some balls? Hey, Kaji, does Kazuki even have a *chinko*?"

"Why are you so interested?" Kaji shot back.

Michi and Tsubasa exchanged a glance of incomprehension at the sniping between their bandmates. "We're going to tune up," Tsubasa said as they headed for the stage. After a long stare at Kaji, Sora followed. Kaji took a couple of steps after the guitarist, but turned back to me.

"What is it, *ichiban*?"

"I was thinking Sora is right. What we do or do not cannot matter if Kazuki will not free himself."

"I'm afraid I agree."

"I am not giving up on him."

"I know. Now get up on that stage. I want to hear some good music."

As Kaji walked away, the sound of cathedral bells rung by a capering hunchback assaulted my ears. I shook my fist at Michi as I took out my phone and answered it.

"Yoshiro," I said warmly, still glaring at Michi who was grinning broadly.

"I say hello to you from Milan, and I am wondering what size shoe you wear."

"Ten and a half UK, twenty-eight point five Japanese, and around a forty-four Euro. Why?"

"I wish to bring you something from Italy."

"You mustn't buy me anything expensive, Yoshi. It would make me a bit uncomfortable."

"Perhaps a bottle of nice wine then?"

"That sounds lovely. We can drink it when you come home."

"I understand that Hayate will accompany Kazuki on his tour. I am glad to hear this."

"Sato-san was not so pleased."

"That was evident in his tone when he called me. He was not pleased when I advised him to honor the contract. He has not been able to force Kazuki to change his will either."

"You're joking! Kaji is still his heir?"

"I believe someone might have cautioned Kazuki to have his fiancée sign a prenuptial agreement and to delay changing any documents until after the paternity test."

"Someone? Like a Buddhist monk who was passing by?"

"I have missed your humor, Ben."

"Do you know how much longer you'll be gone?"

"I have several more visits to make, but the list is much shorter now."

"Yoshi, I want to ask you some questions, but first I need to tell you that you were right about Rune and me. I still love him and I want to give it another go." I paused to swallow. "I know Rune is the one for me, but I'll never forget you."

"That is a great tribute. I am disappointed that my work has taken me away and stolen my chance to know you as a lover, but I am happy that you are happy, my friend."

"Thanks for making this easy for me."

"If I thought I could change your mind, I might be more difficult."

I heard the smile in his voice. "I've a feeling you can be quite difficult if it's called for."

"Ask me your questions, Ben."

"Did you know that Inspector Aizawa is not a real police officer?"

"Aizawa was the man in charge of finding Kazuki when we thought he'd disappeared."

"That's the one."

"Sato-san told me to meet the inspector and bring him to the Murakami house."

"According to the records of the Tokyo police force, Aizawa has never worked for them. I find that disturbing."

"*Hai.* Impersonating an officer is a serious crime. He seemed quite genuine to me."

"I was completely fooled. Did the real police ever find out anything about the people that attacked Kazuki?"

"Unfortunately, no."

"I thought it was odd that he never talked about it. As soon as he was out of the hospital, he acted as though he'd never been injured."

"It is hard for him to admit weakness. It may be hard for you to see, but he is a strong man physically, very fit, and he tries to extend this... toughness into every part of his life."

"I've never doubted his physical attributes, but I think he has one big weak spot. Tell me, Yoshi. Does Sato have some strange hold over Kazuki? I need to know."

"There are facts about the family that I may not discuss. I am sorry."

I made a frustrated noise. "Just a hint, mate?"

"Kazuki's lost necklace that reappeared around Akihashi-san's neck was supposed to be a gift from Kazuki's father to his chosen heir. Mrs. Sato took it with her when she was cast off."

"That's it?"

"It is more than I should have said. You are hard for me to resist, Ben."

"Rubbish. Tell me one more thing: what do you think Kazuki really wants?"

"That is easy. Kazuki wants to be loved and he would prefer to be loved by Akihashi-san."

"You still can't call him Kaji?"

"No, and my shirt is buttoned all the way up."

I chuckled. "I loved what you said that time about Kazuki being a stormy ocean and Kaji being the moon. That was lovely."

"They are from different clans, but their strengths complement one another. The dragon and the tiger should hunt together. Sato-san is a fool to try and keep them apart." Yoshiro was silent for several moments. "Only to you would I say this."

"I understand. It's funny to me that you believe in them as a couple and I'm the doubting Thomas."

"I have a gift for knowing what fits together best. They are like you and Rune-san, halves of the same soul. Only together are you complete."

"If I ever get married, I'm going to ask you to perform the ceremony. I don't care if it's legal or not."

Yoshiro laughed. "For you, I would break the law. What is that noise?"

"That's Hayate warming up. I should ring off or go somewhere else. It's about to get loud in here."

"I will say goodbye then."

"Goodbye. I hope I see you soon."

Sora saw me drop my phone in my pocket and launched into a stomping, crashing version of the intro to "Half-Moon Heart." Michi and Tsubasa picked up the beat, meshing seamlessly with the guitarist's ragged solo, filling in the holes. Kaji let them chug along for a few more bars before he snatched the microphone off the stand and let loose with his signature full-throated howl. I sat down and took a few minutes to watch my lads before I went out to make some more calls.

I didn't mention my conversation with Yoshi until later that evening. Rune and Kaji were as surprised as I to find that Kazuki hadn't changed his will back. As for the necklace, Kaji had returned it to Kazuki. He sketched it as well as he could remember, with the rest of us adding our impressions. We all agreed it was a dragon's claw clutching a silvery-black pearl, but we couldn't agree on a few key details. None of us could remember exactly how many talons it had or whether it had scales or was smooth. I finally had the brilliant idea to look through the photo files and found one of Kaji wearing the damned thing. After doing a quick Internet search, I didn't find anything matching the pendant. I found out a lot about dragons and their claws, but nothing specific about a three-toed dragon with a storm-gray pearl.

*T*he next day, I made sure Hayate and Vudu were at the arena at ten in the morning. We arrived well before Kazuki's crew and Vudu ran through a set of their original songs. While everyone else was taking a break, Sung and Kaji sat on the edge of the stage and worked on the harmony for their duet. I was coming back from the loo, vowing to cut down on the amount of coffee I drank, when I saw Kazuki standing in one of the big doorways at the back of the auditorium. Due to the excellent acoustics, Sung and Kaji's twined voices singing Rune's lyrics could be heard clearly. I think that was the only time I ever surprised Kazuki. He was so intent on listening to the singers with their heads so close together that he didn't hear me come up beside him.

"They sound great, don't they?" I glanced sideways at him, catching the unguarded expression on his face just before it changed. I was instantly sorry for my remark. It sounded too much like I was taunting him.

"Kaji and I would sound better," he said.

There was that grating bluntness again, sandblasting any kind feelings I had toward him. I gritted my teeth and reminded myself that he was right, if rude. "I can't argue. I love the way you and Kaji sound when you sing together: truly magical. A pity you did so little of it."

"I would like to do more."

"I'd say that's up to you, mate."

"Because you do not understand."

"Then help me understand. Help Kaji understand. Stop torturing him."

"Torture," Kazuki repeated softly. "What do you know of it?"

"You have to give me more than vague hints and ominous pronouncements."

"I cannot. I do not think any spies are listening now, but why would I put my trust in you? You do not want me to be with *your ichiban*."

The tone of his voice brought my head around and I met his eyes. "You think I'm jealous?"

"I *know* you are jealous."

"You know something else, mate? You're your own worst enemy."

Kazuki gave me his saurian stare, the one that had me convinced that not all humans evolved from apes.

"I can't help you if you won't let me," I tried again.

"I do not want your help. Is that not clear?"

"I really don't get you. I thought you wanted to be back with Kaji."

"That cannot be."

"This isn't romantic fiction, you know. You're not some tragic *ronin* bound by honor to forsake a lower-caste concubine. You can be with Kaji and you can be happy. Just decide."

"You do not—"

"Understand," I finished for him. "Yes, I'm aware that I'm an ignorant *gaijin* with no appreciation of the subtleties, but speaking as a man who nearly ruined his life by making a willful choice, I'm urging you to reconsider. Don't marry Natsuko if you don't love her. If the child is yours, take responsibility, but don't ruin several lives because you think you're doing something honorable."

Kazuki opened his mouth to reply, but we both turned at the sound of heavy footsteps. Sato came toward us at a fast walk, the bright overhead lights strobing on the shoulders of his silvery sharkskin suit.

I had my smile prepared by the time he reached us. "Sato-san. How nice to see you again."

He gave me a perfunctory bow. "Mr. Blume." Turning to Kazuki, he spoke in a dialect I didn't understand, except for Kaji's name. Kazuki nodded curtly and stalked away without a word.

"What was that about?" I asked bluntly.

"I reminded him of an obligation. I do not wish you to speak with him."

"I understand that."

"I am not certain that you do. I hope you will not require more direct reminders."

"Like the coat and the necklace?" I said just to see how he'd react.

Sato's expression didn't change. "Please honor my request and do not distract Kazuki. It will be difficult enough to keep his empty head on his work with your singer around."

"You should stop there. Every time you talk about Kaji, I end up out of sorts."

"Just keep to your business and I will do the same."

"Aren't we in the same business?"

"You should be more cautious now that you have so much more to lose."

"I've no idea what you could possibly mean by that. Are you referring to our recent success?"

"You have a new partner, yes?"

"You know I do."

"He is more than a business partner, yes?"

"Yesss." I drew the word out. If he threatened Rune, I was going to smack him. I knew it with a sudden and terrible clarity.

Sato's phone rang and he grimaced as he got it out. "*Gomen*," he said, apologizing curtly as he turned his back on me. He spoke for a few seconds in the same dialect he'd used with Kazuki, before hanging up and addressing me again. "I must go. Please follow the schedule my office provided you. If you do not stray from the agenda, you will have no worries."

"Are you serious? This is rock 'n' roll, man. Shit happens."

Sato looked mildly offended, which I took as a victory. "Englishmen: you are all children and you believe the world is your nursery. Your nanny will not come to protect you here."

"You're getting predictable, Sato-san, always ending with a threat."

"Goodbye, Mr. Blume." Sato turned and walked away as quickly as he'd arrived.

Kaji could not believe it when I told him that evening that Kazuki didn't want our help. "That is crazy," he said.

"From what I can see, Sato and Kazuki are both barking mad. Must run in the family."

Rune shook his head. "Sato's an ex-bouncer, that's all. When he has a problem, he goes straight to the strong-arm solution."

"I'm not sure what to do," I said.

"We practice. We attend our press conference. We do our show at Budokan and leave on tour," Kaji said in a matter-of-fact tone.

I ruffled his hair. "We'll do that, for sure."

"And thanks to you, I will be near Kazuki." Kaji rose from his chair. "Good night, Rune-san. Good night, Benny-chan."

"Sato knew we were together again," I told Rune when Kaji was gone.

"Word travels fast."

"I thought he was going to threaten to hurt you and I saw red for a minute. I think I might have actually struck him."

"You really do care about me," Rune vamped, batting his eyelashes.

"I keep getting ambushed by these overwhelming feelings related to you."

"I'm intrigued; tell me more."

"Are you trying to figure out how to ask me if I'm randy without being vulgar?"

"I admit I was wondering."

"Your presence does have a certain effect on me."

Rune slid closer until his thigh touched mine. "That goes both ways, you know."

"So do you." I couldn't resist.

"But I love you best of all," he said, leaning toward me.

Taking Rune's face between my hands, I kissed his forehead, his eyelids, across the lofty cheekbones, down the bridge of his nose to his waiting lips. We strained toward each other as the kiss continued, arms holding tight, legs tangling as we slid downward on the old couch. Just before we slipped off onto the floor, Rune broke the kiss and hauled us back onto the cushions.

"No carpet burns for my Sunshine," he said.

I rolled my eyes. "You're right about that, mate."

"Go out with me tomorrow night."

"The night before the biggest concert Hayate has ever played?"

"That's the one."

"What have you got planned?" I asked suspiciously.

"I'm not going to spoil the surprise. Just say yes."

"Yes," I sighed. "Maybe I'll be able to relax for a while."

"I'll see what I can do. I'd better go make sure my hellions are accounted for."

I kissed him again, savoring the taste of him. "I'll see you for brekkie before the press conference."

Rune hugged me tight for a long moment before letting go. "Sleep well, Sunny."

"I believe I shall. I've been dreaming about you lately."

"Good dreams?"

My smile brought him back to my arms for another long snog. "All right then," I said a bit breathlessly. "Go on now. I'll see you in the morning."

"Don't forget our date," he said from the doorway.

"Let's make it a sleepover." My heart swelled at the look on his face when he realized what I'd said.

"If you insist," he said, regaining his aplomb. "Better bring a toothbrush. I don't keep spares anymore."

"I should hope not." I blew him a kiss when he turned to wave goodbye. I felt a bit foolish, but he pretended to catch the kiss and tuck it into his pocket for later. Silly man.

Chapter Seventeen

"*A bunai!*" Sora yelled, as the boom mike operator narrowly missed clocking Michi in the back of the head. "Watch it, man. What are you doing with that thing anyway? Aren't there enough mikes up here already?"

Hayate and Vudu were answering questions and posing for pictures for the press gathered on the deck of the ocean liner. We'd been on board for about three hours now and hadn't seen anyone from Kazuki's staff, much less Kazuki himself. The reporters had arrived an hour ago and for the last half-hour had enjoyed nearly unlimited access to the two opening acts, but they'd get restless soon. Not even the rather lavish buffet would mollify them for long if the Shining One didn't show. The lads were larking about, giving the photographers plenty of candid shots, but Kaji's gaze went often to the rail and the dock beyond. Past the cordoned area, fans surged, trying for a glimpse of their idols.

About four hours from the time we arrived at the ship, a large black SUV coasted to a stop on the wharf and two large men in suits got out. They opened the rear doors and Sato and Kazuki emerged. Behind Kazuki, Natsuko climbed out of the big vehicle. As one of the bodyguards gave Natsuko a hand, Kazuki started up the gangplank alone. Sato called out to him to wait, but he kept going, quickly widening the gap. The second bodyguard looked conflicted, but went after Kazuki when Sato pointed. Agile Kazuki reached the deck ahead of the security agent and plowed into the swarm of reporters. It took them a moment to realize that the Shining One had not only arrived, but was in their midst. By then, Kazuki was through them like a cheetah through a herd of wildebeest. He spotted Kaji and vaulted nimbly over the table that separated them. Hearing the commotion, Kaji looked up in time to see the whirlwind before it swept him up.

"Sato is going to have an aneurysm," I said to Rune as Kazuki kissed Kaji as though he meant to absorb him. "Bloody hell, look at the photographers. It's like a feeding frenzy."

"Someone's going to get trampled," Rune said. "Shouldn't I care more?"

"You're awful. Oh dear, Kazuki's really going for the gold."

"I should be timing this." Rune glanced at his watch as Kazuki finally let Kaji up for air.

Kaji looked a trifle groggy, but a big dozy grin spread over his face as Kazuki's lips moved against his ear. My lad nodded fractionally and pulled Kazuki behind his bandmates. Kaji put a hand on Sora's arm, said a few words, and began moving backward away from the small crowd. Sato's man made it to the edge of the gathering as his quarry disappeared around the corner. As the bodyguard tried to follow, Sora and the lads resumed their antics, stirring up the press. Rather than shove his way through, the security operative went around.

"I don't like this," I said.

"Come on." Rune started walking in the opposite direction and I followed.

It soon became apparent that Rune had spent time aboard a cruise liner. He made a few turns, took us up and down some stairs, and in a few minutes, we caught sight of Kaji and Kazuki. They were in an open passageway below us, snogging as though they'd just invented it.

"Please forgive the intrusion," I called down. "But Sato's guard dog is hot on your trail."

Kazuki looked up at me, eyes gleaming like a Persian cat's in the shadow. He nodded and then looked Kaji in the face. Speaking quickly and earnestly, he kissed Kaji's forehead and started walking away. Kaji lunged and caught hold of Kazuki's hand. Kazuki looked over his shoulder, shook his head, and pulled his hand away. His lips moved again and I recognized the Nihongo for *hide*. Kaji ducked into a recessed doorway as Kazuki reached the corner and the security man appeared. Whatever Kazuki said to the bruiser convinced the man to walk away with him. When their footsteps faded, Kaji came out of hiding. The look on his face was a punch to my heart.

"This can't go on," I said under my breath.

Rune put a hand over mine on the rail. "I see what you mean. Let's collect your lad and put on our thinking caps."

I loved him so much in that moment that I turned and kissed him tenderly without a thought for who might be watching. Fortunately, that turned out to be Kaji, who'd scaled the metal wall and climbed over the rail.

"So, Kazuki and me were… inspiring?"

"Mate," I said, gathering him into a three-way hug, "you and Kazuki should have set off the sprinkler system."

"I wish we had more time," he sighed. "This is impossible."

"I've never heard that word from you before."

"Perhaps I should accept that we cannot be together as he says I must." Kaji buried his face in my chest. "What have I done, Benny-chan?"

"Nothing so terrible," I soothed him, stroking his hair.

"Do you think Sung would say the same?"

I met Rune's eyes over the top of Kaji's head. "I don't think Sung blames you for anything," I said.

"I used him," Kaji said softly. "I used him to wear out my body so it wouldn't ache for Kazuki. I should have been stronger."

"Probably," Rune entered the conversation, "but none of us is perfect." He paused. "And Sung was more than willing to exhaust you."

"I hear you," Kaji said. "But I will always feel shame when I think of it."

"Yeah, you will," Rune agreed. "But keep in mind that if you really were a bad person, you wouldn't feel the shame or the guilt."

Kaji wiped his face with the ragged tail of his Sora-modified T-shirt and smiled at Rune. Reassured, I called Sora's cell and asked him to meet us at the van with the rest of Hayate. He replied that would be no problem since the Shining One had grabbed all the attention. The habitual derision with which he pronounced Kazuki's name was missing and I swore I heard a smirk in Sora's voice.

"So did Kazuki say anything?" I asked Kaji, as Rune led us off the ship. "If it's any of my business, or did you spend the whole time snogging?"

"Snogging."

"It sounds so cute the way you say it," Rune tossed over his shoulder. "Benj makes it sound like a synonym for mucking stalls."

"I certainly do not."

"Yes, you do, Benny-chan."

I was so pleased to see Kaji smile that I pretended to be affronted. "So I'm a dry stick, am I?"

"I thought the correct word was prude," Kaji said.

Rune stifled a chuckle as he waved breezily to someone in a white uniform. As if he owned the ship, my man strode down the loading gangway with Kaji and me on his heels.

"I am anything but a prude. You can ask Rune."

"You didn't start out that way, that's for sure," Rune said as we reached the wharf.

I faked outrage. "So now I'm an old maid?"

"Not if I have anything to do with it."

Kaji watched as Rune drew me close in the shadow of the van and pressed a sweet kiss to my lips. "Oh, Benny-chan," he said, "you are so lucky."

"Lucky? To be manhandled by this degenerate?"

"*Hai.* You are in the arms of the one you love."

"And the arms of the one who loves you," Rune said, looking into my eyes.

There are moments in your life that stand out like afterimages, glowing against the backdrop of dimmer memories. A nimbus of glory burns them deep in the consciousness where they shine forever. The changing light of a winter afternoon, the smell of approaching rain, the salt tang of the sea on the wind, any one of these or myriad other small changes can bring that moment back with such clarity and perfect recall that we feel once again the overwhelming emotion that imprinted it. I marked this one as Rune and I stood outside time for a brief eternity in a moment of flawless rapport. I was reluctant to let it end, but Kaji was standing to the side with his hands shoved in his pockets and the other lads would be here soon. Rune smiled at me, kissed my forehead, and let me go as though he could read my mind. I haven't entirely ruled out the possibility that he can.

After Rune left to collect Vudu and load them in their van, I started our bus and turned on the air-conditioning. Sora, Michi, and Tsubasa arrived a few minutes later, trailed by a small crowd and signing autographs as they walked. Once the band was on board, I navigated carefully around the fans and drove toward the arena.

"You should have stuck around for the show, *hime*," Sora said, pulling Kaji onto his lap. "Sato tried to stop the press conference, but no one would listen to him. It was… delicious."

"Tell me everything," I said over my shoulder.

"He looked like a blowfish, Blume-san," Michi said.

"He looked like someone who *ate* blowfish," Tsubasa clarified.

Sora grinned like a well-fed wolf. "The reporters kept asking Kazuki questions about Kaji and Sato would tell him not to answer. Those reporters got plenty mad at Sato, you know?"

"*Hai*," Tsubasa snickered. "Sato-san was called a spoiler of fun many times."

"And each time another question came he would look a little more…." Michi paused and asked Kaji in Nihongo for the English word for constipated.

I enjoyed the mental image conjured by their words as I negotiated traffic near the arena.

"Did Kazuki reply to any of the questions?" Kaji asked.

"The first ones," Sora said. "Before the bodyguards came to stand in front of him."

"It was beautiful while it lasted." Michi leaned his head on Tsubasa's shoulder in a swoony pose.

"Now the press has a juicy love triangle to report and Sato can do nothing about it."

"What did he say?" Kaji persisted.

"You want details?" Sora nipped playfully at Kaji's neck. "What is it worth to you?"

Kaji smacked the back of Sora's head, dislodging several hair ornaments that hit the window beside him like a handful of pebbles. "Exactly that much," he said.

"Whack bitch! Ain't tellin' you nuthin'." Sora went rapper sullen.

"Kazuki said he loved you," Michi told Kaji. "He called you his *takara*."

"What?" Kaji and I said simultaneously.

"Of course, he did it in classic Kazuki-style," Tsubasa said. "He rambled in that thoughtful way he has, you know, with all the pauses that make you think he's forgotten what he's saying?"

"I do not care *how* he said it," Kaji prompted.

"The Shining One gave a history lesson." Sora decided to tell the story before the two clown princes messed it up. "He spoke about Greek warriors who had a bond deeper than brothers and I doubt anyone could miss his meaning. He claimed that love between two men was more honored by samurai than any other kind of love. He talked like that for a while and the tabs were swallowing it like warm *sake*."

"Natsuko looked kind of sick, but maybe it was because she was on a boat," Michi said. "You could see she wanted to answer some of those questions, but Sato kept her right beside him."

"She looks cute pregnant," Tsubasa mused. "And I like her new hair."

"Why don't you marry her then?" Sora said.

I laughed as I pulled the van around the back of the Budokan building. As we waited courteously for some workers to settle a crate on the lift tailgate of their truck, I glanced at my lads in the rearview mirror. Michi and Tsubasa were watching the moving men. Kaji was curled on Sora's lap, forehead against the window, Sora's lips moving on the back of his neck as he spoke.

"It was quite a show, but I have to say Kazuki surprised me and showed some stones."

"Must've been the pep talk Kaji gave him," I said, as the workers waved at me, got in their truck, and lumbered away.

Kaji sat up and kissed Sora's cheek. Leaning across the van, he kissed Michi and Tsubasa. "Thank you for covering for me back there," he said.

Michi grinned. "I'd do anything to help a brother get some."

"I was going to say that," Tsubasa whined.

Sora pulled Kaji back into a hug as I parked our bus. "You know that goes for me too. Even if I'm never able to stomach the sight of Kazuki's foolish face, I want you to be happy."

Kaji nuzzled Sora's ear. "*Domo arigato, oniisan.*"

"Am I your big brother again?"

"Always, I hope."

"Then have more respect."

"How can I show you respect?"

"You can get off me; you've put on weight."

"*Baka ne!*" Kaji flung away from Sora. "I am the same as always."

"I don't know, *ichiban*," I said as I got out of the van. "You don't look like you'd fit in anyone's pocket anymore. You've grown a bit."

Vudu's van pulled up while the lads were disembarking and a ball flew out the window. Sora jumped straight up and blocked it with his chest. Michi caught the checkered ball on his knee and bounced it several times before passing it high to Tsubasa. Tsubasa deflected it backward with his head and then forward again with his heel to Kaji. The members of Vudu poured out of their vehicle as Kaji jogged in place, juggling the ball from knee to knee, taunting them. Predictably, Sung charged right in and Kaji passed to Sora. Rune came to stand beside me as the two bands played a very loose game of football. I smiled as Rune kissed the ear that wasn't covered by my phone.

"I have to take care of something," he said when I finished the call. "You mind being stuck with the kids for a while?"

"It's fine. Anything I can help with?"

Rune shook his head, shaggy blond hair moving sensuously against his neck. "Personal."

"Is it really? Well, don't let me keep you." I went from incipient lust to chilly affront in a split second and I realized just how much I cared about him.

With a grin, he pulled me close and kissed the end of my nose. "Don't be cross, Sunshine," he said. "I'll explain later; I promise."

"I'll be all ears."

"I hope not." Rune bugged his eyes comically. "Your ears are delicious, but I like your other body parts just as much."

"You're not right in the head, you know."

"It would certainly explain my attraction to an old maid." He dodged my half-hearted punch.

"Do your lads need anything out of the van?" I got back to business.

"Nothing." He leaned forward and kissed me again. "See you later tonight. You haven't forgotten our date, have you?"

"Call me as soon as you're free."

Rune caressed my cheek in a tender gesture. "The very second," he said and walked away.

I got the pack of musicians into the building and within sight of their instruments. They did the rest, settling down to a smooth practice, despite the fact that there was anywhere between eight and two performers on the stage at any one time. I didn't expect Kazuki to put in an appearance and he didn't, leaving us the run of the place for as long as we needed. I was trying to change my ring tone when I sensed someone behind me. Tilting my head back, I saw Sora.

"Do you need something?" I asked, a lamb to the slaughter.

Sora smiled, pulled the scarf from around his neck, and whipped it over my eyes. I heard the other lads approaching and did my best to get away before they reached me. I'd no idea what they had in mind, but I doubted that my dignity would survive intact.

"Think about this," I advised. "Will it be worth the reprisals?" It was the last thing I said before they gagged me. My hands were gently bound with what felt like another silk scarf and I was helped to my feet.

"We liked your kidnap idea so much that we decided to kidnap you," Kaji said in my left ear.

I made garbled noises that entertained Hayate and Vudu inordinately.

"See you chaps later," Kaji said, and then he and Sora marched me outside. They crammed me into the cabin of some kind of sports car that smelled new and I rode wedged between them for what seemed like a long time. "I hope you won't be too angry, Benny-chan." Kaji helped me out when the car stopped and he led me into a building. He untied my hands and I heard the sound of running feet and slamming doors. Quickly, I removed the blindfold.

I was at Twenty-Third Century Video and I was all alone. Or so I thought. At the far end of the cavernous facility, someone lit a candle. Beginning to get an idea what was going on, I walked toward the light. As I approached, more candles were lit, gilding the hair of the man waiting for me. In front of him was a long refectory table holding an ornate silver wine bucket, a basket of ripe strawberries, and heaps of red and white roses. Behind him was an enormous canopied bed draped in rich brocade.

"What do you think?" Rune asked, spreading his arms and clicking a button on a remote. "Too cliché?"

Beautiful chamber music began to play and the candle flames wavered in my vision until I blinked several times. "It's bloody perfect."

"Special enough?"

I nodded. I couldn't trust my voice. The lovely silly man had trotted out all of the romantic trappings and I loved him for it more than I thought I could bear. I'm afraid I'll have to wax poetic for a few minutes to do it justice. The air was scented with the multitude of petals he'd strewn over the linen and the soft carpet, and the buttery glow of the candles gave a sorcerous sheen to all the satiny textures: fabric, flowers, flesh. All of my senses were stimulated. The feelings that welled in me were too monumental. I had to break the tension. "What's that you're wearing?"

"Come closer where you can see me better."

"This is starting to remind me of a story I heard as a child, but I'm not wearing a red riding hood."

"No, but you do have a basket," Rune leered.

"Are you referring to my package?"

"I'll do more than *refer* to it if you bring it over here."

I couldn't resist him. Never could. Never would. I'd made the decision to take him back with reason and much pondering and now my brain decided its job was done. It was time for the rest of me to put up or shut up, to plunge into the blood-warm sea that had nearly swallowed me once. The truth was that I was frightened by my own passion. My love for Rune had consumed me, subsumed me until I felt I was drowning in him. I didn't want to be so lost and out of control again, but what choice did I have? I loved him and I would surrender all to him and hope I could stay afloat this time. It wasn't his fault I was so weak.

"A kilt?" I exclaimed as I came around the table.

Rune spread his arms and turned in a slow circle so I could appreciate his splendor… and splendor it was. Bare-chested, curling hairs glinting like gold wire, he looked like a Highland warrior in the knee-length kilt fastened around his waist. Candlelight burnished the hard muscles of his arms and legs, throwing the sleek contours into high relief and my fingers tingled at the thought of rediscovering my favorite rises and hollows. The fluttering in my stomach was a storm of wings now and my throat was dry when I tried to swallow.

"Thanks," I whispered, taking the champagne flute from Rune's hand.

"To new beginnings," he said, raising his glass.

We drank and Rune took the crystal from my hand, setting it carefully on the table. "I know you haven't had time for dinner," he said. "I'll try to make sure you don't starve." Picking a large strawberry from the basket, he pressed the tip to my lips.

I opened my mouth and bit into the luscious red berry. Juice trickled over my tongue and down my chin, triggering a rush of saliva. I'd never tasted anything so wonderful in my life until Rune replaced the strawberry with his lips. Swiping at the juice around my mouth, he kissed me in stages, combining licking, sucking, nibbling and berry pulp into one incredibly exciting caress. "Are you trying to seduce me?" I asked when he broke the kiss.

"My consultants thought this setup might do the trick." Rune's summer-sky eyes sparkled as his lips drew up in a sly grin.

"Consultants?" I picked up my champagne and took another drink. I noticed platters of fruit and cheese and a sweating pitcher of iced water among the massed blossoms and wondered idly how long he planned to keep me here.

"Well, it's been a while, Sunshine. Tastes change and I wanted to make sure I had your favorite things."

"I understand that. I'd just like to know who's in on this."

"Mainly Kaji. He's a fountain of information on your likes and dislikes. That boy loves you, you know, pretty much unconditionally."

It was hard to talk past the lump in my throat. "I love him too," I managed to say.

"Maybe we could adopt him." Rune lightened the moment.

"He and the other lads are going to tease me unmercifully about this."

"And?"

"I'm their manager. I have to be dignified."

"Love isn't always dignified," Rune said, taking my hand. "More often than not, it runs around half-dressed with its hair uncombed babbling nonsense. Decorum is difficult when your knees are up around your ears, but the payoff is worth it, in my opinion."

"This isn't easy for me."

"Do you think it was easy for me to approach you after all these years?"

"Well... yes."

"Why?"

"Because you're you, Hagen Rune the Golden Sex God of Rock 'n' roll."

"Is that really how you see me?"

"Roughly. You're ten feet tall with the heart of a lion and the sun rises every day just so it can shine on you."

Rune put his hands on either side of my face and pulled me to him, resting his forehead against mine. "We're the same size," he said.

"Not unless bits of you shrunk."

Rune chuckled softly, his thumbs rubbing lightly against my ear lobes. "That *bit* will never shrink around you."

"Flatterer."

"Whatever gets me into your trousers…."

"Just tell me that you love me and mean it."

"I love you," he said instantly and I do believe he meant it. Before we went any further, he insisted on feeding me, luscious strawberries dipped in whipped cream, chunks of melon so ripe it made my jaw ache, a tart-sweet ring of pineapple that he stuck on his finger for us to nibble. Our tongues brushed, licking the stickiness from his hand, and a bolt of desperate *need* speared me.

"I want you," I whispered.

"I think you really mean that," he said, taking my hand. "It took me a while to understand that you scared yourself back in London all those years ago." He took a deep breath. "When I looked down from the stage that night and saw you dancing…. You were the most beautiful, untamed creature I had ever seen. I had to have to you. Do you know what a kick I got out of just having you at my side, knowing you were mine and that everyone else envied me? Damn, what a dickhead I was!" Rune smiled at my surprised laugh. "It's the same old story: you don't know what you've got 'til it's gone."

"We've covered this," I said, stirring a finger in the chilled bowl of sweetened cream.

"I just want you to know that it's all right if you're nervous. I won't make fun of you."

Idly, I drew a heart on his chest with the whipped cream. "What good manners you have," I said, before I began licking the sweetness from his skin with long strokes of my tongue.

"That sure feels good," he said.

I lifted my head and kissed him soundly. "I am a bit nervous," I said, "but I really want this and I'm ready. If you dare hold back for some misguided reason, I'll never forgive you."

"You are rather good at holding a grudge." Rune groaned as I sucked his lower lip into my mouth and groaned louder when I stepped away from him. "Where are you going?"

"I'm feeling a bit overdressed."

A big grin crept over Rune's face like approaching dawn over a mountain range. Hopping up to sit on the table, he filled his glass and watched me expectantly. "Shall I change the music?" he asked.

I realized he was only arsing about because he was as tense as I was and I didn't let it break the mood. "When did I ever need music to strip?" I shrugged my jacket off my shoulders. The look on Rune's face wiped away any impulse I had to call this off. His obvious pleasure in my inept performance gave me the incentive I needed to shed the useless inhibitions I'd accreted over the years. Letting my suit jacket slip to the floor, I began to unbutton my sunset-colored shirt, taking my time about it.

"Only you would choose that color," Rune said. "Only you could pull it off."

"I thought it was quite cheerful," I said, lowering my eyelids, going for sultry. I probably looked sleepy.

"It's doing wonders to raise my morale." Rune spread his legs wide and hiked up his kilt. He was wearing the garment in true Highlander style, sans undergarments, and his arousal was unmistakable. It drew me as the flower entices the bee, hungry for honey and only staying aloft by a miracle. My knees went weak and I knelt in front of Rune, reaching for him. I smiled up at him as I rubbed my cheek against the silky flesh of his beautiful cock. Turning my head, I kissed the tip of the resilient shaft.

"I love your cock. I love the feel, sight, and taste of it."

Rune sighed and groaned as I took the head into my mouth. Rolling my eyes up to meet Rune's, I bobbed my head gently. He cradled my skull on his palms, sliding his fingers through my hair, caressing my ears.

"I'm glad you still like the old boy," Rune said. "He's missed you."

I let the stiff shaft slide from between my lips. "Next you'll tell me you've named it."

"Stop calling him *it*," Rune said. "It makes him feel like an object."

I raised an eyebrow. "Are you ready to get serious about this?" I asked.

"Doubtful," Rune teased. "I'd rather have fun." He slipped his hands under my armpits and raised me into an ardent kiss. I relaxed and enjoyed the ravishment of my mouth before joining the duel. Swarming over Rune, I bore him to his back on the table. I had to move the pitcher, but by a miracle, didn't tip it over. Straddling his thighs, I aligned my hard shaft with his and took both in my fist. I ran my free hand down Rune's golden-furred chest, bumping over the hard dark pink nipples and the washboard abdomen. A purring growl rose in Rune's throat as I squeezed our cocks together.

"I adore that sound," I said softly.

Rune smiled. "There are a few noises you make that I've been missing. Get up on your knees."

I chuckled and leaned in to kiss Rune as I rose to my knees. My chest was in front of his face and he took the opportunity to lick and suck at my nipples. His hands roamed, fondling me, and I moaned into his mouth as he stroked my hard-on, my sac, and then moved on to my crack.

I shivered when he parted my bum cheeks and rubbed a finger against my hole. The feeling was an exquisite tickle that I couldn't get enough of, each stroke making me crave more. Taking up a bottle of lubricant hidden in a bouquet, my lover anointed his fingers. With small nudges, he coaxed me to relax and eased his finger into me. It had been a while and I couldn't hold in a little whine when a second finger stretched me.

"I'll try not to hurt you," Rune said, and added, "ever again."

I shook his head. "I don't want to miss a single thing, not even the pain. I want to feel you stretching me to my limits. I want to feel the burn and I want to feel it fade. I want to know in my bones that you're inside me. I want to be fully present in the moment."

"We haven't talked about all the drugs we used to do."

"Let's not. I feel like I'm seeing you clearly for the first time and I like the view."

"Look as long as you want," he said as he circled my prostate.

I caught my breath. "That feels utterly amazing. I don't think I can get any harder. Give me your cock."

A crease appeared between Rune's golden eyebrows. "Are you in a hurry?"

"Are you seriously refusing to put your willy in me?"

"Of course not, but—"

"It's all right. We can do it as many times as we want. Right now, I'd like to feel you inside me."

"Condom?"

"You have one?"

"I didn't leave anything to chance this time." Rune ripped open the little foil packet with his teeth. "Want to put it on me?"

"No, but thanks for asking." When he'd rolled the rubber on, I reached between my legs and took hold of Rune's hard shaft. I brought the taut head to my entrance and bore down. As the tip entered me, I met my lover's eyes and held them. Rune took hold of my hips and offered support as I sank slowly, not stopping until I'd taken the full length. Crouched over Rune, I dipped my head to kiss him again, literally on the verge of weeping for joy. Then Rune shifted his hips and I grunted loudly.

"Sorry," he said. "My arse is sticking to the wood."

I grinned. "I really do love you," I said. "I remember when we could shag anywhere, but what do you say we use the bed for now?"

Rune wrapped his arms around my thighs and got to his feet. I braced my hands on his shoulders to relieve the pressure and held on until we reached the bed. He put me tenderly on my back and leaned over me, not thrusting yet, just getting closer. He could hardly get any deeper; I could feel his balls wedged in my crack.

Tentatively, I flexed my interior muscles and Rune's eyelids fluttered. Impulsively, I rolled him onto his back, planted my knees a bit farther apart, and flattened my palms against his chest. Rising a few inches, I settled back down, relishing his gasp of pleasure. With a wicked grin, I repeated the action, the muscles in my thighs flexing and burning. I vowed to take up jogging or biking in the near future.

"Damn, Sunshine," Rune groaned, tightening his grip on my pumping hips. "You're killing me. Mind if I participate?"

I had adjusted to the strain of accommodating his hard flesh and the sliding friction was starting to feel awfully good. "Let's rock," I said, dredging up a phrase from the old days.

Rune got the sole of one foot on the carpet and thrust in counterpoint on my next stroke. I flinched and lost my rhythm and he surged up to reverse our positions. Withdrawing his cock completely, he pushed back in as slowly as he could manage.

I groaned deep in my chest and tried to wrap my legs around him to pull him deeper. Flattening his palms against my inner thighs, Rune pushed my legs wide apart and thrust again at an even more languid pace. I squirmed under him, greedy for more and unashamed.

"Stop mucking about," I panted.

Rune gave me an absolutely evil smile as he hooked his hands behind my knees and bent me double. He pulled out until only the tip of his shaft was sheathed and rocked subtly. "I used to be pretty good at this," he said, as the blunt head of his rod dragged over my prostate twice on each stroke.

I realized the gurgling sound I heard was not a faulty water cooler. It was me in the throes of sensual abandonment. A bit relieved that I could still achieve this beatific state, I let Rune in on the news. "Bloody hell! No one else can make me feel like this. Make me cum. Please, make me cum," I began to chant. "Make me cum, Rune. Make me cum."

"Are you sure?" His grin would have shamed Lucifer.

"Please!" I cried out, my voice echoing in the rafters.

"I've never seen anything so sexy in my life," Rune said as he curved his hand around my arousal.

I jerked as though forty thousand volts had been shot through my system. My hips bucked, tilting my pelvis as I levered myself farther onto Rune's cock while his fist shuttled up and down. When he began to thrust again, I yelped my approval each time he entered me and sobbed my disappointment when he withdrew.

Time and place had no meaning as I rocked against him, surfing the ever-mounting waves of pleasure. The tightness coiled in my groin until it snapped, detonating an explosion that wrung a full-throated shout of fulfillment from me. My cock pulsed in Rune's fist and spurted a powerful stream that broke apart in midair, dappling the hair on his lower belly. He thrust into my clenching arse a few more times before he stopped, buried deep inside me. Leaning as far forward as possible, he filled me to the brim. Rune shuddered, his abs contracting with the force of his climax as he panted in my ear.

"You make me whole." His breath was warm and moist against my neck. "That's the only way I know how to tell you how much you mean to me. Without you, I'm just not complete."

Not trusting my voice, I nodded my agreement and clutched my man tighter. Rune started to ease his cock from my slippery passage, and I clamped down on it. Taking the hint, he let a hand drift down to caress my bum while the other toyed with the damp curls at my groin.

"Everything okay?"

"It's bloody perfect," I sobbed like a prat.

"You had me worried for a minute." Rune shifted to a more comfortable position. "Wow, that was even better than the old days."

I couldn't dispute that. The languor that was spreading through me like honey in hot tea made it difficult to form words, but I felt I had to make the effort. "I feel complete too."

"This is heaven to me," Rune said. "This is success. This is the good life. You're all I need to be happy."

I smiled dreamily as Rune's softening cock began to slide out of me. Shifting a bit, I put my arms around him and hugged him hard. The strong, regular beat of his great heart was a clock marking the moments of a time outside of time as we lay together in the afterglow. Flickering candlelight licked at our skin, leaving no traces of its ardent touch, as I followed its brushstrokes with my fingertips. Rune's half-submerged length began to stiffen and I moaned at the unique sensation.

"Damn it, Sunshine," Rune rasped. "Are you trying to kill me?"

"You've discovered my evil plan," I answered. "I'm going to shag you to death."

"What's taking so long?"

He stopped smirking when I pulled myself off his revived erection. Pinning him to the mattress, I stretched out along his body and buried my face in his crotch. The smell of our combined fluids sent a liquid pulse through my lower belly to the end of my cock. Rune felt me stir against his chest and lifted his head to nuzzle at my cleft.

Wrapping his hands around my hipbones, he raised me up until he could get his mouth on my willy. I left off licking his hard-on from tip to root and took it in my hand. Bending it up, I swallowed it to the base. For several minutes of slurping, sucking fun, we each did our best to make our partner beg for mercy. There was no thought in me but giving my lover the maximum pleasure I could provide. Nothing was too disgusting or too undignified, if it brought that drowsy smile to Rune's face.

"Tell me what you want," Rune said, rubbing his nose against my balls. "I'll do anything for you."

I left off sucking the head of his cock. "Stop reading my mind for a start."

"Really? I'd think that would be an asset when we're making love."

I sighed. "I spoke before I thought."

"Come here," he said in the voice that had always given me gooseflesh. With my willing help, he arranged me on my back against his chest. I bent my knees as he reached down to seat his arousal. The thick head slid easily into me as Rune's fingers closed around my cock. With no sound but our labored breathing, he jerked me off to the same rhythm as his shallow, metronomic thrusts. Measured and even, he stroked me inside and out as the waves of bliss built and built. He plucked at my nipples with his free hand and nipped at my neck in small shivery bites.

I planted my feet against the mattress and matched him stroke for stroke as our skin grew slick with sweat. My orgasm bloomed between one thrust and the next with a sweet ache that felt as though my bones were separating at the joints. Pliant as wax in the furnace heat of an all-consuming climax, I collapsed on Rune with a drawn-out groan.

Rolling me onto my stomach, he rose to his knees and pulled my hips up. I buried my face in the petal-strewn pillow and howled as Rune plowed me. I reveled in the feel of the shaft moving in and out and the cool friction of the satin sheets on my burning groin. He slid down to lie atop me, his legs inside mine, stretching them to their full length as his hands skimmed down my arms, spreading them wide. Lacing his fingers with mine, he flexed his buttocks, barely shifting his cock. His lips moved on my nape, whispering that he loved me, telling me of his need, begging me to say I felt the same. I turned my head until my chin was on my shoulder and met his eyes.

"I love you and I don't want to be with anyone else," I said breathlessly.

He told me later it was the best sex he'd ever had in his life, but at the time, he came like a freight train entering the station with no brakes and passed out. I swear it's true. Rune maintains that he was awake long enough to tell me he loved me, but it was like switching off a light. I teased him, of course, but truthfully, I was glad for the chance to catch my breath. Intending to have a glass of water and maybe a piece of the chocolate, I settled back to watch him sleep for just a minute. When I woke, it was several hours later.

Rune stirred as I sat up and he pulled me into his arms for a kiss. It felt so good being held that I nearly succumbed to his attempt at a hat trick. I explained to him that a double shot of world-class sex was quite enough for the moment and I was a bit sore in any case. He reminded me that I wanted to top him and suggested that this might be a good time, but I was determined to be strong. Giving in to him was what ruined our relationship the first time.

"Today's a big day," I said, pushing him gently away. "Our lads play the top venue in Tokyo tonight. You may think we're prepared, but I know better. And look at this place. We can't leave it like this."

"Sure we can; it's all arranged. Miss Shiori was happy to help me seduce you. All I had to promise her was the rights to the video."

"You're lucky I know your sense of humor. Come on, then. Be a good lad and get dressed."

"All I have is the kilt."

"You're joking." I stared at him. "No, of course, you're not." I threw my arms around him, shaking with laughter, and he nearly tricked me into more sex. I managed to halt the runaway hormones after a very vigorous snogging session and got the length of plaid cloth fastened around Rune's waist. Feeling a bit like a returning astronaut, I walked from the Twenty-Third Century building into the street. "Everything's different this morning," I said. "It's all new."

"It's beautiful. Everything's beautiful." Rune took a deep breath and turned to look into my eyes. "You're beautiful."

"Thank goodness we can agree on something," I answered. He chased me all the way to the car he'd leased for the occasion and nearly nailed me on the bonnet. I finally got behind the wheel and dropped Rune at his place just at dawn. "I really should go," I said reluctantly as the sun edged over the Tokyo skyline.

Rune leaned into the window and kissed me one more time before stepping back to the curb. He looked unbelievably sexy in his uneven kilt and my rumpled jacket, the first rays of sunlight kindling in his hair. I fought the urge to leap from the car and follow him into the apartment building.

"I'll see you in a few hours," he said, his eyes roving the sleek lines of the Aston Martin. "That looks good on you, by the way. Let's keep it as a company car."

Buoyant though replete, I grinned at him. "Why not?" I said as I revved the powerful engine. "If it's good enough for James Bond...."

"I love you, Sunshine." Rune caught my high-bouncing heart in his hands.

"So I've snared you with my wiles, have I?" I answered lightly.

"Well, as wiles go, yours are somewhat stupefying."

"And you are terribly silly, which I love. Now get back inside before someone sees you like this."

"I don't care who sees me."

"Then go back inside because I care." I drew him down for another kiss. "I need to get the band in gear and make sure everything is ready for tonight. I still can't believe we're playing Budokan."

"Didn't you plan on it?"

"Of course, but it wasn't scheduled to happen for six more months in my original estimation."

"That's exactly why I don't make plans. What's the point when one little thing can throw them off?"

"I wouldn't define the Shining One as a little thing," I said dryly. "And it helps to have a bit of structure."

"Fine, you give me structure and I'll give you anarchy; sounds like a fair trade to me."

My heart soared high again and I reeled it back like a wayward kite. "I think we can strike a happy medium."

Rune looked puzzled. "Why would we hit a laughing psychic?"

I took a minute to figure out the lame schoolyard joke. "You're not going to grow up, are you?" I sighed.

"Would you want me any other way?"

"You're a hopeless case."

"Oh, I think you've got the injection that can cure me, doctor," he purred.

I put the car in gear and let out the clutch. "To be continued," I said as I rolled away.

He called my phone before I got to the stop sign. "I love you," he said.

I said "I love you too," but he had already hung up. It was going to be like this from now on, so I might as well get used to the little pranks and spontaneous expressions of affection. I glanced in the rearview mirror and caught the smug smile on my face. Rune was right. I loved him just the way he was.

Chapter Eighteen

I stared at the note, carefully lettered in English. *I am meeting the dragon. See you at Budokan.* I didn't need Kaji's signature to know who'd written it. Bloody hell. The day had begun idyllically but had gone largely downhill from there. Sora had a hangover. Michi and Tsubasa were unaccountably quarreling. I couldn't find Rune and now Kaji had gone missing. I resisted the strong urge to fling my phone at something breakable and tried to call Rune again. Again, I resisted the urge to hurl the phone as I got his voice mail. Bloody bleeding hell.

As I got to my feet, an ache south of my belt line reminded me of last night. For several moments, I stood unmoving behind my desk as a particularly vivid memory washed through me. My cock stirred with a small tickle that brought me back to the present. Banishing all humid thoughts of Rune's magnificent body, I grabbed my sharp new jacket off the back of the chair and left my office. The sooner I got everyone and everything organized, the sooner I could wallow in carnality with my man again. It was marvelous incentive.

I got into the leased car Rune insisted was perfect for the manager of a hot band. As I started the Aston Martin, King Kong roared from my pocket. "Good one, Michi," I murmured as I fished out the cell.

"Blume-san, it's Sung Ke Smith," Sung said, as though his name might have slipped my mind.

"Hi, killer. What can I do for you?"

"I have a text message for you from Rune-san."

"Odd. Why not text me directly?"

"Yeah, Twilight Time."

"I think you mean Twilight Zone."

"*Arigato*," he thanked me for the correction. "Rune-san is at Budokan. He found something interesting that he will tell you about when he sees you. He said to say *payload* to you."

"Oh lovely, now I get to be in suspense." I backed the snappy car out of the garage bay one-handed. "Thank you, Sung," I added.

"No problem. Is my cutie honey there?"

"I'm afraid not," I said as I drove to the main road. "I'm looking for him too."

"You don't know where he is?"

"I know the fact tears a hole in the fabric of the natural order, but Kaji left without telling me where he was going."

"Okay," Sung answered a little uncertainly. "See you."

"Yes, you will. Tonight is going to be great. The best show Tokyo has ever seen."

"*Sugoi!*" Sung agreed, the confidence back in his voice. "*Bai bai*, Blume-san."

I hung up feeling as though I was doing my job well, taking care of the talent. I wish I'd known Sung was going to follow me to Budokan, but I didn't. Obeying the speed limit, I maneuvered the porpoise-gray sports car through Tokyo traffic to the big martial arts complex turned concert hall. I parked near the loading ramps in back, retrieved my laminated pass from the glove box, and entered a security door. Glancing up at the camera that tracked my progress, I walked down the short hall to the checkpoint. An amiable middle-aged man looked at my pass, checked his computer screen, and waved me on.

I found the lads by following the noise. Sora, Tsubasa, and Michi were half-heartedly fooling about on stage. Tsubasa looked up from applying a large spider decal to his bass, but Sora's back was to me, as he worked out a flashy little rhythm duel between his guitar and Michi's cymbals. Michi nodded to me, but kept up the rapid-fire ricochet responses to Sora's stratospheric solo. I went down on one knee next to Tsubasa and asked if he'd seen Kaji. Tsubasa threw his empty energy drink bottle at Sora, hitting the guitar player in the back. Sora glared over his shoulder, saw me, and stopped playing. Pulling the headphones from his ears, he cocked his head inquiringly.

"Have you seen Kaji?" I asked.

"He got a call from Tommy," Sora said. "He told me he was going to meet Kazuki."

"And you let him go?"

"Sure, why not?" Sora shrugged. "He's not a virgin, Blume-san."

"I thought you hated the idea of them together."

"I did." Sora half-turned, nimble fingers tapping lightly against his guitar strings, producing a delicate chiming.

"Sora!" I called him back from whatever musical tangent he'd flown off on. "Do you mean to say you're okay with Kaji and Kazuki as a couple?"

"Not really okay, but I can see that Kaji is serious about the big poser. If I try to keep them apart, Kaji will start hating me."

It was hard to imagine Kaji hating anyone, but I understood what Sora was saying. "That's a good policy. Do you have any idea where they were going to meet?"

"Here," Tsubasa said. "I thought probably in Kazuki's dressing room."

"*Baka ne*," Sora said. "Don't be stupid. They wouldn't have privacy there."

"Never mind." I rose to my feet. "I'm going to walk around a bit. If Kaji isn't here in an hour and I'm still gone, call me, all right?"

"Sure." Sora nodded and wandered back to the drum kit.

"Good luck, Blume-san." Tsubasa smirked as I walked off the stage. "Take your time finding Rune-san."

I pretended not to catch his innuendo as I left the auditorium. Leaving Kaji and Kazuki to their own devices for now, I searched for Rune. I was walking by an area of storage and utility rooms when a couple of synapses connected randomly and Rune's message came clear for me. *Payload*. The word came from a movie we both loved. The picaresque protagonist uses it as he's bragging about his prowess in the bedroom, comparing his equipment to a guided missile. It used to make us howl like baboons and became a sort of safe word. I know I don't have to explain what a safe word is to you. The point is that I was forced to use it during an infamous backstage incident involving a wardrobe trunk, a guitar strap, and a drumstick. It seemed abruptly clear to me that Rune had found something—heroin, illegal arms, rhino horn powder—in one of the crates waiting to be shipped out late tonight. I admit it; I watch too many films, but then again, many films are based on real events.

I exited the rear of the building and found the row of storage sheds, each forty feet long and nine feet high. Once I had thought things through, I realized that the only hanky-panky I was likely to find was being engineered by Rune. Obviously, the code word *payload* was his way of telling me he wanted to meet somewhere out of the way and have it off before the show. Feeling more than a little foolish and somewhat horny, I reached for the door of the first shed and someone called my name.

"Sato-san." I recognized his voice. "Fancy meeting you here."

"It is not a coincidence," he said. "I saw your partner sneaking around and knew you would join him. Come. Your friends are this way and I am sure that Rune-san and my brother's pet will be pleased to see you. Their curiosity has gotten them into a difficulty."

"Where are they?"

Sato gestured to the next storage shed. "After you, Blume-san," he said, swinging one of the end doors open. The interior was lighted and I could see Rune and Kaji seated on the floor with gags in their mouths and their arms bound. Rune's gaze focused on me and he tried to rise, but Kaji was slumped against the crate behind him with his eyes closed. As Rune struggled, making frantic noises around the gag, I hurried through the door. Sato put a hand between my shoulder blades and shoved hard. I stumbled, caught my balance, and spun around to confront him when Kazuki came in behind him.

"What the bloody hell is going on here?" I demanded to know.

"It is time for my brother to grow up," Sato said, glowering at Kazuki.

"Thank you. That explains everything. Why are my friends tied up?" I said as I began walking toward Rune and Kaji. "Why is Kaji unconscious?"

"I lured him here and gave him a taste of some premium heroin," Sato said. "He could not handle it, but it made him extremely manageable."

"You filthy bastard. What reason could you possibly have for doing something like that?" I checked Kaji and Rune visually for injuries as I helped Rune off the floor. When I started to untie him, Sato crossed the room quickly. I saw him coming and prepared to defend my friends. I'd never been in a real fight in my life, but I didn't see what choice I had. Sato was obviously off his nut.

"Get away from them," Sato said.

"I won't," I answered. "You'll just have to try and stop me from setting them free."

"Your foolish courage is tiresome. You are not even smart enough to recognize the danger you are in. You are not a worthy opponent."

"Ouch," I replied and kept working at the fiendish knots.

Kazuki said something in the dialect he and Sato used and a new note in his musical voice made me look up. Sato was pointing his gun at Kaji. "Move," Sato told me.

"All right. Just stay calm, mate. I'm moving. See?" I was contemplating some rash act when the door opened and daylight flooded the interior. Sung shouted Kaji's name and bolted toward him. Sato brought the pistol around and shot Sung from a distance of about ten feet, hitting him in the shoulder. The guitarist was stopped cold and flopped backward as though he'd hit the end of a tether at full speed. The force of the bullet spun him to the left and he hit the floor face down. The size of the exit wound was shocking. I was still staring at it when Sato trained the gun on Kaji again.

"Watch carefully, little brother," Sato said. "You must learn that I have the power to take anything away from you. This is the result of your disobedience."

"Please do not." The words burst from Kazuki's throat as though someone had punched him in the stomach. "I will do as you say. I will marry Natsuko. I will never see Kaji again."

"Ah, but that is what you said the last time you returned to me."

"Please, Ichiro."

"It is too late. Next time, consider carefully before involving others in our affairs." Sato put the gun to Kaji's head and I moved toward him. Abruptly, the enclosed metal space echoed to the roar of a hunting Tyrannosaurus rex, and I reached reflexively for my phone, cursing Michi. Sato's head snapped in my direction and Rune took advantage, lurching into him. Thrown off balance, Sato went down with Rune on top of him. The back of Rune's skull bounced off a crate and he went limp. I couldn't breathe. It was as if a giant pump had sucked every atom of air from the room. Without conscious thought, I hurled myself forward and collided with the side door, as it swung open. I hit the ground and looked up groggily.

"I am sorry," Yoshiro Shin said as he helped me to my feet.

"Never mind. Sato's got a gun. He shot Sung."

"I thought he might do something like that. He is a foolish man."

"Not to mention dangerous." I eyed Sato warily as I knelt beside Rune. Rune was breathing, but unconscious. To my right, I saw Kazuki working swiftly and deliberately on Kaji's bonds and I resumed tugging on the ropes around Rune's wrists. I was absorbed, with no awareness of time or place until a shadow fell over me. "Help me, Yoshi," I said, without looking up.

"Shin is not here to help you," Sato said. "He is here to do his job."

I raised my head and focused on Yoshi. His eyes were as impenetrable as obsidian as he gazed calmly back and I knew Sato was right: Yoshi was not here by coincidence. *What would Rune say if he were awake?* "Are there some contracts that need to be signed?" I asked.

Sato laughed harshly before turning to Kazuki. Wrapping his hand around his half-brother's biceps, he hauled the Shining One to his feet and swung him around. Kazuki tore out of Sato's grasp and placed himself between Kaji and the gun. "Move, *baka*," Sato said, gesturing with his weapon.

Kazuki's expression never flickered. He stared through Sato as though the other man didn't exist, shielding Kaji with the supreme indifference of a brick wall.

"Move or I will shoot you too, and have you repaired." When Kazuki didn't react, Sato called to Yoshi. "Make him obey."

"Yoshi!" The name escaped my mouth like an involuntary reflex.

Yoshiro Shin paused and looked back at me. "I truly am sorry, Ben," he said, as he pulled a wicked-looking gun from a shoulder holster and joined Sato. Kazuki's only response to the new threat was to take a step back so he was standing directly over Kaji.

"Are you having some family trouble?" Yoshiro inquired.

Sato gave the attorney a sour look. "Shoot my brother's concubine and take him home."

"I could do that if it were necessary."

"It is my order."

"*Hai*. However, your orders recently have been... imprudent."

Sato looked thunderstruck at being second-guessed, but he kept his temper. "Do your job," he said coldly. "We will discuss your insubordination another time."

"It is not clear to me why Akihashi-san must die."

"That is why you should rely on the wisdom of your superior."

"It is also not clear to me that my superior is in this room."

"*Nandesuka!*" Sato said. "Kill the whore. Clean up the mess. Take my brother home and guard him until I arrive to deal with him."

Yoshi gazed down at the insensible young man curled at Kazuki's feet. Kaji appeared to be asleep, sooty lashes brushing his cheekbones. He was pale and remote as the moon and just as beautiful, his skin luminous in the dim light. Yoshi looked at him for a long moment before glancing up at Kazuki. "Does it mean nothing to you that your brother loves this one?" he asked Sato.

"Of course it means something. It is the reason the *yarichan* must die."

"Ah, I see." Yoshi raised his gun and took careful aim.

My frozen brain thawed and I ripped my cell phone from my pocket. *Ambulance? Police? Who to call first? Who would arrive most quickly?* With the wild clarity of an adrenaline rush, I punched a number on my contact list. I said a few words to the polite woman who answered and hung up to wait. Across the room, Yoshi's phone rang. As Sato watched impatiently, the attorney answered. I counted off five seconds before Yoshi hung up and turned to look at me.

"You were clever to call the number I gave you, but unfortunately, I am the nearest ninja."

Sato said something angry-sounding. He was really losing his cool, when his words ended mid-sentence with a grunt of surprise. Sung had regained consciousness and grabbed Sato by the ankle, yanking his leg from under him and dumping him on his face. Sato's gun flew from his hand, skidding on the concrete until Yoshi put his foot on it.

"Thank you, Smith-san," the attorney said and kicked Sung in the side of the head hard enough to knock him out again.

"My gun," Sato said, rising from the ground.

Yoshi pointed his weapon at Sato. "Please stay where you are," he said. "Ben, is Rune-san awake?"

"No," I said curtly.

"Then leave him and come stand over here."

After putting my folded jacket under Rune's head, I did as Yoshi asked. Sinking down at Kazuki's feet, I touched Kaji's cheek. To my surprise, he opened his eyes and blinked at me.

"This is quite an interesting situation," Yoshi said as I helped Kaji sit up.

Sato said something else in that dialect that I didn't understand.

"Whatever happens here," the lawyer said, "we are the only ones who will know the truth."

"And just what might that be?" I asked. "Because I'll admit it; I don't have a clue what's going on. Why in bloody hell does Sato want my lad dead?"

"Sato-san miscalculated and now he wishes to restore the old balance. That is why I say he is foolish. He should know that nothing can ever be exactly as it was."

"I still say you would have made an excellent monk."

Yoshi bowed slightly. "In seeking to eliminate Akihashi-san, Sato-san has complicated matters to the point that there are now several liabilities. It is difficult to justify the deaths of yourself, Rune-san and Smith-san, as well as Akihashi-san. It is wasteful and will attract attention."

"You must add my name to your list." The sound of Kazuki's voice was so unexpected that we all turned to stare at him.

"That I could never do," Yoshi told him. "It is my honor to preserve your life."

"What kind of life will I have if you kill what I love?"

Yoshi's gun was not aimed at anyone now, but I had the feeling he was skilled with the weapon and I gave him no reason to point it. Moving very cautiously, I checked Kaji over, but other than being muzzy from the drug, he appeared uninjured. I looked across at Rune, lying so still, and Sung in an ever-widening pool of blood and tried to clear my mind. We needed to resolve this situation and summon medical aid.

"It is complicated," I heard Yoshi say.

"What's so bloody complicated about it?" I asked, as I got to my feet. Kaji started to rise with me and I shoved him back to the floor. "You have a simple choice here: to kill or not to kill. Make your decision, Yoshi, and get on with it. People are bleeding to death."

"It is complicated because I am honor-bound to serve the son of my old master, but I am also compelled to serve you because you called for my help."

213

"Are you going to tell me you're really a ninja?"

The corner of Yoshi's mouth twitched. "Not precisely. I am, however, a soldier of sorts, temporarily under Sato's command. The service whose number I gave you is under the control of Sato's superior."

Sato spoke again, spitting the words.

"*You* may consider him your equal, Sato-san," Yoshi said. "I assure you the reverse is not true." He turned to me again. "So you see my dilemma. To whom do I owe the higher loyalty?"

"My friend Yoshi would have no trouble with that question," I said. "You're about to make a classic blunder. Blind loyalty is not honorable. If you follow a leader you don't respect, how can you respect yourself? Is Sato worthy of commanding you?"

"I love the way you speak, Ben, and I cannot dispute your words. There is, however, an established order and my rank is not so high that I may go outside it with impunity."

"Then I guess you have to decide which is worth more."

"Ah, you do understand. I knew you would. You are a fine person and it would sadden me if you no longer walked in this world. Unfortunately, I know you will never move aside and let me do what I must. To kill Akihashi-san, I must kill you."

"And me," Kazuki insisted.

Yoshi shook his head, blue-black hair gleaming in the fluorescent light. "No, *oujisama*." Stepping closer, the attorney picked up the pendant lying between Kazuki's winged collarbones. "Sato-san was right to be uneasy when you left his control the first time. When he saw this around Akihashi-san's neck in a photograph, he began to panic and to make hasty decisions. It was only a matter of time before he did something so stupid that it could not be overlooked." Yoshi let the dragon claw fall back against Kazuki's chest and stepped back. Kazuki lashed out and high-kicked him in the elbow.

I expected the gun to go spinning out of Yoshi's hand, but he held on to it. Kazuki's next kick took him under the chin and sent him reeling back a few steps. Catching his balance, Yoshi swung the pistol in short arcs, seeking a target. Kazuki's heel crashed into his kidneys and he went to his knees, grimacing at the explosion of pain in his lower back. Before I could think too hard about it, I snatched Sato's gun from the floor. I'd never fired a weapon, but I raised it and pointed it in Yoshi's direction. Yoshi recovered from Kazuki's unexpected attack as Kaji rose unsteadily to his feet and staggered into the lawyer. Yoshi reeled but still held onto his weap0n as he brought his free hand around in a punch aimed at Kaji's head. Kazuki's roundhouse kick connected solidly with Yoshi's jaw as Kaji dropped back to the floor. I pointed the pistol at the ceiling and fired once. I'd heard about recoil, but even forewarned, I was shocked by the way the gun slammed into my palm, flinging my arm backward. I'm sure I looked idiotic, but no one paid the slightest attention to me, especially Sato, who'd produced another weapon from somewhere. The barrel of his gun wavered in figure eights as he tried to follow one of the combatants. Kaji got to his knees to try to help Kazuki and Sato's aim steadied. I saw his knuckle go white and I didn't even think about it. I just pulled the trigger. My shot missed completely, but Sato hit the concrete, his pistol going off on impact. I stared in disbelief at the knife sticking in Sato's hand until Sora yanked it out and pushed the man to the ground with a boot between his shoulders.

"I got tired of waiting for Sung," the guitarist said.

"Bless your impatience. Look after Rune for a minute, would you?"

Kaji was kneeling beside Yoshiro Shin, and I moved behind him to finish removing the ropes from his wrists. Kazuki took my cell and called for an ambulance.

"What happened?" I asked.

"Sato's bullet ricocheted off the floor." Yoshi coughed, "I was standing in the wrong place."

"Is it bad? Can you tell?"

"It is bad."

"Help will be here soon," I told him.

"Let me die," Yoshi said. "That would be the best thing for all of us."

"Forget it." I finished removing his jacket and reached for the top button of his shirt. "Let's give the medical chaps one less thing to do. Whoa!" As I peeled back his blood-sodden Oxford shirt, I gaped at the elaborate tattoos that covered his torso from his neck to his wrists and down to his waistband. "Who would have guessed you had so much ink?"

Kaji edged away from the wounded man. "Blume-san," he said slowly. "Those are Yakuza symbols."

"Yakuza? The Japanese Mafia?"

"Close enough," Yoshi said, groaning as I pressed the wadded sleeve of his shirt against the bullet wound in his side.

"That's... hard to believe," I said. "You're not exactly my idea of a mobster. Kaji, hold this please. I want to check on Rune."

"Emergency services on the way," Kazuki told me.

"Splendid. Help me move Rune and Sung onto these tarps." We wrapped a T-shirt around Sung's shoulder and put him down beside Rune. They were unconscious, but I felt better when they looked comfortable. Only then did I approach Sato again. Sora stepped back, but kept a sharp eye as I wrapped my tie around Sato's hand. "Do you want to tell me what was so important that you'd kill someone over it?" I asked.

Sato clenched his jaw against the pain and kept silent. Aside from the look of pure vitriol he shot at Kazuki, Sato did his best to ignore us. As an afterthought, I dug in his pocket and took his phone.

"Should we see if he has any more weapons?" Kazuki asked.

"Yeah, good call," I said. "I'm a little loopy."

"You will not touch me," Sato told Kazuki, but he was wrong. With Sora's help, Kazuki touched his half-brother plenty and all but stripped him looking for weapons.

"Will you please tell me what's going on?" I asked Yoshi, as I took over the job of keeping pressure on his wound.

"If you will agree to give me five minutes alone with Sato. He and I have unfinished business."

"You've got a bullet in your vital organs. Do you really think that's a good idea?"

"*Hai*, it is the only way that this can be made right."

"I don't understand." I saw Yoshi's gaze waver as Kazuki came to stand over me. I glanced up at the Shining One and then back at the injured man. "How did a publicity stunt turn into all this?"

"He knows nothing." Yoshi's dark eyes flicked to Kazuki. "Sato used him from the beginning."

"For what?"

"The Shining One can travel freely anywhere in Asia, and after this tour, anywhere in the world."

"You're joking! This really *is* a smuggling ring?"

"Smuggling is a very small part of our business, but it is the one that was entrusted to Sato."

"An ex-bouncer?"

"Ben, you are not so naïve. Sato ran a security service that specialized in guarding entertainers. It was a present from his father Masuru." Yoshi coughed and a fine mist of red settled on his chin and neck. "Sato Masuru was a well-respected leader, an *oyabun* of… our organization. Upon his death, his eldest son took his place."

"I'm gobsmacked. And Kazuki didn't know anything?"

"With the drugs he was being given in his food, I am surprised he could think at all."

Kazuki looked over at Sato and said something in their dialect. Sato spat as far as he could in Kazuki's direction and then jerked his head around at the sound of sirens.

"I cannot be taken into custody," Yoshi said. "If I might ask one favor: please leave the room and leave me a gun. You may remove all the bullets but one if you do not trust me."

"Not in a million years would I do that," I said.

"Then you force me to tell you that it was I who put the Yakuza symbol of power around Akihashi-san's neck. I gave him food poisoning to keep him from Kazuki-sama's bed. I told Sato where to find Kazuki-sama after you told me about the mother's house. I was Sato's agent each step of the way and if not for a twist of fate, I would have shot Akihashi-san."

"I'm not falling for it. You did as much good as harm, if you think about it. In fact, it looks to me like you were working to bring Sato down all along."

"Impossible." Yoshi coughed again. "I am a good soldier."

Kazuki's phone rang and he began talking the emergency medical techs to our location. Yoshi's gaze followed him, lingering on the tall, straight-backed figure pacing with careless elegance. The attorney's lips formed a word.

"*Oujisama*," I repeated. "You said that before. I'm not familiar with the word."

"You would say prince," Yoshi whispered. "If Kazuki had his birthright—"

"Perhaps he's better off as a singer. You should probably stop trying to talk now."

"It does not hurt."

"That's shock, Yoshi."

"You are wise, Ben. I had hoped to guide my prince someday, but perhaps it is best if the job goes to you."

"I'm not applying for that position."

"The teacher does not choose the student. When the time is right...."

"Don't you dare go to sleep, Yoshi." I looked up as the door of the storage building burst open and we were inundated with emergency personnel. I got out of the way, familiar with their impersonal efficiency that brushed off anything that got in the way of saving of a life. In order of the severity of injury, Sung Ke Smith, Yoshiro Shin, and Ichiro Sato were put on gurneys and taken out to an ambulance or a helicopter. Without interfering, I stayed as close as I could to Rune until I was assured that his pupils and vital signs were all normal. As Rune was wheeled out the door, Kaji put his hand in mine and leaned against my side, lethargic with the lingering effects of the heroin. His fingers were sticky with the mingled blood of at least two people, but so were mine.

"What do you think of all this?" I asked, feeling a little punchy.

"*Kuso* happens," he replied drowsily.

I glanced at him and a slow grin spread over my face. "I guess rock 'n' rollers have to expect the unexpected."

Kaji smiled. "Sora is going to get such a big head over this."

Kazuki put a hand on Kaji's shoulder and my lad turned from me to be taken in the Shining One's fierce embrace. "*Takara*," he murmured. "I will not let you go again."

"Good, because I cannot stand up."

Kazuki caught Kaji, lifting him in his arms and carrying him over to the med techs. As I started to follow, a man in the uniform of a Tokyo police officer stopped me. He introduced himself, asked me a few concise questions, and strongly advised me to go to the hospital. He assured me that discreet detectives would be sent to take official statements. I started to decline the offer of a police escort, but thought better of it. If they were offering, why not take them up on it? Fame should have a few perks to go along with the arse pains. As I got into the police car, it occurred to me that in that past little while, Rune had come first in my thoughts, even before Kaji. There was no getting around it; I was well and truly in love.

Chapter Nineteen

Three hours later, thanks to his thick skull, Rune was resting peacefully in a private hospital room. The relief that hit me when the doctor told me Rune was all right nearly put me on my knees. I'd spent the time since at my love's bedside, listening to Kazuki and Kaji argue at the other end of the room. If the Shining One had imagined his *takara* was going to take him back unconditionally, he was quickly disabused of that notion.

"You lied to me," Kaji said for roughly the twentieth time.

"I had no choice. I tried very hard to be strong for you. Ichiro sent men to beat me, and I did not leave you, but when he threatened you, I had to do as he said. He proved to me that he could get to you anywhere. He would have killed you if I had disobeyed him again."

"I will not be made the reason for all this tragic stupidity," Kaji said.

"What else could I do?"

"You could have shared your problem with me as if you respected me as an equal. You chose to lie and hide the truth from me as if I were a child and you almost got several people killed; people I care very much about."

"I only wanted to protect you."

219

"Don't you think I want to protect you as well? Or is my love somehow less than yours?"

Kazuki was quiet for several long moments. "I do not know," he said at last. "It is hard for me to imagine that anyone could love as much as I love you. It frightens me, *takara*."

Kaji turned to me. "What am I to say to that?"

"I shouldn't even be hearing this, much less commenting on it."

"Help us," he pleaded.

"Please," Kazuki said.

I sighed. Kaji might not be a child technically, but he was only twenty and though Kazuki was six years older, there wasn't a lot of difference in their emotional ages. I doubt I was qualified to give counseling, but I did have more experience with patching up a relationship than either of them. "You'll be honest with me?" I looked at Kazuki as I spoke.

Kazuki nodded.

"Did you really not know that your father was a Yakuza gangster?"

Kazuki shook his head. "My mother gave me this necklace." He touched the dragon claw with two fingers. "I did not know the... symbol... of it."

"I don't think you lads really have a problem," I said. "Kazuki, you made bad decisions because you believed you couldn't trust anyone. You know better now, right? And Kaji, your only decision is whether or not you love Kazuki so much that you can't live without him. You can forgive him and have faith that he's changed."

Kaji frowned. "That was brief."

"It's all I've got right now. The chat with the police drained me."

Kaji came and sank to one knee beside my chair. "You work so hard," he said, leaning his cheek against my hand. I smiled and ruffled the witch's nest of his hair. Kazuki rose and crossed the room by degrees to hover near us. I held out a hand to him. Kaji looked up at me and then offered his hand to Kazuki as well.

"*Boku-no sei*," Kazuki murmured, accepting his blame as he knelt and Kaji pulled him into a hug. My left hand still rested on Kaji's head and tentatively, I stroked my right over Kazuki's glossy hair. Kazuki reached blindly up and wrapped his fingers around my wrist in an oddly endearing gesture, keeping my hand captive. We stayed that way for several minutes, just existing, breathing in and out, glad to be alive and together.

"Hey, Kazu," I said. "You really kicked arse."

"I think perhaps now my brother regrets… all those dance lessons."

"Did you just make a joke?"

"Stop it," Kaji told me. "Of course, my dragon has a sense of humor."

"I've just never seen it before," I teased.

"Never seen what before?" Rune's rusty voice commandeered my attention.

"You're awake," I said, always a good hand with the obvious. Turning in my seat, I rested my elbows on the side of the bed and put a hand on his arm. For now, it was enough just to touch him, to feel his warmth and assure myself of his solidness.

"Why are you crying?" he asked. "How's everyone else?"

"Am I crying? How odd. I can't remember being happier." I stretched to kiss his cheek. Rune put a hand on the back of my neck and kept me there for a real kiss. When he let me go, my face felt warm and I was sure I was blushing.

"You are blushing," Kaji confirmed with delight.

"You are jealous," I replied.

Kaji glanced at Kazuki and then rolled his eyes at me. "As if."

"My *takara* doesn't need to be envious of anyone," Kazuki said. "I will make sure."

I smiled at Kazuki before I gave Rune the bad news. "Sung's injury turned out to be severe. The bullets Sato used were designed to do maximum damage. The doctors aren't sure he'll be able to use his arm."

Rune sobered instantly. "Playing guitar is his life."

There was a long silence broken by a knock on the door. I called out permission and a police officer entered the room.

"Please forgive the intrusion. I am required to search this room."

"What do you hope to find?" I asked.

"The assassin Shin Yoshiro is missing and we are searching all of the hospital."

"If you don't mind a suggestion, check Sato Ichiro's room. Mr. Shin claimed to have unfinished business with Mr. Sato."

"*Arigato gozaimasu.*" After making a radio call, the officer checked every corner of the room and left with a polite wish for Rune's speedy recovery.

"Assassin?" Rune said. "Someone had better tell me what the hell is going on."

*W*hen we left the hospital, Kazuki insisted that we go to his house in the country. There were no objections; the peaceful surroundings would be a great place to recuperate. A few days later, we had our first festive gathering since the trouble. It was hardly a gala affair: just the members of Hayate, Vudu, and some friends. As people started to arrive, I left Rune in a comfy lounger by the pool and went to the nerve center, also known as the kitchen. Of course, my phone rang as soon as I got my hands wet. Drying off on a tea towel, I listened to the caller, said thanks, and hung up.

"Kazuki-san!" I called. No point in putting off bad news. I heard scuffling and a thump from the sitting room and then Kazuki and Kaji arrived extremely disheveled.

"I have some news from the police," I said. "Kazuki, your brother was found dead in his cell early this morning."

"That is… unlucky," Kazuki said hesitantly.

"It's all right," I said kindly. "I know you have no reason to mourn him. I won't think you're a monster if you don't cry for Sato."

"Didn't I tell you?" Kaji said triumphantly to his lover.

"Yes, you told me." Kazuki crowded Kaji, backing him up to the fridge. Pinning Kaji with his body, Kazuki snagged one of his lover's wrists and brought it over his head. Kaji struggled, but he was more interested in rubbing against Kazuki than getting free.

"Have you two done anything but shag since you got back together?"

Kaji shook his head at the same time as Kazuki answered in the negative. "We have time to make up for, Benny-chan," Kaji said breathlessly as Kazuki bit down on the rim of his ear.

"Nice day for it," I said and left them to it. We needed to have a meeting soon to discuss the postponed Budokan show and world tour, among other things, but that could wait a little while longer. I picked up the big bowl of salad and turned to take it outside, nearly running over someone entering the house. "Sung!" I exclaimed as he caught the bowl one-handed and held it until I took it back. "You look good."

Sung shrugged, his gaze focused on something over my shoulder. I had a good idea what he saw, but I turned to look anyway. We watched Kaji lace his fingers through Kazuki's and pull him down to the couch with much giggling.

"I'm sorry," I said softly, because I felt like I should say something.

"He was never really mine, Blume-san."

"But you still care for him."

"I love him." Sung shrugged.

I put a hand on his good shoulder. "You're a real hero."

"*Arigato*."

"What's the latest from the surgeons?"

"I don't really want to talk about it. Cool?"

"Sure, but if there's anything at all that I can do, you just ask, okay?"

"No worries. I'm going to play guitar again someday."

"I'm betting on it. So you want to watch the rest of this *hentai* show or go outside?"

"Hey!" Kaji yelped. "I can *hear* you."

"Yeah, and we can *see* you," I said.

"Marvel at your good fortune as you leave," Kazuki murmured.

Sung and I exchanged a glance and it gladdened my heart when he grinned at Kazuki's remark. "We're obviously not needed here," I said. "Bring that packet of serviettes and let's get the party started."

*A*fter we devoured the food, I left Rune telling glory-day stories to a rapt audience and went out to my car for the envelope I'd stashed under the spare tire. My man was a legendary ferreter of gifts, but I'd fooled him this time. I smiled as I imagined his face when he read the message on the card, but my glee evaporated when I saw the man talking to Kazuki at the edge of the gravel driveway. Diverting my path, I hurried toward them. The man in the car saw me and pulled away, accelerating rapidly.

"That was Aizawa," I said, taking out my phone as Kazuki turned to face me.

I got another demonstration of the Shining One's disconcertingly fast reflexes as his hand closed over mine on the phone. "Ow," I said. "That hurts, actually." Kazuki let go and I shook my hand a few times. "I take it you don't want me to call the police."

"There is no need."

"You do understand that man impersonated a police officer on Sato's orders, right?"

"*Hai*, you told me."

"Well, what was he doing here?"

"Delivering a message."

"Did he threaten you? I'm calling the police."

"Do not do that, Blume-san."

"Excuse me?"

"It would cause much trouble."

"What did Aizawa say to you?" I waited a reasonable length of time without an answer. "Kazuki?"

"It is... not your business," he said at last.

"Look here, mate. If you have any notion of taking up where your brother left off with these mobsters...." I stopped there as several wild thoughts ran through my mind. Was it possible that Kazuki had fooled everyone? That he had been aware of his heritage all along? That he was an active member of his late father's organization? "If you're involved with criminals, you can bet everything you own that I'll do whatever it takes to keep Kaji away from you."

"You should not count on your power over him."

"I'm counting on the fact that Kaji is a decent person. If he finds out you're doing anything illegal, he'll leave your buff arse so fast you'll feel a breeze."

"I am involved since I was born."

"What shite!"

In the bright daylight, Kazuki's eyes were as pale and cold as the heart of an iceberg. "My father was a very powerful and well-respected man."

I gaped at him. "Your father tossed your mother out on the street with a new baby, which was you, by the way. Your father didn't want you." Cruel words, I know, but they needed to be said.

"My father feared me."

As usual when I was talking with Kazuki, I felt like we were having two different conversations. "Why would a Yakuza warlord be afraid of a newborn?"

"It is not something for *gaijin*."

"You know, I really thought we'd reached some sort of understanding, you and me, but I can see that I was wrong. I think I know the trouble though. I've been trying to deal with one Kazuki, when in fact, there are several. So what do you call this model? The Shining One of the Underworld?"

Kazuki's sensuous mouth curved upward in a subtle smile. "May I use that?"

I drew a harsh breath to retort, but let it out as an incredulous laugh. "Are you having me on?" I paused at his puzzled look. "Are you joking with me?"

"*Hai*."

"Bloody hell!" I laughed again. "You nearly gave me a heart attack. I'll say one thing for you; you have the best poker face I've ever seen. I thought you were dead serious."

"You are not so hard to play."

"Bitch, please," I responded automatically, as though he were Sora or Kaji.

Kazuki bowed.

"You really had me going," I said, as we started up the drive. "So what do you want to do about Aizawa?"

Kazuki shook his head, his hair fracturing the light into glinting needles. "Nothing. I told him I did not want to be his prince."

"Did you really?" I looked sideways at him. "It occurs to me that you might be giving up quite a bit of wealth and prestige. What made you turn it down?"

"I am a prince already in Kaji's eyes, yes?"

"And a dragon prince at that," I agreed.

Kazuki stopped in the atrium and turned to face me. "It is enough," he said.

"Are you telling me you don't need all the power and the glory anymore?"

"Would you give up everything for Rune-san?"

I didn't have to think about the question. "Everything would mean nothing without him."

Kazuki nodded. "I don't know if you will ever believe me, but I loved Kaji from the moment I saw him. I came in disguise to a club where Hayate was playing and after, I could not stop thinking about him and dreaming about him. It was a terrible mistake to let my brother know how much I wanted Kaji, but I was... accustomed to having Ichiro get what I wanted for me. Later, when I saw how he planned to use Kaji to control me, I tried pretending... indifference, but I could never fool Ichiro. He had found a way to hurt me and he used it."

"I've already told you how badly I feel about not believing you."

"I don't blame you."

"And I don't think I'll ever understand you."

"*Sugoi.* I wish to remain a mystery."

"Well, you're doing a fine job, mate."

"*Arigato.*" Kazuki nodded regally.

"You've also done a good job of distracting me," I said as we began walking again. "But not good enough. It worries me that Aizawa, or whatever his name is, has been here. If your Mafia is anything like the Italian one, they won't give up easily when they want something."

"I told the messenger that I would say no to the boss in person if necessary. Now I wait for an answer."

"Great. Look here, if you don't want the police around, at least let's beef up the security staff for a while."

"That is a good idea."

"Really?" His capitulation was so swift that I was caught off balance.

"I cannot risk my *takara*'s life again."

"It's sweet that you call him treasure," I said, and I meant it sincerely.

"He is my treasure and it is also his true name."

"No, his true name is Akihashi Susumu."

Kazuki shrugged, clearly saying I could believe what I wanted, but he knew the truth.

"I notice you're not wearing the dragon claw any longer," I said as we reached the doors to the terraced back garden.

"It does not mean what it once did to me. My father is dead. He will not pass me on the street one day and recognize the necklace. He will not take me in his big car to his big mansion. He will never tell me that he is sorry, that he made a mistake, that he never meant to throw me away like defective goods." Kazuki took a breath. "I gave the necklace to Kaji; he likes it and it looks good on him."

"So he's going to walk around sporting some ancient Yakuza symbol of power?"

"Who will believe it is real?"

"You have a point. In fact, you're getting sharper all the time, though you're still awfully blunt."

Kazuki's eyebrows quirked up over the bridge of his nose.

"That was me being clever," I said. "It probably doesn't translate."

"I understand you. I was only surprised at the compliment."

I narrowed my gaze deliberately. "You're going to be worse than all of the other lads put together, aren't you?"

Kazuki feigned incomprehension extremely well and looked impossibly alluring while doing it.

"Oh do stop," I said, throwing an arm around his neck. "I'm on to you now, dragon. You may look like a sphinx, but you're just another naughty lad with a pretty face."

"Are you hitting on my man?" Kaji said as he joined us.

Whatever I might have said was lost in Kazuki's response to Kaji's change of clothing. Grabbing my lad by the upper arm, Kazuki turned him to the left and right, admiring him from different angles. "*Iroppoi! Chou kawaii!*" the Shining One approved.

I agreed. Kaji looked both sexy and super cute. His shaggy shoulder-length hair was its natural undiluted coffee color again and fell past his shoulders. The black crayon lines of kohl around his eyes gave him a Goth ragdoll look that was enhanced by his pale skin and his wardrobe. Over silver-buckled combat boots and skinny black jeans, he wore a billowy white shirt with ruffles at the neck and wrists. It was Kazuki's shirt and consequently a few sizes too large, but Kaji compensated with a short-waisted jacket of bruise-purple brocade. The black velvet lapels were festooned with silver filigree trinkets, pins, and brooches, a constellation of gifts from the Shining One. More silver circled his wrists and hung from one ear. Against the creamy triangle of skin below his throat, an argent pearl glowed softly in the grip of a dragon's claw. I smiled indulgently as Kazuki hooked two fingers in the studded leather belt hanging low on Kaji's hips and pulled him close. The sound of a fighter jet swooshing past made me duck before I realized it was my phone. I looked around to scold Michi as I answered, waving to Kaji and Kazuki that I'd join them in a minute. As they strolled away toward the pool deck, I turned my back on the party. Before I could say hello, the caller began to speak.

"Hello, Ben. I am glad to hear you are well."

"Yoshi!" I looked around quickly. "Where are you?"

"It seems your destiny to forever ask me that question. I am far away. The location is not important."

"Was it you who sent Aizawa here?"

"You know it was and his name is Sugito."

"Please don't do that again."

Yoshi's soft, soft laugh caressed my ear. "How I wish I could have been your hero, Ben. However, you do not need one. You *are* a hero."

"Will you tell me something? Why does your organization want Kazuki so badly? Is it just his charm and ability to move across borders in mysterious ways?"

"It is his blood, of course. I was… amused when Akihashi-san named him dragon. Tenryu, the dragon of the heavens, was the name chosen by Kazuki's ancestor over two centuries ago when he and some other powerful men formed an alliance. His symbol of power was a dragon's claw clutching the moon."

"And it was his necklace that Kazuki's mother stole," I guessed.

"No, Ben. Tenryu wore a signet ring. The pendant was commissioned by Sato Masuru's great-grandfather when he and a few other samurai formed a syndicate of protection. They were not *burakumin* low-castes, but *daimyos* who lost their estates: aristocrats, you would say."

"I'll grant you that Kazuki is arrogant enough to be royalty."

"Masuru let his pride destroy him. He could not bear to raise another man's son and in his anger at his wife, he ignored our laws. His downfall began the moment he cast her off. I was a lowly *wakachu* at the time and the only servant who would turn a hand to help her carry a few belongings out of my master's house."

228

"But surely, if she cheated on him, he was entitled to a divorce at least."

"*If* she had been of ordinary blood, but Masuru knew that his wife was also a descendant of Tenryu."

"And what does that signify?"

"According to our legend, Tenryu had eyes the color of the finest jade. The leaders of my organization have been waiting for a green-eyed child to be born into the bloodline again. They believe Kazuki is the dragon returned."

"That's… I don't really have an adequate comment. Who was Kazuki's father?"

"The lady did not say."

"Maybe she didn't have to tell *you*. Maybe you knew all along who her lover was."

"Maybe is a very large word. No man has time for all the maybes of this world."

"Now you sound like a monk again… instead of an assassin."

"I hear rebuke in your voice."

"I hear no remorse in yours."

"Listen more closely." Yoshi sighed. "I know what I gave up when I executed Sato Ichiro."

"Let's talk about something else then. Tell me what you see."

"I can see cherry trees in the valley," he said. "And it is almost spring. The wind is cold up here, but the sun is strong. My only company just now is a soaring hawk and your beautiful voice."

"You've been protecting Kazuki for a long time, haven't you?"

"Don't make me sound so noble. I did my job."

"Are you still doing your job?"

"I am on… hiatus?"

"Yes, that's the word you want, I think. If you mean you'll be coming back to work after a break."

"*Hai.*"

"I hope you'll stay away from Kazuki. Kaji likes him."

"It is truly a pity. With Akihashi-sama at his side, Kazuki-sama would be a formidable leader. Sato Ichiro recognized his brother's potential as a rival for power and neutralized him with chemicals, isolation, and wealth. Using Kazuki's career as his cover, Ichiro became a very successful smuggler and earned the respect of his superiors. It was going well for him, but he was not the sort of man who is ever satisfied."

"I sensed that about him," I said drily. I could hear the smile in Yoshi's voice when he spoke again.

"You can imagine that as Kazuki grew older, he grew more difficult and Ichiro used whatever came to his hand to control his brother. When Kazuki told Ichiro that he wanted to meet Hayate's singer, Ichiro saw his opportunity. He thought to use Akihashi-sama as both reward and punishment. He should have remembered that once a dragon has his treasure in his grasp, he will not give it up. Ichiro failed to recognize Akihashi-sama's true nature and refused to listen to counsel. He roused the dragon sleeping in Kazuki-sama's blood and doomed himself."

"How sad for him that there was no one around to remind him about dragons and treasures."

"He would not have listened and I must say that it is pleasant to be vindicated after years of disgrace."

"Are you going to leave us alone?"

"Kazuki-sama has given his answer. He prefers not to take his place in the bloodline."

"And that's an acceptable answer?"

"It will have to be."

"You won't give him any trouble?"

"What are you asking me, Ben?"

"You know what I'm asking."

There was a long silence from Yoshi's end. "If the dragon has need of ninjas, you know what to do," he said at last.

I thought about the phone number I'd added to my contacts as Fixer 1. "Thank you, Yoshi. *Domo arigato*." I paused and I could hear the wind blow across the speaker of his phone. "I suppose you know that the police are looking for you."

"*Hai*. I am a masterless man on the run, a ronin."

I heard the humor in his voice again. "Always the romantic, Mr. Shin."

"I am an old-fashioned man who longs for the old days. I should go now, in case anyone else is rudely listening in."

"I'll miss you," I said sincerely.

"That is something—to know that I will be missed by such a man."

"Goodbye, Yoshi."

"*Sayonara*, Ben. Ah, wait, I thought you would like to know. I am barefoot and I have unbuttoned my shirt. The sun feels very good on my skin."

He hung up then and I never spoke to him again, but I often felt his presence. I liked to think he hovered on the periphery of Kazuki's life, alert for trouble, ready to leap in and save the day. It's not very civic-minded of me, but I was glad that the police never found him.

"Sunshine?" Rune called to me from the deck and I went to him. He offered a penny for my thoughts, but I wasn't so cheap, as I informed him. He knew I was lying and proved how cheap I was by all but shagging me on the lounge chair. When onlookers cheered us like a footy mob, my only reaction was to bow when Rune finally let me up. He raised both arms over his head as though he'd scored, and then pulled me away from the party for a serious ravishing among the peonies. I didn't object to the grass stains. I didn't protest that I was shirking my duties as host. I didn't hold back one ounce of my being. I could lose him so easily, lose everything on the whim of a moment, a subtle shift in the tilt of the scales, an inattentive driver, a weak-walled blood vessel, a gun-wielding Yakuza assassin, and my loved one would be gone beyond recall. I wasn't stupid; I was going to enjoy every minute I was given.

It wasn't until late that night that I remembered to give Rune the card. Inside was a mock-up of a CD cover. The artist I'd used had taken a picture of Rune, faded the colors to sepia tones, and superimposed his handsome features over a woodcut of a Viking longboat, its dragon prow pointed into the storm. In letters like tattered sailcloth, the title read *Return of the Voyager*.

"Just a little encouragement," I said.

"Nag," he said, just before his lips covered mine. Oh sure, he complained, but I could tell he was pleased. And he was right about the nagging. I was going to prod him until he recorded an album. He didn't have forever, after all. Did I mention that life was uncertain?

Chapter Twenty

*I*n case you were wondering, the press never got hold of the story of the Yakuza smuggling ring and its connection with the Shining One. Law enforcement officials were very happy with the amount of heroin they took out of circulation and very understanding about keeping the incident out of the news. Zennousha Music, the company Ichiro Sato built, went through a major shake-up as personnel hastily decamped rather than submit to police questioning. Kazuki dissolved the corporation, signed with Hikage Productions, and got back to the business of making music.

Miss Shiori made a lovely video for Kaji and Sung's version of Rune's "When the Sun Didn't Shine." Putting aside the dramatic themes and big effects, she filmed the two young men on the beach, on a deserted country road, and the steps of a temple. They were dressed simply in jeans and T-shirts and lip-synced the words of the song to each other. The images on the finished video glowed with a golden radiance that Shiori insisted was natural. I don't how she did it, but the two lads looked like the shining ghosts of a pair of star-crossed poets singing the bittersweet but hopeful lyrics.

The video was a hit, but the song was a bigger one. Though it started on the pop charts, it soon crossed over into several other categories. It went from being a big hit to a huge hit and then a monster hit. It played constantly on the radio and became a favorite at Western-style wedding ceremonies. Rune actually claimed to be sick of hearing it after a while. He was proud though, to have written something enduring.

In a virtuoso display of healthy competitiveness, Kazuki went into his private studio at three one morning and came out around nine that night with a new song that he called "The Moon Is My Castle." He recorded it the next day with Hayate backing him on acoustic instruments. It was a sweet song, almost like a nursery rhyme, but as with everything the Shining One did, there was the sense of great passion held in check. It was released as a single with a gorgeous picture of Kazuki with the lads, all of them dressed in white and posed around a huge neon crescent moon. Michi was hanging in a hidden harness from the top point with Tsubasa below him, arms spread wide as though to catch his friend. Sora leaned against the lower point in profile, wreathed in cigarette smoke. Kazuki reclined in the curve of the lighted prop, one leg dangling, making a cradle of his body for Kaji to rest on. His arms encircling Kaji, Kazuki gazed serenely into the camera. Kaji's eyes were closed, his lips slightly parted as though deep in sleep. Stores couldn't stock enough of the recording and so many posters were stolen that we had several thousand more printed as gifts for the fans.

Almost two months after the original scheduled date, the *Pandemic Love* tour got under way with an opening show at Budokan. The audience went wild for the performance that had been rehearsed, but the best bit of all happened spontaneously: when the lads went out for the last encore, they took an extra musician with them.

Rune and I were standing in the wings, listening to the crowd shout, stomp, and clap for one more song. The members of Hayate surrounded us, bathed in sweat and glowing like beatific saints. The energy level in the vast auditorium was so high that I could feel my molecules dancing and when I looked around, I could see that the feeling was mutual. I threw an arm around Rune's waist and drew him close for a kiss before he was pulled away from me.

"Come on," Kaji urged, tugging on Rune's arm.

Bewildered, Rune glanced around at my grinning lads. "Where?" he shouted over the roar.

Sora grabbed Rune's other arm and helped Kaji drag him toward the stage. Seeing their intention, Rune balked, digging in his heels and clutching at me. His look of betrayal was comical as I pushed him out into the lights. Tsubasa and Michi ganged up with their bandmates to compel Rune to the center of the stage. He made a break for the sidelines, but the boys hemmed him in with crossed guitar necks. The crowd fell silent in curiosity and then Hayate swung into the opening bars of "Soho Stomp." Rune's mouth fell open as he recognized his old band's signature song. He glanced stage left and gave me a complicated look that told me he was touched and that he would get even with me in the very near future. However, for now, he had an audience to please, and like the true entertainer he was, he threw himself into it, sink or swim, do or die.

Taking the microphone from Kaji, Rune waited for the intro to end and sang the first line. The second followed at higher volume and by the time he reached the end of the first verse, he was singing fluidly and moving with the beat. The crowd was unsure at the beginning, but the driving tempo and Rune's golden voice stirred their excitement back to a fever pitch. Kaji joined Rune on the chorus, the two of them belting out a rabble-rousing call to arms for a legion of rock 'n' roll rebels. As Rune began the second verse, Kaji grabbed the hem of his shirt and yanked it up to his armpits. The crowd roared their approval as Rune's sculpted, golden-furred chest was exposed under the bright stage lights. As Kaji skipped away, Rune spun and snagged a handful of his long hair. Reeling the other singer in, Rune dropped to one knee and bent Kaji backward over his thigh. Sora and Tsubasa circled as Rune flipped Kaji onto his stomach and then moved in to administer a spanking with their guitars.

Something bright and swift blew by me and the Shining One seemed to materialize beside Rune with a microphone in his hand. Kaji climbed Rune like a short flight of steps to launch himself from broad shoulders. Kazuki caught Kaji and they shared the microphone as they provided a driving backup harmony for the second chorus. Flanking Rune, they raised him to his feet and leaned seductively against him as three voices blended into one impossibly beautiful and powerful siren call.

I watched from the wings and felt not the slightest desire to be part of the spectacle. It was enough for me to know that I had a hand in making it happen and in making my loved ones happy. Seeing Rune drink in the adulation of an audience and deliver a performance that warranted every ounce of their praise was my equivalent of winning an award. I might not get a trophy for my mantel, but I didn't need one. In fact, the only thing that kept life from being perfect was the studio musician who was filling in for Sung Ke Smith.

Well, almost the only thing. There was still the matter of Natsuko's pregnancy.

I asked for another paternity test and Natsuko agreed to the amniocentesis, now that it wasn't a grave risk to the baby. She was very

234

confident that she was carrying Kazuki's child and eager to have it validated. The paperwork was delivered to Hikage's new corporate offices the day after the concert.

"Natsuko's baby has the same DNA as Kazuki," Rune said, his gaze skipping down the report.

Kaji and Kazuki exchanged a look and then Kaji took Kazuki's hand. "I don't care," my lad said. "I just hope Natsuko will let us be in the child's life."

Kazuki kissed the side of Kaji's head. "*Takara,*" he murmured.

I rolled my eyes at the Shining One's dramatics and Kaji stuck out his tongue at me.

"Hang on." Rune paused dramatically and went back to the top of the page. "The baby isn't Kazuki's after all. The DNA was close enough that the lab was fooled the first time, but the baby is Sato's."

There was silence for a few moments and then Kazuki spoke. "So I am to have a niece or nephew then."

"You sound a little relieved," I said.

Kazuki nodded. "I would love any child of mine, but I would not like to be reminded that I hurt Kaji when I slept with Natsuko."

"Then stop talking about it," Rune advised him. Rune was proving to be just what Kazuki needed. Not a father figure exactly, but an older man who wouldn't put up with the Shining One's nonsense. Rune was immune to Kazuki's mesmerizing presence and treated him as just another brash young pup with more ego than brains.

Kazuki shot Rune a narrow-eyed glance that was ignored. "I am sorry," he said to Kaji. "I was stupid then; I am not so stupid now."

"Well, you're still going to need a new lawyer," Rune said. "You don't have to decide right now, but it would be nice if you at least gave it some thought."

"You choose," Kazuki told Rune, burying his face in Kaji's thick hair. "I am busy."

"Done." Rune looked at me. "Kazuki's going to use Hikage Productions' attorney."

"And who would that be?"

"Pending your approval, of course, Hasu Global has offered to assign a member of their legal team to Hikage exclusively. I didn't see how there could be any conflict of interest."

"Don't you?"

"Come on, Sunny," Rune said as he reached for my hand. "I know you're a little gun-shy after the whole Zennousha thing, but I think we can trust Hasu to act in the interests of profit."

"Sorry, but you know how I am."

"Like a she-wolf with cubs?"

I gave Kaji and Kazuki a reproachful look for their snickers.

"It was a compliment," Rune said.

"Really? Because it sounded like *belittlement* to me."

Kaji and Kazuki exchanged a glance, but before they could ask me about the unfamiliar word, Rune spoke again. "No matter what I say to you, every word means *I love you*."

"That is beautiful," Kaji sighed. "If you ever tire of this man, Benny-chan, can I have him?"

Kazuki made an outraged noise. "Shameless slut! You say this in front of me?"

"Yes, so you will know it is a joke."

"I knew it was a joke," Kazuki scoffed. "I was joking also."

Kaji glanced at me, a small smile curving his lips. "Of course, you were," he told Kazuki. "You could never be so weak as to feel jealousy."

"I have only pity for the one who tries to take you from me."

"So fierce, my dragon." Kaji stroked Kazuki's recently highlighted hair, countless splinters of copper among the black creating a brindled look. "I know you would fight for me. You don't have to say it."

Kazuki purred under Kaji's touch, actually purred, an almost subliminal, throaty humming that rose and fell. It put me in mind of Rune's greedy growl that signified his utmost pleasure in bed. As often happened, I found myself becoming aroused at the thought of coaxing that particular sound from my lover.

Rune squeezed my hand and nodded toward the other two men. "If we could bottle the chemistry between them, we could make a fortune selling it as an aphrodisiac."

236

"To the poor bastards that need such a thing," I answered, with a look that promised much.

Rune looked torn and it occurred to me that our roles had reversed. Now he was the one most likely to insist on buckling down to work and I who distracted him with the one temptation he couldn't resist. I lost count of the number of times we shagged like minks at the office, in limos, backstage, anywhere we could be together and enjoy at least the illusion of privacy. All it took sometimes was eye contact. We'd each be busy at some task, placing calls, meeting with journalists, bashing out agendas, and our eyes would meet like flint striking steel. Sparks flew and in moments, I could think of nothing but how to get Rune somewhat horizontal.

Not that I was his harem boy, not by any means. The first time I topped Rune was a revelation for me. It had never been something I craved until I saw his face as I entered him. If I could describe his expression, I would make my living as a poet. All I can say is that I saw the face of love and hope you don't stone me for a soggy git. Maybe my voracious appetite for him will taper off eventually, but I sincerely doubt it. Some hungers are with you for life, and if you're lucky, you find what satisfies it. I consider myself an extremely lucky man.

As for aphrodisiacs…. After the *Pandemic Love* tour ended, Kaji and Kazuki made another video with Miss Shiori. The song was one that Sora and Kaji had been working on for years. The working title was "Anacrusis," a musical term for the lead-in notes before the first down beat. I suppose the word happy in "Happy Birthday" would be the most familiar example. To me, it implies a gathering of energy before really nailing something down, the pause between desire and the act of fulfilling that desire, and, in that sense, it suited the song. The composers claimed that they just liked the way the Latin word sounded.

A love song disguised as science fiction, it was full of big, crashing, anthemic guitar chords that evoked a future of bored hedonists searching desperately for new thrills. The singer-protagonist acquires a sex android and has the bad taste to fall in love with his toy. Shunned by friends and society, he puts the android away, but can't forget what they shared. When he finally opens the closet door again, the android jumps him and makes passionate love to him. While they're in the act, the sex toy slowly becomes human, sort of like Pinocchio, but instead of the nose growing… Well, I'm sure you get the picture.

With a combination of live action and computer-generated effects, Miss Shiori's video presented a world of metal polished to a quicksilver gleam, of light that ran like liquid along every sleek contour, of shadows so dense and black they had gravity. Several android costumes were discussed and drawn up for Kazuki, but the Shining One maintained that his character would have no need of clothing. His final wardrobe consisted of a very long wig of straight silvery hair and a dusting of faintly metallic powder over his entire body.

Creative camera angles and strategically placed tape saved Kazuki from the possibility of his willy being freeze-framed a few million times, and Kaji did his part as well. It amused me greatly to watch Shiori take Kaji's hand and place it to cover a delicate part of Kazuki's anatomy. She did an unusual amount of fussing over the scene where the android takes his master, endlessly arranging the angle at which Kaji's leg rested on Kazuki's shoulder, making sure his thigh concealed any glimpse of the Little Shining One. To be fair, her job was made difficult by the fact that Kazuki was enjoying the whole process immensely and frankly didn't care who saw his bits, which were every bit as handsome as the rest of him. Filming was delayed several times so Kaji could get his laughter under control, but there was nothing faintly laughable about the footage Shiori captured.

Kaji's costume was a jumpsuit of red Spandex with a multitude of zippers strategically placed: vertically, horizontally, and diagonally. When all of the zippers were opened, Kaji's well-defined dancer's musculature appeared to be haphazardly bound in blood-red ribbons. His hair was the color of soot at midnight, plaited tight to his skull in the front and exploding into a peacock's tail of feathery spikes.

The makeup artist had applied faux tattoos to match the bracelets of Egyptian hieroglyphs around Kaji's wrists and upper arms. They framed his eyes and followed the line of his cheekbone down his jaw to his neck. From there, the glyphs flowed down his collarbones to merge briefly before splitting to outline his pectorals and abs, coming together once again at his navel and trailing downward in a single column. The temporary ink continued down his legs to his feet, and just as much attention was given to the back half. That artist earned her pay that day in touch-ups, but the way the tattoos were revealed, zipper by zipper, was worth the effort.

Reclining against a matte black surface, his smooth skin covered in ancient script, draped in the crimson remnants of his jumpsuit and the silver skeins of Kazuki's waist-length wig, Kaji was erotic art.

There's a moment in the video when Kazuki is crouched over Kaji, seemingly in the saddle and near the point of no return. At the crux of climax, as he becomes fully human, his eyes are the last thing to change. I've never be able to figure out how Kazuki did it, even though I was present. I know that there was no trick lighting or photography. No effects were added later, but when you watch the video, you witness an android gaining a soul. Between one moment and the next, something blooms in his eyes and there's a light in them that wasn't there before. I asked him once how he did it and he gave me the dubious look of a man who smells a trick question. His answer? *"I was acting."*

"Anacrusis" is arguably the song and video that kick-started the worldwide craze for Asian rock 'n' roll. Before it was ever released outside Japan, bootlegged clips and full-length versions were posted all over the Internet. The video was eventually officially dubbed in twelve different languages and unofficially in countless others. When it was learned that Kaji and Kazuki's relationship was more than a publicity stunt, far from faltering, their popularity surged again.

It was Rune's theory that most people didn't think of Kaji and Kazuki as being quite real. There was such a theatrical element to their larger-than-life personas that they seemed more like characters in a piece of live performance art. They got away with the most outrageous behavior in public; those who wanted to saw two men in love and others saw two best friends larking about. Kaji and Kazuki didn't care what anyone thought as long as they could be together, which is exactly the same way I felt about Rune.

The summer after the triumphant *Pandemic Love* world tour, Rune and I were married in Norway where he holds citizenship and where they're civilized enough to honor same-sex unions. No one could have been more surprised than I at how I took to the idea once Rune proposed it. I'd always maintained that I didn't need a ring or a legal document to feel married, but damned if I didn't want the ceremony with my friends and family and a big cake. Rune and I exchanged rings and vows and kissed under an archway of white orchids. It was all terribly frou-frou and we each tossed bouquets before our first dance as newlyweds.

The guests were an interesting mix of cosmopolitan Osloensi, Nihon-jin rockers, and my cousin Daniel, the only one of my small family that cared to attend. However, my lack of family and the absence of Rune's more rural relatives did nothing to mar the day. We were surrounded by people who loved us and wished us nothing but happiness. I remember wetting my lips with champagne when toasts were proposed, but I didn't need an intoxicant. I felt fully as blissful as I'd always heard people felt on this day and I wished the world could share it.

"Look at you, Benny-chan," Kaji said as we found ourselves dancing together sometime around ten that night. "You shine!"

"I feel absolutely giddy," I answered as I took his hand and swung him into a waltz.

Kaji followed me easily. "You are giving my dragon ideas," he chided.

"What sort of ideas?"

"About weddings."

"Bloody hell!" I laughed. "Tell him you're too young to get married."

"I think he is just excited about planning a big ceremony."

I laughed again. "I wonder what the costumes will look like."

"Do not encourage him."

"But he needs a new project."

"Yes, like a film about a wedding, not a real one."

"Don't you want to marry your dragon?"

"I am a rocker, Benny-chan, and a rebel. Marriage is not for me."

"Ah, you have to be free."

"*Hai*!"

"I understand completely," I said as the music ended. Rune found me and grabbed me from behind, nuzzling my neck. His arms went around Kaji as well, pulling him into the hug. Kaji put his head on my shoulder and squeezed me. I sighed happily, secure in the embrace of the two men I cared most about in the world. "This moment couldn't be better."

That's when Kazuki took the microphone and fronted the orchestra with his version of "My Funny Valentine." It was certainly a unique rendition and Kaji, Rune, and I rocked gently to the dreamy rhythm Kazuki set as he crooned the old standard. I could guess who'd told him it was one of my sentimental favorites, and I favored Rune with a smoking glance over my shoulder. At some point tonight, I was going to show him just how happy I was to be married to him, but right now, I was content with the simple joy of holding and being held.

When I spoke my vows, I made a promise to be as present as possible in each moment, appreciating it for what it was before it slid irrevocably into the past. I forget from time to time and I take things for granted, but for the most part, I've lived up to that pledge. I have few regrets and heaps of shining memories that I'm not shy about sharing, obviously.

Epilogue

*B*efore I go, I'd like to tell you about another highlight of my life.

Kaji and I were in Los Angeles so he could perform at a benefit concert. It was a full-on black-tie affair with bony women in glamorous gowns being scrutinized and judged on the red carpet. We were almost at the entrance when a woman called Kaji's name.

"Kaji! Kaji Sukoshi! Can I talk to you for a minute?"

Kaji glanced uncertainly at me. We'd been instructed to keep moving until we were inside where we'd be escorted backstage. The planners of the event would probably prefer that we didn't stop, but the woman with the microphone was Leela Silverbeck, roving host of America's top entertainment news show. Surely, we could give her two minutes of face time.

"Welcome to the West Coast!" Leela's plush red lips drew back like curtains in a smile that looked battery-powered. "Congratulations on your sold-out tour."

"Thank you," Kaji replied and Leela moved a little closer, giving her camera operator a better field of vision.

"Hayate is the most successful Japanese rock band in the world and you're known for your wild stage show. Are you a wild man in real life?"

Kaji looked confused. "This *is* my… real life."

Leela chuckled. "You're just as cute and sexy as you are in pictures. I know you have to get inside, but would you answer one more question? The other performers here tonight are mostly opera and Broadway musical stars. You must feel a little out of place."

"Was that a question?"

Leela laughed again, looking into the lens. "Kaji Sukoshi," she said into the microphone. "We're all wondering what kind of performance he'll be giving tonight." She turned back to Kaji. "Thank you! Good luck tonight!"

Kaji bowed slightly and came back to my side. "What am I doing here, Benny-chan?"

"Stop it, you silly prat. You're here because you're a good singer and this is a worthy cause, but mainly because they asked Kazuki and he was too busy."

Kaji punched my arm as we entered the venerable auditorium. "If it were not for the children we are raising money for, I would keep walking."

I rolled my eyes at him. "No, you wouldn't. Even if I weren't here for moral support, you'd go out on that stage and burn it down. You're Kaji Sukoshi."

"I wish the lads were here."

"They were happy to be excused, if I recall correctly."

"Traitors."

I smiled at him as an usher beckoned us down a lushly carpeted hall. "This is a solo gig, babe." I affected a hipster accent. "And you're gonna knock their lacey little socks off."

Kaji smiled back as we reached the green-room area where performers waited to take the stage. I took a step away to inspect his appearance and nodded approval. The Kazuki-chosen tuxedo was a brilliant compromise between formalwear and Goth chic. His glossy hair fell straight to the middle of his back and his only jewelry was one dangling earring and the dragon-claw pendant that he rarely removed. I wiped away a small smudge of eyeliner high on his cheekbone and impulsively kissed the clean spot.

"I'm so proud of you," I said.

"I love you too," he answered.

"I beg your pardon; you're Kaji Sukoshi, aren't you?"

I looked away from Kaji to see Dame Daphne Barrygrove, the queen mother of the English stage, approaching us.

"Do forgive me for interrupting," she said in her plummy voice. "My granddaughter is a great fan of yours." Daphne leaned closer to confide, "And so am I."

After introductions, I left Kaji with his new friend and went to a seat reserved for me. To my shock, Rune was sitting in it. "Where did you come from?" I demanded to know.

"I could say I came from an airplane, but you don't look like you'd appreciate the humor just now."

"You're in my seat."

Rune moved over, grinning cheekily. "How long are you going to pretend you're angry?"

"I don't want to ruin the suspense." I sat down and did my best to keep from smiling.

"I missed you, Sunshine."

"And you're missing several appointments right now."

"They can wait. I had the opportunity to come and I took it. Don't you think I want to be here as much as you do?"

Surreptitiously, I put my hand over his. "I do now," I said, as the lights dimmed. "And I'm glad you're here to share this with me."

"Kaji's just going to dazzle these folks. They won't know what hit them."

I had no doubts about that and I looked forward to watching him win this audience. He'd be singing a song that Kazuki had written for him and tonight would be the first time anyone outside our circle had heard it. It was a soaring, lyrical tribute to the transformative power of love and it required a voice with a broad range and staying power. Kaji had rehearsed it accompanied by a single piano and that's how he'd perform it here. There would be no dense orchestral arrangement to hide behind; just one piano allowing Kaji's vocal to shine.

I applauded loudly as the master of ceremonies announced that Kaji Sukoshi would sing "Me Without Your Love" written by major contributor Naoki Murakami. The stage went dark and the first notes of the piano intro swirled around the vast hall like leaves stirring in the brisk breeze of dawn. A silvery spotlight came on over the black-lacquered grand piano as Kaji rose from the accompanist's bench. As he descended the three steps of the dais, he sang the first verse in tones like a crystal bell.

A bird that's never flown
A child who's never grown
A ship without a sail
A face behind a veil
That's me without your love

As Kaji began the second verse, another singer joined him in a seamless harmony. My lad didn't look at all surprised when Kazuki emerged from the shadows in classic Kazuki-style to stand behind him. The crowd started to applaud, but quickly fell silent again to listen to the exquisite blend of voices.

A butterfly cocooned
The sea without the moon
A horse that's never run
A shadow on the sun
That's me without your love

Kazuki wore a headset mike that gave him free use of his hands and he used this latitude to slip his arms around Kaji's waist as they sailed into the chorus.

Without your love, no reason to care
If I rise or fall
Without your love, I am nowhere
I am nothing at all

The night without a star
An echo from afar
A whisper on the wind
Until you come back again
And bring your love.

Kaji and Kazuki sang the chorus once more with Kazuki dropping out before the final line to give center stage back to his *takara*. Kaji's last note seemed to hang in the air forever, the pure sound of a heart calling to its mate. When it finally faded, the applause was thunderous. I've always wanted to say that, but I'm not exaggerating. I couldn't hear a thing over the sound of hands slapping together. Kazuki tightened his arms around Kaji, hugging him close. Kaji turned his head as far as he could and raised a hand to rest against Kazuki's cheek. The clapping continued as Kazuki dipped his head to give Kaji a soft kiss and then the spotlights went out again.

As soon as we could leave without being rude, we made our way backstage and I received my second surprise of the night when Rune pulled me into an empty dressing room for a very enthusiastic reunion. We emerged a scant fifteen minutes later, rumpled and replete, to find Kazuki holding court outside Kaji's dressing room.

"I thought you had that sport drink commercial to shoot," I said.

Kazuki embraced me warmly as the small crowd politely dispersed. "I acted fast," he said straight-faced.

Rune bear-hugged the Shining One, rubbing his stubble against the other man's smooth cheek. Kazuki recoiled with exaggerated offense and Rune hid behind me.

"You've done it now, mate," I told my husband. "Kazuki never forgives beard burn. You shall suffer the wrath of the dragon."

Kazuki made a fierce face, and I prepared to be smooshed between them when a piping voice rose above the backstage din.

"*Otooji! Otooji!*" The little girl escaped her mother's hand and ran toward us, chubby legs churning in lavender tights. Plowing into Kazuki, she wrapped her arms around his knee and looked up. Her cloudy green eyes were startling in the frame of her inky bangs. "Uncle!" she squealed, switching to English.

Kazuki picked her up and kissed her round cheek. "Hello, Suzume," he said. The toddler's name was Sayuri Sato, but the Shining One called her Suzume Sukoshi, little sparrow, and it suited her. She was small and plump and flitted about like a bird. Sayuri might not appreciate the nickname later in life, but at two years old, she loved the sound of it in her adored uncle's vibrant voice. Enthroned in Kazuki's arms, she graciously granted kisses to her unofficial uncles. I accepted my sticky accolade and watched as she pecked Rune on the cheek, her pink fingers tugging at his mane of pale gold.

Natsuko, who was now going by her given name, Natsuko Fujiwara, caught up with her daughter and scolded her gently for running ahead. "And you encourage her," she accused Kazuki.

"*Takara!*" the little girl said in a demanding tone.

"You should say Sukoshi-san," her mother corrected her.

"Kaji does not care if she calls him *takara*," Kazuki said.

"It's not very proper."

Kazuki gave her an incredulous look. "This is rock 'n' roll," he said.

She gave him a look that said she doubted his sanity. "Give her to me," she said. "I'll take her to the hotel. She didn't sleep at all on the flight and it's late."

Kazuki's demeanor underwent one of his abrupt reversals. "*Arigato*, Na-chan," he said, taking her hand. "Thank you for bringing Suzume."

She gave a little shake of her head. "Thank you for the tickets, for the hotel…."

"Anything for my *ichiban*," Kazuki said, kissing Suzume's cheek again.

"You really are too generous," Natsuko said.

"You are my family. How generous is too generous? Tsubasa talked to me, by the way, about marrying you."

"I told him we should lead up to it. First, he should tell you that we are interested in one another."

"I have known that for over a year."

"And you said nothing?"

"You acted as though you wished it to be secret and I respected that."

"I thought you'd be displeased if you knew. That you would think me a bad mother."

"Then I will try to make my feelings more… clear, in the future."

"I will never know you," she sighed.

"No one understands him," I assured her. "And no one can predict what he'll do, with the possible exception of Rune."

"*Takara!*" Suzume wriggled excitedly. "*Takara!*"

Kaji came out of the dressing room in a series of handsprings to Suzume's crowing delight. "I thought I heard a princess calling me," he said.

The little girl held out her arms to Kaji and he swept her up and swung her around. Natsuko's eyes tightened at the corners, but she didn't interfere. If there was anyone Suzume adored more than her Uncle Kazuki, it was her Uncle Takara. Lifting the toddler high, Kaji set her on his shoulders and led the way to the limo. My phone rang as we reached the expressway.

"*Ohayo*, Smith-san," I said, recognizing Sung's number. "Welcome to Los Angeles."

"*Arigato*, Blume-san. Is Rune-san with you?"

"Yes, and I've already welcomed him… twice."

"He missed you."

"It was only three days, and I reminded him that he's talent now, not management." Rune had been surprised a year and a half ago when the music coordinator of an independent Canadian film wanted to use "When the Sun Didn't Shine" on the soundtrack. Eight months later, the movie and the song were nominated at the Sundance Film Festival. Rune was suddenly sought after as a composer for edgy films by intense young directors with goateed baby faces. I was awed by his output, by the way he could write a piece of music that was intrinsically his, but perfectly personified a film. I refused to let him do any administrative work, so he could use his time creatively. When he complained that he didn't get to spend enough time with me, I moved a piano into the office. It wasn't so easy to fix things for Sung.

After two years of reconstructive surgeries, Sung had limited use of his left arm, but anything as complicated as playing an instrument was still beyond him. He had accepted the position of road manager for the Kazuki/Hayate circus when Vudu disbanded in the wake of Gekko's heroin overdose, but he hadn't given up hope. In between tours, he had designed a guitar that quickly became a gold standard among talented and wealthy musicians. He didn't need the job with Hikage Productions; he just wanted a reason to go on the road. Of course, this rendered him immune to my authority.

"You know, it would have been nice if you'd informed me Rune, Kazuki, and Natsuko were coming over from Tokyo."

"Yes, I'm sure it would have, but I came with them so it's all cool for school."

"Well, it was an awfully nice surprise," I said, brushing Rune's hand off my thigh. "Do you like the hotel?"

"Very nice and easy to secure. I'll meet you in the lobby."

"See you later."

"*Mata ne.*"

I turned to Rune as I slipped my phone into my jacket pocket. "Watch the hands. A child is present."

"If you're referring to Suzume, she's asleep. If you're referring to Kaji or Kazuki, they're not paying us any attention."

Suzume was indeed fast asleep in Kazuki's lap, her chubby cheek pillowed on his chest. Kaji sat next to them, his legs curled on the bench seat, his chin on Kazuki's shoulder, watching the little girl. Natsuko was on the other side, head tipped back, eyes closed, one hand resting lightly on her daughter's foot. They might not be everyone's notion of an ideal family, but they *are* a family and somehow, they make it work. *We* make it work, I should say, for Rune and I are part of the clan along with Sora, Michi, Tsubasa, and Sung and a few others, like Miss Shiori, who became a constant in our lives.

I'm not claiming that anyone lived happily ever after. We're not quite through living yet and this isn't a fairy tale. Well... I suppose it is a bit of a fairy tale, but certainly not in the traditional sense.

A wise friend once told me that the body needs what it needs. When you're hungry, you eat. When you're tired, you sleep, and so on, but there's more to life than filling bodily needs. It's in our nature to seek something beyond the tangible, and blessed are they that find what feeds their soul. I doubt that last sentence is grammatically correct, and neither am I saying anything new. I just think it bears repeating every now and then. If you're looking for a message, I'd offer this one: Don't hold on to hate. If possible, avoid it altogether.

And now I've bent your ear long enough, *ichiban*.

CONNIE BAILEY

Born on an Air Force base, CONNIE BAILEY has been in flight ever since. Her father took the family wherever he was stationed: Spain, Morocco, Turkey, Alaska, and more; then while studying commercial arts, Connie married a musician who turned out to be a pilot in disguise. His job as an aircraft designer and competition pilot has taken them all over the world.

Reading has been Connie's favorite diversion since age four, and books are among her best friends. With her husband's support, she set out to become an author, writing every day and posting at various Internet groups and blogs; she cannot recommend that school of writing highly enough. The candid feedback she received was invaluable to her development.

A few fun facts: she lives at a small grass airfield with a hang gliding school, has what's commonly referred to as a "photographic memory," and collects words as a hobby.

Visit her Web site at http://www.conniebailey.com/ and her blog at http://baileymoyes.livejournal.com/.

Other titles from Connie Bailey…

Available at Dreamspinner Press
www.dreamspinnerpress.com

BIN TRAVELER FORM

Cut By: _Pedro Castillo #19_ Qty _32_ Date _07-06-26_

Scanned By: _____ Qty _____ Date _____

Scanned Batch ID's

_____

Notes / Exceptions

_____